RAMAGE'S
TRIAL

DUDLEY POPE

HOUSE OF
STRATUS

This edition published in 2001 by House of Stratus, an imprint of House of Stratus Ltd, Thirsk Industrial Park, York Road, Thirsk, North Yorkshire, YO7 3BX, UK.

www.houseofstratus.com

Typeset by House of Stratus, printed and bound by Short Run Press Limited.

A catalogue record for this book is available from the British Library and the Library of Congress.

ISBN 1-84232-481-0

Dudley Bernard Egen ... into an ancient Cornish seafaring family. He joined the Merchant Navy at the age of sixteen and spent much of his early life at sea. He was torpedoed during the Second World War and his resulting spinal injuries plagued him for the rest of his life. Towards the end of the war he turned to journalism becoming the Naval and Defence Correspondent for the London *Evening News*. Encouraged by Hornblower creator C S Forester, he began writing fiction using his own experiences in the Navy and his extensive historical research as a basis.

In 1965 he wrote *Ramage,* the first of his highly successful series of novels following the exploits of the heroic Lord Nicholas Ramage during the Napoleonic Wars. He continued to live aboard boats whenever possible and this was where he wrote the majority of his novels. Dudley Pope died in 1997 aged seventy-one.

BY THE SAME AUTHOR
ALL PUBLISHED BY HOUSE OF STRATUS

FICTION
ADMIRAL
BUCCANEER
CONVOY
CORSAIR
DECOY
GALLEON
RAMAGE
RAMAGE AND THE DRUMBEAT
RAMAGE AND THE FREEBOOTERS
GOVERNOR RAMAGE RN
RAMAGE'S PRIZE
RAMAGE AND THE GUILLOTINE
RAMAGE'S DIAMOND
RAMAGE'S MUTINY
RAMAGE AND THE REBELS
THE RAMAGE TOUCH
RAMAGE'S SIGNAL
RAMAGE'S DEVIL
RAMAGE'S CHALLENGE
RAMAGE AT TRAFALGAR
RAMAGE AND THE DIDO

NON-FICTION
THE BIOGRAPHY OF SIR HENRY MORGAN 1635–1688

For the Ballengers
with thanks

CHAPTER ONE

Southwick walked slowly across the quarterdeck to where Ramage stood trying to find some shade from a small awning which, having done so much service in the Tropics, now comprised more patches than original cloth and in places was so threadbare from sun and wind that it provided only a little more shade than a piece of muslin.

"This current is stronger than I'd allowed for," the master said. "I'd be glad if you'd make up your mind in the next few hours, sir, because it might save us a hard beat against both wind and current..."

Ramage nodded agreeably because in fact he had at last decided. The choice had been simple – they had sailed northwest along the South American coast from French Guiana, shepherding their two prizes captured off Devil's Island, and he had to decide whether to make for Barbados or Antigua.

Barbados, being further out in the Atlantic, a sentry box guarding the Windward and Leeward Islands running north and south like a fence dividing the Caribbean from the Atlantic, meant they had to turn a point or two to starboard and hope that the flagship of the admiral commanding "His Majesty's ships and vessels upon the Windward Island station" was anchored in Carlisle Bay.

With luck the admiral would be very short of frigates and only too glad to buy in the two prizes to add to his force – no

1

commander-in-chief ever had enough frigates, and two unexpected prizes coming up from the south would be like a quart of fresh water to a parched man.

The admiral might let the *Calypso* sail at once for England – he should, since she was sailing under another admiral's orders. However, many convoys assembled at Barbados for the long haul across the Atlantic to England, and what admiral could resist ordering an extra homeward-bound frigate to join the escort? Ramage guessed that, even worse, few if any admirals could resist putting Captain Ramage in command of a convoy and escort, which would mean a long and tedious voyage home.

Antigua, the alternative choice, was likely to have the other admiral there, the one commanding the King's ships on the Leeward Islands station. Whoever he was at the moment – Ramage seemed to recall that it was Hervey – would be in a very bad temper because he probably had his flagship in English Harbour, which with its mosquitoes, unpleasant and windless anchorage, and notoriously corrupt dockyard staff, made most officers rage against it. One of the most vocal had of course been Rear-Admiral Nelson (when a captain), whom Ramage once remembered getting very angry over the corruption of the Antigua merchants who were busy trading with the Americans in clear defiance of the Navigation Acts.

Ramage recalled the long days and nights spent in English Harbour refitting the *Calypso* after capturing her from the French and the constant rows with the master shipwright, master attendant, boatswain and (worst of all) the "store-keeping and naval officer", each of whom regarded the King's stores as personal investments upon which they could draw, selling cordage, canvas (and probably even spars) to merchant ships, illegally and at grossly inflated prices.

Men who were likely to know reckoned that the dockyard minions vied with local businessmen for the size of their profits – with the advantage that they took no risk (the King's stores being delivered there in the King's ships) and faced no competition: a merchant ship with blown-out sails was forced to buy more canvas; those with sprung masts or yards rarely carried any spares and the master might visit the dockyard with a sorry story but he had to have hard cash in his purse.

After all the strain of the past few weeks, which had started when he had been forced to leave his new bride on board one of the King's ships off Brest as the Treaty of Amiens collapsed and war started once again, Ramage decided he could not face the heat, stink and corruption of English Harbour.

He turned to Southwick. "Make it Barbados," he said.

The master, his white hair streaming in the wind like a freshly dried mop, gave a knowing grin. "I'd already put my money on it, sir, and took the liberty of keeping up to windward. Is it all right if I pass the word to the ship's company, sir? Most of them hate Antigua, too, but they like Barbados, even if it does mean a convoy for us."

He waved towards the two prize frigates following the *Calypso*, one on each quarter. "It's been a profitable voyage for the lads – I reckon they're a fair way to becoming the wealthiest seamen in the Navy. You don't often come home with less than a couple of prizes!"

"That makes you one of the Navy's wealthiest masters!" Ramage said, teasingly.

"Reckon I am," Southwick said cheerfully, "and all of it safe in the Funds."

Ramage's curiosity overcame his usual tact. Southwick had served with him from the day he was given his first command (it seemed so many years ago that a very young Lieutenant Ramage was given seemingly impossible orders by Commodore Nelson, and by a glorious stroke of luck had managed to carry them out successfully). Now he and Southwick shared the bond that comes from having death beckon them many times. "Who inherits the Southwick riches?"

Southwick looked so embarrassed that Ramage could have bitten his tongue. "My sister (as you know, she's my only living relative, and she's been a spinster all her life), well, she's provided for, so she'll never need again, and then what's left will be a sort of thank you." With that the master excused himself, saying he had some more work to do on the chart.

The three seamen sitting at the table were chatting and teasing each other with the easy familiarity that comes from often-shared dangers. The tall, sandy-haired man who had a natural authority ran his fingers through his thinning hair. "So it's Barbados," he commented. "I guessed the captain wouldn't choose Antigua, after the trouble we had refitting this ship there."

"Nor me neither, Jacko," said Stafford, the Cockney in the trio. "Not after the way those dockyard people behaved. Reckon they're rich men now, on the *Calypso* alone. Nasty lot, they are; they've turned on their own people."

"But the *Calypso*'s just one of dozens of ships," said the plump, black-haired man whose accent betrayed his Italian origins. "They all get cheated."

Rossi, known to most of his shipmates as Rosey, in fact came from Genoa and was a volunteer in the Royal Navy, although since Bonaparte had later turned Genoa into the capital of the Ligurian Republic, the French might now claim that Rossi was a traitor to the French cause. Ramage had always assumed Rossi's original departure from Genoa was connected more with disagreement over the law rather than any personal disagreement with Bonaparte's politics. Not that it mattered; he was a fine seaman with uncomplicated loyalty: he was loyal to his friends (who were serving in his ship) and particularly Jackson and Stafford. He reserved for Captain Ramage what a priest (if Rossi had ever talked to one, which was doubtful) would call idolatry. Ramage's fluent Italian – he could mimic most of the regional accents – and deep love and knowledge of Italy made him Rossi's liege lord, if such things still existed.

"Still," Stafford said cheerfully, "the *Calypso*'s made *us* rich too. And the *Triton* brig before her, and then the *Kathleen* cutter."

"Ah," Jackson interjected, "they've made us rich because we've risked our necks: we've used them to kill Frenchmen and capture their ships. If there's no risk, there's no profit; I've learned that much. But what did the storekeeper at English Harbour ever do to justify making a penny out of us? Or the boatswain, or the master shipwright, and all the rest of that sticky-fingered crowd of time-servers who are always lurking around there? Still, yellow jack or blackwater fever might yet take 'em off before they get home to spend their loot. It's an unhealthy spot, Antigua. Especially English Harbour, which has a fine cemetery ready for 'em. Come to think of it, some of the early ones must be there already!"

"The survivors should all be put in the Clink," Stafford said emphatically.

"The Clink?" asked a puzzled Rossi. "Where's that? We've never been there – have we?"

"You and I haven't," Jackson commented, "but I couldn't be sure about Staff. Go on, you tell him, Staff."

"I don't know what Jacko is being so clever about. The Clink – well, it's the prison in Southwark. Leastways, *any* prison's called a clink by the villains: comes from the clinking of their leg irons. But the original Clink was at Southwark – in London, on the south side of the river – where the vagabonds couldn't be arrested. A sort of…"

"Sanctuary," Jackson supplied.

"Yus, that's it: a sanker wherry. Dunno whether it was legal or if them as was going to do the arrestin' was just scared of goin' in there."

"I'll remember that," Rossi said.

" 'Ere, now listen," Stafford said hurriedly. "The sanker wherry bit was long ago. 'Undreds of years, maybe. Today, that Clink is a clink, like all the other clinks: just a prison."

"I'll remember," Rossi assured the Cockney. "If I go to London it is to collect my prize money and I'll stay at an inn, not a clink."

"They don't always give you the choice," Stafford said darkly and shook a warning finger. "And watch out for them women; very light-fingered, some of them."

"We have them in Genoa, too," Rossi said reassuringly. "What do you reckon we'll share out for the two French frigates, Jacko?"

"Depends," Jackson said. "If the admiral in Barbados is short of frigates (he probably will be) he might pay a good price. Though of course his price has to be approved by the Admiralty. The Navy Board, rather. But they're good ships: no rot; no action damage; sails, spars and cordage in good condition – for Frenchies, anyway. Maybe he'll pay £10 a ton for each hull, so that'll be about £7,000 apiece, plus sails, cordage and stores. Hmm…about £10,000. That'll be some £2,500 shared out among us seamen. Doubled, of course, 'cos there are two ships."

Rossi was faster than Stafford in working out an individual share, which in any case varied with the man's rank. He nodded contentedly, and said: "If this war ever ends, and if we all live to see that day, I shall go back to Genoa a rich man. I may even become a *latifondista*: ha, *that* would be a joke!"

Stafford tried to repeat the word but said sympathetically: "It's somefing you get from rich livin'? Perhaps mercury'll cure it, since it helps the venereals. Seems unlucky if you get it, having fought so hard for your money."

Rossi laughed and waved a reassuring hand. "No, Staff, is not a disease, a *latifondista*. Is a big landowner who lives somewhere else on the rents. He has tenants on his land."

"Oh, so it's all right being one, then?"

"If you can afford it, yes. Maybe I'll be able to live a rich life in London knowing my tenants are working hard in, say, Piedmont, which is near Genoa."

Jackson saw that Stafford was still puzzled and explained: " 'Landed gentry' – that's what he'll be. Like the Duke of Shinbone living in Whitehall although his money comes from a big estate up in North Britain."

Stafford's eyes lit up. "Say, Jacko, if Rosey can live in London on his prize money like the Duke of Shinbone, what about me? I'd make a good Duke of Hambone, and I'd buy an estate nearer to London than North Britain. Somewhere down in Cornwall, say."

"So you can watch the pretty ships sail out of Plymouth, eh?" Jackson said sarcastically. "And all your pretty daughters can stand on the Hoe with their chaperones and wave the sailors goodbye!"

"It'd suit me," Stafford said happily, "s'long as the sailors don't get too close."

"Why so?" Rossi asked.

"I wouldn't trust those dam' sailors wiv my daughters," Stafford declared. "I know what they're like with pretty girls!"

Jackson shook his head. "No dukes and *latifondisti* for me. Just a nice comfortable coaching inn; I just fancy myself as 'mine host'."

"All that truckling to the rich gentry," Stafford complained. " 'Fetch some more port, my good man!' "

"Won't worry me because I'll be truckling them a big bill as well. And if they aren't the likes of Mr Ramage, then we shan't have any rooms available."

"We?" Stafford asked derisively. "So the Jonathan will take himself a wife, eh? Some poor and innocent English girl will get herself lured by your sweet American promises…"

"I'll keep 'em, that's for sure," Jackson said, and Rossi recognized another lonely man who had come to terms with the unpleasant fact that he would never settle down in the land of his birth. That, Rossi knew well by now, was the penalty of travelling. A man crossed distant horizons and sometimes found beyond them lands which were greener or more welcoming…where it was easier to find a good job, a comfortable home, a sympathetic wife…Where one did not have to lock the door and secure the windows, nor risk arrest by secret police who spirited a man away so his family never saw him again. England, Rossi had long since decided, did not have as much sun as Genoa, but it bred the likes of Mr Ramage, and every man was born with as much freedom as he needed. And anyway he now had enough prize money to stay well clear of the clink…

The *Calypso* seemed to be sliding into Carlisle Bay like a skater on ice: the light wind scattered wavelets across the half-moon bay. Looking over the side, Ramage was once again delighted by the deep blue of the sea gradually shading into the faintest of blues and greens as it shallowed and was edged here and there by coral reefs. He had spent enough time in the Tropics to be able to judge the depth of water by the colour – what seemed barely a fathom, hardly enough to float a jolly-boat rowed by half a dozen men, was often deep enough to let a ship of the line swim without risk. Still, when approaching an anchored flagship it was wise to have a man in the chains heaving the lead and singing out the depths in the monotonous voice that it was all too easy not to notice.

The gunner was standing by ready to fire the salute to the admiral (a rear-admiral received thirteen guns, but if he was also a commander-in-chief he received seventeen). Paolo Orsini, midshipman and rapidly growing into a lean and handsome youth, as well as being a fine seaman, was standing by with his telescope, ready to read off immediately first the flag which would reveal the exact rank of the flag officer and then the hoist of flags by which the flagship told the *Calypso* where to anchor.

The place indicated by a bearing and distance was usually where any reasonably competent captain would in any case anchor his ship, but admirals (or more likely those around him) liked to exercise the brief authority granted them by pointing out the obvious.

"Red ensign with a white ball," Orsini reported and added, unnecessarily, "the commander-in-chief is a rear-admiral of the red." A few minutes later he followed that with: "Flagship about to hoist a signal, sir," having caught sight of a couple of seamen handling coloured bunting and preparing to hoist away at a signal halyard.

Ramage glanced forward to the fo'c'sle where Southwick was waiting with a couple of dozen seamen, like a shepherd standing on a hillock with his flock, ready to let go an anchor at the given signal.

More men were standing by, preparing to trim the yards and braces; others were at the shrouds, ready to swarm aloft to furl the *Calypso*'s topsail. The fore and main course were already furled, and Ramage was taking the ship in under topsails. With the wind as light as this it was a slow job, but as far as Ramage was concerned few admirals worth their salt were impressed by young frigate captains tearing into crowded anchorages under a press of sail, anchoring and furling with a flourish. Too many admirals had seen too many anchored ships hit by new arrivals to offer any encouragement, and signalling a ship where to anchor certainly slowed down the gamblers and calmed show-offs.

Paolo read out the signal giving a bearing and distance, and by eye, without having to bend over the azimuth compass, Ramage saw that he had guessed correctly and the *Calypso* was already heading for the position, with her two prizes astern like two swans obediently following the cob.

Ramage lifted the speaking trumpet to his lips after giving an order to the quartermaster, who swiftly passed it on to the two men at the wheel. Slowly the frigate turned into the wind; another order saw the maintopsail furled, followed by the mizentopsail. As she headed into the wind it pressed on the forward side of the *Calypso*'s foretopsail, pushing it against the mast like a hand on a man's chest and slowly brought the ship to a stop. Ramage then bent over the compass, checking the bearings given in the flagship's signal. He noted the distance, and waited for the *Calypso* to gather sternway. He walked to the ship's side and looked down at the water. A tangled strand of floating seaweed which had been floating past now slowly stopped alongside and then began to move ahead. Or, Ramage corrected himself for the thousandth time in his career, the ship had begun to move astern. He gave another order to the quartermaster because now the rudder's effect was being reversed and, looking ahead to make sure that Southwick was watching him, he lifted his right arm vertically.

Seamen let go the anchor. The splash of its thirty-seven hundredweight, almost two tons, hitting the water was followed by the cable (it was hemp, seventeen inches in circumference, as thick as a man's lower thigh) which snaked over the side, leaving a haze of smoke at the hawse as its friction scorched the wood. Southwick watched from the bulwark and as it slowed and stopped for a few moments gave the signal for the men to snub it round the bitts. The *Calypso*, pushed astern by her backed topsail, which was being braced round to keep it square to the wind, then kept a steady strain on the cable, and Southwick gave the order to veer more. Finally he signalled to Ramage that the *Calypso* was safely anchored. The holding ground in Carlisle Bay was good, but in many islands weed on the bottom, or sunken palm fronds, made anchors drag.

Ramage shouted down to the gunner: "Begin the salute!"

The first gun on the starboard side spurted smoke and its sharp crack – being unshotted there was no boom – echoing and reechoing across the bay sent the sleepy-looking pelicans into the air after their usual ungainly run across the surface of the water, and it set the black-headed gulls wheeling and screaming in protest at the interruption in their hunt for the fish scraps left by the pelicans.

Ramage could imagine the gunner muttering the time-honoured phrases used to time the salute – words which when spoken reasonably quickly took five seconds: "If I wasn't a gunner I wouldn't be here…Number two gun fire!" And repeating the phrase to himself reminded him yet again that he must replace the gunner: the man was useless, running a mile faster than take a ha'porth of responsibility and completely unsuited to the *Calypso*. But changing a gunner was a tedious business: it was not a question of applying to the commander-in-chief, as one would to change an unsatisfactory lieutenant. No, a gunner was appointed by the Board of Ordnance, which of course was part of the Army. Guns and gunnery in the King's ships was the Army's affair – at least by tradition. Gunners were examined and given their warrants by the Board of Ordnance, which also arranged for the casting of guns and shot and provided the powder. Thus changing a gunner (or such an application by a ship's captain) was likely to be seen by the Army as a criticism, and the application would end up in the pigeon-hole reserved by the clerks for the paper to smother in dust.

Fifteen, sixteen, seventeen…and that was it: the commander-in-chief of His Majesty's ships and vessels upon the Windward Island station had received the salute due to him by a ship visiting his station from some distant part.

Southwick joined Ramage at the fore end of the quarterdeck and commented: "I can almost see the sun reflecting on the telescope lenses! They must be wondering how the devil we collected those two!" He gestured to the two prizes now anchoring astern.

"Yes, any moment the flagship will hoist the signal for me to go over to report. But I want you to start getting our men back on board here from the prizes as soon as they have anchored. Just leave a dozen behind in each one."

Southwick nodded: no explanation was needed because everywhere in the world any one of the King's ships was short of men, but here in the West Indies, where sickness was the enemy, not the French, many of the frigates and smaller ships were being sailed with half their official complement of men. Since sickness, mostly the black vomit, did not distinguish between officers and men, promotion could be rapid for both lieutenants and captains – but equally the appointments could be brief, and one of the most prosperous men in Barbados was the mason carving names and dates on marble headstones in the cemetery (the wording was carefully copied out and sent home to relatives).

"Boat leaving the flagship with a lieutenant on board, sir," Paolo Orsini reported. "Heading our way."

"The admiral smells his share of prize money," Southwick muttered as Ramage went below to his cabin to change his uniform and put on his sword. A brief but comprehensive "Report of Proceedings" waited on his desk: it lacked only the name of the admiral, which he had yet to discover.

Ten minutes later a young lieutenant arrived on board and was brought down to the cabin, where he introduced himself as Lieutenant Newick. He told Ramage that the admiral wished him to make his report as soon as possible. "The two prizes," he said hesitantly. "We had no idea that there were two such French frigates in the area, although we guessed we might see you."

"Oh – why was that?" asked a puzzled Ramage. What could have brought him to the commander-in-chief's notice?

The lieutenant looked embarrassed. "Perhaps I shouldn't have mentioned it, sir. There's a letter from the Admiralty waiting for you, and the admiral had one at the same time. Came out in the last Post Office packet that arrived a week ago."

"Let's go," Ramage said. He could think of no reason why Their Lordships should be writing to him, but despite the heat of the tropical sun coming down through the *Calypso*'s deck, he felt a sudden chill. The unexpected was usually unwelcome: so far he had learned that much about life.

CHAPTER **TWO**

Rear-Admiral Edwin Tewtin greeted Ramage at the entryport of his flagship the *Queen* with what Ramage later described to Southwick as well controlled amiability lightly cloaked with a curiosity which was clearly as painful to ignore as a nagging toothache.

After all the formalities of a little-known rear-admiral (commanding one of the Royal Navy's smallest stations) finding himself greeting one of the most famous of the Navy's young frigate captains had been completed – with a pardonable amount of wariness on either side – Tewtin led the way down to his cabin and waved Ramage to the comfortable chair, sitting down opposite him while Lieutenant Newick perched nervously to one side in a straight-backed seat.

Ramage saw at once that Tewtin had probably not (so far, anyway) done well from prize money: the furniture in the great cabin verged on being spartan; the curtains bunched on either side of the sternlights would have been appropriate in one of the public rooms of a small but busy coaching inn; the rows of wine glasses nesting in a rack on the bulkhead above the sideboard could have come from the bar parlour, and the buckles on the admiral's shoes were made of pinchbeck, not gold.

None of which, Ramage told himself, necessarily made Rear-Admiral Tewtin any less efficient as a flag officer, and might indeed indicate heavy expenses at home – many a man had been ruined through inheriting a large estate without the money to run it, or acquiring a wife whose style outranged his purse.

Although Ramage waited a minute or two, expecting Tewtin to hand over the Admiralty letter, the man made no move, and his desk was bare. He looked up at Ramage and asked: "You have a written report of your proceedings?"

Ramage bent down to open the canvas pouch he had leaned against the side of the chair, but Tewtin said: "I'll read that later. Just tell me what brings you here with two French frigates as prizes."

And now, Ramage thought to himself, choose your words carefully. He had written orders from the commander-in-chief of the Channel Fleet, Admiral Clinton, for the operation he had just carried out, and these concluded that the *Calypso* should then return to England and report direct to the Admiralty (leaving Admiral Clinton happily distant in the event of failure). There was nothing to prevent Rear-Admiral Tewtin holding on to the two prizes (indeed, Ramage hoped he would, *after* he had bought them in).

"It's a bit of a long story, sir," Ramage said apologetically.

"Well, keep it short: you're here now; where did you start from?" Tewtin smirked at Newick, as if to indicate that famous young captains were really rather silly fellows who needed a guiding hand from admirals like Tewtin.

"At a friend's château near Brest, where I was spending my honeymoon, sir."

The smirk left Tewtin's face, but now he was clearly puzzled: was Ramage teasing him, or…"Honeymoon? Did you finally marry that Italian woman?"

"You mean the Marchesa di Volterra, sir?" His voice was just cold enough to point out Tewtin's lapse.

"Yes, I think that was her name."

"No," Ramage said shortly. "At the signing of the Treaty she returned to the Kingdom of Volterra – of which she is the ruler."

"But...well, Bonaparte must have had her arrested when the war started again."

"Probably. I have her nephew serving with me. She was not to be persuaded to stay in England."

Now Tewtin realized he had blundered but he could see no way out. "Er, you did say you were on your honeymoon? Who was the lucky woman?"

"Yes, sir – I married the daughter of the Marquis of Rockley."

The embarrassed smirk vanished from Tewtin's face as though a barber had wiped off shaving soap: he realized that with a few ill-chosen remarks he might have antagonized the son of the Earl of Blazey (who was still an admiral of the white although retired), referred to an Italian woman as though she was a tart (and now found out she in fact ruled an Italian state) and then discovered that this young puppy Ramage had married the daughter of a marquis (who had been the most powerful man in India and presumably had enormous influence with the present government in London).

It would be hard, Tewtin thought ruefully, for a rear-admiral near the bottom of the flag list who had been lucky enough to get this job (and it was luck; he admitted that) to drop so many bricks in so short a time – less than five minutes. Anyway, the last had hit the deck; now he would handle Ramage carefully.

"May I congratulate you?" Tewtin said. " 'All the world loves a lover', eh? You were describing your honeymoon."

"Hardly that, sir," Ramage said tightly. "I said I was staying near Brest on my honeymoon."

"Of course, of course. At a friend's château when the war started again, I think you said."

Ramage nodded. "Yes sir. Bonaparte's police arrested my friend, but my wife and I managed to escape. At the same time, the ship's company of one of our brigs mutinied and ran into Brest with her – "

"Yes, yes, I've heard from Their Lordships about that."

"Good," Ramage said, "that shortens my story. So when we reported to the Channel Fleet – "

Tewtin held up a hand. "Wait! Their Lordships simply warned me that the men had carried the ship in and sent me a list of their names."

Ramage deliberately gave a gentle sigh, hoping Tewtin would take the hint. "You asked me to start at the beginning and keep my story brief, sir, but there are some details I have to give to make sense of it."

"I do understand, my boy; go on," Tewtin said encouragingly.

"After my wife and I escaped from the château we had to think of a way of getting back to England, and also see if we could rescue our host – "

"Your duty was to return to England and report at once to the Admiralty," Tewtin said heavily, like a bishop admonishing an errant deacon.

"Of course, sir, but we had no transport, and our host was a friend – "

"Friend!" Tewtin almost exploded, slapping the arm of his chair for emphasis. "Surely you put your duty to your King before your social obligations to a friend – a Frenchman, I presume!"

" – a friend of the Prince of Wales," Ramage finished his sentence.

"You don't mean that you were staying with…"

"The Count of Rennes is an old friend of my family, and of course apart from being a leader of the French Royalists who fled to England, he is a close friend of the Prince."

Tewtin hauled a large handkerchief from his pocket as though, Ramage thought, he was letting fall the *Queen's* foretopsail. The admiral mopped his brow, rubbed the sides of his nose vigorously to give himself time to think, then found he had wiped the whole of his face and brow without thinking of anything: the crash of falling bricks was leaving him stunned. "Do go on," he urged Ramage.

"Well, sir, at the same time that we found the Count had been put on board a French frigate with many other Royalist prisoners to be transported to Devil's Island, my wife and I and some French fishermen (Royalists, of course) managed to recapture the *Murex* brig that had mutinied after the villains had been taken off by the French, and sailed in time to meet the Channel Fleet, which was just arriving off Brest to resume the blockade."

Tewtin had many questions to ask but managed to restrict himself to nodding approvingly. A nod was safe, he realized.

"By chance my own frigate, the *Calypso*, was in the Fleet and I was put in command again." Ramage saw no reason to elaborate on how that came about. "Anyway, as soon as Admiral Clinton heard that a French frigate was already on its way to Devil's Island with the Count and many other Royalists, I was sent in pursuit, my wife returning to England in the *Murex* brig."

Tewtin, thinking that was the end of Ramage's story, nodded and said: "But you picked up a couple of prizes, anyway. I'm sure the Count will survive, although he's in a very horrible place at this moment."

"Oh, he'll survive, sir," Ramage said reassuringly, a tight smile on his face. "Just a touch of fever."

"What is?" asked a puzzled Tewtin. "Fever?"

"The Count, sir. He is on board the *Calypso* but developed a bout of fever a couple of days ago."

Tewtin jumped to his feet. "Good God, man! Bring him over to the flagship! He must be my guest. Here – " he waved at Lieutenant Newick, "have this cabin prepared for him. Warn Captain Woods that I shall be moving into his quarters – "

"Sir," Ramage said quietly, "I don't think the Count will move from the *Calypso*. Apart from anything else, his main concern is to get to England as quickly as possible."

"I don't want any argument from you about this," Tewtin said firmly. "He will be my guest, and that's that. Have him sent over in a boat – no, I'll send over my barge. That will be more comfortable for a sick man."

"Sir, please leave the Count where he is: he anticipated your kindness," Ramage said tactfully, "and was most emphatic that he should stay in the *Calypso*." Suddenly Ramage thought of another excuse. "He prefers to talk French: in fact, he is so weakened by the fever that he has great difficulty in speaking English. Do you have a fluent French speaker…?"

"Well, as long as you have faith in your surgeon," Tewtin said grudgingly. "But I would be most distressed if the Prince of Wales…most distressed," he repeated, without elaborating.

Ramage thought of his men on board the prizes and then decided not to mention them. Southwick would be retrieving the men as soon as the prizes had been cleared by the quarantine authorities. It would be better to leave Rear-Admiral Tewtin to sleep on the thought that he had two extra frigates if he wanted them, and to reflect on why he should not delay a friend of the Prince of Wales.

"I have a number of other Royalists on board, sir," Ramage said and, noting the gleam in Tewtin's eye, hurriedly added:

"They are very frightened that Bonaparte will take reprisals against their families in France, so they are very anxious that their names be kept secret. You will appreciate that they do not want to be invited to any receptions. In fact, I rather fear the Count will expect to hear our sailing date when I return on board."

"But you have to water and provision, surely?" Tewtin said. "And the prizes – buying them in: I have to have them surveyed and valued…it all takes time."

"Indeed, sir," Ramage said soothingly, knowing that having Tewtin on board to meet the Count in a day or so would work wonders: it would give the admiral something to tell his wife about in his next letter home.

Tewtin suddenly snapped his fingers and shook his head, as though irritated with himself. "There's a letter for you from the Admiralty – from Lord St Vincent, I believe." He waved a hand at Newick. "Fetch it – you should have reminded me."

Again Ramage felt the strange chill. It was not a change in orders, telling him to take the *Calypso* or the Count to, say, Jamaica instead of England, because Their Lordships had no idea that Jean-Jacques had been rescued. There were (he finally forced himself to face the fact) no letters waiting for him from Sarah when he had expected a couple of dozen at least: she would have written every day, even if only writing letters like a diary, but she would have posted several. Lord St Vincent would certainly have sent a message telling her that a Post Office packet left for Barbados on regular dates and would carry any letters she had ready.

"Sir," Newick said, and Ramage realized he had been repeating the word several times as he held out a packet with the familiar Admiralty seal.

"Thank you," Ramage said automatically and picked up the canvas pouch. He dropped the packet into the pouch and took out his report of proceedings, handing it to Tewtin.

The rear-admiral saw it was a lengthy document and realized it was bound to take several pages to reduce to writing the story which Ramage had paraphrased.

"Very well, my boy, I will read this and we'll have the prizes surveyed and valued as soon as possible. You'll soon be on your way," he added jovially. "You to return to your new wife; the Count to call on the Prince of Wales. Although I haven't read your report yet, it does seem to me you have done an outstanding job. Off you go, then, and do assure the Count he would be very welcome and I will get passages for the other French Royalists in the next convoy for England."

The *Queen's* boat taking Ramage back to the *Calypso* seemed to go so slowly that to him the seamen might have been ancients rowing through molasses. He climbed on board, nodded to Aitken who, as first lieutenant, was waiting at the entryport to greet him, and went straight down to his cabin. The canvas pouch seemed to be weighing a hundredweight by now; Lord St Vincent's letter appeared in his imagination as a harbinger of some nameless evil he could not imagine.

He tossed the pouch on his desk and sat down at the chair. Steady, he told himself, it's only a packet. Probably just a private letter from St Vincent with a message for the Count from the Prince of Wales, or perhaps some advice on how to deal with it all (the Earl would have to assume that Ramage had been successful). And judging from the thickness of the packet, there were fresh orders, too. Nor would that be unusual. He had been sent across the Atlantic on the orders of Admiral Clinton, commanding the Channel Fleet, but it had all been a highly irregular proceeding because of the emergency. With the Prince of Wales now involved, it would be quite normal for the Admiralty to take control again. Which is what the letter must be about. And, he asked himself, what was he getting so depressed about? Just break the seal and read the stylized wording, hallowed by tradition …He reached for the paper-knife and slid it under the seal. Slowly he unfolded the cover. Inside was one sealed letter marked "Personal and Private", and another which was clearly orders.

"My dear Ramage," the letter began (a glance at the signature showed it was from the First Lord), "regard this letter as relaying a rumour, not necessarily fact, but I feel it my duty to keep you informed about such a delicate matter. As you know, Admiral Clinton sent back to England the *Murex* brig which you so skilfully cut out of Brest, and she was bringing home Lady Ramage and the former captain of the *Calypso*."

And that, Ramage noted, was a very discreet way of describing that drunken scoundrel, and he could imagine the Earl then wondering how to describe Sarah. The First Lord knew Ramage did not use his title in the service, but Sarah was titled both as the daughter of the Marquis and as the wife of an earl's son who bore one of his father's titles.

Ramage suddenly jerked himself out of the reverie: Earl St Vincent, a man who could make sword steel look like putty, was not a man who ordinarily relayed rumours.

"The *Murex* brig was due in Spithead two weeks ago. She has not yet arrived. The weather has been good with a brisk southwester blowing – and a messenger was sent to Plymouth with orders that I should be notified the moment she arrives. All the other southern ports have been similarly instructed.

"Thus it is my unpleasant duty to inform you that at the time the messenger leaves for Falmouth with this letter in tonight's pouch, we have no news. I have talked with your father and with the Marquis, and while both agree with me that there are many possible reasons why the *Murex* should not have arrived, ranging from dismasting to taking a prize and having to shepherd her in, we all felt that you should be informed, which I have now done, and remain your obedient servant, St Vincent."

Sarah was, at best, a prisoner of the French. At worst she had been killed or drowned when the brig was captured or sunk by bad weather or a French ship of war or privateer. A brief honeymoon and, because of some mutinous scoundrels and a drunken young post-captain, she was dead. Killed because she had been witless enough to fall in love with Nicholas Ramage.

The cabin darkened and shrank round him: his body tightened as an uncontrollable spasm drove out every thought except the one that he had dreaded – Sarah was dead. He was alone, and had lost the love he had begun to despair of ever finding. Yes, he had earlier loved Gianna, but that had eventually only served as a yardstick by which he could measure the depth of his love for Sarah. He began to curse the injustice of it: many couples had twenty, thirty and even more years of marriage before one or other of them went over the standing part of the foresheet. But he and Sarah had been together, as man and wife, for how long – a month? They had known each other for a few months. The stark, blinding unfairness of it all. Why Sarah? Why hadn't a roundshot cut him in half instead? This thought calmed him down. Lord St Vincent was not saying that she was dead: only that she was dead *or* a prisoner, and given the usual ratio of casualties in an action, the odds were ninety-eight to one that she had been taken prisoner.

How a crowd of French privateersmen would treat a woman prisoner sent another muscle-tightening spasm of rage through his body, but to have her alive...Then he felt himself calming slightly: it was impossible to imagine Sarah dead. Yet surely all lovers must feel their partners were immortal: bereavement was what happened to other couples.

He suddenly realized that for two or three minutes there had been a steady knocking at his door, and the Marine sentry's call was now being reinforced by the agitated calls of Aitken and Southwick.

"Come in!" he called and the door flung open, Aitken almost sprawling as he rushed through, crouched so that his head did not hit the beams. He stared at Ramage sitting at the desk but jerked as Southwick, head down, bumped into him.

Aitken was quick to recover. "Sorry, sir, but you didn't answer."

"I was thinking," Ramage said lamely, "but come in and shut the door." He saw both men were pale under their tans, and although Aitken might be satisfied with the explanation, Southwick certainly was not: the old master had served with him so long that his role had slowly changed to – well, what? A benevolent grandfather dependent on his grandson's largesse? Anyway, the old man was now standing over him, a puzzled look creasing his face. "Are you *sure* everything is all right, sir?"

Ramage thought for a moment. If he did not tell them now, he would have to keep the news to himself all the way to England, like a man nursing a guilty secret, so now was the time. He held up the First Lord's letter. "If you can't read the signature, it's from Lord St Vincent."

Southwick sighed, as though he knew from long experience that letters from such heights never carried welcome news, and sat down, giving the page a shake to straighten it out. As he read, Aitken said quietly, by way of explanation: "When you came back from the *Queen*, sir, your face was white as a sheet. You seemed to be trembling. We thought you'd been struck by one of these sudden fluxes."

Ramage shook his head and nodded towards the letter that Southwick had just finished reading. The old man's features were frozen as he handed the letter back to Ramage without a word. Ramage gave it to Aitken, who took the precaution of sitting on the settee first: he had seen the effect on Southwick. He read it through twice, folded it and gave it back to Ramage without comment, but the skin now seemed too tight on his face.

Then Ramage remembered Jean-Jacques. The Count had been entranced by Sarah. And the four Frenchmen, Gilbert, Louis, Auguste and Albert, who had come to serve in the *Calypso* after helping to capture the *Murex* brig: they regarded Sarah as a woman among women for the part she had played.

He was bewildered; he pulled himself together enough to realize that. But the news of Sarah had torn a piece of himself away: the part that had feelings, that told him what to do...

He then remembered the second enclosure in the packet which was still lying on top of his desk. He opened the seal, more to take his mind off St Vincent's news than because of any curiosity about new orders. For that was what they were.

They were signed, as usual, by Evan Nepean, the Secretary to the Board of Admiralty, and began in one of the time-honoured fashions, "I am directed by My Lords Commissioners of the Admiralty to acquaint you..." which told Ramage at once that whatever the orders were, they would not be radical: new orders usually began: "You are hereby requested and required to..."

Ramage glanced quickly through the copperplate writing and, having assured himself there was no petard smouldering among the sentences, waiting to hoist him into more trouble, read through again, more slowly.

For a bizarre moment he pictured Their Lordships sitting solemnly round the long polished table in the Boardroom with a box in front of them full of slips of paper on which was written the word "whereas". While dictating their instructions to Nepean they would, every minute or so, skim another "whereas" slip across to him, to insert in the letter he was drafting.

Anyway, whereas Captain Ramage had been on Admiralty approved leave in France when hostilities had again broken out, and whereas he had managed to escape in the *Murex* brig and join Admiral Clinton upon the commander-in-chief's arrival off Brest with the blockading force, "and whereas Admiral Clinton had given Captain Ramage command of his former frigate the *Calypso*" (and there Ramage recognized the gentle rap over the knuckles: although he had applied to the Admiralty for leave to go abroad, as laid down in the Instructions, and been granted it, the fact was when the war suddenly broke out again he was not with his ship. The Admiralty never sought or listened to excuses – officers went on leave by their own choice – and generally had a bovine disregard for fairness or logic).

" – and whereas Admiral Clinton gave certain orders concerning the capture of the French frigate *L'Espoir* and the release of French Royalists, among them the Count of Rennes, and whereas Their Lordships have now assumed that these orders have been successfully executed" (an indication, as if one was needed, Ramage thought to himself, that there was no excuse for failure), "Their Lordships direct that having called at Barbados with the prize and the Royalists, the refugees, the Count of Rennes among them, are to be given passages in suitable merchant ships and sent back to England with the first convoy.

"Their Lordships further direct that you are to remain in command of the *Calypso* frigate, which should also return to England and is now again under Admiralty orders." Which meant, Ramage noted, that Rear-Admiral Tewtin could not interfere.

Any prizes taken in the course of the original operation, Nepean continued, should be handed over to the commander-in-chief, the Windward Island Station, who would buy them in for service or otherwise dispose of them. And Nepean had the honour to be, etc.

So there it was. Their Lordships (which probably meant in fact a quorum of three members of the Board) blithely assumed one could do the impossible, and afterwards punctiliously sent out fresh orders to keep one gainfully occupied, just as one leaned back to rest a moment and take a deep breath. Still, it was better than facing a court of inquiry (or even a court-martial) because of failure.

But now there was all the irritating detail, although arranging passages for the refugees should not be difficult – there were a couple of score of merchant ships already anchored in the Bay, and obviously a convoy was being assembled.

Admiral Tewtin would no doubt present a few problems (no local flag officer liked a ship in his waters receiving direct Admiralty orders) but Ramage could use the actual orders as a talisman: they were as binding on Tewtin as on Ramage himself. The two prize frigates – well, whatever price Tewtin decided on had eventually to be approved by the Admiralty and Navy Board who, to be fair, were just as likely to raise a low one as reduce another that was too high. So within the week the *Calypso* should be on her way across the Atlantic to England, with the Royalists following in the convoy.

The *Calypso*, he remembered with a shock like a gun going off beside him, would be going to an England where Sarah would not be waiting to greet them. And now he must go to tell Jean-Jacques.

CHAPTER **THREE**

Admiral Tewtin read through the Admiralty's orders once again and then looked up at Ramage, who was sitting opposite him across the big desk in the *Queen*'s great cabin, the sun reflecting harshly through the sternlights and almost blinding Ramage when each wave threw up a flash of sunlight, as if deliberately trying to dazzle him. "Yes," Tewtin said, folding the page, "it all fits together very well: I'll buy in the prizes because I need frigates to escort this next convoy: we'll arrange passages in the merchant ships for the refugees – for the Royalists," he corrected himself, "and then you can command the convoy when it sails for England."

"But...but that's not my understanding of the orders, sir," Ramage protested.

"It's *my* understanding," Tewtin said shortly, "and that's what matters."

And Tewtin was right: it would be six months or more before the Admiralty could reprimand him for delaying the *Calypso*, and only a fool would think that the Admiralty valued the frigate's speedy arrival in England more than the safe arrival of a large trade convoy.

The Count was safe, which was what mattered as far as the Prince of Wales was concerned, and would be coming home in the convoy. In addition, Ramage reflected, from Tewtin's point of view there was a good chance of the convoy arriving unscathed if Ramage commanded it: all too often convoys were commanded by frigate captains who were fit for nothing else or had fallen out of favour with the admiral. It was not too difficult to fall out of favour with some admirals – when sent to "cruise", a euphemism for hunting for prizes, it was no good coming back too often with stories of bad luck. The admiral's share in a prize was an eighth of its value; a couple of years on a good station usually meant he could buy a large country estate and put enough in the Funds to run it, apart from buying a knighthood or baronetcy and, with luck, having a seat in Parliament, being in effect issued one of those like Rochester which, with several others, the Admiralty regarded as its own property…Admiral Sir Hyde Parker was thought to have made £200,000 in prize money during his recent four years as commander-in-chief at Jamaica, generally reckoned the most lucrative station of all. So no doubt Tewtin had high hopes, and those hopes rested almost entirely on his frigate captains. That in turn depended on having frigates. No commander-in-chief ever had enough of them, so Tewtin was very lucky to have three arrive unexpectedly out of the south, a bonus he could use for the convoy without losing any of his own yet two of which he could fill with his own people. Each of the two prizes now needed a captain and three lieutenants, apart from warrant and petty officers. The commander-in-chief of the station made all such promotions, although they had to be approved afterwards by the Admiralty.

Watched by Tewtin, Ramage picked up the Admiralty orders and read them through once more. They had been drafted in good faith and neither Their Lordships nor Nepean could have anticipated the present situation. Tewtin could not interfere with a ship acting under direct Admiralty orders, but he was too cunning for that. The Admiralty had ordered the *Calypso* back to England, but they had not added a phrase like "with all possible despatch", or "without delay". This, Ramage noted bitterly, allowed Tewtin to claim that since the *Calypso* was returning to England anyway, she might as well take the convoy under her protection.

There was just one more card to play, a poor and miserable card but the only one he had left.

"To be perfectly honest, sir, I'm worried about the Count of Rennes. He is in a desperate hurry to get back to England, to see the Prince of Wales – and of course he has large estates in Kent. I had been wondering whether or not I should keep him on board the *Calypso* and make a dash for it."

Tewtin nodded understandingly. "I see your problem, but I hope the Count is grateful to you – and the Royal Navy – for rescuing him. Now is not the time to show impatience – why, but for you he would be rotting on Devil's Island. From what I hear, the prisoners don't last very long down there. If your Count of Rennes makes a fuss," he said portentously, "I'll have a word with him. In the meantime, transfer him to that merchant ship – what's she called? – where he has a suite awaiting him."

At that point Ramage knew he was beaten: at the end of a week in Barbados, he was going to have to command a convoy back to England, and all he could do now was hope that the merchant ships were not too undermanned, that their sails were not so ripe they were furled in anything of a breeze, that their spars were not so sun-dried and shaken that they would forever be signalling to one of the escort that they needed assistance – which meant sending across a carpenter and his mates to fish a spar.

All of which meant that all too many shipowners sent their ships to the West Indies with too few men and ancient sails, with rigging and cordage that should have been replaced a year ago, spars and yards that had shakes in them wide and deep enough to trap a man's finger, if not a whole hand

– and always relying on the Royal Navy in an emergency to help them. And usually the Royal Navy had no choice: a disabled ship left behind by the convoy could be a ship lost to French privateers, and there would be violent letters of protest arriving at the Admiralty from the outraged owners and the insurance underwriters, and woe betide the poor frigate captain who was exasperated beyond control by these constant demands on his men and resources. Not for nothing did most commanders of convoys and the escorts refer to the masters of merchant ships as "mules".

When would the Admiralty in its collective wisdom put its collective foot down and stop these profiteering shipowners from running their ships at the taxpayers' expense? With very few exceptions, shipowners were making their fortunes, thanks to the war. To begin with, the convoy system stopped any rush for a ship to be among the first dozen or so to arrive in England with the new harvest of sugar, tobacco, nutmeg or whatever it was to reap a high price in the market place. The convoy system meant all the ships arrived at once, their cargoes swamping the market, which was bad luck for the shippers (the planters in the West Indies, in this case) but fine for the shipowners. In peacetime, the faster ships (well kept and well commanded) could reasonably charge the highest freight because the planters, first at the market with their produce, made a good profit. In wartime there was no need for fast ships, and unscrupulous ship owners were quick to buy up any hull that would swim and could be insured: the convoy system ensured that she would not be beaten into port by faster ships and the Royal Navy was forced (blackmailed, in fact) to keep her afloat. And, to save any strain and wear on sails, spars, masts and cordage (costs, in other words), the damned mules always reefed at night, no matter how scant the breeze.

In turn that meant that each could sail with a smaller crew: with no risk of having to reef in a squall, many of these smaller traders sailed with only a master, mate, a couple of apprentices (whose indentures meant they were paying to be on board) and half a dozen men. Food, from what Ramage heard, was bad, and any complaints by the crew to a master met with a standard response: a man or two could easily be handed over to the next pressgang that came in sight. The choice was simple: serve in a merchant ship with bad food but higher pay, signing on for a single round-trip voyage, or be swept into one of the King's ships, serving until the next peace, which at the moment seemed a lifetime away.

When he returned to the *Calypso* and stepped through the entryport, Aitken met him with a broad grin on his face. "Mr Southwick wanted to talk to you before you go below, sir," he said, "and I've passed the word for him."

"What's all this about?" Ramage asked impatiently: he had been sitting in his cutter so long that the heat now soaking him with perspiration seemed to come from inside his body, as though it was a glowing coal. At that moment Southwick, also grinning, bustled up.

"You have visitors, sir, and I took the liberty of taking them down to wait in the cabin, where it's cooler."

Why was Southwick so concerned about visitors? Why the grin? Why the "I've got a surprise for you" way he was rubbing his hands like a parson with the Easter offering? Ramage, still at the entryport, looked outboard along the boat boom, rigged out at right angles to the ship's side and to which the painters of boats were secured. Only the *Calypso*'s cutter was now secured there, so how had the visitors arrived? Had they dropped from a passing cloud? And who wanted visitors at this moment: he was still so angry over Tewtin's behaviour that he just wanted to go down to his cabin and brood in peace and quiet. Sulk, really, because Tewtin had trapped him with an Admiralty order, and the prospect of driving a convoy of a hundred mules back to England at an average speed (if he was lucky and found the right winds and persuaded the mules to keep enough canvas set) of perhaps four knots. Days and weeks must pass before he could discover anything about Sarah.

At such a time a man wanted solitude, just as a sick animal hid away in a dark corner. He did *not* want to be surrounded by a noisy throng, all of whom would be fortifying themselves with rum punches and determined to cheer him up, not realizing that trying to cheer up a man in these circumstances only emphasized his loneliness: one was never more alone than in a crowd.

But Southwick and Aitken were still waiting expectantly, and he walked aft to the companionway. He clattered down the ladder, acknowledged the salute of the Marine sentry outside his door, pushed it open and walked into the cabin which, because his eyes had been dazzled by the sun reflecting up from the sea and the scrubbed decks, seemed very dark. There was a man sitting at his desk and he was just conscious of another smaller figure on the settee.

As the man stood up, Ramage recognized him and suddenly realized that of all his friends – few as they were – this was the one he most wanted to see at this moment. No wonder Southwick was grinning: the three of them had been shipmates several years ago, when Ramage had been under orders to find out why so many of the Post Office packets were being captured by French privateers.

As a startled Ramage just stared the man laughed. "You didn't expect to find that fellow Sidney Yorke sitting at your desk, eh?"

Ramage shook his head, trying to gain a few moments while he collected his thoughts. "No, hardly! I expected you to be in London, chasing clerks, bullying your shipmasters, and becoming very rich. Oh yes, and marrying and beginning a large family."

As he finished the last sentence he followed Yorke's eyes round to the settee and saw that the person sitting on it was a woman of such beauty and poise that he felt dizzy, almost disoriented by the surprise. Yorke had found an exquisite wife, and Ramage found himself walking forward in a daze to kiss the proffered hand and muttering "Daphne".

"You two have never met," Yorke said, his voice revealing a pride in both of them.

"But I have heard so much about you, Captain," the woman said, "that I feel I have known you for years. Why Sidney never persuaded you to visit us I don't know!"

Ramage hurriedly thought back across the years. Yorke had never mentioned a wife.

"The gallant captain was always rushing about in those days," Yorke said, "and of course there was the beautiful Marchesa!"

"Ah yes," the woman said, "the Marchesa. But we heard before we left England that she had returned to Italy..."

She broke off, as if realizing she should not have mentioned it, but Yorke said: "It's all right: Nicholas must know she was caught in France when the war started again. Have you any news of her?"

Ramage shook his head. "Not a word. I know she stayed a few days with the Herveys in Paris, but whether or not she had left for Italy, I don't know."

Ramage pulled himself together and realized he was still holding the woman's hand, and Yorke introduced them formally: "Captain the Lord Ramage...Miss Alexis Yorke..."

Ramage kissed her hand and then said politely: "Sidney, I trust you and Mrs Yorke will stay to dinner? Are you travelling in one of your own ships?"

As Yorke accepted the invitation, the woman laughed: the charming and tinkling laugh of a happy person who had just heard something amusing.

"Answering the last question first, yes. We came out in the *Emerald*. We planned a nice quiet voyage to celebrate the peace, and who knows, I might have found out here what I can't find in England!"

"And what is that?"

"*Who* is that," Yorke corrected, grinning.

"Very well, who. And have you succeeded?"

"A wife, and no, I haven't succeeded."

A dumbfounded Ramage turned to the woman, who burst out laughing. "I *thought* you heard Sidney introduce me as 'Mrs', but he said '*Miss*' Alexis Yorke. I am (thank goodness) his sister, not his wife. In fact I have been sorting out the widows, fortune-hunters and desperate mothers among the islands and – "

" – and she has rejected the whole lot of them," Yorke said.

"Out of hand," Alexis said firmly. She looked up at Ramage, who realized she had large eyes which seemed in the shade of the cabin to be black, and she gave what could only be described as an impish grin. "You see, it isn't just a question of a wife for Sidney, but a sister-in-law for me."

"Quite," Ramage said carefully. "It could be a problem."

"Not 'could', but 'will'. Sidney will expect his bride to be immune from seasickness and as fond of going to sea in his ships as he is. She won't, of course; she'll hate the sea and will get sick even in a well-sprung carriage going down the Mall, so she will stay at home when he goes off on his voyages and every day she will come round and weep on my shoulder."

"You have no sense of family loyalty," Yorke chided. "You should be only too glad to console a grieving sister-in-law."

"I'll console a *grieving* sister-in-law," Alexis said, "but not a moping one, and if I don't keep an eye on you we'll end up with a moper."

"You could get married and live at the other end of the country," Ramage commented, but she shook her head.

"Don't suggest that," Yorke said. "She's already inspected all the eligible men and found them wanting. If she lives at the other end of the country, I'll have my house forever cluttered up with a brother-in-law complaining that his wife has just gone off on a sea voyage..."

"I love sea voyages," Alexis said, and her laugh seemed to make the *Calypso* come alive. "But not every man does."

"What she means is that when the suitors come knocking on the door, the first question she asks is whether or not they like sea voyages. If they say no, they don't cross the threshold."

Ramage excused himself for a moment: he had to give instructions to his steward for the meal. Silkin, sensing that with two guests the captain would at last allow him to fetch out all the silver and cut glass that stayed so long in drawers amid green baize, and napery that yellowed with disuse, listened carefully. The courses he and the captain would like to serve were limited by the frigate's cooking facilities and the fact that he could not get on shore and buy a prime cut of meat in time to roast it. Roasting food was a time-consuming job in a frigate's galley.

"Lobsters," Ramage said. "You can do much with lobsters. The wardroom bought a lamb yesterday. See if they will sell me enough to make up a plate of cold cuts."

"The prizes," Silkin reminded him. "All those salami sausages, or whatever the French call them. There are those what likes that sort o' thing, sliced thin. And we've a couple of hams left that go ten pounds each."

The midday meal, traditionally eaten by the captain about two o'clock and called dinner, was going to be a pleasant one. At that moment, Ramage realized that he had never enjoyed a meal he had to eat alone: it was as if guests were needed to give food any piquancy.

He went up on deck into the dazzling sunlight to find Aitken and explain why Southwick and not he was being invited to dinner, but the Scotsman understood only too well: the master had already told him how Mr Yorke was with them in the Post Office packet.

Ramage turned to go back down the companionway and found that Alexis had come up the steps and was now looking through one of the gunports. She turned and smiled as he approached.

"Are visitors allowed on deck?" she asked.

"Visitors such as yourself are *encouraged* to be on deck," Ramage said lightly. "The sun seems brighter."

Again that impish smile. "You are very gallant, Captain."

"The opportunities are very rare," he said dryly.

"Who is 'Daphne'?" she asked quietly.

"Daphne? I don't know anyone of that name," he said lamely. The name had sprung to mind the moment he saw her in the shadowed cabin; but surely he had not spoken it aloud?

"I heard you say it and I saw your lips forming it," she said, "but I must not pry into your secret."

"Secret? No secret, I assure you," he said, trying to hide his embarrassment. He managed to muster a laugh. "Oh indeed, no secret!"

"Very well, then who *is* Daphne?"

She was wearing a long, close-fitting olive dress which was pleated below the knees, obviously intended to give her free movement in awkward places like ship's companionways. Her hair was long and the colour of honey except on the top and sides, where the sun had bleached it. She had left her hat below in the cabin, he noticed. Her face was heart-shaped but with high cheekbones, and her nose –

"I shan't allow myself to be inspected until you tell me about Daphne," she said with feigned sternness.

"I really can't tell you," Ramage found himself stammering.

"You are blushing," she said. "Is she very beautiful?"

The devil take it, Ramage thought: she is a stranger who through Sidney has known of me for years; she is being persistent, and if I do not answer now I shall never hear the last of it.

"She's very beautiful, yes; but she's cold and lifeless and ignores me completely."

"You set me a puzzle," she said. "Now I have to guess who Daphne is! Could I have met her?"

"No, you could not possibly," he said, now alarmed. "She doesn't exist. She's imaginary."

She stood closer and murmured: "The Daphne I saw in your eyes existed: I was watching you. You looked round, saw me and said 'Daphne'. Had it not been so quiet I might have thought you said 'Damn me!' from surprise, but I was sure you said 'Daphne' and you've just confirmed it."

"Confirmed it?" Ramage exclaimed. "How? I said I didn't know anyone of that name!"

"There's some association, then. Ah – you *are* blushing under all that sun-tan. Tell me, or you'll never have a moment's peace."

"Oh, very well," Ramage said ungraciously. "A marble statue. Of Daphne. You've never seen it."

"I hope I have," she said. "As a very young girl when I felt clumsy and ugly, when I was making the Grand Tour and seeing what Italy had to offer. Let me see, Daphne is tall and slender, both arms are lifted in the air, and most of her is naked. Except for her left leg, which is turning into the bark of a tree trunk, and her hands too are changing into sprigs of laurel, and she is crying out to her father for help to stop this terrible metamorphosis – and close, holding her with one hand but helpless to do anything, is Apollo, from whom she is fleeing. You flatter me, Captain!" She moved back a pace, as if to let him see her more clearly. "Surely I am not really like the Daphne created by Bernini!"

His eyes dropped to her breasts, outlined perfectly beneath the dress, and he could imagine the flat belly on which, in the statue, Apollo's hand rested.

He looked up to find two grey eyes watching him. Daring him? Certainly far from offended. Yes, she understood: she knew that her warm body had just been compared with one of the most exquisite female bodies ever revealed in marble, and the comparison apparently neither offended nor embarrassed her. Those grey eyes, the calm look, the complete composure seemed to be saying: "Well, what is the verdict?"

And he heard her say, softly: "Well, what is the verdict?"

"You know already," he said. "I recognized you at once."

"I always thought," she said conversationally, "that Bernini's Apollo was too young. In my imagination I had always thought him older – about your age, I suppose."

"Daphne is as I always thought her," he muttered, finding his breath reluctant to go down to his lungs.

"My brother will be wondering where we are," she said. "Or what we are talking about, anyway."

The meal was the most sparkling that Ramage could remember: the long and dangerous voyage that Yorke, Southwick and he had made (with Jackson, Stafford and

Rossi) in the Post Office packet to discover why the ships were being captured now turned into a tale of teasing and hilarious episodes (hilarious when told now; terrifying at the time) which kept the three men glowing with reminiscence and many times brought protests from an almost incoherent Alexis, weakened by laughter and hiccoughs as the narrative began in Jamaica and proceeded to Portugal. The afternoon was finally brought to an end when Aitken passed the word that a lieutenant had arrived from the flagship with a pouch full of papers for Ramage.

They comprised, as he complained sourly to Southwick, just about every paper an admiral's imaginative clerk could draw up. For the two prizes – a bundle of papers including the surveys of their hulls by the master carpenter of the Barbados yard and two carpenters from the fleet; on their sails by the *Queen*'s master and the master attendant at the yard; on their guns by the flagship's gunner and two more from other ships; on their provisions by the flagship's purser and master, assisted by two other masters…and so it went on. In one of the French frigates, a cask of red wine with a loose bung had turned to vinegar – so the contents were valued as vinegar, not wine…

Yorke, Southwick and Alexis waited while he turned the pages – he had wanted to glance through all the papers, in case any were urgent, before saying goodbye to the Yorkes because at the moment he had no hint when the convoy was to sail.

Ah, there was the final valuation for one of the frigates: £11,384 11s 6d.

He skimmed through the second survey until he came to the valuation: £1,284 6s 2d less. That made a total of £21,484, which in turn meant that Admiral Clinton's eighth (which he did not have to share with a second-in-command because he had not joined Clinton off Brest at the time the *Calypso* sailed) was about £2,600, with £5,300 or so for himself, £2,600 for the *Calypso*'s officers, master and surgeon, the same for the midshipmen, other warrant officers, Marine sergeant and so on, and the rest of the ship's company would share £5,300. Considering the pay of an ordinary seaman was 19 shillings a month, the wild hour it had taken to capture each of the frigates had been profitable.

He saw Southwick watching him and guessed the old master realized he had reached the valuations – which were in fact the prices at which Rear-Admiral Tewtin was prepared to buy in the prizes and put them into service with the Royal Navy. Fortunately these sort of purchases rarely led to disputes: the Admiralty and the Navy Board had long ago put a price on ships' tonnages with allowances for age and condition, and on just about every object to be found in a ship, so the various surveys carried out by men who did not stand to gain or lose a penny were usually very fair.

Ramage read out the total figures.

Alexis, who knew that the two frigates concerned were the prizes the *Calypso* had captured at Devil's Island, gave a contemptuous sniff. "That doesn't seem a very good price for two splendid frigates!"

"Please excuse my sister," Yorke said jocularly.

"But no," Alexis protested, "there's not a ship in *our* fleet whose hull is not insured for more than three times one of those frigates."

"They carry more than three times the cargo!" Yorke said.

"I'm talking of the hull insurance only. Anyway, they're not so dangerous to capture," Alexis protested, to be calmed by a smiling Southwick.

"If we captured such a French merchant ship laden with cargo, ma'am, we'd probably get three times the prize money."

Ramage nodded in agreement and opened the next packet. His orders for the convoy. "Seventy-two ships," he commented to no one in particular. "All the ships rendezvous here, thank goodness."

"Why is that a good thing?" Alexis asked, collecting a frown from her brother. "Oh, pardon me: these are not matters concerning women!"

"They concern the *Emerald*, so they concern you," Ramage said idly, his eyes skimming down the copperplate hand-writing of Tewtin's clerk. "The advantage of sailing from here is that all seventy-two ships must assemble here by the set date, and then we all sail together. But if we started with, say, twenty-five from here, and then went on to pick up ten from St Vincent, and another fifteen from St Lucia, and the rest from Tortola, we'd be delayed a month...at St Vincent there'd be three ships still waiting for the last of their cargo, and they'd have a sorry story that if I did not wait they'd have to sail in the next convoy and they'd be ruined...and so it would go on. Here, if there are only sixty-five ships ready when the convoy is due to sail, Admiral Tewtin will send us on our way..."

"I love Barbados," Alexis said. "Can Sidney and I persuade you to come to the races with us tomorrow afternoon – after a meal on board the *Emerald*?"

Ramage looked at Yorke for confirmation but he grinned. "You'll get used to it," he said cheerfully. "I own the shares in the company but she runs it."

"You don't own *all* of them," she protested.

"Not *all*," he said mockingly, "but enough that I don't *have* to listen to you."

"But you do, though."

"Just out of politeness," he said, and Ramage saw the affection in his glance.

CHAPTER **FOUR**

As the captain's coxswain, Jackson always commanded the boat carrying Ramage to and from another ship; while he steered the *Calypso*'s cutter towards the flagship he reflected on the years he had served with Mr Ramage, and how often they had been in action together, frequently side by side.

From there it was an easy daydream trying to remember how often each had saved the other's life. Jackson eventually gave up trying to reach a total because how did one count a shouted warning which saved death from a slashing sword or a well aimed pistol, compared with actually warding off the sword, or shooting down the man aiming the pistol?

It was a pointless exercise anyway because, as far as he could see, the two of them were running about equal, and if they were to stay alive and die of old age, they were going to have to carry on as before until this war ended – if it ever did.

Apart from the recent year and a half following the Treaty of Amiens, which did not really count, Jackson found he could not remember what peace was like: the war had been going on for – well, it must be eight or nine years now.

Ramage, sitting in the sternsheets and trying to get some shade from the brim of his hat, although as many rays reflected up from the waves as came directly from the sun, suddenly had a shock. He had been thinking of Sarah, and how many more tedious weeks of worry must pass before he had any definite news, when he found that he could not recall her face.

Every time he called on his memory, he saw only a blur. Yes, her voice came, and a few of her mannerisms: he could hear some of her little jokes and many of the whispered endearments. But her face, like an elusive word or name, refused to appear.

In her place he saw Alexis, and guiltily he dismissed her immediately, telling himself that as he had been talking to her only a few hours ago it was hardly surprising she came to mind so readily.

And here was the *Queen*: already her lookouts had hailed, already Jackson had shouted back the answer: "*Calypso!*", warning the flagship that the approaching boat carried the captain of the named ship, and ensuring that sideboys would be ready, holding out the sideropes.

Ramage grasped the canvas pouch which had been resting on his lap. Rear-Admiral Tewtin would want to talk about the convoy: what route Ramage intended to take back to England (and the answer to that would be that it depended on wind direction), and no doubt a few ships would be mentioned as being of special concern – meaning the owners were friends of the admiral, or friends were shipping cargoes in those ships.

In fact, Ramage found the admiral in good humour. Or, to be more exact, once he found that Ramage accepted the valuations of the two frigates, he stayed in the good humour with which he had obviously greeted the dawn.

"You read the papers about the convoy?"

"Yes, sir, and the sailing date. No delays if ships haven't arrived?"

"Indeed not. The merchants throughout the islands have had the date for weeks. But can *you* be ready?"

"Yes, sir: we've started provisioning, and wooding and watering shouldn't take too long. But you didn't mention what other ships I'd have."

"Why, bless my soul!" Tewtin said, "the two prizes, of course!"

"But sir, they've neither ships' companies nor sufficient provisions. And *L'Espoir* is only armed *en flûte*." Ramage had a sudden picture of Tewtin expecting him to sail the ships to England with the original prize crews – two thirds of the *Calypso's* ship's company, in other words, leaving him with three virtually defenceless frigates to defend both themselves and the convoy.

Tewtin apparently correctly interpreted the reasons for the dismay showing on Ramage's face. "I'm making two of my lieutenants post, to command; two other promising young lieutenants will become first lieutenants, and four young lieutenants who should never have gone to sea will be getting their last chance…All thanks to you bringing in a couple of prize frigates, Ramage. Now I've been frank with you. I've put in good captains and good first lieutenants…"

"And the ship's company, sir? Aren't you short of seamen?"

The admiral looked slightly embarrassed. "Well, yes, I wish I could give you more men in both frigates, but you know how it is out here in the West Indies. I've lost a thousand men from yellow fever in the last year."

"So what's being done to make up the shortages in those two ships, sir?" Ramage asked, although, since he knew, the answer would be a formality.

"Take what you need from the best-manned ships in the convoy," Tewtin said nonchalantly. "Tell any masters who complain that the men will be more useful protecting the merchantmen by serving a gun in a frigate than cowering behind a few casks of molasses."

That was one thing about Tewtin, Ramage admitted: he did not beat about the bush. He had just found a way of sending the June convoy to England without having to use even one of his own frigates; he had been able to use two of the prizes to make post two of his favourite lieutenants and give two more of them hefty promotions (and at the same time get rid of some duds).

The hint that the Count of Rennes was a friend of the Prince of Wales and that it might be unwise to delay his return to England had made little impression: Tewtin might only be a rear-admiral but obviously he knew (or guessed) enough about Court life to know that Prinny's attention could be held at most for only a couple of minutes, unless the subject concerned women or the latest fashion in men's clothing.

"Lieutenant Newick has all your copies of the convoy instructions, one for each master, although God knows by now they should know them by heart. Secret signals – I haven't received the latest ones from the Admiralty (who nevertheless are trying to dissuade flag officers from issuing their own). So you'll have to draw up a set. Send them over here for copying – I know your clerk won't be able to make seventy-two copies in time."

Tewtin bellowed a hearty "Come in" when the sentry at the door announced a name, and Newick walked in, holding a bundle of papers and to be met by an angry Tewtin.

"Do you expect Mr Ramage to carry those convoy instructions round as though he's selling copies of the *Morning Post*? Have them sent down to his boat.

"When you reach flag rank, Ramage," he added, "if you haven't discovered it already, you'll find you're surrounded by dolts. And in my experience so far, the higher the rank the more dolts it attracts."

At that moment Ramage felt he could grow to like Tewtin, who said: "Hold the meeting of the convoy masters the day before they sail. Any earlier, they'll forget all your warnings. And it's just early enough in the hurricane season that all those scoundrels wanting to cadge sailcloth or a topsail yard or cordage can be told there's no time for any of that nonsense: hoist in boats and get the capstans and windlasses turning!"

Ramage sat at the far side of the room on a small dais – in fact a platform used by the auctioneer in Bridgetown when taking bids for whatever luxuries (like armchairs, crockery, cutlery and cloth) the latest convoy from England had brought in. The masters were coming in to Bridgetown's only large hall for the convoy conference, but Ramage knew from experience they were men who could only demonstrate their independence by being late. It was like the old and tedious story of a senior officer keeping you waiting fifteen minutes and unwittingly giving you a good insight into the uncertainty he felt about himself. A confident man had no need to play such silly games.

Southwick sat on his left and Aitken on his right, and in front of Ramage was a pile of twelve-page booklets, each measuring a dozen inches by eight. The title, in small type and neatly displayed between double rules, said: "*SIGNALS and INSTRUCTIONS for SHIPS under CONVOY*". In tiny type was the announcement: "Printed by W Winchester and Son, Strand."

"Forty-three of the mules up to now," Southwick growled.

"Don't be impatient, you're going to have their company for weeks..." Ramage chided as he turned over the first page of one of the booklets. The title was repeated, with the extra explanation: "*INSTRUCTIONS explanatory of the SIGNALS*".

As Ramage glanced down the seven numbered paragraphs on this first page he felt the all-too-familiar despair. Number III, for instance: "No signals are to be made by the ships under convoy besides those appointed by the Commander thereof." What would happen, in fact, was that proper signals made by the commander (himself) would be ignored and incomprehensible flag signals would be hoisted by mules. Days later it would transpire that the mules were using an old signal book from some past convoy.

The next instruction was almost a mockery: "The ships of the convoy out of their stations are to take advantage of all opportunities, by making sail, tacking, waring, &c to regain the same."

What forbearance (or plain stupidity) the Admiralty had shown in not making it a direct order that unless the weather made it necessary, the mules must not reef at night, or furl topsails, and drop so far astern that by dawn they would be specks on the horizon, just the trucks of their masts showing up in a powerful glass. Or, even worse, they would be below the horizon, and the whole convoy would have to heave-to until noon while they caught up. Well, Ramage thought grimly, if Yorke played his agreed role at this convoy conference, perhaps this time there would be less of all that nonsense.

The next instruction followed on logically: "In case of parting company (which the ships of the convoy are to avoid by all possible means) and being met with by an enemy, the Commanders of the ships are to destroy the rendezvous, these signals, and all other papers whatsoever concerning the destination of the fleet, *SEE PAGE 13.*"

Idly Ramage turned to page 13, although he knew what it said. It began by quoting the Act of Parliament under which it was enacted that "if the Captain of any merchant ship, under convoy, shall wilfully disobey signals or instructions, or any other lawful commands of the Commander of the convoy, without notice given, and leave obtained for that purpose", he was liable to be hauled into the High Court "at the suit of the Crown", and fined up to £500 or jailed for up to a year.

The next section warned a master that he could be fined £1,000 for sailing alone from a port where a convoy was being arranged, and more important, Ramage reckoned, he could be fined £1,000 if he should "afterwards desert or wilfully separate or depart from such convoy without leave obtained from the Captain or other Officer in His Majesty's Navy entrusted with the charge of such convoy..."

Ramage noted that the cheapest infringement for a master seeking a bargain was, ironically, for one of the most important tasks falling to a master in time of attack – he would have to pay up to £100 if, "being in danger of being boarded or taken possession of by the enemy", he "shall not make signals by firing guns, or otherwise convey information of his danger to the rest of the convoy, as well as to the ships of war under the protection of which he is sailing; and, in case of being boarded or taken possession of, shall not destroy all instructions confided to him relating to the convoy".

On the final page, a paragraph set by itself in solitary splendour and headed *MEMORANDUM* said:

All Masters of Merchant Vessels to supply themselves with a quantity of False Fires, to give the Alarm on the approach of an Enemy's Cruizer in the Night; or in the Day to make the usual Signal for an Enemy. On being chased or discovering a suspicious Vessel, and in the event of their Capture being inevitable, either by Night or Day, the Master to cause the Jeers, Ties, and Haul Yards to be cut and unrove, and their Vessels to be otherwise so disabled as to prevent their being immediately capable of making Sail.

Aitken muttered: "I think they're all here now, sir."

Ramage looked up to find the hall now almost full, and if a complete stranger looked at all the masters and tried to guess who they were, the chances are he would choose farmers attending an auction to bid for some well-favoured grazing land.

"Very well, Aitken: bring 'em to the starting post!"

Aitken rapped on the table. "Gentlemen, your attention please, and I introduce the commander of your escort, Captain Ramage."

There was an immediate buzz of conversation, and from what Ramage could hear of the masters in the front row, they were commenting on the name. One of them waved an arm like a schoolboy with a question.

"Is that the Captain Ramage we've read about in the *Gazettes*?"

"Aye, the very same one," Aitken answered, his Scots accent very pronounced.

At that moment Yorke's voice shouted from the back: "Captain Ramage, eh? Last time I saw you, you were firing across the bow of one of the convoy and then towing a slow ship – nearly towed her under, I recall, with the master crying for mercy from the fo'c'sle."

Ramage stood up and slowly looked round the room. Nearly eighty pairs of eyes were focused on him; their owners were looking at him with interest and, he thought, in some of them there was fear.

"Good morning, Gentlemen. As Lieutenant Aitken has just told you, I shall be commander of this convoy." He tapped the pile of *SIGNALS and INSTRUCTIONS* in front of him and waved towards Jackson and Stafford, who were standing behind the table. "Each of you will now be given a copy, which you've read as many times as you've sailed in convoy – I *hope* you have, anyway, because there are some interesting points in it.

"Now, to answer the question put by that gentleman at the back, who must have been in that particular convoy. He forgot to mention that the convoy reached England without loss, although we were attacked four times. Still, I should be misleading you if I did not warn you that anyone dropping astern at night because of unnecessarily reefing and furling, will get towed back into position by one of my frigates. That reef-and-furl nonsense can delay the convoy for half a day while you catch up at your leisure..."

"But that's outrageous!" bellowed one of the masters, a man whose complexion revealed his tippling. "I shall resist! To the utmost!"

"That is your privilege," Ramage said dryly. "Just remember that my orders are to get this convoy to England safely and your anticipated tardiness could endanger every other ship in the convoy. Look around you, sir: your desire for quiet nights in bed under reduced canvas will put every one of these other gentlemen and their ships at risk. The French are at sea, you know."

Ramage could hear the muttering now, like waves on a distant beach, and it seemed to be directed against the truculent master, who had to try to save face. "Well, if your fellows try to board me, they'll get a hot reception."

"I'll tell them," Ramage said coldly. "Less than a month ago the men in my frigate – 'my fellows' – captured two frigates from the French and you saw them being brought in as prizes. Those two frigates will be part of your escort. Your threat will no doubt fill 'my fellows' with alarm..."

Many of the masters began laughing and the original man contented himself with a gruff: "I know my rights."

"Yes," Ramage said pleasantly, "and you should know your obligations – they are set out in the booklets now being issued to you."

And now, he thought, thanks to Yorke's well-timed remark, none of these mules are under any illusions about what will happen if they delay. Perhaps one or two will go over to the *Queen* and complain to Admiral Tewtin, but Tewtin was so delighted with the idea of getting rid of the convoy without losing one of his own frigates that he would send the grumblers packing – probably adding his own threats as well.

"Well, gentlemen," Ramage continued, "let us get on with the serious business of the convoy. You will find tucked into the *SIGNALS and INSTRUCTIONS* a plan showing the position of every ship in the convoy. You'll see that the ships are spaced two cables apart. I want to warn you that I have chosen two cables, four hundred yards, not because it is my favourite number but because, first, that is a reasonable separation to avoid collisions and, secondly, it is a practical distance that gives the frigates room to manoeuvre among you should there be an attack by French privateers – or the French fleet."

"Is there any intelligence that the French fleet is at sea?" one of the masters asked nervously.

"No – but there's always a chance."

"Aren't we blockading Brest?"

"Yes, but French ships of war can sail from Toulon, Marseilles and a dozen other ports; they can also arrive from the East Indies, from Martinique..." Having got the idea across to the masters Ramage was reluctant to let it go, but for the moment he could not think of any other French ports. But the main threat was not from French ships of war.

"Gentlemen, we must all be on our guard against the main enemy – privateers. You've sailed in convoys before, most of you many times, but I must emphasize this. There's not much chance of a privateer being able to capture one of you if you stay in position in the convoy: your positions and the shape of the convoy have been selected to give the frigates in the escort the best opportunity of defending you.

"But if one of you straggles, drops astern during the night so that at dawn we just see your topmasts on the horizon, you are inviting a French privateer to snap you up.

"Any privateer with experience knows there's always a straggler – your reputation, gentlemen, is well known – so the privateer gets astern of the convoy during the night and chooses his straggler. Just before dawn he is ready, and then he swoops. In ten minutes you are his prize – and no doubt you will complain the escort is not doing its job. You'll forget you straggled five or six miles astern. I put it to you: why should each of the other seventy-one ships in the convoy be put at risk so that a frigate can stay with the straggler, who is only trying to save pennies on canvas, or make sure he has a quiet night without a squall making him furl or reef?

"Gentlemen," Ramage said bluntly, "if you don't want to be roused out at night to furl or reef, or tack or wear, then you should not have come to sea: you should have opened a grocer's shop, or set up as a farrier or, if you feel bloodthirsty, set up a knacker's yard."

The choices set most of the masters laughing: in fact, Ramage decided, that sorted them out: the men laughing were those who did not straggle; those with long faces, like mourners attending a debtor's funeral, were the stragglers...

He then ran through the SIGNALS and INSTRUCTIONS, emphasizing the seven instructions, going through the signals from the commander of the convoy which would be made without flags, and then the signals which would be made with one flag or with a pendant under a flag. Then very carefully he covered the signals to be made from ships in the convoy to the commander of the escort – they ranged from "An enemy is in sight" and "Being in distress and wanting immediate assistance" to "Sticking on a shoal" and that the commander's signal was not understood (a favourite way of being stubborn). Fog signals and the various combinations of lights used at night rounded off the working part; then Ramage emphasized the penalties printed on page thirteen.

"I want you to note, gentlemen, that at the bottom left-hand side of the page is written your name and that of your ship. To the right, where it says 'Given under my hand on board of…' you will see my signature.

"Those of you who know me – and I recognize some faces – also know that I am a man of my word. I promise you I shall try to get this convoy to England safely. But in turn I rely on each of you to play your part. We shall sail tomorrow morning, as soon after dawn as possible. So thanking you, I bid you all good-day."

"You got them," Southwick muttered. "There wasn't one of them, except Mr Yorke, who couldn't see the *Calypso* towing 'em under in a high wind and a rough sea!"

As the masters filed out of the hall, Ramage said: "I hope they could also imagine it happening in a light breeze, if necessary!"

CHAPTER FIVE

The day began with a typical tropical dawn: the first hint of daylight showed a low bank of cloud on the eastern horizon looking more like a mourning band worn round a hat, with none of the jagged lines associated with squalls or thunderstorms.

The *Calypso* was alive with excitement and bustle, as though the frigate herself was excited at the prospect of sailing. Southwick strode the decks with the bounce of a suffragan bishop about to hold an unexpectedly large confirmation; Aitken had the firm walk of a landowner in the Highlands setting off on the ten-mile walk that would bring a prime stag in front of his musket. Young Paolo, with a telescope tucked under his arm, was watching the flagship for signals (not that any were expected, but one should never trust flagships) but more important watching every one of the anchored merchant ships: now was the time for them to start signalling all their defects, all the reasons why they could not weigh anchor (too few seamen), hoist sails (same excuse), sheet them home or brace them up (they needed new cordage or had sprung a yard), and why they had run short of water (having been too lazy or too cunning to send their men on shore to fill casks, they now hoped the Navy would send men and boats, in order to get the convoy moving). Or, as Southwick had commented bitterly, the kind of cunning excuses invented by sly men to get something for nothing.

Just as Paolo (the slight accent in his voice suddenly reminding Ramage of Gianna) reported that a merchant ship called the *Beatrice* had hoisted a wheft from the foretopmast, showing that she wanted to communicate with the commander, Ramage said briskly: "Loose the foretopsail and fire one gun…"

Aitken gave a bellow that sent a dozen men up the foremast and out along the yard: Southwick shouted an order to the gunner while having the men on the fo'c'sle heave a few more turns on the capstan and haul up more of the anchor cable, which had already been taken in to "short stay", the last position before Southwick would report "Anchor aweigh…up and down."

"The *Beatrice*, sir?" Paolo asked.

"Take a turn round the foredeck and then report it to me," Ramage said and Paolo grinned and walked forward.

Ramage sighed: none of the mules seemed to be making a move towards weighing, and from the look of the bedraggled ship with the wheft, the *Beatrice*, she probably needed everything, including men to man the pump…Well, this damned convoy was going to be sailed to England "by the book". Ramage had his orders from Tewtin to take the convoy to England: the *SIGNALS and INSTRUCTIONS* gave the mules their orders; his own conduct was governed by the large volume of the *King's Regulations and Admiralty Instructions*, and the very slim volume comprising the Articles of War; and that was that. Any mule wanting anything was going to be charged at the rate set down; those that did not keep up with the convoy without a good reason would get a tow to frighten them; after that they would be left to disappear astern, prey for French privateers.

Captain Ramage in the *Calypso* and the Count of Rennes in a large merchantman each had their own reasons for getting to England in a hurry, and Ramage had decided that the urgency of him getting news of Sarah more than justified sticking to the rules: there was no regulation saying that the King's ships were responsible for getting merchant ships under way or keeping them afloat: this had become a habit because most convoy commanders were (quite reasonably) frightened of the effect it could have on their career if some wretched master of a merchant ship complained to his owners, telling a self-serving story, and they in turn complained to Their Lordships, naming the captain and listing his alleged misdeeds.

As too many frigate captains had found to their cost, it was harder to answer allegations than to make them, and Lloyd's wielded influence far greater than most officers expected. And, of course, masters trying to justify their own conduct or shortcomings or that of their owners, did not always pay strict attention to the truth. However, frigate commanders understood one thing – Their Lordships appeared to fawn over Lloyd's, and a frigate captain found he was never employed again after a collision with them. There was a desperate shortage of frigates; there was a glut of post-captains to command them.

Ramage looked round the great bay. It was a good many years (a couple of centuries in fact) since it was named after Lord Carlisle, who had been made, as though by a whim, "Lord Proprietor of the English Caribbee Islands" by Charles I. Since then a good many thousand merchant ships had anchored in the Bay at the beginning or end of the long voyage to or from Europe. Once again another convoy was preparing to sail – though, he admitted sourly, at the moment there was little sign of it. The *Calypso's* foretopsail hung down like a curtain, slatting in the breeze; she had fired a gun, and the very first of the *Signals from the Commander of the Convoy* gave the explanation: *Foretopsail loose…One gun, To prepare for sailing.*

Both the other frigates were under way, and Ramage was pleasantly surprised at the men Tewtin had put in command.

But it was now time for the second signal from the convoy commander listed in the *SIGNALS and INSTRUCTIONS*: *Maintopsail loose…One gun, To unmoor.*

Ramage waved at Aitken, who was standing at the other side of the quarterdeck rail, and the first lieutenant lifted the speaking trumpet to his mouth, shouting an order which sent men racing up the ratlines and then out along the maintopsail yard. The sail billowed down as another spurt of smoke tried to race the echoing crash of the signal gun.

Pulling out the tube of his telescope, Ramage began inspecting the merchant ships and was reminded of a herd of cattle spread across a meadow. Left alone they would slowly chew the cud, clumsily rising every few hours, and if the wind got up or it began to rain, turning to face away from it. But the *Calypso* was now the barking dog coming into the meadow (not rushing, but slowly, like a well-trained animal) to disturb not just a few but every one of them.

The circular image in the glass revealed desultory movement on the fo'c'sle of two-thirds of the ships. But the only thing moving on board the *Beatrice* was the wheft, the knotted flag flapping at the foretopmasthead. Sidney Yorke's *Emerald*, by far the smartest in the anchorage, with hull and spars newly painted, the cordage showing the golden colour of new hemp, already had her anchor apeak and, with a foretopsail set, the ship was about to thread her way to leeward, away from the rest of the anchored ships and to the area well clear of the anchorage and off the town where the convoy was to form up. Form up, Ramage thought bitterly…easier to teach cows the quadrille than get these mules into their proper positions without broken bowsprits, ripped out jibbooms or, the more usual, having at least one ship locked in tight embrace with another, its jibboom and bowsprit stuck through the other's rigging, its bow locked amidships by torn planking…

Now Paolo was back. "Are you ready for my report, sir?" he asked with a grin.

"Yes – tell me, Mr Orsini, have you seen if any of the merchant ships have made me a signal?"

"Why yes, sir: I've just seen that one of them, the *Beatrice*, has a wheft flying at her foretopmasthead: I assume she wishes to communicate with you, sir."

"Very well, acknowledge it. If I remember rightly, hoisting a blue, white and red at the mizentopmasthead merely says: 'The Commander of the convoy sees the signal that is made to him'."

"Yes, sir, it doesn't specify which signal or who is making it," Paolo said, enjoying the game.

Ramage nodded and then, still looking through his glass, he groaned. "That horse won't start – the *Beatrice* is hoisting out a boat. We'll have the master on board in a few minutes with a list of requests…"

" 'Bout time for the next gun, sir," Aitken reminded him, overhearing the conversation with Orsini and looking across at the *Beatrice*, a ship which was of no colour: her paint was worn off the hull by the combined attacks of sea and sea air, time and the wind. Time had turned the bare wood grey, so that she looked as if she had been built of driftwood. "The boat they've just hoisted out doesn't look as though she'll swim this far!" Aitken added.

And Ramage saw that the first couple of men who had climbed down into the boat were now busy bailing: obviously the planking of the boat, stowed on deck without a cover to protect the wood from the scorching sun, had split as the wood shrunk: "shakes", like the wrinkles on an old man's neck, would let the water leak through. It would take hours of soaking for the wood to swell up and staunch the leaks enough for the boat to be usable. Stowing the boat with water in it would have saved them a lot of trouble because the rolling of the ship would have kept the water swilling round.

"Very well, Mr Aitken, the last signal!"

The first lieutenant, after checking with Southwick that the anchor was off the ground, gave the order for the topsails to be sheeted home, and another gun to be fired. That was the final order to get the convoy under way and given in the *SIGNALS and INSTRUCTIONS* as *To Weigh, the outward and leeward ships first.*

"Let's get out to seaward of them," Ramage said. "If we stay here, one of them is sure to hit us."

"The *Beatrice*, sir," Orsini reminded him.

"You are the Keeper of the Captain's Conscience, eh?" Ramage teased him. "They've signalled that they want to communicate – and we're waiting for them."

"She's in sight of the flagship, sir," Paolo pointed out.

Indeed, the *Queen* was perfectly placed to see all that was going on, and if the *Calypso* left the anchorage without attending to the blasted *Beatrice* there would be plenty of sycophantic lieutenants on board the flagship only too anxious to make sure that the admiral was kept well informed.

He was going to have to do something about the damned ship sooner or later, but in the meantime it would not hurt to scare the *Beatrice*'s master. "We'll circle the anchorage a few times while these mules get under way," he told Aitken. "Once we've got the leaders of the columns in position, Orsini can take a boat over to the *Beatrice*. I'm more concerned with seeing how these two frigates are handled...They'll all be nervous for the first few days, let alone the first few hours."

And he had made a few more hours slide by without thinking of Sarah. Plenty of work, plenty of bustle, plenty of alarms and emergencies...It was a good theory, but in practice it was going to be days and weeks and perhaps months of boredom, watching these mules making no attempt to keep position and knowing there was nothing he could do about it, except tow one or two – and leave some behind if necessary.

Ramage had chosen a convoy formation which gave him a broad front: the seventy-two ships were formed up in eight columns, each of nine ships. There were almost endless variations – some commanders preferred a long thin column of ships, claiming it was easier to control them. That might be so, but it was almost impossible to defend them: even a single privateer, let alone a couple of enemy frigates, could cut the convoy in half.

Having the ships advancing in a broad box-shaped formation meant that escorts could patrol ahead and astern, whence attacks were most likely to come, and since the box had narrower sides there was less room for a stray privateer to sneak in. But the real advantage, from Ramage's point of view, was that the mules had less chance to dally and drop astern.

With the convoy now formed up and heading northwards along the west coast of Barbados, the sun dipping low on the larboard beam, Ramage was weary but satisfied: getting under way could have been a lot worse. Even the abominable *Beatrice* was in position after Paolo had taken over half a dozen men to help the fools to weigh their anchor. Because of some tedious dispute about pay owing to some of her men, four of her six seamen had deserted last night in Barbados, swearing they would kill the master rather than sail with him again (and Paolo reported that he would not blame them). Four men short meant they could not turn the windlass to weigh the anchor, hence the wheft at the foretopmasthead.

As every drill sergeant knew, the most important man on a parade was the "right marker", the man against whom all the other files positioned themselves. Ramage realized how lucky he was in having Yorke and the *Emerald* as his right marker. But by giving Yorke the position of leading ship in the starboard column (and thus the pivot on which most convoy movements would be made) he had put the *Emerald* in the most vulnerable position of all if the French attacked with a squadron. However, in war there was always risk, and Yorke would be the last to complain. Yet he was not thinking of Sidney Yorke: if he was honest with himself, Ramage was worrying about Sarah, who had been caught up in the war by accident: she had gone off on a peacetime honeymoon with her new husband and the war had started again to wrench her away. To what, he dare not think.

At least the two former prize frigates were turning out well. John Mead, the young lieutenant just made post and given command of *L'Espoir*, seemed a good shiphandler and had imagination. The sail handling was taking too long, but obviously during the next few days Mead would have his men working against a watch. Sail handling was second nature with most captains; but less popular was gunnery exercise. Guns firing meant scorched paint. There was always a spurt of flame upwards from the touch-hole and there was the muzzle blast, a mixture of smoke, unburnt powder and powdered rust from the shot. No matter how carefully shot was hammered and given a coat of blacking, there were always rust scales, and gunnery exercises (or a bout of action) always left the first lieutenant's scrubbed and holystoned decks stained and greasy – and badly marked by the wooden trucks of the carriages. There was no way that four wheels supporting a gun weighing a ton and a half being flung back in recoil were going to avoid scarring the deck planking, even if it was already grooved from previous years. Carpenters could plane and seamen scrub with holystones, but the marks were there, like cart tracks on a country lane, and a couple of hours' shooting worked the soot and rust powder well into the grain so that it looked like a chimney sweep's neck. Anyway, that was the problem for *L'Espoir*'s new captain: Ramage's only concern was that he carried out gunnery exercises.

Summers, commanding *La Robuste*, was a completely different man: where Mead was lively and talkative, full of ideas which Ramage noticed he sometimes expressed without sufficient thought, Summers was dour; he gave the impression of never speaking a word (expelling it, almost) without chewing it ten or twenty times. It was not the hesitation preceding deep thought, of that Ramage was sure; the dourness came from a brain which turned over slowly, like a roasting pig revolving on a spit. Would Summers be as slow in reacting to an emergency – when a privateer rushed out of the darkness to cut off one of the convoy? Why had the admiral put Summers in command of *La Robuste*? If he had been an unsatisfactory first lieutenant in one of Tewtin's ships, it was of course a convenient way of getting rid of him. It wasted an opportunity to promote a favourite, but there must be times for flag officers when the need to get rid of a really incompetent (or irritating) subordinate overcame the demands of favouritism.

Summers, then, was the question mark; the convoy was sufficiently large and the escort of three frigates (one, *L'Espoir*, armed *en flûte*, so that virtually she carried no guns) was pathetically small: it averaged out at twenty-four merchant ships for each frigate. The escort was just large enough for

Tewtin to avoid criticism from the Admiralty – unless it was heavily attacked and suffered disastrous losses. In that case Tewtin would probably be agile enough to make sure all the blame rested on the shoulders of the convoy commander …after all, admirals could not be everywhere, and had to rely on subordinates…

Still, it was a beautiful evening and Barbados was drawing astern on the starboard quarter, or rather the *Calypso* and the convoy appeared to be stationary on the sea, like small ornaments on a polished table, while the island itself seemed to be moving slowly away, distance softening the low outlines and turning the pale greys into misty and distant blues that would challenge a water-colourist.

What was Sidney Yorke (and his sister Alexis, for that matter) thinking about as they passed this northwestern coast of Barbados? It was out here, in the time of Cromwell, that one of Yorke's Royalist forebears had to escape from the island just a few yards ahead of the Roundheads and, according to Sidney, taking with him a French mistress, wife of some besotted Roundhead planter. He must ask Yorke to tell the story of that particular forebear, because he ended up in Jamaica as the leader of the Buccaneers, and the estates he then acquired now belonged to the Yorkes, though Ramage was far from sure that it was Sidney Yorke's branch of the family. It must be strange, though, looking across at an island and knowing that one and a half centuries ago, or whenever it was, all that parcel of land belonged to your family and, but for Cromwell's antics, would now belong to you.

Ramage realized that Southwick was standing nearby, obviously anxious to say something but unwilling to interrupt. Southwick always knew when he was away in another country and often another century.

"Ah, Southwick, this is probably the last time we'll ever see these mules in such good order!"

Southwick laughed and dismissed them with a wave of his hand. "I was watching those masters at the conference: that question you put Mr Yorke up to asking had an effect! You looked so fierce that every one of them could see the *Calypso* towing them under. Worth five dozen warning shots, that bit o' play-acting."

"I hope no one got the wrong idea," Ramage said. "I'll tow when needed, but I'll also leave 'em behind if they keep dropping astern at night."

"I heard you threaten that, sir, but you wouldn't really, would you?" Southwick's doubt was quite clear.

"They'll get a couple of warnings, maybe three, but after that I'm not keeping the convoy jilling around until after noon. Otherwise it means we get only six hours or so's sailing out of twenty-four. We have to heave-to at daylight, say five thirty am, and the mule finally gets into position by noon. By six or seven o'clock at night he's reefing or furling again and snugging down for the night – and we've had the pleasure of his company for six or seven hours, making perhaps five knots. So in the twenty-four hours the convoy's covered thirty-five or forty miles, plus a bit for current if we're lucky. Remember, Southwick, we've got to sail 3,500 miles before we reach the Chops of the Channel. Does a hundred-day passage appeal to you? I'm damned if any of these mules are going to make me wait a hundred days for news of my wife."

"I understand that, sir," Southwick said, looking round to make sure no one else could hear them, "but I was thinking of Their Lordships."

"*What* about Their Lordships?"

"These damned shipowners have a lot of influence, sir. If we left one of their ships behind and they complained to

Their Lordships…why, they could even cast you in damages. You personally, sir. If a shipowner cast you in damages in the High Court, and Their Lordships then decided you should face a court-martial under one of the Articles of War…"

"I'd be in a pickle," Ramage admitted ruefully. "But I'll have some witnesses in my favour – the Count of Rennes, which means the interest of the Prince of Wales, and Mr Yorke and the master of the *Emerald*."

"Mr Yorke, yes, and all the King's officers in the convoy, but beyond that, remember the old saying, 'Put not thy trust in princes'."

"We could trust the Count."

"Ah, yes, more than most men – particularly since he owes you his life. But," Southwick said carefully, "I had in mind some of his friends in England: those who'd mistake the Board of Admiralty for another kind of gaming table."

Ramage nodded because the old master's warning made a great deal of sense. Fame was a high place surrounded with traps set by jealous men. Without intending or wishing it, Ramage had become one of the Royal Navy's most famous frigate captains, not a role he had sought or particularly wanted but one which was the result of many actions, many desperate fights, many prizes taken, many of his own men killed or wounded and more of the enemy. He had taken many chances too, and occasionally disobeyed orders deliberately, but for the good of the King's service. And he always had loyal shipmates like Southwick, and seamen as brave and faithful as Jackson, Stafford and Rossi.

Yet Southwick was thinking beyond all this: his memory was going back to Ramage's childhood, when his father the Earl of Blazey was one of the youngest and certainly the most brilliant admirals in the Navy and who had been serving a government that needed a scapegoat for having sent out too small a fleet against the French and too late to do any good. Their scapegoat had been Admiral the Earl of Blazey, and his subsequent trial had split the Navy and the country.

"Let's hope the mules behave themselves," Ramage said, and Southwick nodded: he had understood all the unspoken additional qualifications, ranging from Sarah to Sidney Yorke's support and the bad luck which put at least one *Beatrice* in the convoy. Another half a dozen *Beatrice*s would most probably turn up in the next week. It was remarkable how these ships generally needed extra canvas and cordage before the weather turned bad as they reached the more northern latitudes...

Yes, the convoy was in good shape, the box of ships sailing along easily to the northwest to skirt Bermuda, the wind steady from the southeast, with *L'Espoir* out ahead, *La Robuste* tacking and wearing along the western edge, and to windward, placing her astern of the convoy, the *Calypso* under easy sail, in a good position to hurry down to the convoy in an emergency – and swoop on any merchantman showing signs of furling her wings for the night.

It was time for the watch to change. In a few minutes Southwick would be relieved by Kenton. Over in the *Emerald*, hidden from the *Calypso* by the rest of the ships in the convoy, Sidney Yorke and Alexis would probably be drinking tea and talking of – what? Their forebears in Barbados and Jamaica? He shrugged and wished Sarah's face would come clearly in his memory.

Sidney Yorke spread some soft butter over the slice of bread on his plate, and nodded towards the jam dish. Alexis pushed it towards him and said: "If only this weather would last all the way to England."

"We'd take a year to get there!"

"I don't think I'd mind. London is so boring…"

"*Really* boring – for a beautiful young woman like you?" Yorke asked with mild sarcasm. "Think what it must be like for a plain young woman!"

"It's much easier," Alexis said unexpectedly, "if you're plain and your father is only moderately wealthy, then you can dance and talk vapid nonsense. But if Nature made you beautiful and you happen to have a fair competence, as everyone seems to know I have, every man in the room, whether a pimply youth or some jaded old roué, is chasing after you."

"Beauty and the beasts," Yorke teased.

"Yes," Alexis said crossly, "and even when you are there they ogle me and whisper suggestions."

"You never tell me!"

"I should think not! If you knew what some of them said, you'd call them out, even tho' duelling is forbidden now."

"Why don't you find yourself a nice husband," Yorke said banteringly. "Then he can protect you from the pimply youths and jaded roués."

"Oh yes, one looks around and finds 'nice husbands' are thick on the ground, like ripe apples after a thunderstorm. I notice you're still a bachelor and certainly you rarely approve of anyone I happen to talk to for more than four minutes."

"Well, you do seem to choose the most extraordinary men. No chins, noses like beaks, ears like mug handles, wispy moustaches and with 'fortune-hunter' embroidered all over their elegant coats."

"Dear brother," Alexis said patiently, "you don't understand and you never listen. I've met only one real man in the last two or three years. *One*."

"Why didn't you marry him, then?"

"He didn't ask me," she said, blushing in spite of herself.

"Oh? So being rich and beautiful isn't enough, eh?"

"He was already married," she said bitterly, and as Yorke went on to tease her she burst into tears and, gathering up her skirt with one hand and trying to hide her face with the other, she ran from the cabin.

Yorke sighed and cursed his crude tongue: the girl was probably frightened to death of ending her days as a spinster, surrounded by lapdogs of all varieties and visited daily by a fawning parson hoping to be remembered in her will...Alexis who, even though she was his sister and he was prejudiced, was among the half dozen women he had ever met who combined beauty, elegance and wit with a natural warmth that prevented her being distant and forbidding.

But who was this man? Yorke was curious, but searching his memory he could not remember seeing her with any particularly outstanding married man. In the last two or three years, she had said. Well, he had not been away very often, so who the devil could it be? He knew of only one man he'd care to have as a brother-in-law. Anyway, he would have to go and make his peace with her.

She had been badly upset when she saw the Kingsnorth plantation and the old house as they had passed the northwestern corner of Barbados: she had wept when he told her what he could remember of Ned Yorke, their great-great-great-great-uncle, who had been driven from his estate by Cromwell's Roundheads, and she had wanted to know more – with what seemed to him to be a fierce longing – of the French woman who had escaped with him to become his wife and their distant aunt. That was the trouble, sailing the turbulent islands, be they British, French, Danish, Swedish or Dutch: there were too many Yorke family memories entwined in their violent history. In fact, what few people seemed to realize was that the history of the West Indies was simply the combined history of settler families, be they English, Scots, Welsh, Irish, Dutch, French, Danish, Swedish…yes, and Spanish and Portuguese, of course; the other half of the coin, as it were.

At that moment the door of the saloon opened and Alexis, now dry-eyed, came in and said briefly: "I'm sorry; I made a fool of myself."

He wanted to ask her about the man, but he knew her too well: he was sure her tears were at least partly caused by vexation with herself for having said so much.

"Let's go up on deck," he said. "It's going to be a glorious sunset, and we can watch Nicholas chasing up anyone starting to dawdle."

"His ship is so far astern it's impossible to see her – will she stay there the whole voyage?"

"No, probably not. The escorts usually shift about according to the wind direction. The *Calypso* will probably always stay to windward as you can see, we have a quartering wind, but as it hauls round I expect you'll find the *Calypso* closer to us."

"We might invite him to dinner – on a calm day, of course."

"Indeed, we shall. And he'll invite us back, and you'll see what it's like for a young lady to be controlling her skirts while she's being hoisted on board one of the King's ships."

"*Hoisted*? What, like a bullock, slung over a strop?"

"No, no! The Royal Navy are very polite where women are concerned. Instead of the strap under the belly they use for a bullock, they lower a small seat, like the one for a child's swing. You climb into it and settle your skirts and arrange a brave smile on your face, and they hoist you right up into the air out of the boat on to the deck, where – if you are beautiful or important enough – the captain and all the officers are waiting to salute you and kiss your hand. A glimpse of an ankle as you alight from the chair and they are your slaves for – well, until the next beautiful ankle comes on board, which is unlikely to be within the next five years if they're on a foreign station!"

"Why don't we have such a chair in the *Emerald*?"

"We probably have, but we usually have the gangway rigged. You'd sooner walk up a gangway, I know."

She smiled. "It depends on the naval officers," she said.

A few moments later she asked: "What shall we have for dinner?"

Yorke looked puzzled. "When?"

"Oh wake up. Why, when we have Captain Ramage for dinner."

"We'll have to invite some of his officers as well, so we'll kill a sheep."

She had already produced a tiny notebook from a pocket in her dress. "Whom shall we invite, apart from Captain Ramage?"

"For Heaven's sake call him Nicholas. It's embarrassing when you are so formal with my best friend!"

"But I've only just met him," she protested. "He's not *my* best friend!"

"If anything happened to me, you'd find he was," Yorke said quietly.

"Well," she said cheerfully, "he's good company, so why not stay alive and let's all be friends. Now, who else are we inviting – that delightful Mr Southwick, for one."

"And the nephew – Paolo Orsini. He is a nice lad and I know Nicholas is very fond of him."

"He speaks excellent English. Who is he exactly? Is he really related to Captain Ramage – to Nicholas?"

"Dear me, that's a bit of a long story. Once upon a time," he said, dropping his voice as though beginning a fairy story, "there was a handsome young lieutenant in the Royal Navy who landed from an open boat on the coast of Tuscany and rescued a beautiful young marchesa from under the very feet of Bonaparte's cavalry."

Alexis nodded. "That sounds a very romantic story – but I'm sure it doesn't finish there, does it? All proper fairy stories have a happy ending."

"We don't know yet if this one has: it's still happening. Anyway, Nicholas rescued her with some of his men, fellows like Jackson and Stafford, who came on board the other day with the lieutenant who brought a message."

"*Then* what happened? Didn't I hear that she came back to England? I seem to remember her family were old friends of the Ramages – or perhaps her mother was."

"Yes, her mother. The Marchesa is the ruler of Volterra, so you can see Bonaparte was angry that she slipped through his fingers."

"Sidney, come *on!*" Alexis said firmly, "you can't leave the story there."

"Well, that's more or less all there is to it. Everyone thought Gianna and Nicholas would get married – until they realized the religious problems, she being Catholic."

"Were they in love?" Alexis asked casually.

"Blessed if I know. He didn't talk about her much when we were together in that Post Office packet – yet she was waiting for him when we arrived in Lisbon."

"But he eventually married someone else…"

"Yes, very recently."

"But why is the story of the Marchesa unfinished?"

"Well, it seems she was very anxious to get back to her people in Volterra. It's not a large country but as soon as Bonaparte signed the Treaty of Amiens she decided to go back."

"She trusted that dreadful man?"

"Don't forget that most of the British government did, too. Addington and his half-witted friends thought they had pulled off a great coup, whereas they were falling into Bonaparte's trap. But with the Marchesa, I think it was a sense of duty."

"Why didn't Captain Ramage dissuade her?"

Yorke stifled a smile: the "Nicholas" quickly reverted to a formal "Captain Ramage" when Alexis disapproved of something. "He told me that he and his parents spent days trying to warn her that she might fall into the hands of Bonaparte's secret police."

"Yet she went..."

"Yes, and during the Peace the Admiralty sent Nicholas with the *Calypso* on a long surveying voyage down to Brazil, and there he met his wife."

"She is Brazilian?"

"No," Yorke explained patiently. "I'm not sure of the details – damnation, I've only had time to speak to him a couple of times. Her ship was captured and he rescued her and her parents."

"He seems to make a habit of rescuing beautiful damsels in distress."

"Yes, doesn't he," Yorke said, ignoring the sarcasm. "Very lucky for the damsels, wouldn't you say? Saved the Marchesa from Bonaparte's assassins, and Sarah (that's his wife) from a crowd of half-breed pirates."

"All right, all right," she said, "I was just being catty. If he wasn't married I'd sit on a rock and imitate a Siren..."

"But the Sirens lured poor sailors to their doom," Yorke protested.

"So they did," Alexis said dryly and with a straight face.

CHAPTER SIX

Shortly after dawn next morning Ramage stood at the forward end of the quarterdeck staring into the greyness, although his thoughts were several thousands of miles away. He heard the traditional hail from the lookouts on deck at six different positions round the ship, "See a grey goose at a mile" – the signal for a couple of men to go aloft, one to the foremasthead and the other to the mainmast, and watch the horizon.

Because Admiral Clinton would be continuing a tight blockade of Brest, and there had been no frigate flying into Barbados with a warning that the French Mediterranean fleet had left Toulon and broken through the Gut into the Atlantic, the Royal Navy for the time being could take one thing for granted: that the chances were that any squadron or fleet of ships they sighted would be friendly, although single ships could be privateers.

Anyway, the *Calypso*'s eyes could now see a good deal further and almost every minute, as the sun, although still hidden, came up the eastern side of the earth heading for the horizon, the circle of visibility widened. After spending a moonless night unable to see more than a couple of hundred yards (the advantage of a tropical night was the clarity of the stars, which made their own light) the lookouts would soon be able to see to the horizon; from a height of eye of one hundred feet, they could see a distance of ten miles, and a ship beyond that would be visible the moment the tips of her masts began to rise over the far side of the horizon.

The officer of the deck, the small and red-haired third lieutenant Kenton, whose heavily freckled face was continually peeling because of the sun, came up to Ramage and formally reported that the lookouts were aloft.

Kenton waited for the next step in the routine by which one of the King's ships greeted a new day at sea in wartime. At the moment, every one of the *Calypso*'s 12-pounder guns and six carronades were ready to fire: the ship was at general quarters, the way every King's ship met the dawn, at sea, ready to defend herself or attack.

Ramage took one last look round the horizon (almost a formality, since Kenton's telescope would have spotted even a distant gull perched on a bottle).

"Very well, stand down from general quarters."

Kenton saluted and then turned away, grasping the japanned speaking trumpet. The son of a half-pay captain, he had inherited all his father's seagoing characteristics except a stentorian voice. Kenton's shouted orders needed the help of the speaking trumpet to lob his voice as far as the fo'c'sle.

The men ran in the guns and secured them, covered the flintlocks with aprons, small canvas hoods that tied down securely to protect the flint and mechanism from salt spray, put pistols and muskets back into the deck lockers, slipped the ash staves of the long boarding pikes into the racks round each mast, and then made their way below.

Ramage saw the fourth lieutenant coming up the quarterdeck ladder to relieve Kenton. Young Martin was, with Kenton, the newest of the *Calypso*'s lieutenants but at twenty-three or four – Ramage could not remember which – Martin had already experienced as much action as most officers saw in a lifetime. The son of the master shipwright at the Chatham

Dockyard, Martin was known throughout the ship as "Blower", an improbable nickname used openly by his fellow officers and discreetly by the rest of the ship's company and bestowed out of admiration, because Lieutenant William Martin was a superb flautist. He played the wooden tube as though it was a part of his own body: the sheer pleasure that it and music gave him found an echo among the men, who did not care whether he was playing an obscure piece of baroque music or one of the traditional forebitters, used when the men were heaving at the capstan, bringing the anchor home.

Ramage watched the two young lieutenants: Kenton reporting the course and any orders from the captain that remained unexecuted (there was none), plus any unusual occurrences, thus carrying out the captain's standing orders for handing over the deck. The two lieutenants now faced forward, and Ramage guessed they were discussing the convoy. Yes, there were still seventy-two ships, and considering all things they were in reasonable formation. For that Ramage knew he could thank a night of steady southeasterly winds and probably the impression he had made at the convoy conference. But steady winds and past impressions did not last; one should never trust the weather or one's memory...

A convoy under way with dawn breaking is always an impressive sight, and he continued looking at the ships. The increasing pinkness now spreading over the eastern horizon like a water-colour wash gave the flax of the merchant ships' sails a warmth which was gently shaded by the curve into which the wind pressed them. Yet it was hard to believe the ships were more than toys being pulled by unseen strings across a village pond: at this distance each seemed much too small to be carrying hundreds of tons of valuable cargo in her hold. For all that, cargoes from the West Indies were smelly rather than exotic, he reminded himself, mostly molasses and hides…Sometimes there were more aromatic spices such as nutmeg, but molasses were a touchy cargo, liable to absorb the smell of anything else stowed near it.

In England it was an hour before noon. In France about the same. What was Sarah doing at this moment? Could she be at home with her parents – in London, or their estate in Norfolk? Or was she a prisoner in France? Bonaparte must be a vile man: never before had women been treated as prisoners of war – at least, among civilized people. Nor, for that matter, were civilians accidentally caught in a country by a sudden war – oh, to hell with it; continually worrying would not tell him whether or not she was safe, although worrying was all he could do. Worry and watch over these damned mules across 3,500 miles of the Western Ocean – more if the winds played tricks and headed them.

"The *Emerald*, sir," Martin reported, his voice seeming to come from another planet. "Wheft at the foretopmast – 'To communicate with the commander of the convoy'."

"Very well," Ramage said in the usual response. "Can you see any other sail beyond her? Has the *Robuste* hoisted any signal?"

If there was an emergency – a privateer in sight or a French man-o'-war – then the *Emerald* would have hoisted the appropriate signal, and the *Robuste* would have sighted her as well. No, Sidney Yorke had a routine message to pass – probably, Ramage guessed, the opening round in the social invitations exchanged between the more important merchant ships and escorts. In fact it was usually restricted to the commander and one or two merchant ships whose masters were old friends. Whatever the circumstances, such invitations broke up the monotony of the voyage, both for the officers invited and the men who had to row them over: the hospitality usually included the men, and it was a wise coxswain who kept an eye on the drinking in the fo'c'sle.

"Well, Mr Martin, let's pass within hail of the *Emerald* and see what she has to say."

"Aye aye, sir."

"And Mr Martin, let's do it in the fewest tacks and gybes possible, from this position. Over to her and back here again."

"Aye aye, sir," Martin said doubtfully, knowing this was a test.

Just half an hour later, with the rising sun bringing a freshening wind, the *Calypso* bore away a couple of points and surged close under the *Emerald*'s quarter, the frigate's bow butting up sheets of spray as she sliced through the bulky merchantman's big quarter wave.

Right aft Ramage could see Sidney and Alexis waving: the girl seemed to be jumping up and down with excitement, and even the ship's master stood at the taffrail, a hand upraised.

Now Sidney had a speaking trumpet to his mouth and Ramage rapidly reversed the one he was grasping, holding the mouthpiece to his ear like a deaf beggar.

"Dinner...today...you...nephew...Southwick...as many officers as you..."

And then, as Ramage waved an acknowledgement, the *Calypso* was past her and angling across the bow of the ship leading the next column, which had her rail lined with white faces – it must be disturbing to have a frigate steering at you, even though for only a minute or two.

Then the *Calypso* was out ahead of the convoy and just as Martin was going to bring her about, to tack round the eastern side of the convoy again, Ramage stopped him. "That was well done, but we'll carry on and do a circumnavigation of the whole convoy. Won't do any harm to let the mules know we can turn up alongside 'em while they're busy having breakfast. Hey, what's the matter with you? You look as though you're going to faint!"

"I'm all right now, sir; it was just those last few minutes!"

A startled Ramage stared at the youth. "Blower" treated musket shot and cannon balls with contempt. What on earth could make him go white like that? "What 'last few minutes'?"

"Passing under the stern of the *Emerald* so close, sir. I know the owner is a friend of yours, and the lady was watching, too."

Ramage smiled as he shook his head. "Martin, remember this: the fact the owner of that ship is a friend of mine didn't make her one foot nearer or farther away."

"No sir," Martin agreed, "but if we'd hit her the crash would have sounded a thousand times louder."

Poor "Blower", he had been determined to bring the *Calypso* close enough for them to hear the *Emerald*'s hail, even if he scared himself to death. He did not realize that if there had been a collision the responsibility would have been Ramage's but, Ramage realized, this was not the time to point that out: "Blower" had handled the ship splendidly under the impression that one mistake would see him court-martialled and dismissed the Service. It was an experience which added to his confidence.

"At *least* a thousand times louder," Ramage said.

Southwick knew he had eaten too much but the dinner given by Mr Yorke was more like a banquet than anything he had eaten on board a ship for a long time. Those John Company fellows were supposed to live like pashas (indeed he had eaten some good meals on board ships of the Honourable East India Company), but nothing to compare with what the *Emerald* had to offer. John Company masters ran to heavy and highly spiced food; a curry so hot you lost the taste in the furnace created in your mouth, and found comfort in the stream of perspiration erupting on your face. A course like that, Southwick thought sadly, was the kind of thing that "old India hands" loved, and once they had caught their breath again they could make half an hour's animated conversation out of the piquancy. Well, usually they had not much else to discuss, so curry often became a staple subject, the rules and standards as well defined (and as boring) as a political speech.

Yes, he was going to pay for this present meal in an attack of wind, but it would be worth it. It was curious that on board a John Company ship the master felt it necessary to emphasize India instead of wanting a change. Yet by the same token in the West Indies everyone seemed to drink the local rum – anyone offering something else like gin was assumed to have bought a few cases cheaply.

Curious...the thought struck Southwick as he reached for his glass of port that the real curry lovers, the men who became excited at the prospect and then discussed the memory as though recalling a loved one, were almost without exception extremely dull fellows. Was there any relationship between brains and a liking for a particular food? He was just parading people he knew and putting them in categories when he realized someone was speaking to him.

It was Mr Yorke's sister, and she wanted to know if the sherbert had been too sweet for him.

"No, ma'am, it was just right."

"But you hardly ate any; you left most of it on your plate!"

"No discredit to the sherbert, ma'am: I have to admit I've eaten too much of everything – or nearly everything. The meal is a credit to – " he hesitated: could such a beautiful young woman arrange a dinner like this? Would she? Or would Mr

Yorke leave all the details to the purser and the cook – to the chef, rather?

She gave him a mischievous smile and Southwick blessed whoever had arranged the seating for having put her next to him. She guessed the reason for Southwick's pause.

"You can give me the credit for choosing the menu. My brother deserves credit for finding the chef – he is a Scotsman who had a French mother."

"A remarkably successful combination, ma'am," Southwick said. "I have never eaten so well afloat before."

She whispered: "Do you think that Captain Ramage has enjoyed the meal? I mean, is it the kind of food he likes, or would he have preferred curry, or anyway spicier food?"

Southwick thought for a moment. This was going to be a long and probably slow voyage, and Mr Ramage would be dining on board the *Emerald* several times before they reached the Chops of the Channel. It was worth the risk of being tactless.

"Ma'am," he whispered back, "I was praying you wouldn't give him curry or food that's too heavy or spicy. He really hates curry. Leastways," he qualified the remark, "I've never been too sure whether it's really curry or the people that eat it. Anyway, take my word for it, ma'am, he's not one for too much spice."

"He likes more subtle food?"

"That's just the right description," Southwick assured her. " 'Subtle' – that's just the word. Not that we ever eat anything subtle in one of the King's ships! The galley is just a big copper."

"So you can boil clothes and plum duff, but that's about all!"

Southwick grinned again, running a hand through his mop of white hair. "So you've heard about duff, ma'am. Best thing to fill a hole when you're hungry and warm you up on a cold day!"

"You've served with Captain Ramage a long time?"

"Since he was a young lieutenant given his first command," Southwick said. "You were a little girl then!"

"He's not so old," she said unexpectedly, and Southwick glanced at her in time to see her blush.

"Depends how you measure time," the old master said dryly. "In many ways he's as old as Methuselah."

"And in others?"

Southwick shrugged his shoulders. He was getting into shoal waters in what could be a twisty channel. "In others? Well, he's been at sea in wartime since he was a young lad, so there hasn't been much time for social life or horseplay."

"Just killing Frenchmen?" she teased.

"Yes," Southwick said seriously. "And trying to avoid being killed by them, too. He's been wounded enough times; I've mistaken him for dead – oh, half a dozen times or more."

"The voyage you both made with my brother in that Post Office packet – that was dangerous."

Southwick suddenly realized that Miss Yorke must know a good deal more about Mr Ramage than she had let on, and he knew he was being used to satisfy her curiosity. Well, the captain was a handsome man and attractive to women, and she was one of the most beautiful and lively young women that Southwick had ever met; a mild flirtation with Mr Ramage on this voyage, whether Mr Ramage was married or not…Anything, Southwick thought, that took the captain's mind off the fate of Lady Sarah. After all, Mr Ramage had always regarded Mr Yorke as one of his best friends (although they had little chance of seeing each other) and Southwick had been surprised to find that Mr Ramage and the sister had never met before. He found himself speculating about what might have happened if they had met before the *Calypso* had sailed for Ilha da Trinidade, where Mr Ramage had met Lady Sarah.

"Captain Ramage must miss his new wife," she said, her voice carefully flat.

"Yes. It's a terrible worry for him, not knowing if she's alive or not."

"Alive?" She sounded shocked and he saw her glance across the table at Ramage, who was talking to her brother. "Why, has she been ill?"

Quickly, before the whispered conversation was noticed by the others, Southwick told her about the Brest escape and how Lady Sarah had left for England in the *Murex* brig, and how Ramage had learned in Barbados that the *Murex* had never arrived in England.

As the old man told her the story, Alexis realized the depth of his feeling for both Nicholas and this daughter of the Marquis of Rockley. She longed to quiz him about Lady Sarah, but if they continued whispering everyone would notice. Why had Nicholas not mentioned the *Murex* business when he told them he was married? Had he in fact told Sidney?

So Southwick had "mistaken him for dead" more than half a dozen times. That meant that each time he had been so badly wounded that he was unconscious. There were two small scars on his brow, and a tiny circle of white hair on his head which Sidney said was where there was another wound. How many times, she wondered, could a man be wounded badly enough to be "mistaken for dead" before eventually being wounded so badly that he died – or was killed instantly?

It was curious how (even when he was just sitting there, a hand playing idly with a long-stemmed glass) he seemed to be the centre of the room. Sidney once showed her how a knife blade affected a compass needle, pulling it round by an invisible (and, as far as she was concerned, inexplicable) force and holding it there until the knife was removed. Nicholas seemed to have that effect, and it was not just because he was a handsome man: no, if anything that would tend to make other men jealous, but with Nicholas he seemed to have a magnetic hold. She was not sure, remembering her own comparison of a minute or two earlier, whether he was the compass needle or the knife, but just by being in the room he seemed to dominate it without any of the eccentricities of dress, loud voice, affected accent or manner that some men (lesser men, she realized) adopted to make themselves stand out in a crowded room. No, he had a quiet voice, and a naval uniform reduced everyone to the same fashion. No mustard-yellow waistcoats, gaudy green cravats, absurdly patterned coats…No extravagant gestures. Then suddenly she realized what it was.

Captain Ramage – Nicholas – was sure of himself. Not cocksure, like so many of the young men who seemed to haunt London's most fashionable drawing-rooms; not dogmatic like so many of the older men, especially disappointed politicians. No, Nicholas was just sure of himself. Sure in the social sense – his background and title meant he could mix with whomever he liked without feeling uncertain. Sure in the naval, or professional sense: he was at a very early age (maddening that she could not discover exactly how old) a famous frigate captain. Mr Southwick had given more than a hint that his naval promotion was due to coolness and bravery; the influence of his father, Admiral the Earl of Blazey, may well have been a disadvantage.

The purser was at her elbow, asking in a whisper if everything was satisfactory, and she assured him it was, and as soon as he had left the saloon, Sidney was standing beside her.

"At this point the ladies withdraw," he said, "and leave the gentlemen to their cigars."

"They do indeed," Alexis agreed. "I'll follow them..."

Sidney Yorke knew he was beaten and with a grin he turned to the men. "We must forget the social niceties, I'm afraid: my sister was brought up among savages..."

"Only one," Alexis retorted, "and that was my brother, and the only manners he has, I regret to say, are those I've taught him."

"It must have been an uphill struggle," Ramage said. "But as an hostess you more than make up for his deficiencies."

"Hear, hear!" Southwick said gruffly, followed by Aitken, who was still slightly out of his depth, finding the mixture of a formal meal and the easy informality of old friends hard to follow. He knew that only himself, Paolo and Mr Yorke's sister had not sailed together in the Post Office packet, and he now appreciated for the first time that it had been a desperate business, with Britons committing treason.

The Yorkes, Aitken now saw, were not just "trade": he had picked up enough of the social rules and regulations to know that "society" as typified by the Marquis of Rockley, for example, who was Mr Ramage's father-in-law, would not normally mix with "trade", in this case a shipowner. But it was now very clear that Mr Yorke and Mr Ramage were extremely good friends and Mr Yorke was from an old family and descended from the famous Ned Yorke, who, a century and a half ago, led the Buccaneers and later became the most powerful man in Jamaica (and probably in the whole West Indies) – certainly the man most feared by the Spaniards on the Main. And Mr Yorke was his several greats nephew. How many of that old Ned Yorke's pieces of eight and Jamaica plantations were still in the family? Both brother and sister had that ease of manner that came with wealth, and they both had the good taste and restraint that came from good breeding. Aitken realized that somehow he had learned while serving with Mr Ramage how to distinguish all this. He knew well enough that he had learned from Mr Ramage a good deal of seamanship and all he knew about sea warfare, but he had not (until this moment) realized he had also learned something about society. He did not live "in society" naturally, but he had discovered that the real society (as opposed to the *nouveau riche*) was quick to open its doors to men of ability. The door stayed shut to those who knocked on it with a bouquet of pretensions, but it was flung wide open for men like Southwick: brave and honest men who were recognized as being more at home with a sword and pistol than cut glass and spotless napery.

Aitken was just realizing that Mr Ramage had been unconsciously showing him how to open some of the social doors, when he saw the door of the saloon open and one of the ship's officers signalled to Mr Yorke, who immediately left his seat, spoke to the man, and came back to Mr Ramage.

"Sorry, Nicholas, but the *Calypso*'s hoisted a signal with our number over it, so I presume it is for you." He described the flags.

"They've sighted a strange sail," Ramage said. "Well, it's time we made our farewells." He walked round the table. "The memory of today's visit will last a long time, thanks to our hostess. I'm afraid we have very plain fare in the *Calypso*, but the warmth of our welcome will – I hope – make up for the culinary deficiencies." He kissed Alexis' hand and led the way to the door, followed closely by Aitken, who saw that the *Emerald*'s officer had already called the *Calypso*'s boat's crew.

CHAPTER SEVEN

Ramage was already settling down in the boat's sternsheets as Jackson began giving orders to the men at the oars when he saw the *Calypso* fill her backed foretopsail and start to run down towards the *Emerald*.

"Mr Wagstaffe's going to make it easy for us," he commented to Jackson. "He'll come across the *Emerald*'s stern and heave-to to leeward of us."

"He's spoiling us, sir," the American coxswain replied. "It won't put muscle on these men's backs just letting them row down to leeward. They need a couple of miles to windward!"

"I don't, though," Ramage said. "I've just had a splendid dinner and I'm damned if I want to be soaked with spray. Nor does Mr Southwick – he's about ready to doze off."

As he spoke Ramage was looking round the horizon. He had not wasted time looking round while on the *Emerald*'s deck because a distant sail would already have been closely inspected from the *Calypso*'s masthead, and whatever the identity or intention of the stranger, he could do nothing about it until he was back on board the frigate.

Wagstaffe met him as he stepped through the *Calypso*'s entryport and his quick salute was followed by: "Over to the southeast and well up to windward, sir: a frigate about five miles away and closing. She was steering north when we first spotted her. I think she was slow to see us, because it was a good ten minutes before she bore away to head for us. Her lookouts must have been dozing."

"Hmm. Ten minutes! Time enough for a good snooze. I trust you've assured yourself she is not enemy?" Ramage asked ironically.

"Yes, she's British-built, sir, and British-cut sails. As you see, she's not close enough yet for us to be able to read flags."

"Very well. Beat to quarters, Mr Wagstaffe."

The second lieutenant looked startled. "Standing orders, Mr Wagstaffe," Ramage said sharply. "We must meet every strange sail ready for action."

"Yes, I know sir, but…"

"Mr Wagstaffe," Ramage said patiently, "we captured the last two prizes without too much trouble just over a month ago when they assumed that because this ship is French-built she is still in Bonaparte's navy. That ship over there – " he nodded towards the approaching frigate, still little more than a faint smudge on the horizon, " – might have been built in an English yard, but since then she could have been captured by the French who intend playing the same trick on us that we've just played on them. Anyway, it's time that young drummer gave his goatskin another good thumping."

"Aye aye, sir," said an embarrassed Wagstaffe, who realized that the combination of escorting a convoy of merchant ships (which could hardly be less warlike than the mules they were called) and the fact that the destination was England had combined to dull his normal sharpness. On the way up to Barbados from Devil's Island, he recalled ruefully, any sail, be it even a wretched dugout canoe spreading some old cloth to help her to leeward, put him on his guard.

And that, he told himself, is why some men become admirals and others stay lieutenants. Not an invariable rule, admittedly, because in all too many cases influence and patronage helped, but to be a competent captain or admiral, then you had to react precisely as Mr Ramage had done. He recalled the exchange. Lieutenant Wagstaffe had said, in effect: "Ah, a British frigate has just hove in sight." But Mr Ramage had said: "Ah, a British-built frigate has just hove in sight. *But is she British?"*

The other thing, Wagstaffe thought to himself as he looked round for Orsini, was that Mr Ramage would not have wasted two or three minutes with his head full of idle thoughts. "Orsini!" he bellowed, "tell the drummer to beat to quarters! Step lively there and be thankful that's not a French fleet up there to windward!"

Ramage noticed that the little drummer was thumping away in only a matter of seconds, making up in volume what he lacked in skill. The drum was regarded by everyone on board the *Calypso* with a good deal of pride. Carefully painted on the front were the arms of Bonaparte's France (Revolutionary France, in other words) and below them the name *L'ESPOIR*.

Ever since they had captured the *Calypso* from the French, the men had been sent to quarters by bosun's mates shrilling their pipes and shouting. Yet nothing was more unmistakable (and more thrilling, getting the men into the right martial mood) than the beat of the drum. The Marine lieutenant, Rennick, had often bewailed the lack of a drum, claiming to have a lad who could beat out a tune, and Southwick had often sniffed and said that the song of a bunch of Spithead Nightingales was no way to send men into battle. Well, the bosun's calls deserved their nickname, but on the few occasions he had been in London Ramage had forgotten to buy a drum (he had to pay for it out of his own pocket because they were not issued to frigates).

So, when Sergeant Ferris found this drum in the prize and presented it to his senior officer, Rennick, the Marine lieutenant had brought it in triumph to Ramage, complete with a well-reasoned argument why they should ignore the sentence in the Articles of War about not removing any objects from a prize before "a proper inventory" had been taken. The Army, Rennick had pointed out, was very proud of itself when soldiers captured the colours of an enemy regiment, and always kept them – usually in some special place at their own headquarters, where they were displayed with pride. The Navy had no such mementoes. He had to agree with Ramage that soldiers did not get prize money and that, given the choice, soldiers and sailors alike would probably choose prize money in place of captured regimental colours.

For Ramage the choice was easy. He knew that although he did not want to see the arms of Revolutionary France so frequently, the drum itself was in good condition (and, as Sergeant Ferris had been quick to point out, there were five spare goatskins so they were well off for replacements when the drummer beat his way through the present one). Nor was Ramage concerned with the drum as the naval equivalent of regimental colours: to him a drum (any drum, even a tom-tom made out of goatskin stretched over a butter firkin, a favourite in the West Indies) was a more effective way of sending men to quarters, quite apart from the other orders that could be passed by the beat of a drum.

As Ramage turned to go down to his cabin and change out of his best uniform, he saw a grinning Rennick standing by Wagstaffe, and the Marine snapped to attention as he saw Ramage looking at him. "The drum, sir," he explained, "first time it's beat to quarters in earnest: it's always been daily routine up to now."

Ramage smiled and nodded and went below. It was startling to find out what gave the men pleasure, and what made them proud. Bashing away on an old French drum delighted the Marines – and probably the whole ship's company – so it was a good thing he had forgotten to buy one in London. The fact that this one was French, and had the French arms painted on it, and came from one of their prizes, was what mattered: it gave it a martial tone, Ramage realized, that could not be equalled (as far as the Calypsos were concerned) by any other drum. This was *their* drum, and whack it, lad!

The rat-a-dee-tat-a-dee-tat of the drum, Wagstaffe noted, had the same effect on the *Calypso* as scooping the top off an anthill: suddenly dozens of hitherto hidden bodies swarmed out, apparently running about aimlessly, but an experienced eye saw that every man knew exactly where he was going.

By now the cutter used for the captain's visit to the *Emerald* was towing astern – with the ship going to quarters there was no time to hoist it in and stow it on the booms amidships (where an enemy shot could shiver it into a thousand splinters which would be more lethal, because more numerous, than a keg of grapeshot).

The *Calypso* had already turned back to the southeastward, and her yards had been braced sharp up as she began to beat to windward to meet the frigate, now steering northwest.

Now Aitken came up on deck to relieve Wagstaffe so that he could go to the maindeck and stand by the division of guns that were his responsibility. Already he could see Kenton and Martin watching the men load and run out the guns in their divisions.

Aitken moved up to the quarterdeck rail, noting that Jackson had taken over as quartermaster and another two seamen had joined the two already at the wheel, not because four men were needed in this weather but they were usually the target for sharpshooters. Now Mr Ramage had come on deck, wearing a sun-bleached uniform, coat, white breeches that had long ago lost their shape, a hat which was getting decidedly floppy from a diet of spray and hot sun, and shoes that made up in comfort on the hot deck what they lacked in smartness. The uniform worn for social visits (especially where the hostess was such an elegant woman) was not the one most suitable for going into action. Except for the silk stockings – that was one of Mr Ramage's rules, and the surgeon Bowen reckoned it a very good one. Officers had to wear silk stockings in action, even if they had only one pair. The danger (and trouble for the surgeon) of wool in the wound was apparently very great.

Aitken admitted it was a damned nuisance at times, particularly if the ship was in a busy sea lane, where one might sight a dozen strange sail in an afternoon, but out here in the Western Ocean, where sighting a strange sail might happen only once a week, it did not matter. Unless, as now, one was replete with quite the most splendid dinner he had ever eaten.

"Deck there! Foretopmast here!"

Aitken snatched up the speaking trumpet and answered the hail.

"The frigate's hoisted a couple of signals, sir."

As Orsini hastily reported: "I can see them, sir!" Aitken told the man aloft to continue to keep a sharp lookout.

Orsini put down his telescope and flipped through the pages of the signal book.

"She's the *Jason*, sir," he reported to Ramage and added, a puzzled note in his voice: "But she's not making the right challenge."

"Is it last month's?" Ramage inquired.

That was a not infrequent mistake, or sometimes the ship concerned had been at sea so long she did not have the latest

list. But it left the question of what reply did one make? A
challenge was a challenge...

"You've got our pendant number and the correct challenge
bent on?" Ramage asked.

"Yes, sir. And the correct reply bent on another halyard."

"Hoist our numbers and the challenge," Ramage ordered.

As Wagstaffe had already reported, the approaching ship
was obviously a British frigate: her sheer and the cut of her
sails were borne out by her using the Royal Navy's signal book
(quite apart from the fact that one was most unlikely to meet
an enemy ship so close to Barbados). Nevertheless, she had
hoisted the wrong challenge, and it was now important to see
what reply she made to the correct one.

Ramage watched the large flags flog and flap as seamen
hauled down briskly on the other end of the halyard until the
top of the uppermost flag reached the block.

Orsini was watching the frigate, balancing himself on the
balls of his feet to compensate for the *Calypso*'s roll, and
the telescope seemed a part of his body.

"She's lowering her challenge, sir," he reported just as the
lookout aloft reported the same thing. A few moments later
Aitken reported to Ramage that the *Calypso*'s guns were now
loaded with roundshot, carronades with grape, "pistols, pikes
and cutlasses issued".

"Very well, Mr Aitken."

The advantages of the "Captain's Standing Orders" were
only too obvious at a time like this: the guns and carronades
had been loaded with the correct type of shot; the small arms
routinely issued without orders (which wasted time); and
people like Bowen had made their own preparations.
Bowen's surgical instruments would be ready, with bandages
and dressings to hand, tarpaulins spread for wounded to lie
on. Some captains liked to rig boarding nets, but Ramage

considered they were for defence: they stopped (hindered, rather) an enemy trying to board, because like thick fish nets it took a minute or two for a cutlass to slash through it. More important, a net designed to stop the enemy from getting on board also prevented one's own men from swarming over the bulwarks and boarding the enemy.

Ramage looked across at the approaching frigate but knew that the sharp eyes of Orsini, Aitken and the masthead lookouts would keep him informed, so contented himself with an inspection of the *Calypso*. She was ready for battle, or for lining the bulwarks and giving a friendly ship a cheer.

All the guns were run out; half a dozen men were gathered round each breech, their different shirts making splashes of colour. Most of them had narrow bands of cloth tied round their heads, across their foreheads, to prevent salty perspiration running into their eyes. Cutlasses were stowed along the inside of the bulwarks where they could be snatched up in an emergency; pikes and pistols were all placed near at hand. The muskets were still in the arms lockers, thanks to Ramage's long-held view that a musket was a clumsy and bulky weapon in an open boat or a frigate, and useless (except as a heavy object to hurl at the enemy) after firing one shot.

The 12-pounder guns were shiny black cylinders: the last job for the ship's company before the *Calypso* left Carlisle Bay was to give all the guns another coat of blacking. Curious how every ship's gunner kept secret his particular recipe, but they were all much the same, depending on soot, although he recalled one gunner who swore by rust which was pounded into a fine dust and bound together by lacquer. Anyway, most of the shot the *Calypso* would need if she went into action had just been scaled of rust by men tapping away with chipping hammers. It was hard to prevent them hammering too hard and pitting the roundshot with tiny dents. Almost more important, each shot had been passed several times through a shot gauge, a brass ring with an inside diameter precisely the correct size for a 12-pounder shot, just under four and a half inches. If there were any tiny hummocks of rust, or flakes of scale, the shot would stick in the gauge and the gunner would reject it, returning it to the men for more chipping.

Now those shot were ready for use, sitting in the racks round the hatch coamings in scooped-out recesses, so that they looked like large black oranges. More shot were close to the guns held in small pyramids by shot garlands, small rings of thick rope put flat on the deck and preventing the shot in the lower tier from rolling away as more tiers were added to form a pyramid. This time they would not be needed and would have to be stowed away again as soon as the *Calypso* stood down from general quarters, but Ramage noted that each garland was full; each pyramid was finished off with a single shot at the top, so the men were not saving themselves work.

From up here on the quarterdeck the flintlocks, carefully oiled small rectangular blocks of steel which could be fitted to the breech of each gun by wing nuts in a matter of seconds, glinted in the sunlight. The lock was the most important part of each gun, holding the flint in what looked like a cockerel's head and beak. At the breech end the firing lanyard was secured to a ring so that a steady pull by the gun captain (standing behind the gun and beyond the recoil) released the powerful spring and, in effect, made the flint peck against steel, showering sparks which ignited the powder in the pan and sent a flash down the vent into the breech of the gun, firing the charge. Until the flintlock was brought into use fifty years ago, Ramage reflected, guns were fired by slowmatch (in effect a burning cord) wound round a linstock, a method little better than jabbing with a red-hot poker.

Yet flintlocks did not always work – heavy rain or a shower of spray as a ship punched to windward could put them out of action until they were carefully wiped dry, and in action there was usually no time for that. As an insurance, a couple of feet of slow match for each gun was kept alight, fitted into notches round a tub of water so that the glowing end hung over the inside, ensuring that sparks should not ignite any stray grains of gunpowder.

Sparks were not the only risk: the trucks, the wide wooden wheels on which the gun carriages recoiled, caused a good deal of friction. The metal-shod handspikes, the heavy wooden levers like massive broom handles and used to shift over the breech end of the carriage to traverse the gun, could make a spark. So the deck, drying fast although the sun was getting low on the horizon, was sluiced down with buckets of water, with sand scattered on top so that the bare-footed gunners should not slip.

All these preparations, Ramage mused, because of the approach of another frigate which had almost certainly left Barbados a couple of days after the convoy, probably calling in on her way to England for routine despatches from Rear-Admiral Tewtin after visiting English Harbour, Antigua, braving the mosquitoes and general unpleasantness there to collect letters to the Admiralty and Navy Board, letters of absolutely no consequence. English Harbour had never been anything but an expense to the Royal Navy: even Rodney, after the Battle of the Saints (fought within seventy miles of English Harbour), had scorned the place and taken all his prizes (including the *Ville de Paris*, then the largest ship of war afloat) to Port Royal, Jamaica, seven or eight hundred miles away, giving Jamaica a sight still remembered, the largest fleet of ships of war ever assembled.

Ramage suddenly became aware that Aitken was talking to him and he quickly emerged from his reverie.

"That ship hasn't answered the challenge, sir."

Yet she had hoisted her numbers and *a* challenge. Probably some muddled lieutenant with the wrong edition of the private signals (they were changed monthly), having made the wrong challenge (therefore receiving what seemed the wrong reply), would now be scrabbling about trying to find the current signal book, being harassed by an alarmed captain.

In turn the captain would be angry because his lieutenant had made a fool of him over the challenge – and at the same time would know the seriousness of approaching a convoy and its escort without having made the correct reply to *her* challenge. Ramage was thankful not to be the lieutenant – though the fault was ultimately the captain's because the particular book of private signals with the daily challenge and reply was in his care and he should know them in case a strange sail came into sight.

He sighed: it was *always* the damned captain's responsibility, just as now he had to decide what to do about this approaching idiot...

He reached for his telescope, pulled out the tube and lined up the focusing ring. He balanced himself against the roll and was able to ignore the pitch. The view now brought closer by the telescope lenses showed a lower semicircle of dark-blue, almost purplish sea with an upper semicircle of duck-egg-blue sky, and right in the middle was the foreshortened frigate running down towards them. In a hurry, it seemed: she was still running under all plain sail, though surely a prudent captain would be clewing up the courses by now, if not actually furling, and certainly furling the royals, leaving the ship under topsails, ready to heave-to close to the *Calypso*.

Ramage studied her carefully. Sails – a few patches but everything in good condition. Paintwork – the black paint of the hull was still black (mottled with dried spray) but did not have that purple tinge which showed age, too much sun and too much sea. And the copper sheathing on the bottom, showing frequently as the ship pitched heavily in the following seas, was bright and seemingly new, as though she was not long out of drydock.

Ramage turned to Aitken. "She doesn't *look* French, from her condition. Sails and sheathing look almost new."

"That's what I thought, sir; but ploughing down under all plain sail and not making the correct reply to the challenge…"

Ramage shrugged his shoulders. "Well, we're at general quarters so there's nothing more we can do until she gets closer."

Aitken nodded. "That's one thing about her, sir; she's steering directly for us and not trying to dodge round to get at the convoy."

That had been the first thing that Ramage had considered: to him a natural reaction on first sighting a strange sail was, did she menace the convoy?

"I think we'll accept that the *Jason* – if that's who she is – doesn't have such efficient officers as the *Calypso*."

"Probably has a less tyrannical captain," Aitken said in one of his rare flashes of dry humour.

Certainly a more erratic one, Ramage thought: the *Jason* was leaving herself with less than a mile in which to clew up courses, furl royals, round up and then back the foretopsail ready for the *Calypso*'s approach, and unless she had a full ship's company (which was unlikely: if she had 150 men out of an establishment of 210 she would be lucky) the next few minutes could provide an object lesson in how not to handle a ship. A lesson which would not be lost on Aitken, Wagstaffe, Kenton and Martin, he noted grimly.

He was always thankful when some other ship, friendly or enemy, made mistakes which provided lessons for them: he had taught them just about all he knew; they had reached the stage where they were eager and well prepared to work things out for themselves. In effect he had taught them to add, multiply and subtract; now they had to tackle the various sums that sea life threw at them. So far, each one (and Orsini, too, of course) had come up with the right answers.

Suddenly his mind slipped back several years and he saw himself through Southwick's eyes, a green young lieutenant put in command of the *Kathleen* cutter, knowing how to sail the damned ship but with precious little idea how to *command* her. That was the hardest part of teaching leadership – making young men realize that being able to tack a frigate in a high wind through a crowded anchorage proved only that they could sail a frigate, not necessarily lead men into battle. Yet going into battle and winning was their ultimate task.

And all that, he told himself crossly, is how Captain Ramage spends valuable seconds daydreaming instead of displaying the leadership he is always talking about.

But that damned *Jason* was showing no sign of getting ready to heave-to; she was surging along like a runaway horse tearing down a lane dragging a laden haywain.

Ramage walked over to the compass and glanced at the quartermaster, Jackson. There was no need to ask the question.

"She's just steering straight for us, sir: her bearing hasn't changed from the time we went to quarters."

So the *Jason* was approaching with the wind on her starboard quarter. To pass the *Calypso* or to round up at the last moment without the risk of a collision, she would almost certainly turn to starboard and then back a topsail. By the same token the *Calypso*, beating up to her on the larboard tack, with the wind on the larboard bow, would have to come round only a point or two to larboard to back her foretopsail, or bear away to starboard if there was any risk of a collision.

Southwick came up to the quarterdeck, obviously expecting that there would have to be some smart sail handling in the next few minutes and knowing he would be needed.

"Hope the captain of this frigate isn't senior to you, sir," he muttered.

"That thought just crossed my mind, too," Ramage said. He was sufficiently young and his name was low enough on the Post List that the odds were that the captain of the *Jason* was senior to him, and therefore safe from anything Ramage could say about the way he handled his ship. But should he be junior…Ramage would take perhaps two minutes and never raise his voice, but the *Jason*'s captain would not act so stupidly again.

"From her pendant numbers she's the *Jason*," Ramage said.

"Aye, one of those three Thames-built frigates launched just before they signed that peace."

Southwick's comment was followed by one of his famous contemptuous sniffs which were a language of their own. Ramage recognized this one as referring to the peace treaty: a comment, on the stupidity of Addington in falling for Bonaparte's carefully baited agreement which gave him breathing space to restock his empty armouries, granaries and shipyards. The peace had lasted eighteen months, and the politicians were congratulating themselves instead of being impeached. Ramage dare not think of the Navy's condition if the First Lord had snatched that brief period of peace to carry out the threatened reforms. They were laudable and long overdue, aimed at rooting out corruption in high places and low, but not something to start in the middle of a war. Except, of course, St Vincent and Addington had been too shortsighted to realize that Bonaparte's Treaty of Amiens was simply an eighteen-month pause between campaigns.

And still the *Jason* came on. He lifted his telescope again and examined her carefully. She was getting too close in view of her odd behaviour. Her guns were run out on both sides, tiny, jutting black fingers. Her ensign was British, but she had lowered her pendant numbers. Ah...they were beginning to clew up the courses, but slowly, as though the ship was manned by cripples or the old and infirm. No, he was not being fair because the *Calypso*'s ship's company had served together for years and as far as sail handling was concerned it mattered not at all whether it was blowing a gale or the ship was becalmed, whether tropical sun dazzled or it was a dark night.

"Took long enough," Southwick commented. "Perhaps half the ship's company's down with black vomit – could be," he added. Ramage wondered – sickness usually hit a newly arrived ship, and the *Jason* did not look as though she had been very long in the West Indies. A ship serving in the Tropics somehow acquired a bleached look; the sails would be faded, the paint on the hull would show it, even though recently applied...Somehow the frigate *looked* as though she was fresh from England. It was a feeling that Ramage could not have explained, and when he mentioned it to Southwick the master nodded. "Not a sheet of copper sheathing missing, as far as I can see. That alone rules out much service in the West Indies!"

Ramage looked astern at the convoy. The great mass of ships was now far enough away that they merged into a narrow band on the horizon, a band which now took on the colour of the sails like a faintly reddish blur of smoke. Yet the *Jason*'s lookouts would have spotted it: her officers must have examined it with their telescopes. It must be obvious to the captain of the *Jason* that the *Calypso* was one of the convoy's escorts, so why all this prancing about?

Ramage lifted his telescope once more. Yes, the other frigates had obeyed his instructions: *L'Espoir* had moved out to starboard, up to windward of the convoy and able to cover the front by running down to leeward. *La Robuste* had moved across from the leeward side to take the *Calypso*'s place astern and to windward. So the convoy was still covered: until they were all well away from the islands there was always a chance of French privateers attacking from Guadeloupe. That butterfly-shaped island had plenty of bays providing perfect bases for privateers. They could sail westward to intercept ships bound from Barbados to the more important islands to the northwest, like Tortola; or eastwards to intercept the Europe traffic. These privateers should be kept under control by the Royal Navy ships based in Antigua, but these days few people placed much reliance on English Harbour, which seemed to have an enervating effect on anyone based there.

Meanwhile what the devil *was* the *Jason* up to? Now half a mile away and steering an opposite course to the *Calypso*, she was perhaps five hundred yards over to larboard, which meant she would pass too far off to hail. She had no signals hoisted; nor would there be time to answer if she hoisted one now. And Ramage had no idea who commanded her… someone senior, or some young fool at the bottom of the Post List who wanted to cut a dash?

The *Calypso* was slicing her way up to windward but unable to close the five-hundred-yard gap. Considering she had not been careened, her bottom must be cleaner than he thought. But what the deuce was he to do with this *Jason* idiot? Just bear away as she passed and run back with her to the convoy? Why the devil did he not hoist a signal?

Probably, Ramage decided, her captain was a man sufficiently high on the Post List who had identified the *Calypso* and guessed who commanded her and now wanted to catch him out in some silly game – like, hoisting a signal at the last moment and demanding an instant answer. The price of a little hard-earned fame in the Navy, Ramage had discovered, was to be the object of envy (jealousy was perhaps too strong a word) of all the failures who were senior on the Post List. They wanted, it seemed, to prove that he had feet of clay, and Ramage could almost hear the refrain – "There, that shows him he's not as clever as he thinks he is!" It was tiresome, boring even, for someone quietly doing his job.

"Watch out!" Southwick bawled just as Ramage saw the *Jason* suddenly turning to larboard to cross the *Calypso*'s bow. But was there room? Not if the *Calypso* continued slicing her way up to windward: there would be an almighty collision in a minute or two, with the *Jason*'s starboard bow slamming into the *Calypso*'s larboard bow.

"Back the foretopsail!" Ramage shouted at Aitken and turning to Jackson snapped: "Hold her steady as she goes; the moment we get the foretopsail backed I don't want her to make a ship's length of headway."

A ship's length would make all the difference whether the *Calypso*'s jibboom missed or touched the *Jason*'s shrouds and that in turn would decide whether the *Jason* tore out the *Calypso*'s foremast by ripping away the jibboom and bowsprit, or the *Calypso* sent the *Jason*'s masts by the board as her jibboom scraped along her shrouds like a small boy running a stick along a fence.

Seamen raced from the guns to the foretopsail sheets and the braces to haul round the foretopsail yard by brute force.

Ramage had already seen that he could not help them by turning the *Calypso* into the wind because that could carry the frigate those few yards extra which could bring the *Jason* crashing into him.

But a quick look at the other frigate showed that she was making an attempt now to avoid a collision: it seemed that she was just determined to shave across the *Calypso's* bow and if there was any risk of a collision it was up to the *Calypso* to make the appropriate move.

Ramage was aware that Jackson was cursing the *Jason's* captain with a monotonous fluency but his words were drowned as the *Calypso's* foretopsail slatted and banged when the yard was braced round, and a glance over the side showed the frigate slowing down, as though she was sliding on to a sandbank. And there was the *Jason* running obliquely down towards them from only a hundred yards away: Ramage could now see patches stitched into her sails; her bow had grey patches of dried salt on the black paint. Her figurehead, brightly painted, was probably a representation of *Jason* himself. Although the guns were run out, black and menacing, there was not a man in sight: no seamen's faces at the gunports, no one on the fo'c'sle waving a cheery greeting (perhaps after thinking the captain had run things rather close), no one shouting a message through a speaking trumpet.

Suddenly the gun poking out of the first port gave an obscene red-eyed wink and then gouted smoke and, as the thunder of the explosion reached the *Calypso* the second gun fired, then the third and fourth in a ripple of flame, smoke and noise.

The *Calypso* was being raked by a British frigate, Ramage realized in a shocked rage and the shots were passing over with a noise like ripping calico: raked at a few yards' range and both ships had British colours hoisted.

The French poltroons who had captured the *Jason* were using a perfectly legitimate *ruse de guerre* when approaching under false colours, but the rules of war required that she lowered them and hoisted her own proper colours before opening fire.

And there was not a damned thing that he could do about avoiding the rest of the broadside because by now the *Calypso* was stopped hove-to, dead in the water and a sitting target as the *Jason* raced by.

But the *Jason* would pass in a few more moments and as Ramage listened for the crash of the *Jason*'s shot tearing through the *Calypso*'s hull and the screams of his men torn apart by shot or splinters, he shouted at Aitken to brace up the foretopsail yard and get the frigate under way again, otherwise if the *Jason* was quick she could wear round and pass across the *Calypso*'s stern, raking her again with the other broadside.

Ramage saw, however, that if *he* was quick enough he could turn the *Calypso* away to starboard in an attempt to follow the *Jason*, preventing her from passing astern. Everything depended on whether or not the *Jason*'s captain had anticipated him heaving-to, suddenly stopping the ship. Ramage thought not: anyone foolish enough to pass so close ahead, risking a collision but (more important in the light of the raking) making it harder for his gunners, who had to fire at a sudden blur passing the port instead of having a good look at the target fifty yards away, anticipated nothing.

The last of the *Jason*'s guns fired and out of the corner of his eye Ramage could see the *Jason*'s transom as she continued on the same course as before. Both Southwick and Aitken now joined him, the master bellowing through the speaking trumpet from time to time as the foretopsail began to draw.

Jackson gave hurried orders to the men at the wheel to meet her as the bow began to pay off in the moments before the frigate came alive, moving through the water so that her rudder could get a bite.

"Damage, casualties?" Ramage demanded of Aitken and was startled by the puzzled look on the Scotsman's face.

"No casualties, sir, but a few sails torn and some rigging cut – nothing important."

Southwick saw the unbelieving look on Ramage's face. "That's quite right, sir: those gunners were all aiming high."

Oh yes, an old French trick: dismantling shot to tear sails and rigging to pieces but leaving the hull and spars undamaged so that when they boarded the helpless ship they need only hoist up some spare sails and bend them on, and knot the parted standing, and splice the running rigging, and they had a ship they could use.

But what *were* the French doing? They were not racing for the convoy, nor were they tacking or wearing round to attack the *Calypso* again. What was their target? Their objective? The attack on the *Calypso* had been more like a flippant gesture than an act of war...

"You'd think they were just passing on their way to Guadeloupe!" Aitken exclaimed wrathfully, "and they didn't even bother to wave..."

"Follow in her wake," Ramage instructed Jackson, and Aitken began giving the orders to trim the sheets and brace the yards.

Ramage found himself tapping his cupped right hand with the barrel of the telescope, which he was still holding in his left hand. His brain had apparently stopped working: the shock of what had just happened had, in its unexpectedness, numbed him.

"Well," he asked Aitken, "we've a few minutes before we catch up with that scoundrel. Any ideas?"

"Absolutely none sir!" Aitken admitted. "Why, I was waving at her when you ordered me to back the foretopsail, and that – well, that woke me up as I watched to see how close we were to a collision. Thirty yards, I reckon. Then the broadside started."

Ramage turned to Southwick, who shook his head as a woman might spin a mop after it had dried. "Same with me, sir. I was waving to the scoundrels when they began firing. I thought her captain was being very silly and showing off by passing so close across our bow. She looked like the *Jason*, though."

"She was the *Jason* all right," Ramage said. "I recognized her and remember her figurehead, and she had it carved on her transom and nicely picked out with real gold leaf..."

"So why did she open fire on us?" Southwick asked. "Must have been captured by the French. But those damned French gunners were drunk or something to have aimed so high."

"After our sails and rigging," Aitken said.

"Don't believe it," Southwick exclaimed. "They were firing roundshot. The *Jason* probably doesn't have dismantling shot in her locker, since few British ships carry it, but if you're after sails and rigging you use grape or case. A keg of case or grape through a sail shreds it well enough. A roundshot – well, you can see – " he gestured aloft, " – just a hole punched through the cloth; nothing that can't be patched or stitched."

"Very well," Ramage said, watching the *Jason* as the *Calypso* finally turned into her wake, "all that's over. What's she going to do now?"

"Beats me," Southwick admitted. "She's not even heading for the convoy. I'd understand her raking us in the hopes of sending one of our masts by the board, and then carrying on to attack the convoy – she's nicely placed to windward for that."

Aitken took his hat off and scratched his head, a signal which Ramage interpreted as meaning he had a suggestion about which he was doubtful. Ramage looked at him with raised eyebrows.

"I was wondering, sir, if whoever commands the *Jason* is puzzled because the convoy is surrounded by three French-built frigates? If he's a Frenchman, could he have thought three French frigates had captured the convoy and he was coming down to join us to drink a toast to Bonaparte? Then suddenly at the last moment he saw we had British colours and bore up to rake us? That would account for her captain staying on the same course now and not making for the convoy."

Before Ramage had time to answer, Southwick had seized on the same flaw that Ramage had spotted. "Why was she flying the *Jason*'s pendant numbers and British colours, then? If she thought the *Calypso* was also French, surely she'd have been waving a Tricolour and some French signal or other? But approaching another French frigate under British colours – that'd be asking for trouble, apart from being quite unnecessary."

Aitken nodded. "Yes, you're quite right: I didn't think long enough before I spoke."

"We haven't much time," Ramage said, "so let's hear thoughts when they arrive!"

"What do you reckon, sir?" Southwick asked.

The more Ramage thought about it, the more puzzled he became. He acknowledged Jackson's report of the *Jason*'s course. "I'm certain of only one thing: we aren't going to find any answers by following her so far astern: let fall the courses, Mr Aitken. Out with your quadrant, Mr Southwick, and let's have some angles on the *Jason's* masts: I want to know the minute we start overhauling her."

As Aitken turned away, calling out orders, Paolo, obviously annoyed at having no role to play so far, asked: "No signals for *La Robuste* or *L'Espoir*, sir?"

"No, they know that they have to stay with the convoy. This is just the moment that a privateer lurking on the horizon would be praying for."

As Southwick left the quarterdeck to get his quadrant and seamen swarmed up the ratlines and out on to the great lower yards to untie the gaskets securing the lowest and largest sails, Ramage relived the few brief minutes when the *Jason* raced across the *Calypso's* bow and her guns started firing.

There had been something he had noticed, something which, even while he was shocked by being raked by what everyone thought was a British ship, seemed odd. Something discordant, something which did not fit into the picture either of the French attacking under a *ruse de guerre*, or a – a what? Anyway, he'd noticed it in those split seconds but now he was damned if he could remember what it was. If he *could* remember, would it provide an answer? He was not even sure of that. It was in fact little more than a nagging thought, as though he had forgotten something but could not remember whether it concerned a button missing from a coat or to remind the butler that the dining-room clock had stopped and needed winding.

The maincourse dropped from the yard with the gracelessness of a fat woman flopping into a low chair, but Aitken's staccato orders snapping across the deck from the mouth of the speaking trumpet sent some men forward hauling on the mainbrace and others aft, hardening in the sheets. A few moments later the forecourse came tumbling down, freed of the gaskets, and the yard was braced as the sail was sheeted home and trimmed.

Southwick bustled up with his quadrant, cursing that the courses would now get in the way, spoiling his view of the *Jason*.

"Not if you come over here," Ramage said from the starboard side of the quarterdeck.

The master stood, legs wide apart to balance himself against the rolling, and carefully adjusted the quadrant until it showed him the angle between the *Jason*'s mizenmasthead and her waterline. He scribbled the figure down on the slate kept in the binnacle box drawer.

"Timed that nicely," he commented. "Just as our courses started to draw. We'll soon see what effect they're having."

Ramage nodded. "But we'll have to get up the stunsails unless…" He did not finish the sentence for a few moments. "We have to keep the convoy in sight. If we haven't caught up with her by the time the convoy's drawing astern, we'll have to let her go."

"Then we'll never know what the devil's going on, sir," Southwick grumbled.

"Maybe not, but our job is to protect the convoy, and anyway, I'm anxious to get home!"

Southwick nodded in agreement about the convoy. "I can see that, sir: we don't want a long beat back. You can bet the wind'll die on us."

"Or *La Robuste* won't be tough enough on the stragglers, so that at dawn we'd find the convoy spread right over the horizon."

Southwick sighed as he lifted the quadrant once again. "They're like a crowd of schoolchildren, those mules," he grumbled. "Turn your back for a moment and they're up to all sorts o' mischief."

Then he gave a more contented sigh after looking at the scale. "Well, that's good news, sir: we're catching up fast!" He lowered the quadrant, yet Ramage could see that the old man was puzzled. "We're catching up faster than setting the courses can account for – at least, by my reckoning."

"Those Frenchmen may have only just captured the ship," Ramage said. "It'd take a few days for them to get the best out of her."

"Not if her officers are proper seamen," Southwick said contemptuously.

"Come on, be fair," Ramage chided. "The poor beggars spend most of their time swinging round an anchor in places like Brest. Our blockade doesn't give them much chance of getting experience at sea."

"My heart," Southwick said, giving his chest a thump, "it fairly *bleeds* for them."

"And well it might, right now," Ramage said teasingly. "Just put yourself in their place on board the *Jason*. They nearly collided with an enemy they were trying to rake, failed to send even one mast by the board or cut any important piece of rigging, or destroy a sail. Now, as if that wasn't enough, their target is not only chasing them but catching up. And there isn't a damned thing that they can do – that they *know how to do* – to make their ship go faster."

Southwick sniffed as he lifted the quadrant. "Don't go on, sir, you'll have me in tears...Ah!" he exclaimed as he looked at the curved scale and read off the angle. He then looked up at the frigate ahead, took another reading and then said: "If they weren't French, sir, I'd say they were deliberately dawdling, trying to trap us into coming alongside."

"They're not actually going any slower, surely?" Ramage asked. "I get the impression that they're still making about the same speed as when they crossed our bow, and that once we bore away and followed in her wake we didn't start overhauling her until we let fall the courses."

"Yes, sir," Southwick agreed. "I just meant that with the same canvas set, we're overhauling her."

Aitken had just joined them and, hearing Southwick's remark commented: "Perhaps the difference is that the *Calypso*'s hull was designed by the French and the *Jason*'s by the English."

"Aye," Southwick said sourly, "and I notice the Scots never seem to design anything– except new shapes for haggises."

Aitken did not answer, knowing he had made his point.

"Stunsails, sir?" he asked Ramage.

"Not for the moment: we're overhauling her nicely, and I want to have a leisurely look with the glass."

He thought a moment and then told Aitken: "Jackson has the *Jason*'s course. Look at the chart and see if you can work out where she's bound. She's not changing course. Too far south for Guadeloupe, I think, but she is not steering for the convoy."

"She might yet," Southwick said grimly. "She might be trying to pluck up enough courage. If Aitken's guess is right, she had as big a shock as us, only she got hers a few minutes earlier!"

"How are we doing?" Ramage asked pointedly, not wanting to start the inquest over again.

Southwick raised the quadrant, adjusted the arm and looked at the scale. "Overhauling her fast, sir. Do you want distances? I have a table of mast heights of most British and French ships o' war."

Ramage shook his head. "We need only get within gunshot, and we can judge that by eye!"

CHAPTER EIGHT

The six men serving number four gun on the starboard side were as puzzled as their captain. Stafford was by far the most outraged at what he regarded as the perfidy of the *Jason*, although his anger was mixed with contempt for her poor shooting.

"Beats me," he declared, "how they could all miss. I mean ter say, if it was a single broadside fired all at once, then the ship could have rolled at the wrong time. But there she was, sailing across our bow, bang, bang, bang…"

"For me it is enough that those gunners *did* miss," Gilbert said, his French accent more pronounced, as though the sudden shock had affected his English, which was normally good.

Rossi had no doubts. "She is captured by the French," he declared. "She comes down with the enemy's colours – we've done it, so we can't make of the complaining. And she rakes us. But the gunners are not used to the guns."

"A gun is a gun," Stafford pointed out. "You load it, aim and fire it. Doesn't make any difference whether the gun was cast by a British or a French gunfounder."

"Is true," Rossi admitted, "but if these were privateersmen, used to shooting 6-pounders and smaller from the deck of a tiny privateer, then they would not find it so easy firing 12-pounders from a frigate."

The other Frenchmen, Louis, Auguste and Albert, demanded a translation and Gilbert explained. Louis made the only comment: "I do not think a French privateer could capture a frigate, and she was not damaged…"

Gilbert translated and Stafford exclaimed: "Good for Louis, I never noticed that. All right, then, how *did* they capture her?"

Rossi sighed and said: "We must remember to ask them. But it can be done."

"Rubbish!" Stafford said flatly. "Bound to be shotholes in the hull: you can't repair them and paint 'em over at sea."

Rossi pointed towards the convoy and said triumphantly, "What about *L'Espoir* and *La Robuste*? We captured both of them without scratching the paint!"

"Oh well, that's *us*," Stafford said with a dismissive wave of his hand. "You're not suggestin' a lot of Frogs could do that, are you?"

Gilbert said quietly: "Four Frogs helped Lord and Lady Ramage capture the *Murex* brig and sail her out of Brest…we did not scratch the paint, either…"

"All right, all right," Stafford said. "I was wrong. But Gilbert, when I say 'Frogs' I mean Frenchies, I don't mean you four."

"But we're 'Frenchies', too," Gilbert said mildly.

Stafford sighed, the picture of a schoolmaster trying to keep his patience as he explained a complicated point to an obtuse pupil. "Listen, Frogs and Frenchies is Boney's men. They're the ones we're fighting."

Gilbert grinned, enjoying himself as he led Stafford into the trap. "Then what are we?" he inquired in the tone of a man genuinely seeking enlightenment. "Louis, Auguste and Albert were born in France (admittedly under the Ancien Régime), and I doubt if they'd even been twenty miles from Brest until they joined Mr Ramage. I was born near Brest but occasionally accompanied the Count to places like Paris. But I never left France until we fled to England. Yet, we're all French – why, those three speak no other language."

"But you are *Royalists!*" Stafford seized the word with the same energy as a drowning man grasping a rope. "That's the difference."

"Is not," Rossi announced. "Is *French* and is a *Royalist*. You, Stafford, are two things, just like them."

"I'm *not* two things," Stafford declared emphatically. "I'm me, and that's that!"

Jackson had been sent down to his gun and arrived in time to hear Stafford's protest.

"What Rosey means," Jackson explained, "is that you are English and a Royalist – you support the King. Gilbert and his mates are French but they support the King, or did until he was murdered."

"What about you, then?" Stafford demanded suspiciously. "You and your lot are revolting. You don't even have a king now."

"No, I'm a bit different," Jackson admitted. "It doesn't matter after all these years, does it Staff?"

"Well, no, I suppose not," the Cockney admitted. "I mean, I don't fink you'll suddenly turn on me with a barker in each hand and shoot me."

"Jacko is like me," Rossi said. "You and Bonaparte have a fight, and Jacko and me like a good fight too, so we join in."

"Why didn't you choose Boney's side, then?"

"*Accidenti!* Are we the cat in the hiding?"

"The what?" Stafford was startled at Rossi's sudden anger. "What cat, for Gawd's sake?"

"*Gatto in covo* – an Italian expression. I don't know the English."

"He means 'A snake in the grass'," Jackson said. "No, Rosey, don't get cross with our friend from London. He thought he could beat Boney by himself and doesn't like having to admit he needs help."

Stafford looked round at all the men and said with quiet pride: "All right, I get a bit muddled at times, but this I do know: my country started fightin' the French more'n ten years ago, and we're the only country left still fighting 'em. All the rest have quit or changed sides or– like your crowd, Jacko – been careful to stay out of it. But when Boney's beaten it'll be because my country kept on fighting him. Thanks for any help you lot give us – but just remember my words."

"Yes, yes," Gilbert said soothingly, "you are right and this is a silly argument. We all hate Bonaparte, and surely this gun's crew is a good example – four Frenchmen, an Italian, an American and an Englishman."

"All right, then," said a mollified Stafford and, acknowledging Jackson's tap on the shoulder and pointing finger, said: "We're overhauling her fast. Soon be raking 'er – and I 'ope she's not relying on *us* to aim high."

Ramage walked from one side of the quarterdeck to the other, pausing every couple of minutes at the quarterdeck rail to look forward. In the past, just before going into action, he had been frightened, apprehensive, cheerful, miserable, exhilarated and doubtful. But, he now admitted to himself, he had never before been just puzzled.

There she was, the *Jason* frigate. Still the British colours flapped in the wind. Still she steered the same course which would, in a few minutes' time, take her (if there were no interruptions) five miles astern of the convoy. None of her sails were particularly well trimmed, but they would satisfy a slack captain. Her guns were still run out, but there was still no sign of men moving about on deck – even though, as the *Calypso* closed on her, one would expect to see a few bright shirts through the glass as seamen moved about.

Nor was there any sign of officers on her quarterdeck. Surely there must be an officer of the deck, and the captain too, considering that a hostile frigate was overhauling her fast and indeed was now barely five hundred yards astern and so placed in the *Jason*'s wake that she could sweep down to attack either side. Surely a captain would be on deck, trying to guess which side the *Calypso* would choose, since his crew could not man the guns on both sides at the same time. Were all the officers at their divisions of guns, crouching down and peering through the ports, like voyeurs?

He lifted his telescope as a thought struck him. That was strange – there was not a single lookout aloft. In fact for all one could see, the *Jason* was a ship being sailed by phantoms. That was a fanciful thought until one remembered that these phantoms fired guns (and presumably could reload and run them out again, too).

Which meant that the *Jason* had another neat trap for him. What was it? This one, if he did not spot it, might be a complete success. Like a headmaster reviewing an erring pupil's activities for the day (before administering a painful caning), let us go over the events, he told himself. First, Aitken was right: the Frenchmen in the *Jason* recognized the *Calypso* as being French-built and were being wary in case she had been captured by the British, and finding that she was they had tried to rake her. It was an attempt that deserved better luck – yet it was damned odd that all those gun captains aimed high. He shrugged his shoulders – yes, privateersmen might be used to smaller guns and shorter ranges, and might have called for more elevation (and thus range) than was needed with the 12-pounders. Yes, that was it! Why the devil had he or Aitken or Southwick not thought of that before? Anyway, after the raking by the *Jason* had failed to bring down any of the *Calypso*'s masts she had carried on to leeward and, in effect, tried to lure the *Calypso* into following her – that could be the only explanation of why she was being so badly sailed. But what exactly was the trap they were trying to set?

The choices for the Frenchmen are limited, he thought. If there are two or three hundred of them on board the *Jason* (unlikely, unless she is now a French national ship, part of the French navy and not a privateer's prize) they would not want to get alongside the *Calypso* and try to carry her by boarding.

So she would want to keep the *Calypso* at a distance, fighting a battle of broadsides. But having seen the failure of his attempt to rake the *Calypso*, would the French captain rely on his gunners? No – unless the raking was just part of the trap, a deliberate attempt to make the *Calypso* think the French gunners were fumbling and inexperienced, so that she would get close alongside – to find the French guns firing with deadly accuracy.

Yes, the more he thought about it, the more likely that seemed. It meant that the French captain of the *Jason* thought fast and had a well-trained crew.

Very well, what now? Ramage turned yet again as he paced from one side of the deck to the other. From his own experience, captains planning ingenious ways of gaining that all-important advantage of surprise were also more likely themselves to be taken by surprise: they were much more prone to underestimate the enemy. He was himself a good example of that: having captured those two frigates, *L'Espoir* and *La Robuste*, by legitimate *ruse de guerre*, the very next time he met the enemy, which was now, he had fallen for the same trick.

It was important now to accept that the *Jason* was being commanded by a cunning enemy, and try to guess what he was trying to make the *Calypso* do. Once you start having to react to what the enemy does, Ramage told himself sternly, you have lost the battle: the whole art of combat, whether with swords, fists, armies or ships of war, is to make sure the enemy always has to respond to *your* move: always keep him off balance, wondering where or when the next blow will fall. Ramage almost laughed at the lecture he was giving himself: it was all quite correct, but hard to apply while chasing an enemy frigate across a bright tropical sea under a bright tropical sky with both ships heading into a gaudy tropical sunset which turned flying fish skimming the surface into pink darts.

Very well, he could not see any men on board the *Jason*, What did that mean? Was it intended to make him think the ship was short of men and lure him into boarding her? No, that was too crude a trick; a ploy intended to puzzle the *Calypso*, perhaps, but otherwise of no significance. And the slow progress? Probably nothing more than the *Jason*'s wish to bring the *Calypso* into action before there was any chance of the other two frigates now escorting the convoy joining in the action.

There is only one decision to make, Ramage told himself sternly; all the rest is idle speculation. How are you going to attack the *Jason*? Are you going to get a hundred yards away on her starboard or larboard side, and pound her with broadsides. Or slap the *Calypso* alongside and try to take her by boarding?

He looked across at the *Jason* as she rolled her way to leeward, now almost directly under the sun and dazzling the eye. Five hundred yards away? The *Calypso* was overtaking her, all right, but the wind was dropping with the sun, and the swell waves, with the wind waves rippling over the top of them like muscles, were flattening.

The decision seemed to make itself, and he turned to Aitken.

"I want grapnels rigged from the starboard yardarms, and a dozen more ready on deck in the hands of men who can throw them accurately." Already, before Ramage had finished giving his orders, the Scotsman was grinning, his worry that the captain had at last run out of ideas, or not yet recovered from the trick just played on him, now dispelled. "All men except the afterguard to have pikes, half-pikes, pistols, cutlasses or tomahawks; whatever they choose. And pass the word for Rennick, there'll be work for his Marines."

Southwick was still standing close and he nodded approvingly as Aitken started giving a string of orders.

"Only thing is, sir," he said quietly, "do we want those Frenchies to *see* us rigging grapnels? It might give the game away."

Ramage nodded and called down to Aitken: "Tell the topmen to rig those lines as though they're working on the sails. Don't hoist a grapnel high enough for the *Jason* to see. It's to be a happy surprise for them," he added.

"Glad you're going to board, sir," Southwick commented, his voice low.

Ramage was curious why the old master had reached that conclusion – one that Southwick seemed to have had in mind for several minutes. "Why board? Their shooting was lamentable."

"By keeping the men hidden, seems to me, sir, that French captain is trying to make us think he wants us to board. But he's not such a fool as to think we'd fall for it, so I reckon he *doesn't* want us to board. He just wants us to think he wants us to, so that we'll do something else.

"That makes me think – what with his poor shooting just now, which was so poor it must have been deliberate – that what he really wants is to have us a hundred yards away on his beam where his guns can either smash our hull to matchwood or tear our sails to shreds. I reckon you're going to do just what he's scared of and what he's trying to lead us away from – like a lapwing running lame to lead you away from her nest."

"I hope you're right," Ramage said. "I don't fancy that frigate running around loose in the convoy, with us lying out here dismasted and those new captains on board *L'Espoir* and *La Robuste* – "

" – running around like moulting hens," Southwick finished the sentence. "You've just got time for a word to the men, sir – if you wanted to say anything."

Southwick knew quite well that Ramage hated these eve-of-a-fight harangues which many captains liked – those who made time for long speeches full of rounded phrases and stirring thoughts designed to make the men fight better. Ramage knew the Calypsos would fight well if no one spoke another word, but Southwick always disagreed, not because he thought the men would not fight so well, just that he reckoned they liked to hear a few words from their captain.

Very well, there was nothing worse than having Southwick walking round with a disapproving look on his face. Where was the speaking trumpet? He would just have time to include the topmen before they went aloft to reeve the lines for the grapnels. He gave a bellow which had every man turning to look up at him.

"Calypsos, I think the King would like to have that frigate (she's the *Jason*, by the way) back again before the reek of garlic stinks out the bilges. So we'd better retake her. It'll also mean we have a stronger escort for the convoy too, and yet more prize money. Not that any of you need it!"

Every man in sight seemed to be waving his arms and cheering and slapping each other on the back, so perhaps Southwick was right, though why fifty words, a sneer at the French and a joke about prize money should make any difference was beyond him. "So we'll board her," he concluded, "and I want the boarders away in a flash when the order is given. Once you are on board her, don't stand around gossiping; I want those prisoners secured quickly, otherwise it'll take all night to beat back to the convoy."

He tapped Southwick on the arm and nodded towards the quartermaster, who was continuing to watch the set of the sails and the compass and the four men at the double wheel. "Let's make sure we all know exactly what we're going to do," he said. "I don't want to have to be shouting orders at the last moment."

Southwick looked at him suspiciously. "You're not planning on leaving me behind again, are you sir?"

"Being left in command of a frigate is hardly 'being left behind'," Ramage said mildly.

"You know what I mean, sir, and you've used that argument at least a couple of dozen times. It's my turn now. Leave one of these youngsters behind – they all had a chance with those two," he added, nodding at the convoy where by now it was easy to see *La Robuste* and *L'Espoir*.

Southwick, old enough to be the grandfather of each of the officers and most of the petty officers and seamen, liked (indeed, craved) a good fight on the decks of an enemy ship as a drunkard craved a pull at a bottle except, Ramage thought ruefully, that he knew of a few drunkards who had been cured of their craving whereas Southwick's seemed to grow with each passing birthday.

"Very well, just this time. Martin or Kenton?"

Southwick shook his head. "I'd sooner see Wagstaffe left here, sir. The *Jason*'s a well-found ship and looks to me as though she's commanded by a shrewd devil. Whoever stays on board here might...well – "

" – might have to take the convoy back to England, eh?"

Southwick grinned, but because that was what he had in mind he nodded. "We're all mortal, sir, and we've had a good run for our money."

"Very well, just listen to what I have to say to the quartermaster, then go down and find Wagstaffe. Tell him what I'm going to do and tell him he'll be left in command. And don't forget to collect that dam' meat cleaver!"

Southwick's enormous two-handed sword was famous. Most of the men in the *Calypso* carried a picture of Southwick, in some action or other, sweeping down the deck of an enemy ship, white hair flowing in the breeze, bellowing like an enraged bull and whirling the great sword over his head, scything his way through a crowd of the enemy as powerless to defend themselves against this apparent monster as a rabbit to evade a ferret.

Quickly Ramage explained to Southwick and the quartermaster what he planned to do, and both men nodded. There was nothing particularly subtle about it; both men understood that, given the circumstances, it was the only plan that stood a chance of success without a heavy loss of life.

Aitken and Wagstaffe both arrived on the quarterdeck together, and Ramage looked questioningly at the first lieutenant. "We haven't much time, Mr Aitken," he said.

The Scotsman recognized the tone because it was the nearest Mr Ramage ever came to being querulous, and he grinned cheerfully. "Lines for the grapnels are already rove, sir, and I have a couple of dozen men hidden below the bulwarks and securing the grapnels."

Ramage nodded. "Well, if I don't see them at work presumably the *Jason* won't. Now listen, the pair of you, this is what I intend doing." Quickly he explained that Wagstaffe would be in command of the *Calypso*. This brought an immediate protest from the second lieutenant that he would be left out of any fight and Ramage looked at both Aitken and Southwick. "There are times," he said with mock exasperation, "when I wish the three of you would go up on the fo'c'sle and settle all this among yourselves."

Southwick, fearing Ramage would change his mind, said hurriedly to Wagstaffe: "You're greedy. You had a good scrap with the last prizes and took command of one of them while I had to stay in the *Calypso*."

"Well, I *am* the second lieutenant."

"And I'm old enough to be your father and grandfather," Southwick growled, "and even if you are a commission officer, if you're not careful I'll put you across my knee!"

The remark was just enough to set them all laughing. Wagstaffe agreed it was Southwick's turn and looked serious when Ramage pointed out that having command of the *Calypso* gave him responsibility for the convoy, "Even though the captains of *L'Espoir* and *La Robuste* will take it from you the moment they know anything has happened to me."

Ramage left the deck for a few minutes, going down to his cabin and returning with a cutlass and belt slung over his shoulders and a mahogany case containing a brace of pistols. He knelt down at the case to load the pistols while Aitken hurried below, promising to collect Southwick's sword because the master was still busy with his quadrant.

Finally, as Aitken returned wearing his own sword and with a Sea Service pistol tucked in his belt, handing Southwick his sword and a pistol, Ramage told the master:

"Put your quadrant away somewhere safe: we can rely on our own eyes now!"

Eyes, he thought bitterly, but not brain. What the devil was going on in the *Jason*? Was she really being sailed badly to lure on the *Calypso*? Why were all the men hidden – it could not be from fear of sharpshooters. At least the mythical Jason had a ship full of heroes to help him when he sailed in the *Argo* to find the Golden Fleece. Still, the equally mythical Calypso offered immortality and eternal youth to Odysseus when he was shipwrecked on her island. All of which, Ramage reflected, shows that recalling Greek mythology is a great help if you want to pass the time and keep your thoughts from getting occupied with more troublesome matters.

The *Jason* was on the starboard tack, with the wind fine on her starboard quarter. She would expect to be attacked on that side, from to windward, and no one but an idiot would attack from to leeward. From the *Jason*'s point of view the *Calypso* would be unlikely to attack from to leeward because the wind would blow the smoke from her guns straight back on board, blinding her officers and choking the gunners. More important, if the *Calypso* attacked from to leeward, the *Jason* could drop down on to the *Calypso*, while the British ship would have to get up to windward to close the range. *The weather gauge*...to many admirals they were the only three words that mattered, although they were as confining as a canvas straitjacket.

Yet those three words explained, Ramage reflected sourly, why several famous admirals had won peerages for what were tactical disasters, complete failures which the politicians (ignorant of tactics) had, by the judicious distribution of peerages and knighthoods, turned into great victories with stirring speeches in Parliament.

That was why Vice-Admiral Nelson had not made himself very popular among the Navy's senior flag officers: before his victories at the Nile and Copenhagen, it was enough for the admiral commanding a fleet to break the enemy line and capture three ships – then England rang the bells for a great victory and gave him a peerage. St Vincent took four ships in his victory – but two of those were captured by Nelson.

But the Nile and Copenhagen had set new standards: for three, read a dozen or more. Yes and give credit to Admiral Duncan at Camperdown because his victory over the Dutch was hard won and complete, and Rodney at the Saints. But the Glorious First of June, so proudly hailed by the old guard, was by the new standards a disaster, a Glorious Failure.

Very well, Captain Ramage, prepare for your attack on this strange ship the *Jason*…There's four hundred yards to go, you've made your little speech to rally the men, all the guns are loaded, the men have cutlass, pikes and tomahawks to hand, and pistols too; the grapnels are ready to fling on board the enemy.

He turned to the quartermaster, Pegg, who had taken over the job usually carried out by Jackson. He was a wiry, gipsy-faced seaman, famous in the *Calypso* for his hatred of Welshmen. "A point to starboard – as though we are going to pass the *Jason* five hundred yards to windward."

Pegg gave the order to the helmsmen as he brushed his carefully plaited black hair to one side and, grinning happily, muttered to himself: "But we ain't though, I'll bet all the takings from a Michaelmas Fair." Since he had been given instructions, Pegg was not taking much risk.

Ramage caught the sense of the gipsy's words and smiled to himself: the "takings" that Pegg had in mind were not the profits made by the stallholders, but the haul made by the "dips", the light-fingered pickpockets who regarded the fixed fairs as the times in the year when they could clear good profits to see them through the winter. Like a "dip" planning his campaign, Pegg could see that the obvious way of attacking the *Jason* was to overhaul her and settle down five hundred yards to windward and pound her with the 12-pounders, later perhaps closing in to give her a taste of the carronades loaded with canister or grape. But Pegg had sailed with his captain too long ever to expect the obvious: he had also learned that the obvious was the most easily countered.

A broadside first? Ramage knew there was no time to reload, so that the starboard broadside would be no better than a single pistol shot. What would be best, smoke, noise and confusion – or just silence: a cold-blooded silence?

Well, he was doing the unexpected and it had better be right: looking forward, he could already see Aitken going to each division, explaining to the officers in charge and the men serving the guns exactly what they were to do when the time came. Aitken stood, and was apparently talking, with all the authority of the man who knew for certain what would happen. A lucky fellow, Ramage thought and glanced at the two pistols in his belt. The flints were good and Ramage thought of the flint knappers tapping away with their special hammers so that the flints flew off like someone slicing a crisp cucumber. A man's life could depend on a good flint...

CHAPTER **NINE**

Ramage stood at the starboard side of the quarterdeck rail with Wagstaffe beside him. The quartermaster Pegg had moved between Ramage and the men at the wheel so that he should not miss a hurried order, but almost imperceptibly the *Calypso* was closing with the *Jason*. Even without a glass they could see the gingerbread work on the scroll on the transom: *JASON* was carved there, the letters picked out in gold against a red background. The scrollwork enclosing it all was picked out in blue. Not my choice of colours, Ramage thought, but obviously some other man's personal taste clashed with the normal dictates of heraldry. At least the name *was* gilded – the man who sought the Golden Fleece did not have to suffer the indignity of having his name painted in tawdry yellow.

There was Southwick, crouched down behind the bulwark, trying to hide the fact that he had occasional twinges of rheumatism. There was Paolo, still loyal to the midshipman's dirk but covering himself by having a cutlass in a belt over his shoulder and a pistol tucked into his belt. Yes, Paolo was as excited as an eighteen-year-old boy was entitled to be. He would be the target of every French sharpshooter in the *Jason* if they knew he was the heir to the Kingdom of Volterra (might even now be its ruler, if Gianna had been murdered by Bonaparte, which seemed very likely). Young "Blower" Martin had a pistol and a half-pike. Interesting that this time he had picked a half-pike against a cutlass, but he was small, and with a half-pike you could jab the enemy four and a half feet away, whereas you had to be breathing in each other's face to have much effect with the cutlass.

Martin's father, the master shipwright, would probably not recognize his son at this moment. Ramage had a feeling that the father regarded the flute as an unmanly instrument without realizing "Blower's" skill with more lethal instruments.

And there was the irrepressible third lieutenant, Kenton. There was no mistaking his red hair, heavily freckled face which was always peeling because he could not protect it from the sun, and his four-square stance – even though he too was crouching. Kenton's father, a half-pay captain, would be delighted at the eagerness with which Kenton awaited action.

Finally there was Aitken, brought up as a boy in the Highlands and the son of a former master in the Royal Navy. Aitken, tall with a thin, almost gaunt face, black hair and deep-set eyes, at first meeting seemed dour and spare with words, issuing them with the reluctance of a purser handing out candles (which he had to pay for out of his own pocket). But in fact Aitken had a droll sense of humour: he and Southwick sparked teasing remarks off each other which made the rounds of the ship.

All the *Jason's* guns were still run out, and even though he had looked carefully at each gunport, Ramage could see no sign of the guns' crews. He could now see two men at the wheel (two, not four as a British ship o'war usually had when going into action) and a man was walking round them who could be either the officer of the deck or the captain, but who certainly was not wearing the uniform of a post-captain in the Royal Navy. Or the uniform of anyone's navy. Trousers (did that mean he was a *sans-culotte*? Presumably) of dark-green material and a long coat one would expect to see on an English parson visiting the dying: it was black with a deep velvet collar. Who but a madman would wear a coat like that in the Tropics? Well, Ramage admitted, the fellow commanding the *Jason* seems quite at home in it.

Ramage turned to Pegg, eyebrows raised, and the gipsy face nodded to show that he understood the moment was fast approaching and knew what he had to do. It was not a straightforward manoeuvre, because no one would be tending sheets or braces, but Pegg had the kind of confidence that Ramage had spent years instilling into his ship's company against such a day as now.

Fifty yards…the black paint of the *Jason*'s hull was in even better condition than he had thought. Forty yards…there were a dozen brightly coloured shirts strung out on a washing line on the fo'c'sle. Thirty yards…although the *Calypso* was overhauling her, the *Jason* was making good speed: her wake formed the usual fascinating pattern of whorls. In a few minutes the *Calypso*'s jibboom would be overhanging the *Jason*'s stern like a fishing rod over a stream.

Ramage nodded to Pegg, who snapped out an order which had the four men spinning the wheel. To the captain of the *Jason* the *Calypso* was at last beginning to turn to starboard, sidestepping so that instead of following she came up alongside to starboard: on the windward side, with her whole broadside ready.

The *Jason*'s captain would be making sure that all his gunners were at the starboard side guns: no frigate could man both broadsides at once, and if it was needed the men fired one side and ran across to fire the other.

There were still several yards between the *Calypso*'s jibboom and the *Jason*'s transom, even though the British frigate had begun her swing out, ready to overtake and come alongside.

Ramage watched the gap, narrowing his eyes as if to see more clearly. All he really saw was every one of his officers and Pegg anxiously watching him.

"Right, Pegg," he snapped and the gipsy, certain the order had been left a moment too late, shouted at the four men and flung himself on the wheel too, clawing at the spokes.

Slowly, as though with enormous dignity, like a dowager changing her mind, the *Calypso's* bow began to turn to larboard. To the watching men, it seemed as though the *Jason* was being pulled slowly to starboard and then, as the *Calypso's* extra speed became obvious, the *Jason* was gently pulled astern.

Ramage watched the *Jason's* quarterdeck. Twenty yards …that curious black-coated figure was striding up and down and he had not looked at the *Calypso* for several minutes: it was as though he was unaware that she had been following and was now overtaking. All part of the play-acting, all part of whatever trap he was trying to set? Ramage was far from sure: all he knew was that the man would look perfectly at home striding among the dark-green yews and the moss-packed tombstones in an English cemetery, perhaps quietly muttering some prayer or psalm in memory of those who had taken up permanent residence.

He said to Pegg: "Now!"

The quartermaster snapped a third order to the men at the wheel, who hauled on the spokes and then stopped at another order from Pegg as the *Calypso's* bow started to swing in towards the *Jason*. After she had travelled to within a dozen yards, the wheel was spun back amidships and the *Calypso* came back on to a parallel course.

Wagstaffe sighed, but Ramage had the feeling it was more from disappointment than relief: the *Jason's* guns had not crashed back in a full broadside, even though the *Calypso* was a perfect target. Then once again Pegg, after a quick glance at Ramage to receive an approving nod, gave more orders which sent the wheel spinning again, except this time the *Calypso* turned on to a course which would converge with the *Jason* in two ships' lengths.

As the ships approached to crash alongside each other Ramage shouted: "Stand by those grapnels," and ran down the quarterdeck ladder to join his men waiting on the maindeck. Pegg calmly gave the order which turned the wheel enough to lessen the shock of the forthcoming crash. An excited Wagstaffe, for once ordered to remain on the quarterdeck instead of leading a boarding party, contented himself with shouts of "Hurrah, Calypsos!"

Ramage squeezed alongside a gun barrel and peered down into the water between the two ships. Only five yards separated them.

"Over with the grapnels!" he shouted. "Swing the others out from the yards. Take your time and aim true!"

The clinking of metal was men's cutlasses banging against gun barrels and metal fittings as they slid to the ports; the sharp metallic clicks were men cocking their pistols. Moments now – and there it was: with a crash that men felt right through the hull rather than heard, the *Calypso* drove alongside the *Jason*. The grapnels swinging out to lodge in her rigging and bulwarks were hauled in to hold the two ships together, and before Ramage had time to give the order the Calypsos were swarming on board the other ship, led as far as Ramage could see by Southwick, who looked like a demented bishop as he ran, white hair streaming, across the *Jason*'s deck, his great sword like an immense crozier.

Ramage scrambled up and over the *Jason*'s hammock nettings and dropped down on to her deck, vaguely noticing that the nearest men to him were Jackson, Rossi, Stafford,

Gilbert and the other three Frenchmen. With a pistol in his left hand and cutlass in his right, he headed for the quarterdeck, for the man in the black coat, and was surrounded by dozens of men shouting excitedly: "*Calypso! Calypso!*"

But there was a strange atmosphere, as though they had met the coldness of a crypt. The excited dash that surged the Calypsos over the *Jason's* bulwarks was slowing down: far from men being in desperate cutlass-against-pike, pike-against-tomahawk, pistol-against-pistol duels, they were slowing down to a walk and looking round with all the curiosity of bumpkins at a fair. And beyond – or was it round them? – other shouting: that of frightened men shouting in English, as though desperately trying to establish their true identities before being run through, spitted by a pike or cut down by a tomahawk.

Was this the trap? English prisoners forced to shout for quarter at the instant the Calypsos boarded? Creating confusion and making them pause just long enough for the French to shoot them down?

Ramage looked round wildly, saw no immediate explanation and carried on his dash towards the man in the black coat who (Ramage blinked but kept his pistol raised) was now walking towards him, arms outspread in a welcoming gesture: just as a parson would greet a valued parishioner or, more likely, the patron of his living.

Above the din Ramage could hear the man saying in a normal voice: "Ramage, isn't it? I've heard so much about you, my dear fellow, and I'm so glad we meet at last!"

Was this the trap? Ramage stopped and motioned with his pistol that the man should stand his ground. Southwick and Aitken stood warily, like hunters waiting for the prey to walk into their gun sights, and the *Calypso's* boarders had all stopped and were watching Ramage, waiting for a signal or order.

Ramage glanced at Aitken and snapped: "Talk to her gunners!"

The first lieutenant, as he took the few paces to the nearest gun's crew, realized how quickly his captain was thinking: the gunners would reveal their nationality, why they had fired high when raking the *Calypso*, and who or what their captain was.

There were six men grouped round the nearest gun, all crouching, and none was armed: there was no sign of a cutlass, pistol, tomahawk, pike or musket; in fact a glance showed Aitken what they should have noticed from the *Calypso*, that the boarding pikes were still clipped into the racks fitting round the masts like dogs' collars.

The nearest man, holding the trigger lanyard, was obviously the gun captain but his face was white under a superficial tan and his eyes avoided Aitken's glare. He still stood in a half-crouch, as though he had just been kicked in the belly. To Aitken he looked like a pickpocket caught in a congregation and singled out by the parson up in the pulpit for special castigation.

"Do you speak English?" Aitken demanded.

The man nodded nervously.

"Well, stand up straight and tell me what's going on." Aitken suddenly realized something else. "Where are all the officers apart from the man in the black coat and a few midshipmen?"

At last the seaman threw the lanyard over the breech of the gun, out of the way (Aitken noticed the lock was not cocked, so the gun could not be fired), and stood to attention.

"All the officers are down in their cabins, sir. One of them could tell you. Yes, sir," he said eagerly, the idea becoming more appealing as he thought about it, "they'd all be able to tell you, 'specially the first lieutenant."

"*You* tell me, quickly!" Aitken snapped, slapping the flat of his cutlass against his leg, "or else you'll all be dead men in a couple of minutes: you fired on one of the King's ships. That's treason, to start with."

"Oh no!" the man protested in an agonized voice, and several of the others round the gun now stood up straight and added their protests. "We fired over you sir," the man said excitedly "All of us did, even though we'd been told to rake you."

Ramage, out of earshot, called impatiently and Aitken said: "Quickly now, this is the *Jason* and one of the King's ships?"

"She's that," the man said. "Commissioned in Plymouth the week after the war started again. Bound from Barbados an' Jamaica with despatches."

"Why did you open fire?"

"Go on, sir; ask one of the officers," the man said evasively, his body wriggling like a hooked fish.

Aitken's brain felt numbed: if the man in black was the captain, the officers were down in their cabins, and the men were crouched down round guns whose locks were not cocked, then what the devil was going on?

"What were your orders if and when you were boarded by us?"

"Orders, sir? Oh Gawd, sir, it ain't like that at all: please go an' ask the officers 'cos they know all abart it."

"So none of you are going to fight us?"

"*Fight* you?" the man said in alarm. "Strike me, we bin 'oping fer weeks something like this would 'appen."

Aitken turned and reported to Ramage, who thought for a moment and then snapped out orders. "Renwick," he told the

Marine lieutenant, "get all these men at the guns lined up on the fo'c'sle, with your Marines surrounding them."

Then, with his pistol covering the man in the black coat, he told Southwick: "Have all the *Calypso*'s grapnels unhooked and hauled inboard. As soon as she's free I want Wagstaffe to get her clear and keep a gunshot to windward of us."

He looked round for Jackson and waved him over. "Collect half a dozen men here."

Then he turned to the man in the long black coat who was still standing there, calm and not a bit alarmed at having men from another ship swarming over the deck of his own ship; in fact, Ramage realized, the man had a strange remoteness, like an effigy in a church which had watched over the funerals, weddings and christenings for centuries and would continue until the church fell down, unless another Cromwell came along.

Ramage tucked the pistol in his belt and slid the cutlass back into the frog and deliberately looked the other man up and down. He said loudly to Aitken, aware that the words might well have to be remembered as evidence at a court of inquiry: "I wonder who this man is – you notice he is not wearing any sort of uniform. Green trousers, a long black coat, no hat…"

"Aye, sir," Aitken said, realizing the point of Ramage's remark. "There's no telling who he is."

"Come, sir," Ramage said, "you have the advantage of me: you have guessed who I am, but I only know your ship has just been firing at mine."

"Shirley, my dear Ramage, William Shirley at your service, a captain in the Royal Navy but lacking, I fear, your distinction."

"You have your commission?" Ramage asked sharply.

"Oh yes indeed, it's in a drawer in my desk. Shall we go down to my cabin and find it?"

"Later," Ramage said. He wanted witnesses to all the conversation with this man. "Less than half an hour ago you approached my ship in the *Jason* flying the wrong challenge and then giving the wrong answer when my ship hoisted the correct challenge."

"My dear fellow, you don't say so?" Shirley seemed genuinely upset. "How careless of me. Still, no harm came of my omission, I'm glad to say."

"No harm?" Ramage looked round at Aitken to make sure he had heard, and noticed that Jackson, Stafford and Rossi were among several other seamen who had, almost without realizing it, grouped round Shirley, covering him with their pistols. "You narrowly missed colliding with my ship and then fired a raking broadside into her. Do you call that 'No harm'?"

"A raking broadside?" Shirley repeated in a puzzled voice. "My dear Ramage, you are mistaking the poor *Jason* for someone else. Why should we want to rake one of the King's ships?"

"That's the point of my questions," Ramage said, adding heavily: "It is rather an unusual situation."

"Yes, it would be," Shirley agreed. "By the way, do I address you as 'my Lord' or just Ramage? I've heard it said you don't use your title in the Service."

"Ramage will do. Why did you open fire?"

Shirley shook his head sorrowfully, as though regretfully refusing some importunate request. "Must have been some other ship, my dear Ramage. Anyway, now we've settled that, I hope you can be persuaded to stay and dine with me. That is one of the complaints I have about the King's Service: at sea and on foreign stations one does meet such a poor class of person, and that is why it's such a pleasure to meet you."

Ramage gestured to him. "Come with me." He walked over to one of the starboard guns, ordered the crouching men to stand upright, and told the captain of the gun to step forward.

The man was in his early thirties, clean shaven, his hair tied in a neat queue. He had a green cloth tied round his forehead to absorb perspiration and did not wear a shirt above his white duck trousers.

"Name and rate?" Ramage asked.

"George Gooch, sir, rated able."

"Very well, Gooch. Tell me, have you fired this gun today?"

The man glanced at Shirley, looked down at the deck and said woodenly: "No, sir; ain't fired no gun."

Ramage nodded towards Jackson, who walked to the muzzle and sniffed. "It's been fired recently, sir. Inside half an hour."

"What have you to say to that?" Ramage asked Gooch. The man shook his head and refused to look up.

Ramage took Shirley's arm. "Come, Mr Shirley, let's examine that muzzle ourselves."

"By all means." He stood back a pace and made a sweeping gesture indicating that Ramage should lead the way.

Ramage bent down at the muzzle. The smell of burnt powder was unmistakable. He pointed. "Smell that," he told Shirley.

The man clasped his hands behind his back and bent forward. He inclined his body, Ramage thought, like the patient parent leaning over to listen to a mumbling child.

"Well?" Ramage demanded.

"I can smell nothing, but I have a poor sense of smell anyway."

Aitken and Southwick had come down the other side of the gun.

"This one has been fired; those on the larboard side haven't, sir," Southwick said firmly. "I'll check all these on the starboard side." With that he turned and made his way along the row of guns, ducking under barrels and holding his sword clear, sniffing at the muzzles like a terrier at rabbit holes.

"Please wait with these men," Ramage told Shirley and gestured to Jackson to guard him. He noted that Kenton was standing by the men at the wheel giving them orders while Martin was busy with a party of men, helping bear off the *Calypso*.

With Aitken beside him he made for the officers' cabins.

"What do you make of it, sir?" a bewildered Aitken asked. "Seems like a dream to me: each time you reach out to touch something you find it has no substance, as though everything was made of smoke."

"And we're trying to shovel it," Ramage said sympathetically. "But no, I haven't anything more than a suspicion. Captain Shirley looks crazy enough to be the next Archbishop of Canterbury. Have you noticed he's not perspiring under that black coat?"

"He's not moving very much, either, sir," Aitken pointed out.

Ramage led the way down the companionway, blinking for a few moments in the half-light. But within five paces of the gunroom, a burly Marine lunged forward with a musket and bellowed: "Halt, who goes there?"

Ramage stopped and inquired in a quiet, polite voice: "Who are you expecting?"

"That's none of your business," the man snarled, taking another pace forward.

"Do you recognize my uniform?" Ramage asked, his voice still low. "And the officer beside me?"

"Aye, I recognize both uniforms but they don't mean nothing to me. Captain Shirley's the only one I take orders from."

"Not even from the Marine captain or lieutenant commanding your detachment?"

" 'Specially not 'im; 'e's one o' them."

"Who are 'they'?" Ramage inquired sympathetically.

"That lot in there," the Marine said, turning and pointing with his musket. He turned back to find Ramage's pistol aiming at his right shoulder, the eye looking along the barrel deep-set, brown, and as far as he could see, without a glimmer of mercy in it.

"Tell me," Ramage said, "don't you think it would be a wise insurance to take your right hand away from the trigger and then hand your musket over to the lieutenant standing beside me?"

The man's right hand came clear; he was making the movement unmistakable. He gave the musket to Aitken as though presenting a large bunch of flowers.

"Where are the other Marines?" Ramage demanded.

"Dunno, sir. On deck, I 'spect. I'm not due to be relieved for 'bout half an hour, I reckon."

"Who are you guarding in there?"

The Marine looked puzzled, as though Ramage's question was one even an imbecile could answer.

Ramage, feeling himself near the answer to the whole puzzle, jabbed his pistol for emphasis, wanting to hear what the sentry had to say before blundering into the half-darkness of the gunroom, whose occupants were regarded as dangerous enough to require a Marine guard.

"Guarding, sir?" The man misunderstood his meaning, and Ramage realized the two senses in which the word could be used, to protect, or to prevent escaping. "Well, sir, they're all in there; the whole bloody lot."

"Damnation, man, who *are* 'the whole bloody lot'?"

"Why, sir, all the commission and warrant officers. Them wot mutinied!"

Commission and warrant officers mutinying? Against a captain who was walking the quarterdeck wearing a long black coat and denying that every gun in his starboard broadside had just raked the *Calypso*? Aitken was right: all this had the insubstantial atmosphere of a dream! If only he could wake up and find the *Jason*, the man in the black coat and the gunroom full of alleged mutineers had all vanished, and his steward had brought him a cup of proper coffee bought in Barbados, whence it had been smuggled from somewhere on the Spanish Main.

But this was no dream: he was down below in the *Jason* with his pistol held at the head of a Marine who was startled to find that Ramage did not know the gunroom was full of mutinous officers.

Aitken, realizing that Ramage intended to walk into the gunroom, said hurriedly: "Wait, sir, I'll get Rennick and a brace of our Marines. They can flush them out. Come with me," he said sharply to the Marine, gesturing with the musket, and disappearing up the companionway.

Ramage, left alone, listened to the slap of the water against the hull – he should have given orders for the *Jason* to be hove-to, before she and the *Calypso* were carried too far to leeward of the convoy. And those two newly promoted captains – would they protect the convoy while he was away? Supposing French privateers out of Guadeloupe suddenly attacked, just a couple of them from different directions: would *La Robuste* and *L'Espoir* be able to drive them off? They were powerful and weatherly enough, but no ship was better than her captain. And anyway, the commander of the convoy was standing in half darkness outside a gunroom door, waiting for some Marines to act as good shepherds.

Yet Aitken was right: he was the commander of the convoy, not the leader of a boarding party, and if the convoy came to any harm, Their Lordships would quite reasonably want to know what the devil he was doing.

He stuck the pistol back in his belt, suddenly conscious that his wrist ached from holding it. Damn and blast, all he wanted to do was get this wretched convoy safely back to England and find out what had happened to Sarah. The devil take frigates commanded by men who looked like run-amok prelates in long black coats and whose gunroom (according to a Marine sentry) was full of mutinous officers.

Supposing the captain was not mad. Supposing, instead, that the officers had mutinied. What happened now? Captain Ramage had the responsibility of sorting it all out, along with nursing his convoy, and he owed the Yorkes a dinner, he thought irrelevantly, but found he liked thinking about them. Sidney owned a fleet of merchant ships that were among the best kept and best sailed at sea today, and he was an amusing, erudite and lively host, apart from having become one of Ramage's closest friends. Strange how he had so few friends. Yet not so strange really, because most of his adult life had been spent at sea, where the only people he met were naval officers (with the exception of Sidney).

A clattering on the companion ladder heralded Aitken, followed by Rennick, Southwick (his great sword in hand), Sergeant Ferris and several Marines. Ramage moved back a few steps to make room for them all, and to avoid explanation and any more delay, pulled both pistols from his belt, cocked them and then kicked open the flimsy door of the gunroom, striding in with the shout: "No one move!"

No one moved because the gunroom itself was empty: the table in the centre was bare, there was a form at each of the long sides and a chair at either end, and all round were the doors of the officers' cabins. Hats hung on hooks over several of them, and there were empty racks which normally held swords, telescopes and pistols. But in view of the heat, it was significant that all the doors were shut. Ramage stood by the table until the men behind him had come into the gunroom, pistols and cutlasses at the ready.

Rennick's whole stance showed that he considered this was a job for the Marines, and remembering how there had been no work for them as sharpshooters, Ramage told him: "All right, look into the cabins one at a time, starting at that end."

Rennick did not wait for Ferris or one of the Marines: instead he stepped forward quickly, pistol in his left hand, and flung the door open. Inside a man crouched on a small, folding stool that took up the space left by the cot and small chest of drawers.

"Out!" Rennick snarled, "slowly, with your hands clasped in front of you."

The deckhead was too low for a man to hold up his arms: everyone in the gunroom was having to crouch, and Ramage pulled round a chair and sat down. Whatever was going on, there would be no violence. The officer now coming out of the cabin which was neatly labelled "1st Lt" looked as if he had not slept for a month nor changed his clothes.

"Sit here," Ramage said, pointing to the form on his left. "If you are the *Jason*'s first lieutenant, tell me your name and explain why you are skulking in your cabin."

"Ridley, sir."

"That answers my first question…

The man ran a finger along the grain of the deal table but avoided looking up at Ramage, who examined the man's pale and unshaven face closely.

"Ridley," he said quietly, "you haven't been up on deck for two or three weeks." He recalled the man's stiff gait. "And I doubt if you've been out of your cabin, either. Why?"

"My duties kept me down here," the man said sheepishly, his eyes still fixed on the table.

Ramage pointed to the next door.

Rennick flung it open and another man came out. Ramage glanced up at the lettering over the door and waved the man to sit next to Ridley.

"Are you the third lieutenant?"

"Yes, sir. Owens. Henry Owens."

"And what are you doing in your cabin at a time like this?"

"Captain's orders, same as Mr Ridley."

"When were you last on deck?"

"I…er, I'm not sure, sir. Within the last two or three weeks, I think."

Ramage sighed and looked up at Southwick. "Is everything all right on deck?" When the master nodded, Ramage signalled to Rennick, who opened the door over which was written "Master".

The *Jason*'s master was, Ramage noted in amusement, the opposite to Southwick in just about every way: he was tall, thin to the point of being cadaverous, completely bald – his head seemed to be polished like the ivory top of a Malacca cane – and his nose was not just long but tilted up, as though something should be hung on it.

"If you're the master, tell me your name and the date of your warrant," Ramage said wearily, and then felt a finger poking into his side. He looked up to find Southwick signalling that he wanted to whisper something.

"I know this fellow," the master whispered. "A good man."

Ramage looked at the man questioningly. "Well?"

"Price, sir. Warrant dated August 1793."

"Very well, go with Southwick – I believe you know him. Take your hat, the sun's still bright."

As Price collected his hat and then followed Southwick out of the gunroom, Ramage said impatiently: "All right, Mr Rennick, winkle out the rest of 'em – the second lieutenant, surgeon and purser, I believe." He raised his voice, so that they could all hear. "I'm getting tired of all this play-acting. None of you seem to realize you're probably going to spend the next few weeks in irons."

The first lieutenant's head jerked up. "But sir!"

"But sir, *what*?" Ramage demanded, hoping to provoke him into revealing some details. "Do I need to remind you of the Articles of War? Numbers 12, 13, 14, 15 and 16 come immediately to mind, but no doubt 19, 20 and 22 could apply. You'll recall that most of them end up with the phrase 'shall suffer death'."

"But...but well, it's not like that, sir," Ridley wailed.

"What is it like, then?"

"Oh, I can't say!" the man said and, collapsing on the table with his arms clasped over his head, he burst into uncontrolled tears.

Ramage stood up, feeling completely helpless, and said formally to Rennick: "All these officers are under arrest and confined to the gunroom."

"The captain, sir?"

Ramage tried to look stern, although he felt more sympathy for the sobbing Ridley than it would have been proper to admit. "I'll decide about him later, after I've had a chance to talk with him."

CHAPTER **TEN**

Back on board the *Calypso*, with the *Jason* abeam as the two ships beat back towards the convoy, Ramage tried to make up his mind. There was a choice: although he had by no means finished questioning the *Jason*'s officers and ship's company, he was still just near enough to take the *Jason* back to Barbados and hand over the whole wretched and puzzling business to Admiral Tewtin. Or he could keep the *Jason* with him, carry on with the convoy, and hope to get it all settled in England.

If there were six reasons why he should do one thing, there were half a dozen why he should do the other – and that was only choosing between returning to Barbados or going on to England.

There were plenty of variations lurking around to distract him. He could escort the *Jason* back to Barbados with the *Calypso*, leaving *La Robuste* and *L'Espoir* to carry on with the convoy and arranging a rendezvous for, say, a week's time. (But what hope was there of clearing up this business in a week? Tewtin would want dozens of depositions: Shirley, if he had any sense, would want even more. Very well, forget that choice.)

What about sending the *Jason* back to Barbados with, say, *La Robuste*, giving her captain a written report for Rear-Admiral Tewtin? How the devil could he describe all this in a written report that was not as long as the *Regulations and*

Instructions, the largest volume a King's ship carried? And what yarn was Shirley (and his officers, whatever their role was) likely to tell, if Ramage and the Calypsos were out of sight and sound, even if not out of mind? Shirley could have the *Calypso* raking the *Jason*, and those officers of his would probably back him up, judging from the story Southwick brought back after his talk with the *Jason*'s master.

Yet if he was honest, his main concern was that the *Jason* business was so unusual and complex that Rear-Admiral Tewtin was not the man to deal with it: this was something for Their Lordships at the Admiralty, and the Judge Advocate's department.

And he was involved in it only because he – well, first he had got married, then he and Sarah had had to escape from Bonaparte, and all that had led to him crossing the Atlantic to Devil's Island, to rescue Jean-Jacques, the Count of Rennes. In turn he had brought two French prizes into Barbados...and been stuck with the job of escorting this convoy back to England. But why – *why, why* – had the *Jason* chosen to interfere with his convoy? Why could she not have gone on to Britain, where her orders sent her?

He answered the Marine sentry's call and Southwick came into the cabin. Ramage waved him to a chair, and the master threw his hat on to the settee.

"I've been reading the Articles of War again, sir."

"They don't help," Ramage said, "unless you want to get into more of a muddle."

"But there must be *something* we can do, sir."

"There isn't," Ramage said shortly. "Not so long ago, while I was escaping from the French at Brest, none of you could do anything about a drunken captain sent to the *Calypso*. Their Lordships in their wisdom have drawn up the Articles of War on the assumption that a captain can do no wrong."

"A surgeon can have him replaced on medical grounds," Southwick offered hopefully but without much conviction.

"Oh yes. What do you suggest Bowen diagnoses in Captain Shirley's case? That the black coat proves he has a poor tailor? That a bulge in his right shoe shows he has a bunion? The fellow doesn't drink, doesn't smoke (or even chew tobacco in secret), he doesn't swear or keep a mistress on board. He seems identical with dozens of other post-captains, except perhaps he reads his Bible more frequently."

"Those officers," Southwick said. "Apart from Price…"

"Apart from the master they seem a weak-kneed crowd," Ramage said. "I wouldn't want to go into action with them, especially Ridley, who is a fool as well. But apart from keeping their mouths tight shut, they haven't done anything to harm us. Indeed, keeping their mouths shut isn't *harming* us; it's just puzzling."

"It's not my place to say this, sir, and I'm presuming on the years – "

"Oh, for God's sake," Ramage said impatiently, "out with it!"

"Well, sir, are you sure of your ground in putting Captain Shirley under an arrest? You were just saying about the Articles of War."

"What gave you the impression that Captain Shirley is under an arrest?" Ramage asked innocently. "I've no grounds for arresting him. No authority, rather. I may have, but I can't find any backing in the Articles of War or the Admiralty Instructions."

Southwick frowned, the wrinkles on his brow like a much folded leather pouch. "But when you spoke to him in his cabin and left Wagstaffe there, I thought you said…"

"I know you did, and so did Aitken and so did Wagstaffe. More important, so did Captain Shirley. You all expected me to arrest him – and so you heard words I didn't actually say."

Southwick was by now grinning broadly. "Well, as long as Captain Shirley and that sorry collection of commission and warrant officers accepted it, and continue to do so until we reach Plymouth, we'll have no complaint."

"No, we just have to hope for an understanding port admiral at Plymouth. Once we have the convoy safely dispersed, everything should be all right."

"But if he talks to the wrong people in Plymouth?" Southwick asked.

"Half-pay for my officers, if they are lucky."

"But what about you, sir?"

"Best for you not to think about it."

Southwick shook his head and picked up his hat. "You said the *Jason*'s station is a cable off our larboard beam?"

"She'd better stay a cable to leeward of us, unless she gets a signal to the contrary. Wagstaffe understands."

"Yes, I had a word with him before he went across. It was a good idea putting him in command. It'd be risky with Aitken."

"Yes, Aitken is too near being made post: if there's trouble, it could count against him."

"If there's trouble it'll count against you," Southwick said gloomily.

Ramage shrugged his shoulders. "If I am dismissed from the Service, I've plenty to keep me occupied, but it's Aitken's whole life. Though thanks to prize money, I doubt if he depends on his pay."

"Pay! Thanks to you no one in the *Calypso* now depends on his pay, even allowing for the villainy of the prize agents."

Ramage grinned at Southwick's forthright statement. "Still, I expect Aitken would like to get his flag eventually, so that when he retires to his estate in the Highlands, it'll be as Rear-Admiral Aitken. Perhaps even Vice-Admiral, with a knighthood."

"Could be," Southwick agreed. "He would if it just depended on merit. This stepping into dead men's shoes is no good. Promotion by seniority is just an insurance policy for the dullards. If you live long enough you're bound to end up the most senior admiral in the Navy."

"Providing you make that first jump on to the Post List," Ramage pointed out. "Unless he is a post-captain, he doesn't even put a foot on the bottom rung…"

"That's understood, sir. Don't forget he's already refused one chance. Admittedly that was because he reckoned he wasn't ready, and would learn a lot more by staying with you."

"Yes, but now he's learned all he can from me. He's ready for the Post List, and I don't want anything like this – " he gestured in the direction of the *Jason*, " – getting in the way. Now, leave me to write up my journal. Between now and the time we reach the Chops of the Channel, I have to write a full report on all this business…"

"Aye, and if you'll allow me to stick an oar in, sir, you'd be well advised to get signed reports from the *Calypso*'s officers, and perhaps some of the senior petty officers."

"You *are* gloomy," Ramage commented.

"I just wonder who this Captain Shirley has for friends. As I see it, his friends are going to be our enemies, if all this business comes to trial."

Southwick was right, of course: whatever happened, it was all bound to come to a trial which would clear or condemn Shirley. It could even turn into a situation where clearing Shirley meant condemning Ramage…All the Calypsos were certain that Shirley was mad. Perhaps not permanently, but at least temporarily. Touched by the sun, perhaps. Anyway, Bowen was going to examine him tomorrow and would write a report, but all that would not stop Shirley getting a fair trial.

It was more likely, Ramage thought ironically, to bring odium and attacks down on the head of Captain Ramage, if Shirley had friends in high places and money to pay off the press and get lampoons and pamphlets sold in the streets. Ramage knew how vicious were the attacks made on his own father, when the Earl of Blazey was made the government's scapegoat for sending a fleet too weak and too late to deal with a French attack on the West Indies. And most shameful of all (perhaps the most shameful episode in recent British political history) there was the Byng affair: there a not-very-bright but honourable admiral had been accused of cowardice and shot to disguise the vacillating weakness and stupidity of the First Lord, Anson, and the prime minister, the Duke of Newcastle.

Stupidity? No, it was the very essence of politics: viciousness, self-interest, hunger for power and cowardice. In the case of Admiral Byng the whole crowd of them, the Duke of Newcastle, the Earl of Hardwicke (and his son-in-law Anson) and most of the rest of the party were trying to cling to power in Parliament, and they were quite prepared to murder Byng (judicially, of course: why use a stiletto when you have the law to do it?). Byng was executed and they kept power. Byng, Ramage reflected, lost his life, but the government under Newcastle and the Admiralty under Anson lost their honour (without realizing what it was).

Ramage knew he should talk again to Shirley and his officers before drafting his report. Yet after talking to any of them he came away with the feeling that he had been dreaming; their answers were so incoherent or remote from reality that recalling them later was like trying to remember how you had behaved while drunk at a party.

Captain Shirley had never seen such grim-faced men sitting round his dining table, and he seemed more puzzled than alarmed. Both Wagstaffe and Aitken held pens and had to share the same inkwell as they wrote down the questions, and Shirley's answers, making him slow down or repeat an answer. The demands for repetition were frequent because many of Shirley's answers were difficult to credit.

The *Jason* was rolling her way along, astern of the convoy, in good weather. Wagstaffe had the big awning stretched over the quarterdeck and the captain's coach, cabin and sleeping place were cool. Ramage had thought deeply about making Shirley move down into one of the officer's cabins in the gunroom but had finally decided to leave him in his quarters and instead put Wagstaffe in the first lieutenant's cabin, making all the lieutenants shift round one.

As soon as Ramage had come on board and Wagstaffe had the frigate under way again (at the speed the convoy was making good, nothing was lost by heaving-to the frigate to avoid getting soaked by spray which would be thrown up if the ship had to tow the *Calypso*'s boat alongside), Shirley – still in his long black coat – had walked over and greeted Ramage.

"Ah, my dear Ramage, how thoughtful of you to pay us a call," he had said in a completely sincere voice, rubbing his hands as though washing them. "Can I persuade you to dine with me this time? No – then a cup of green tea, or a glass of something stronger?"

The man had been genuinely upset when Ramage refused, and again Ramage was reminded of an anxious parson who felt he was being rebuffed by his patron.

Even now, sitting round the dining table, Ramage at the head, Shirley to his left and with Aitken and Wagstaffe on his right, facing Shirley, the man exuded sincerity. Sincerity? Well, again and again Ramage was reminded of the last occasion he had met the Archbishop of Canterbury, who proved to be a most unctuous individual exuding the secretive bonhomie expected of the doorman at one of the better houses of pleasure in Westminster.

Ramage tapped the table to emphasize what he was going to say.

"Captain Shirley, for the eleventh time I must ask you why you raked the *Calypso* although she was displaying British colours and her pendant numbers, and was flying the correct challenge?"

"My dear Ramage, why should the *Jason* fire at the *Calypso*?"

"Don't dodge the question," Ramage snapped. "I am asking you."

"On what authority, pray?"

Ramage waited until Aitken and Wagstaffe had finished writing. It gave him time to think, although God knew he had already given the subject enough thought.

"On the authority of a captain of one of the King's ships trying to discover the reason for a traitorous and treasonable attack by another of the King's ships."

"But no one attacked you, treasonably or traitorously. Ask my officers. Ask my men. You have done so once already, but you have my permission to ask them again."

This man was so calm and cool. Both Wagstaffe and Aitken were perspiring – although that could be from the effort of writing fast and concentrating. But this man Shirley – there was not even a single bead of perspiration on his brow. A belly of pork! Ramage suddenly realized that the man's complexion, dead white and only wrinkled by lines running from each side of his nostrils to the corners of his mouth, reminded him of a familiar sight in a pork butcher's shop. The man's baldness heightened the effect: not only was the skull utterly hairless, but Ramage was sure (probably because of some illness, malaria, perhaps) no hair grew on the man at all. Did he have to shave? There was none of the shadow on his face that most men had by late afternoon (and even earlier in the Tropics, where the heat made hair grow faster).

His eyes were small but unusually widely spaced. However, the nose seemed to belong to another face altogether. This face was cadaverous, the skin tight over the bones, with no pouches beneath the eyes, no hint of middle age in jowls. No, there was not much flesh to wrinkle, apart from the lines beside the nose. But the nose!

It seemed to belong to a much bigger and heavier man; someone with Falstaffian girth and a plump face, and a great club of a nose that commanded attention like a blunderbuss when its owner aimed it. In keeping with the rest of the face it was bloodless, yet for its size one would have expected a healthy pink glow, something that would show up on a dark night.

Both Aitken and Wagstaffe had written down the answer. Ramage looked at Shirley again.

"Have you threatened any of your ship's company so that they are frightened of answering my questions?"

"Why should I? I have nothing to hide! Ask them anything you like, my dear fellow."

"When I asked to smell the muzzle of that gun – number nine gun on the starboard side – you said you could smell nothing."

"Nor could I! Just the usual blacking, of course."

"In your opinion the gun had not been fired recently?"

"No. Nor was that just my opinion; it was the opinion of the men serving that gun."

"But *my* officers and those of my men who were asked all smelled burnt powder and gave their opinion that the gun had been fired within the last half an hour."

"Yes, they did, and most singular I found it. Had you threatened *them*?" Shirley asked archly.

"Why were you the only commission officer on deck when the *Calypso* came alongside?"

"Apart from two or three midshipmen, who were running messages, my officers have various different duties, of course! Really, Ramage, I do find some of your questions naïve."

"Perhaps so, but why were all your officers at that moment confined to their cabins with a Marine sentry guarding the gunroom door?"

"There you are, that's what I mean. You know as well as I do that in a frigate like the *Jason* or the *Calypso* there is always a Marine sentry at the gunroom door, just as there is one at the door to the captain's quarters and, in hot weather, at the scuttle butt, so what is so singular about this particular sentry? What *is* curious is that you choose to go down to the gunroom at a time when the officers are in their cabins. I was on the quarterdeck – you saw me – and surely you agree that I am competent to handle the ship without assistance from some callow lieutenant?"

Ramage had a mental picture of the *Jason* racing across the *Calypso*'s bow, her shrouds missing the jibboom by inches, but this was not the time to thrash it out: it was not a subject that could be reduced to questions and answers even though, according to lawyers (indeed, the whole legal system), every situation must be, even when a man's guilt, and thus his life, depended on answering yes or no to particular questions. "When did you stop beating your wife?" Everyone but lawyers and judicial authorities had heard that "Answer yes or no" joke but whether a man was on trial for murder or treason, or stealing a trinket or poaching a hare, it was "yes" or "no".

Shirley turned and faced Ramage squarely. "Tell me, my dear fellow, are you attempting to remove me from my command? I am your senior by dozens of places on the Post List, as I am sure you are well aware."

And that first question was the one I hoped you would not ask, Ramage thought to himself. He was now standing on the edge of the great pit dug by the Articles of War to trap scoundrels but also equally dangerous to officers trying to carry out their duties in the King's Service.

Board him in the smoke: a good rule when you are not sure what to do next. "Don't you think that attacking the *Calypso* justifies you being removed from your command?"

No sooner had Ramage asked the question than he realized he had provided a loophole, and Shirley was quick to stick his musket through and open fire.

"I keep telling you, Ramage, and so do my officers and men, that I did not attack the *Calypso*. You have questioned all of us, yet you persist in this absurd allegation."

Ramage considered for a minute or two, considered the risk of the *Jason* suddenly attacking ships in the convoy or one of the other frigates, and made his decision. Shirley did not dispute that Ramage had the authority to remove him from his command if there was sufficient justification (something about which Ramage was far from certain). No. Shirley was only disputing whether or not the *Jason* had fired on the *Calypso*; whether or not, in fact, he had provided the justification.

"We do agree on this point, then," Ramage said. "We agree that you say your ship did not fire on the *Calypso*, and we say she did."

"Yes, indeed," Shirley said, "that seems a very fair summary."

Both Wagstaffe and Aitken wrote quickly.

Aitken pushed the paper across to Ramage with the quill resting on top. "I've written down your question and Captain Shirley's answer," he said. "There's nothing else written there."

Ramage immediately guessed his first lieutenant's purpose. He took the pen, wrote in the date and headed it "On board His Majesty's ship the *Jason* frigate" and, dipping the quill again, said to Shirley: "To avoid any misunderstanding later, perhaps you would care to read that and sign it?"

Shirley read it slowly, nodded as though there could never be any doubt that he would agree, and wrote his signature with a flourish. He gave the pen back to Ramage and slid the paper along the table. "Now you sign it, eh? Then there can be no question of what we disagree about."

Although Ramage did not use his title in the Service, this sheet of paper was becoming (was already?) a legal document, so he signed simply: "Ramage".

"Ah yes," Shirley said jovially, "you fellows with titles don't have so much writing to do as we more common folk."

Ramage smiled. "Our tailors charge us twice as much, so in the long run I'm sure you gain."

"Ah yes, innkeepers too, no doubt," Shirley said sympathetically. "Even ostlers would expect half a guinea tip from a lord, whereas an impoverished post-captain like me in the lower half of the list gets away with a shilling."

Yes, Ramage thought to himself, you look the sort of fellow who would tip a shilling when half a guinea was appropriate: no doubt you would also take mustard with mutton.

"Well, is that all?" Shirley inquired.

"You are so obliging," Ramage said hypocritically and hating himself for it, "that there are two other things I'd like to get cleared up while we're at it. Three things, actually."

"You have only to ask," Shirley said expansively.

"Your orders, what are they?"

"You have no right to ask, of course, but as there is nothing particularly secret about them, I've no objection to telling you. I am taking despatches to the Admiralty from the commanders-in-chief at Barbados and Jamaica."

How the devil could one dislike a man like this? Ramage asked himself. He was not a man one liked in the sense of making him a friend, but he was thoughtful and courteous (when he was not raking you: do not forget that).

Ramage nodded his thanks as Shirley said: "And the second thing? You mentioned three, if I remember correctly."

"Yes. I would like my surgeon to examine you. I presume you would have no objection to that?"

"Ah, back we go to removing a captain from the command of his ship. You know it can only be done on medical grounds, so it follows your sawbones has to make an appearance."

"Yes, but my surgeon is far from being a 'sawbones' – he was in a practice in Wimpole Street before entering the King's Service."

"He must have done something very dreadful to cause the change, then," Shirley commented. "Still, I'll agree – as long as he doesn't bleed me. I won't be bled. Achieves nothing, bleeding a sick man; just drains the life from him. Remember Ramage, if you want to kill something you cut its throat to let the blood run out. Yet these doctors try to say it does human beings good. Rubbish, sheer rubbish! Hold on to your blood, never know when you'll need it. Very well, now what's the third on your list?"

"I would like to leave Lieutenant Wagstaffe on board with you."

"I'll be glad to have him on board. I'm sure he'll find the experience invaluable. Experience – it's everything for the young naval officer. Battles, boarding parties, hurricanes, wooding and watering – everything!"

Ramage glanced at Wagstaffe who, red-faced but apparently more amused than angry, was writing with great concentration.

"Speaking of surgeons," Shirley said, "always remember one thing." His voice was solemn and Ramage expected he was about to go back on his agreement to be examined by Bowen. "Two things, rather, and stand by them no matter what the surgeons might say. Three things, in fact. There are only three sovereign remedies. Just three. Mind you, the sawbones don't like to admit it because knowing the three sovereign remedies puts them out of business. Would you care to know them?"

Anything, Ramage thought, which throws any light on what is going on in your head and keeps you agreeable to Bowen's examination. "I would regard it as a favour on your part," he said.

Shirley nodded agreeably. "Yes, well, for any common distemper – upset of the bowels, for example, then rhubarb. I carry a good supply of dried sticks and use it ground up and dissolved in water. In wine, if you prefer it. For headaches, general malaise, muscular pains – brimstone and molasses. Fresh mixed and well stirred, a large spoon four times a day. And last, for any agues, feverishness, or trembling of the extremities, then the bark. I know that many surgeons use the bark. I expect they have heard of my success with it."

Shirley ran his thumbs under the collar of his coat, as if he was going to turn it up because of a chill wind, but then Ramage realized he had done it several times and it was a nervous gesture, the only thing that Shirley did that was not absolutely normal.

"Thank you," Ramage said politely, "I'll make sure my surgeon has supplies of those items. Now," he said as he stood up, "we'll leave you in your cabin while I have a chat with your officers."

"Ah yes, indeed," Shirley said with unexpected heartiness. "You don't need my inhibiting presence, do you!"

"No," Ramage agreed because there was no point in disguising the fact that no one in the ship would dare say more than "Good day" with that black-coated figure pacing up and down, like a crow on the lawn presaging a death in the family.

It was humid and almost dark down in the *Jason*'s gunroom, which reeked of the sickly-sweet smell of bilges that needed pumping. The officers and warrant officers, Ramage quickly realized, were still sulking from yesterday, although at first it was not obvious whether their resentment was directed at Shirley or against Ramage, who had freed them from their arrest and put them back on normal watches.

The atmosphere, Ramage decided, was not ripe for either comfort or the exchange of confidences. "Join me on the fo'c'sle," he told Ridley, noting that the man still had not shaved.

The *Jason*'s bow lifted and fell as she stretched along astern of the convoy under topsails only. The wind was light and she needed little canvas set to keep up with the merchant ships, which were jogging along under all plain sail and, Ramage noted, in good formation.

Ramage found some shade made by the fortopsail and waited with Aitken and Wagstaffe.

"What do you make of this Ridley fellow, sir?" Wagstaffe asked.

"Scared stiff of something," Ramage said. "Reminds me of an animal trapped in a cage. Eyes flicking from side to side, looking for a way out. Apart from that, he looks intelligent ...or, rather, not too stupid."

Wagstaffe laughed as he saw the man coming up the ladder. "I'm glad you qualified that, sir; I was thinking he got this job because his father knows Captain Shirley."

"His tailor, perhaps," Aitken said, and the other two laughed. It was one of the oldest jokes in the Navy that a certain type of captain would pay for his uniforms, shirts and hose by taking the tailor's son or nephew to sea as a midshipman (officially a captain's servant) – a gesture which cost him nothing since he was allowed to take a certain number and he did not pay them, nor did they act as servants.

Ridley walked up and stopped in front of Ramage, saluting with a listless gesture, as though all spirit and energy had been drained out of him.

Ramage looked him up and down carefully, noting the unshaven face, uncombed hair, creased breeches and jacket, soiled stock.

"Is that your usual rig? Do you always sleep in full uniform and has the carpenter borrowed your razor to split wood? Is there a shortage of soap in the ship?"

Ramage spoke quietly but contemptuously, his voice intended deliberately to provoke the man, who straightened his shoulders and sighed. Ramage recognized it as a sigh of despair and ignored it.

"I'm sorry sir. I didn't expect you, otherwise I'd have tidied myself up."

Ramage took the watch from his fob pocket, looked at it and slowly put it back. "Is the *Jason's* first lieutenant usually still *en déshabillé* at this time of the day?"

"Sir, these are not normal times for the *Jason's* officers," Ridley muttered plaintively, as though that sentence alone explained his appearance.

"In what way?" Ramage said, encouragingly.

Ridley shook his head. "I can't explain, sir; but I'd be grateful if you'd just take my word for it."

"Ridley," Ramage said sharply, "your ship opened fire on the *Calypso*. I'm trying to find out why."

Ridley shook his head. "I'm sorry, sir, I know nothing about it. You must ask Captain Shirley."

"Have you and the other officers been threatened?"

"I'm sure the captain can tell you all you need to know, sir. I'm only the first lieutenant," Ridley said doggedly.

"Which means you are the second-in-command and take command if anything happens to the captain."

Ridley stared at the deck and said, almost absently: "But nothing *has* happened to the captain…"

"Listen," Ramage said quietly, "tell me in confidence what has happened. I'll tell these two officers to move out of earshot so there will be no witnesses to whatever you say."

"It's no good," Ridley said miserably, "there's nothing to say, witnesses or no witnesses."

Very well, Ramage decided, persuasion will not work so it has to be a threat. "You realize there will be courts of inquiry and courts-martial when we reach England. You are going to be asked about the *Jason's* guns firing. You are going to have to give your evidence on oath. Your word against mine. Your word against that of all my officers and men. Can you guess which the court will accept?"

"You must ask Captain Shirley, sir," Ridley said woodenly. "I know nothing about courts and oaths." He looked at Wagstaffe as he asked Ramage: "If you have no further questions, it's my watch in a few minutes."

"Run along," Ramage said sarcastically, "you don't realize the depth of the water you're standing in. Send up Mr Price."

As Ridley went down the ladder, Ramage shook his head wonderingly. "I've got it!" he exclaimed. "There was something about these men that seemed familiar, and I've just realized what it is. Two things, in fact. One concerns the officers, warrant officers and men; the other Captain Shirley."

Aitken and Wagstaffe waited expectantly but after a minute or two Aitken realized his captain's thoughts were miles away.

"What's familiar, sir?"

"Voodoo! I last saw this sort of thing in Grenada. The witch doctor had a spell put on the local people. He threatened terrible things if they didn't keep a secret, so when they were questioned they denied everything in the same way, as though their minds were not in their bodies. And the witch doctor (of course he denied he was one or that he had anything to do with Voodoo) was just like Captain Shirley: friendly, polite, apparently willing to answer questions – yet for all that remote, as though the real man was hidden behind a pane of glass."

"I've a slight idea of what you mean, sir," Aitken said. "Not from having had anything to do with Voodoo, but in the Highlands there are some very odd happenings: people with strange gifts and strange powers…"

He broke off as the *Jason*'s master, Price, came up to Ramage and saluted.

"You wanted to see me, sir?"

"Yes, and you can guess what it is about because Southwick mentioned it yesterday."

Price shook his head and glanced aft at the quarterdeck.

"The captain is down in his cabin," Ramage said. "You can talk in absolute safety."

"What's there to talk about?" the man said insolently. "I'm sure Captain Shirley or the first lieutenant can answer all your questions."

"Different men give different answers," Ramage said carefully, deciding to accept the man's insolence for a few more minutes in the hope that his attitude would change. "There are just a few questions."

Price shrugged his narrow shoulders indifferently.

"Tell me Price, why do you think the *Jason* fired at the *Calypso* yesterday? Was it an accident?"

The *Jason's* master ignored the suggested excuse. "I never heard tell of ships firing at each other yesterday," he said. "Leastways, nothing until Southwick asked me, and you too."

"Sir."

"You too, sir," Price amended. "You'd better ask the captain."

"Price," Ramage said slowly, "Southwick speaks highly of you, and you know as well as I do that when we reach England there'll be a court of inquiry and courts-martial. Obviously if you help us now, I will speak up for you."

"You want me to turn King's evidence, eh?" Price sneered.

"Don't be absurd. Just look at it from my point of view: my ship comes up to greet another of the King's ships, and gets raked. I could have had masts sent by the board and dozens of men killed."

"But you didn't, though," Price said slyly and for a moment Ramage thought the man would reveal more, but he simply waved an arm towards the *Calypso*. "I see she has a full complement of masts…"

"Price, I'm giving you a last chance. I'm not threatening you. But you know the danger you're in. You know my offer to speak on your behalf is your only chance – "

"No one's got a chance," Price interrupted angrily. "We had one chance but we lost, and that's that."

"A chance to do what?"

"Forget I ever said that," Price said, suddenly nervous. "I said too much. S'more than a man can stand being up here on the fo'c'sle and 'terrogated like this by strangers. If you've got questions, ask Captain Shirley, don't pick on us – sir. And don't go telling Captain Shirley we said anything, 'cos we didn't." With that Price quickly saluted, turned and bolted down the ladder, hurrying along the main deck back to the gunroom.

"They 'had one chance, but we lost'," Ramage murmured to himself. "Who are 'we'? The gunroom officers? Everyone on board the *Jason*? Is Captain Shirley included or excluded?"

"I think we'd be better off if Price hadn't said that," Aitken said bitterly. "It's just tantalizing, and no one is going to tell us any more."

Ramage nodded in agreement. "I had the impression that 'we' probably referred to the gunroom officers. I don't think the men were involved."

Both Aitken and Wagstaffe reminded Ramage that the guns' crews denied the guns had been fired, but Ramage said: "No, I'm not talking about the whole business. I think the 'chance' is one thing and the attack on the *Calypso* is another."

Aitken agreed. "I'm thinking about the way everybody seems…"

He paused, and Ramage finished his sentence: "Wrapped in fear and apprehension."

"That's it, sir; like schoolboys who have been told to see the headmaster in the morning, and not sure whether they're going to get a good beating or not."

"Well, we're only getting ourselves more puzzled by staying on board here. Keep an eye open," he told Wagstaffe, "and sleep with a pistol to hand."

"Sir," Wagstaffe began tentatively, "supposing Captain Shirley starts doing something that is, well…sort of…"

"You'll have to decide whether or not what he's doing (or proposing to do) is prejudicial to the King's Service. If it is, you have to do whatever you think fit. I can't give you orders to cover everything, but I'll back whatever you do."

"Supposing one of the officers refuses to carry out an order…"

"Look, Wagstaffe, what we're doing is by way of being a bluff: I am trying to get the *Jason* back to England without Captain Shirley attacking some other ship. Unless Bowen gives me a report tomorrow showing that Captain Shirley is mad, there's nothing I can do about him, officially. Putting you on board, sending Bowen to examine him, questioning the officers, questioning Shirley himself – all this lays me open to various charges, I expect, if we can't prove that Shirley attacked us without cause and that he's crazy."

Ramage warned both men: "Don't forget that at the moment we're safe as long as we can prove that the *Jason* raked us, and we have all our own people as witnesses. Shirley, on the other hand, can produce witness for witness to deny everything. So it depends who the members of a court want to believe. However, I think Shirley's missed his most plausible defence."

"I'm glad to hear that, sir," Aitken muttered. "What would that be?"

"Shirley would have had a good defence for raking us if he'd sworn he never saw the convoy in the distance. Then he could claim that because the *Calypso* has French lines, he assumed she was French, flying British colours as a *ruse de guerre*."

Wagstaffe said: "He could have claimed he thought we were about to attack the convoy and that he arrived just in time to save it."

"That's true, but keep the thought to yourself," Ramage said dryly. "I haven't even thought of it in Shirley's company in case he has the same powers as some of those old biddies in the Highlands, and reads my mind."

"He's got some weeks to think of it," Aitken pointed out. "They say there's nothing like a sea voyage to clear the mind."

"No," Ramage agreed, "but he denies firing a gun, so he'd have to change everything to use that defence."

"You'll have to tell Bowen to think of some vile disease that Shirley has, sir," Wagstaffe said. "Something that'll keep his mind occupied, worrying!"

"They get damned ethical, these medical men," Aitken grumbled. "At least, ones like Bowen do. He'd faint if you suggested he prescribe a dram of brandy on a cold night 'for medicinal purposes'."

"Damnation take it!" Ramage swore. "The *Jason*'s surgeon! We haven't questioned him."

"Haven't *seen* him," Aitken said. "And I remember that when we were down in the gunroom yesterday, winkling out the officers from their cabins, I noticed the only open door and empty cabin had 'Surgeon' painted over it."

Ramage was already hurrying down the ladder to the maindeck and a couple of minutes later the Marine sentry was announcing him at the door of Captain Shirley's cabin.

Shirley was sitting back on his settee with his feet up reading a book. He closed it and swung his feet down, but Ramage waved him to remain seated. "Please don't get up. I'm sorry to interrupt your reading."

"My dear Ramage, you are always welcome, as I continually tell you. I am beginning to think you have a poor opinion of yourself!"

"Certainly you make me a welcome guest. There was just one question I forgot to ask you. Your surgeon. I have not seen him."

Shirley shook his head sorrowfully, and Ramage thought that being the possessor of such a sad, long face would make Shirley an excellent professional mourner: all he needed was a tall hat with a thick ribbon of black silk round it, and a pair of black silk gloves: he already had the long black coat.

"Ah yes, a sad business. Died very suddenly – just off Barbados. We don't know what it was, since we have no medical knowledge – " he permitted himself a slight smile, " – but we all agreed that it was something in the nature of a stroke. Yes, a stroke; that's what we agreed to enter in the log and I put it in my journal. A moving funeral because he was a popular man. Not as well qualified medically as your fellow, I imagine, but widely experienced, especially in the diseases of the East. He had served in John Company ships as a surgeon's mate, I think."

CHAPTER ELEVEN

Ramage leaned forward over his desk, finding his chair hard, and he was tired of the sound of his own voice. He looked round at Aitken, Bowen and Southwick and said: "There you have it. That was all the information that a morning's work yielded us. I haven't forgotten anything, have I?" he asked the first lieutenant.

"No sir, except the strange feeling you had about Captain Shirley and the men." When Ramage looked puzzled, Aitken reminded him: "You did mention about Voodoo, sir – some experience you had in Grenada?"

"Voodoo?" Southwick exclaimed, startled. "Don't say…"

"Mr Southwick was with me at the time in Grenada," Ramage explained to Aitken. "And so was Mr Bowen."

"Tell us about it, sir," Bowen said anxiously. "Don't say that Captain Shirley is mixed up with Voodoo!"

"No, no, no!" Ramage said emphatically. "I was just describing its effect to explain to Aitken and Wagstaffe what the atmosphere reminded me of – there was no sign of Voodoo as such."

Southwick looked at Bowen and nodded his head. "The captain is right. When we talked to them on board the *Jason* yesterday I couldn't put my finger on it then, but now I've got it. It's the same as going down into a crypt – no reason why you should feel uneasy, but you do. You know about the coffins, you know the stonework makes the atmosphere cold, you expect the air to be stuffy because the door has been shut…but you can still get a strange feeling: the hair on the back of your neck wants to stand up. There's no reason, but it just does."

"And talking to the witch doctor and his victims," Bowen added, "you feel they're hiding behind a pane of glass; you can see and hear them but if you reached out you'd never touch them."

Ramage tapped the desk top. "Now then, let's not attach too much importance to that. I'm more interested in knowing how Captain Shirley makes his whole ship's company deny everything."

"Well, they're not exactly *denying* everything, sir," Aitken said. "I noticed that more often than not they told us to ask Captain Shirley about it. They shifted the responsibility for an answer on to him."

Ramage shrugged his shoulders. "Yes – which is the same as them dodging the responsibility."

"I'm more interested in the death of the surgeon," Bowen said. "Most unfortunate that they don't have a surgeon on board. His views would have been very significant."

Aitken waved a deprecating hand. "Don't you believe it. If he knew anything of the slightest use, he'd have bleated about medical ethics. But he wouldn't have noticed anything – he was one of those bleed-and-purge chaps. Started as a surgeon's mate in a John Company ship."

"Probably knew some sovereign remedies for belly aches brought on by too much curry," Southwick said, unable to resist teasing Bowen. "Anyway, as far as a court-martial in Plymouth is concerned," he said, a practical note in his voice, "all we know is that the Jasons deny firing at us, and we heard the shot whistling over our heads, and we had some holes, since patched, in our sails and some rigging cut, all of it since replaced."

"That's it," Ramage said. "So it's up to you now, Bowen."

"Don't expect too much from my report, sir," Bowen warned. "A walk across Parliament Square or down Whitehall is enough to prove that there are more madmen walking around than sane ones, simply because the mad are usually very cunning."

Sidney Yorke shook Ramage by the hand. "Alexis wanted to invite you to dinner again but I told her we must observe the formalities. Now, Jackson knows – " He watched as the cutter's painter was led aft, so that the boat trailed astern like a dog on a lead. "Ah yes, he knows," he said with a smile as the American led the boat's crew forward. "I told the cook to make them up something with cold cuts."

"That's why they like coming over," Ramage said. "All the food is boiled in the King's ships. You look well. How is Alexis?"

"Come below now and see her or she'll get impatient. Is everything arranged to your satisfaction?" he inquired ironically, waving towards the *Calypso*, which was now stretching along a couple of cables to windward of the *Emerald*. "It's a good idea of yours to take a turn round the convoy occasionally: I've never seen such good station-keeping. You scared them at the convoy conference!"

Alexis, wearing a high-waisted morning dress of white cambric, sprigged muslin and yellow morocco slippers, was sitting in Yorke's day cabin, and when Ramage kissed her hand she smiled up from the settee. "I thought you'd decided to leave us when you suddenly headed for Africa! And then that frigate began shooting at you, although she seems to be on our side!"

"We needed the exercise," Ramage said teasingly. "I for one was feeling quite jaded."

"You should come over and see us, then," Yorke said, "and bring any of your officers who can be spared."

He pushed forward an armchair for Ramage. "It's a hot day. Rum punch or lemonade – or lime, or orange?"

"Lemonade, please," Ramage said and Alexis commented: "I thought you'd prefer a rum punch."

She blushed as first Yorke and then Ramage laughed, and Ramage quickly explained: "It's an old joke between your brother and me: he knows I hate rum."

"Alexis hates it too," Yorke said. "She nearly faints away when a planter leers at her and then whispers sweet nothings through a smokescreen of rum fumes."

"You certainly know how to put our guests at ease," Alexis told him crossly. "Now the poor man is worried in case I don't like the smell of lemons!"

"I doubt it," Yorke said. "He's not about to give you a planter's leer."

Seeing Ramage's eyebrows raised questioningly, Alexis laughed and explained: "And that's an old joke between Sidney and myself. The ladies out in the islands – wives of the planters, merchants and soldiers – tend to have shrivelled up minds and figures, so that…"

She broke off in embarrassment, having started off on an explanation without considering where it might lead her.

Yorke rang a small silver bell for the steward as he finished her sentence. "So that the husbands, bored and boring, flock round a beautiful woman like moths round a candle and singe their wings with what they think is wit but is simply bawdy, almost barrack-room humour."

"Actually the wives are worse," Alexis said unexpectedly. "You men never notice it but they're so jealous they're very, very polite, yet everything they say has hidden implications."

"Implications?" Yorke exclaimed. "What implications? Most of them are so stupid they couldn't distinguish an implication from an imprecation!"

"Oh, they imply that I'm trying to run off with their husband or have come out to the islands looking for a husband."

"Wasn't that the idea?" Yorke asked with feigned innocence. "A handsome husband, ten thousand a year and 20,000 acres no further north than the Trent?"

"It might have been your idea, so that you could get rid of me, but it wasn't mine. I must admit," she added sharply, "I *was* looking for a wife for you: it's high time you married. Nicholas – "

She broke off, her face flushed with embarrassment as she realized what she was about to say.

"You are quite right," Ramage said quickly, "it's high time he married. I have just the sort of woman in mind. I can recommend some names."

Alexis was clearly intrigued. "What sort of woman?"

Yorke shook his head: he had known Ramage too many years to have much doubt about the well-cushioned little trap into which Alexis was walking.

"Well, first one has to assess what Sidney has to offer. He's wealthy, and even if he proves an incompetent shipowner, you'll be there to keep an eye on him. He's not very handsome – but his fortune compensates for what his features lack. A poor card player– that's a great advantage because wives can get very resentful if their husbands constantly beat them at quadrille. He's hopeless at backgammon, which makes him an even better prospect. He has good taste – he's always in the company of one beautiful woman, his sister…"

"Oh, do go on," Alexis urged, laughing at Sidney.

"Well, this woman should be a widow, because while a widow understands marriage, I'm not at all sure that Sidney does. A *mature* widow, and preferably the late husband should have been a dull fellow who left her verging on debt, so that Sidney dazzles her with his wealth. You see," Ramage explained to Alexis, hard put to keep a straight face because she was concentrating on every word, "his money can make up for some of his shortcomings."

Alexis was nodding in agreement. "Yes, but did you see anyone suitable in Barbados, for instance?"

"No, I didn't go on shore. But London – I know of several in London. The advantage there is that their tipple is likely to be gin, not rum, so their breath won't trouble you."

At that she glanced up warily, saw Yorke grinning and told Ramage crossly: "You are an unfeeling brute: I thought for a moment that you really cared about Sidney's happiness."

"I do," Ramage assured her. "I care enough not to interfere. One day he'll meet the right person and he'll recognize her, and it won't be someone we've discreetly introduced into the family circle."

"You seem very certain. Anyway, it won't be anyone we approve," she said, with a trace of bitterness in her voice. "But it hasn't happened yet."

"Sidney and I are the same age," Ramage said gently. "I married only a few months ago and I met my wife on board a John Company ship anchored off a tiny island in the South Atlantic that few charts even show. Until fairly recently, everyone expected me to marry a woman I met in Italy."

"The beautiful Marchesa whom you rescued?" she asked softly.

"Yes, *la bella marchesa*. But I finally met my wife a quarter of a world away."

Yorke said: "I'm flattered at the attention of two such experienced marriage-brokers, but when are you going to tell us what happened yesterday, Nicholas?"

"Yes," Alexis said. "What did you do to make that poor frigate fire at you?"

"That 'poor frigate' should not have fired at us," Ramage said mildly, "so have a care where you scatter your sympathy!"

For several moments both Yorkes were silent: both knew enough of ships and the sea to know that something had gone dreadfully wrong.

"From here it seemed that she fired her starboard broadside at you," Yorke said. "We saw the smoke between you."

"The frigate is the *Jason*. The smoke you saw was from her starboard broadside: she suddenly cut across our bow and raked us. Fortunately without doing much harm."

"But why?" Alexis exclaimed. "She's British, and you must have been flying all the right flags."

"We were, but I don't know why she did it." Ramage stopped talking while the steward came into the cabin and set down the glasses, putting the jug and sugar bowl in front of Alexis. "Shall I pour, madam?" Alexis shook her head, obviously preoccupied with what Ramage had just said, and the steward left the cabin.

"Sidney always tells me I mustn't interfere in men's business – but can you tell us any more? It is most intriguing. No, alarming. I have visions of a British frigate suddenly sailing across *our* bow and raking us. Surely, if one rakes you, then another might attack us?"

Ramage gave what he hoped was a reassuring smile. "I have a hundred questions of my own, but no answers. In fact," he admitted, "I'm here as a refugee. I've discussed it so much on board the *Calypso* that my brain is overflowing. I was hoping you two might have some fresh ideas."

"It is sweet of you to include me," Alexis said, "but what can a woman know about naval matters?"

"This doesn't concern naval matters," Ramage said grimly, sipping his lemonade. "It concerns a madman, and I think we all know as much as each other about madmen. This one seems to be straight out of Bedlam, although who unlocked the door and gave him the King's commission I don't know."

"It's the captain, is it?" Yorke asked.

Ramage nodded. "This is what happened," he began, and finished half an hour later, during which time Sidney Yorke and Alexis listened with all the concentration of children hearing a thrilling fairy story, asking only an occasional question.

At the end of it Yorke said promptly: "I don't know for sure about this man Shirley, but I'm certain *you* are crazy!"

Alexis, now white-faced and almost in tears, looked at her brother as though he had suddenly hit Ramage, and instinctively reached out to touch his wrist, as if wanting to reassure him.

"You're crazy because you've got yourself involved. The *Jason* was bound for England. Very well, her captain is mad and opens fire on you – but without doing much damage and not killing or wounding anyone. If you had any sense you'd have sheered off, left her alone to carry on to England. All right, you didn't know she was bound for England, but she obviously wasn't coming to reinforce you. At that point you'd have been simply (in lay terms) the injured party, and when you got to England you'd have reported to the Admiralty all you knew – that the *Jason* had raked you without cause and then sailed off over the horizon.

"That is what a sensible man would have done. But what did you do? Since you obviously haven't noticed yet, I'll tell you what you've done – and remember I speak as a layman: I know nothing of Admiralty rules and regulations. You have in effect captured one of the King's ships, removed the captain from his command and put one of your officers in his place, and discovered that not a man on board the *Jason* will back up your story that she opened fire on you – oh yes, yes, I believe you, but I am trying to see it through the eyes of the president of the court of inquiry, or court-martial, or whatever it is.

"The masters in the convoy would back you if they knew what had happened. Both Alexis and I will – if our word matters a damn. But why did you get involved with the damned ship?"

Alexis, now in tears and trembling from her brother's harsh words, stood up and without realizing what she was doing put her hands on Ramage's shoulders in a gesture partly to protect, partly to comfort him.

"Sidney's wrong, oh so wrong," she said, the words tumbling over each other, tripped by sobs. "You had to take command, otherwise who knows what other mischief that madman will do. He's terrified his officers. He's a mad dog!" she exclaimed, turning to her brother. "Don't you realize that? You shoot mad dogs, you don't let them run off to attack the neighbour's children!"

Yorke held out both hands despairingly. "I'm sorry, Nicholas, you seem to have run into more trouble on board the *Emerald* than you had in the *Calypso*."

Ramage reached up and held Alexis' hands. "No, I wanted to hear what both of you thought. You've put your finger on it, Sidney: you've seen the choice I had, and you think I made the wrong one. You, Alexis, think I made the right one. But so far you're the only people who see clearly that there were only two choices. The rest of them – Aitken, Southwick and probably Bowen, although I haven't seen his report yet – are too close to the problem and," he gave a grim laugh, "too loyal to me to consider that I might be wrong."

Yorke held up a warning hand. "No, both you and Alexis have misunderstood me. I say you made the wrong choice in getting involved. I repeat, you made the wrong choice. But knowing you and considering what's at stake, the choice you made is the only honourable one for a naval officer. It's just not the sensible one. But if I'd been in your place I hope I'd have done the same thing, although I'm a coward and doubt it. But it frightens me to think of the trouble this man Shirley could cause you in England *if he can convince people he is sane.*"

"I'm not so much bothered by that as wondering what patronage he has," Ramage said. "His patrons can cause the trouble. A court of inquiry might clear him and then pressure on the Admiralty from his patrons could get me brought to trial on some trumped-up charge."

"Why don't you send him off to England?" Alexis said impetuously. "Let him go on and say nothing more about it. Don't report to the Admiralty or anything. Just act as though it never happened."

"There are about two hundred men on board the *Calypso* and two hundred more in the *Jason*. All of them know what happened, even if Shirley has cast a spell on his men. There are seventy or so ships in the convoy and two other frigates, *L'Espoir* and *La Robuste*. Up to a couple of thousand men, in other words, who will gossip. Oh yes, I'm sure if I asked them the Calypsos would keep their mouths shut, but is it a thing that a captain should – or can – ask of his men? No. Apart from anything Shirley might do, there will be gossip and rumour and speculation and exaggeration…the story will be around Plymouth within hours of our arrival; the Admiralty will soon know about it."

Yorke poured himself more lemonade with sufficient deliberation to make Ramage watch him.

"When you chased after the *Jason* and went alongside her," Yorke asked, "you had guns run out, and all that sort of thing?"

"Yes, in fact we boarded her. Just managed to stop the men firing in time. As I told you, we thought she had been captured by the French."

"Yes, I just wanted you to repeat all that. You don't see what a madman (with all his witnesses terrorized, somehow or other) can make of that?"

Ramage shook his head, puzzled at the tone in Yorke's voice. "No – it seems natural enough that the *Calypso* should assume that any ship that fired a broadside at her must be enemy."

"That's not what I mean. A madman (or anyone trying to hide a mistake for that matter) could claim that *you* were attacking one of the King's ships. Deny the broadside and accuse you: any sane man covering up a mistake would say that. I hate to think what embellishments a madman could add."

Ramage offered Alexis a handkerchief but she shook her head, gathered up her skirts and left the cabin.

"I'm sorry," Ramage said lamely. "I've wrecked your day with my problems."

"On the contrary, I'm glad we were here to listen to them. You know that anything..."

"Yes, I know," Ramage said humbly, almost resenting that for the first time that he could remember he was in this position. "I'm sorry that Alexis had to be involved – and I've just upset her by offering a handkerchief. I was trying to help."

Yorke laughed unexpectedly, and it sounded to Ramage like a conspiratorial laugh; everyone in the room laughing at a family joke. "My dear Nicholas, there speaks an only child. Indeed, there speaks a man without a sister. So help me, there speaks a man who must have been spending his life with some very unusual women. Alexis, bless her heart, is not upset with you!"

"Then why…?"

"She was so completely engrossed in your story that she forgot she had been crying. When you offered her a handkerchief she suddenly realized her face was tearstained and that she probably looked more like an upset schoolgirl than the *grande dame* she would rather Captain Lord Ramage saw."

"*Grandes dames* frighten me. Anyway, Alexis would stop all the conversation in any salon merely by walking through the door."

"I know that because she's been on my arm so many times when it's happened. But you can't convince her. She thinks the conversation stops because her dress is unsuitable, or she is wearing too many or too few jewels, or her hair is in the wrong style…there's always some damned thing!"

"I may have no sisters, but you sound like the eternal brother!"

"When you have a sister as beautiful and vulnerable as she is, and both parents are dead, believe me, you are mother, father, chaperone, brother and trustee, with a few other roles thrown in from time to time."

"Like matchmaker!" Ramage said lightly.

"I wouldn't mind that," Yorke said. "Unfortunately, I have to be just the opposite. When Alexis complains that someone's attentions are becoming 'tedious' – the ultimate sin in her calendar – I have to warn him off."

"I can just imagine you being stern!"

"Stern be damned. One young buck, a captain in a fashionable regiment and the heir to a barony and a fortune, wanted to call me out! Swore that it was lies, and I had Alexis locked up so that she could not see him. Gave me a choice of pistols or swords!"

Intrigued at the picture Yorke had drawn, Ramage asked: "How did you get out of all that?"

"Oh, I chose the coward's way out. Rang the bell for a maid, sent her for Alexis, and told her that unless she gave this tradesman's son his *congé*, I'd have to meet him at dawn and kill him, except that I had a strict rule against duelling with tradesmen's sons."

"And that did it?"

"As far as this dandified soldier was concerned, yes: he retreated with a red face. Alexis then nearly fought a duel with *me!*"

"What on earth for?"

"Oh, she felt sorry for the fellow (after I'd got rid of him) and said there was no need to throw 'trade' in his face just because his father owned half a dozen mills in Lancashire and recently bought a title."

"She had a point," Ramage said sympathetically.

"You're as bad as she is," Yorke complained. "I'm the innocent party carrying out his sister's orders, and the damned soldier wants to spit me on the end of an épée or put a pistol ball in my gizzard. All because my sister gets too flirtatious and – "

" – and what?" Alexis said from the door.

"I was telling Nicholas about that wretched soldier who thought I'd locked you up and wanted me to get up at dawn and clang swords or pop pistols with him."

"Oh yes, you really did behave disgracefully towards that poor fellow," she said.

Yorke looked at Ramage and sighed. "Don't encourage her," he said, "otherwise she'll expect me to send him a case of claret with an apologetic note."

She had changed into a close-fitting wine-red dress, so close-fitting that Ramage found himself wondering how she had got into it. Her hair was now swept up in a style which emphasized her profile, and she looked every inch the calm hostess: not a hint of a stifled sob, her eyes clear.

Ramage suddenly realized that she was watching his eyes.

"A good maid is worth a queen's ransom," she said and smiled. "Dinner is being served in five minutes."

CHAPTER TWELVE

In his cabin on board the *Calypso*, Ramage was sleepy from too large a dinner but otherwise clear-headed because he had refused all wine and the Yorkes had not pressed him. He waited for Bowen to make himself comfortable in the armchair; both Aitken and Southwick sat on the settee.

Bowen had only just returned from the *Jason*: he had not waited to change his spray-spattered breeches, although his dry boots showed he had paused to get out of ones which had been sodden by the water in the bottom of the boat.

"You mentioned a written report, sir," Bowen began tentatively. "At least, I thought at first that you did. I now realize that I was completely mistaken: that all you really wanted was a verbal report on any conversation I might have with Captain Shirley."

Ramage sat back and considered carefully what Bowen had just said. He had told Bowen to go over and examine Captain Shirley, and return to write a very detailed report on the man's condition which he should sign, with one of the *Calypso*'s officers witnessing his signature. Name, date and location. Now, Bowen is saying, in a roundabout way, that he did not hear him refer to a written report. Something has happened, or Bowen has discovered something (or not discovered it) that he does not want to put into writing and he is trying to avoid involving Aitken and Southwick in anything that can later be construed as conspiracy.

"Yes, indeed, you were mistaken," Ramage said. "Well, now we're all together can I offer any of you gentlemen a drink?"

They all shook their heads. "I was offered enough on board the *Jason* to have floated her out of a drydock," Bowen said. "Those gunroom officers…" He shook his head at the memory. "The third lieutenant stuck his head in a bucket of sea water before going on watch."

"To make his hair curl, or does he find it puts him in the right mood for handling the ship?" Southwick inquired.

"To sober himself up enough to walk comparatively straight. It's not a bucket but a tub: they have one outside the gunroom door. One day someone is going to be so tipsy he falls in and drowns, unless the Marine sentry fishes him out."

"Come now, Mr Bowen," Ramage said, assuming a suitably formal manner. "Tell us about your visit to the *Jason*. It must make a pleasant change for you to visit another of the King's ships. I trust you were also able to deal with any medical matters arising since the death of the *Jason*'s surgeon."

"Yes, indeed, sir. Nothing like a dead surgeon for increasing the sick list. There's not a man in that ship, from the captain downwards, who hasn't got an ache or pain somewhere since the day they buried the surgeon. That is why I've been such a long time," he explained to Ramage. "I've treated more men on board the *Jason* in an hour than I've had sick in the *Calypso* in six months."

Southwick sniffed and brushed his hands together in a dismissive movement. "That's easily explained," he said. "Our chaps are scared stiff of you. Belly? Here, take this soap pill. Chest? Here, take this soap pill. Head? Ah yes, a soap pill is a sovereign remedy for afflictions of the head. You work miracles, you scoundrel. No matter what any of our fellows may contract, there's nothing that doesn't vanish the moment the sufferer thinks about one of your 'sovereign remedies'."

Bowen looked carefully at the master. "Tell me, old friend, for how long have you been suffering with this acute pain in the back that almost cripples you on a cold, damp day? And those rheumy eyes – shouldn't you be thinking of retiring? Perhaps we could get you a berth somewhere as 'mine host' – the landlord in a comfortable old hostelry with a blazing log fire, a lad to help roll the casks off the brewer's dray when it calls once a month (and lift the kegs of brandy from the smugglers' horses, too), and all you need to do is give a sharp tap to start the bung…"

Southwick grinned, admitting that Bowen had won this round in the continual teasing between the two of them.

"We were talking about the *Jason*," Ramage said, "but somehow we became involved in finding Mr Southwick's bung-starter…"

"Ah yes. Well, sir, I went on board the *Jason*, as you know, and Captain Shirley was expecting me. He was wearing that black coat but was otherwise quite normal. He invited me down to his cabin and offered me rum, gin or wine: he made rather a point that those were the only choices. But I am afraid that was the only example of slightly strange behaviour, and even that is not very strange if he does not have much choice of drink in his locker."

"So what did you talk about?" Ramage asked.

Bowen laughed quietly, as though enjoying a private joke. "Well, he told me about the surgeon dying, and how good a man he was, then described the size of his sick list and asked if I would examine some of the men. I agreed because it seemed it might give me a good chance of questioning them about other matters of more immediate interest to us. Then, very tactfully (by his standards, but rather like a particularly clumsy bull trying to cross a flower garden undetected), he started to ask me about you, sir."

"*Me?*" Ramage exclaimed. "What on earth did he want to know about me?"

"He asked in a very roundabout way with about thirty very carefully phrased questions, but there was no doubt what he was asking."

"Bowen, stop grinning like a parson who has just received ten times as much as he expected from Queen Anne's Bounty!"

The more he thought about it, the funnier it seemed to Bowen. "The trouble was, sir, I didn't know what answer to give. It all depended on one's point of view."

"Oh do stop guffawing like a schoolboy. What was Captain Shirley trying to find out?"

"If you were mad, sir."

Ramage joined in the laughter. "What point of view did you put forward, eh?"

"I avoided committing myself," Bowen said.

"Oh, you did…well, you could have risked perjury and given a definite answer."

Bowen shook his head. "Remember, sir, I was trying to get Captain Shirley on my side. I told him I could not discuss the condition of a patient with anyone else and he agreed – forgetting that surgeons have to give daily reports on every man reporting sick. He wanted to know how long I had served with you, how often you had been wounded, and so on. He belongs to that school of medical thought (dating back about five hundred years) that believes all madness is the result of a blow on the head. Have you ever had a blow on the head, sir?" Bowen asked innocently.

"No, only on my soup."

Bowen nodded. "I thought as much. Well, Captain Shirley and I talked, and he answered all my questions without hesitation. The only trouble is that when a man behaves quite sanely, it is very difficult (impossible, in fact) for a medical man to frame questions that would reveal insanity. You see, sanity or insanity is not like a fever, fractured limb, rash, sprained ligament or anything like that. I give you an example. Two men are sitting side by side, quietly daydreaming. One man is thinking how much he loves his wife. The other man has just murdered *his* wife and has her fortune in a leather bag beside his chair. One man is sane, the other insane. But looking at the two of them, and in ninety-nine cases out of a hundred, by talking to them, there is nothing to distinguish the mad one."

Ramage sighed with relief. "That was the feeling that Aitken, Southwick and I had – that the man seemed sane even though he had just behaved like a madman. Been a madman, rather."

"That's the problem, sir. I could take you to Moorfields and we could walk through the wards of Bethlehem Royal Hospital – better known perhaps as Bedlam – and men and women would come up to you and I defy you to distinguish whether they are inmates or visitors like yourself. Oh yes, there are many palpably insane – screaming, making faces, claiming to be Genghis Khan, and so on."

"They are the dangerous ones!" Ramage said.

"Not always, sir. A screaming man who wants to take an axe to all piebald horses is probably less dangerous – because one sees at once that he is deranged. But those only rarely insane are usually not violent."

"You mean, they don't get screaming mad?" Ramage asked. "They just go mad in a quiet way?"

Bowen smiled and acknowledged: "Yes, sir, I admit I may have been simplifying a little too much!"

"Anyway, you learned nothing about Captain Shirley. Very well, then what happened?"

"I then held a sick parade, beginning in the gunroom. The gunner and the third lieutenant were both sick. I noticed that all of them were drunk, in varying degrees. And all of them seemed to be frightened of something. Apprehensive, in the way men would be if they'd been told the day the world would end, and it's next Thursday but they have to keep it secret."

"Did you find out anything from the gunroom?"

"Nothing, except that they're all frightened and drunk. Then I saw about twenty of the rest of the ship's company. Nothing serious: just the 'illnesses' you find in an unhappy ship."

Ramage realized that Bowen had made a shrewd observation that applied to just about every ship in the Navy. Unless there was something about the station (the West Indies and the black vomit, for example) then a glance at the surgeon's journal, more formidably known officially as the *Journal of Physical Transactions* of the particular ship, probably told you all you needed to know about her captain – and her officers, too. In a well ordered ship there was no need to sham sickness. But the *Jason*'s copy was missing: Bowen had just confirmed that...

Which did not get over the fact that Bowen had also confirmed that Shirley's form of madness was easy to hide, and dam' nearly impossible for anyone else to prove. And there was no clue to how (or why) Shirley was holding a whole ship's company in silent terror.

Looking on the bright side, he had another frigate to help escort the convoy. In fact by normal standards the convoy now had a strong escort – four frigates for just over seventy ships: almost unheard-of these days. Providing, of course, that the *Jason* was not entirely useless as a fighting ship: a mad captain and drunken officers did not inspire confidence, but it meant –

"He's senior to you on the Post List, but you command the convoy," Southwick said.

"I've been thinking about that."

Southwick nodded because finding himself and his captain thinking alike was nothing very new. "Mind you, sir, that's not to say he has to *obey* any orders you give if he doesn't want to."

"No, but it does mean he can't use his seniority to take the command away from Mr Ramage," Aitken interjected. "Mr Ramage has his orders in writing from Admiral Tewtin."

"Let's not get too involved in that," Ramage said. "All that concerns us is that if I give the *Jason* an order concerning the safety of the convoy it's up to Shirley whether or not he obeys it. I think he will. He's obeyed my orders up to now – that's why the *Jason* is on our larboard beam."

"I dream of the day the Lizard comes in sight," Southwick said.

"I alternate," Ramage admitted. "Sometimes I dream about the day we anchor at Plymouth; at other times I have nightmares about it."

"Have pleasant dreams," Southwick advised. "There's not a damned thing we can do until we get there, and you know my advice – don't fret about something you can't do anything about."

Ramage stood at the quarterdeck rail wishing he could ignore his own rule, that no one was allowed to lean on it with his arms. Evening was the pleasantest part of the day with the sun sinking on the larboard beam and taking with it the heat and glare of the Tropics that eventually seemed to bake and dazzle you into impatience sabotaged by listlessness. Each day the wind had veered a little more. As they left Barbados the Trade winds had blown briskly from the east, with never a touch of north in them, as though to emphasize what many sailors had long suspected, that the old geographers had been teasing when they called them the "North East" trades. Anyway, they had left the islands behind, islands which for the Yorkes and for Ramage had been or become part of life – Grenada, St Vincent, St Lucia and the Pitons, the almost unbelievable matching pair of sugarloaf hills which Nature had dumped on the southwestern corner…Martinique, Dominica with its cloak of thick cloud and heavy rain which made it a favourite island for the Spanish plate fleets to make a landfall if they were short of water…Guadeloupe which looked on the chart like the two wings of a butterfly, Antigua, parched and mosquito-ridden, then the tiny island of St Barts, and St Martin, the island split between the Dutch who owned the southern half (and called it Sint Maarten, reminding Ramage of a lamb bleating) and the French. Then low-lying Anguilla and beyond Sombrero, a barren rock which seemed to guard the entrance to this wide channel joining the Atlantic to the Caribbean.

From there the convoy had really started its long voyage across the Atlantic and Ramage was thankful their luck had held: the wind had veered to the southeast a day past Sombrero and then held steady for a week so that they were able to steer for Bermuda.

Within a hundred miles of the collection of reefs, wrecks and legends of what used to be called Somers' Island, after its former owner, Sir George Somers, but now more generally known as Bermuda (after the Spaniard who discovered it, Bermudez), the wind had begun to haul round to the southwest and was now starting them off on the great sweep which should carry them into the Chops of the Channel.

Please, Ramage said in silent prayer, do not let it head us; the prospect of much beating to windward with these mules, tacking the whole convoy even once a day, made the patient

Southwick blench. But now, as the latitude increased, they were abeam of Madeira away to the east across the Atlantic, while Savannah and Charleston were on the American coast to the west.

Already the real heat had gone: there was a nip in the air at night. Those hating the heat as the sapper of energy and father to a long list of vile diseases, almost all fatal, and those hating the cold northern latitudes with their rheumatism, colds and consumptions, generally reckoned the temperature dropped one degree for every degree of latitude made good towards Bermuda.

Yesterday the big awning which kept the sun from beating down on to the quarterdeck, making the caulking runny so that if one was not careful the pitch stuck to the soles of one's shoes and made black marks on the scrubbed planking, had been taken down and this morning the sailmaker and his mates had been checking it over, putting in some patches and restitching along the roping where the constant fluttering in the wind and the rays of the sun had rotted the thread. The last job today had been to roll it all up and lower it below to be stowed until the *Calypso* next slipped back into the Tropics or Mediterranean.

The *Calypso* was, Ramage reckoned, a hot-weather ship: he had captured her from the French in the Tropics, and she had fought most of her actions in the Tropics or Mediterranean. Her guns would probably warp or miss fire in the cold of the North Sea!

During a near-tropical evening, an hour before darkness and as the last of the cottonball clouds vanished for the night, there was no finer sight created by man than a well-ordered convoy. However patched the sails of the ships, they were brushed a reddish-gold by the setting sun, the heavy shadow on the eastern side of each hull and the light playing on the western making pleasing patterns. Because it was a falling wind, none of the ships was going fast enough to leave a turbulent wake to disturb the pattern of waves and all the ships seemed to be uncut gems set down on deep-blue velvet.

Standing here admiring the convoy as an object of beauty was almost dangerous because he nearly forgot that seventy-two ships were his responsibility: ships laden with valuable cargoes for a country at war and heavily insured, and with probably a couple of thousand men on board. And many women, of course: most of the larger ships carried passengers – plantation owners, tradesmen and soldiers and their wives returning to England. And Alexis, too, who might well at this moment be looking astern from that ship leading the starboard column – although it was unlikely that she could distinguish the *Calypso* from all the rest of the ships, even if she wanted to.

The quartermaster spoke quietly to the two men at the wheel as the ship wandered a few degrees to windward, and they hove down on the spokes, hoping the bow would swing back before the captain glanced round with a scowl. He never actually said anything but somehow, the quartermaster thought, that was worse: as though Mr Ramage had made an entry in some great ledger and one day he would bring them all to account.

The quartermaster on watch was a Lincolnshire man named Aston, one of the most agile men in the ship but also one of the plumpest. Like a fat pigeon, his body carried extra flesh wherever there was room for it. Although less than thirty years of age, he had jowls and paunch more appropriate to a cleric, although he had a sharper wit and a better understanding of his fellow men. Now he was concerned that the swinging bow should not distract Mr Ramage because he could see that the captain, alone at the quarterdeck rail, was miles away in his thoughts. Aston knew that Mr Ramage had more to trouble him than was a fair load on a man. Commanding a convoy of merchant ships would make a saint run amok, but on top of that there was this strange business of the *Jason*. Why had she opened fire?

Jackson was with the captain when the *Calypso* boarded her, and he had been back again with him, but if Jacko was to be believed, Mr Ramage still did not know why it had happened. There was one thing about Jacko – if he could not reveal something out of loyalty to the captain, he always said so. When he just did not know, he usually said so. So Aston was inclined to believe him now – that if there was any explanation at all, it was that the captain of the *Jason* had gone daft.

That would account for Mr Wagstaffe going over there – it was said he was in command now, which meant Mr Ramage had taken on himself the responsibility of replacing the captain, and Aston knew the Articles of War were hot and strong against that.

But even worse than all that, and something that Aston, recently and happily married, could understand very well, there was the worry about her ladyship: Jacko had heard that the *Murex*, taking her ladyship back to England, had just vanished after leaving them off Brest. A short enough distance – must be about a hundred miles and the weather was not out of the way. The *Murex* could have sprung the butt end of a plank and sunk like a stone: she could have been sunk by a French man-o-war; or she could have been captured by a French privateer. It must be awful for Mr Ramage, just not knowing.

Aston was thankful that he knew his wife was at home in Lincolnshire, looking after his mother and tending the half-acre of land with occasional help from her young nephew.

The boy was an idle youngster, but since Rebecca had cut off his meals for a day or two, then cuffed him once when he was insolent, he had mended his ways a bit. In fact Rebecca had been so provoked by him that once she turned him out of the house so that he had nowhere to sleep. He had gone off and told the parson a tall story and without even bothering to ask Rebecca, whom he had known since christening her twenty years before, the parson gave the boy a whack across the shins with his walking stick, made him sleep the night in the parsonage stables and sent him home again next morning with orders to beg Rebecca's pardon.

That sort of parson was good for a village, but all too many of them seemed to reckon that only the squire and his lady were likely to go to Heaven and the rest of the folk were not worth bothering about, damned because they were poor. Well, luckily the local parson was a good old chap because the fact of the matter was (and not even Rebecca knew much about it: she would go telling her mother, then it would be all over the village), thanks to Mr Ramage and the number of prizes they had taken, he had quite a bit of money now. And head money too, for all the prisoners taken. So when the war ended and he had all his prize money together, he was going to make old Swan an offer for Lower Farm. Eighty-four acres and good land. The tithe ran at seven pounds eleven shillings a year, but that field behind the wood was hard to get to and was just right to let out to grazing, leaving exactly seventy acres to farm and the rent would pay the tithe.

He had talked to Mr Ramage about it, and Mr Ramage reckoned Swan's price was about right and also reckoned letting that field for grazing would be a good idea. In fact he had suggested it. The captain said that one of the secrets of good farming was being able to get to all your land all the year round. Having a big field cut off by thick snow or thick mud meant you might as well not own it for many months.

Aston admitted he would never have seen it in that light, but it was true. Mr Ramage also said he would have his man of law go over all the papers with Swan when the time came and make sure everything was in order. That was Mr Ramage for you. Aston knew of other men that Mr Ramage had helped, and he never talked about it, or behaved any differently towards the men: he never expected more than a good day's work. What a landlord he would make!

Ramage, was inspecting the columns of ships, looking at each one through the glass, not from any particular interest but because he knew that for the next few weeks there would not be many more tranquil sunsets. In fact in the next few days he would have all the storm canvas stretched out on deck to be patched where necessary and to make sure the stitching holding the bolt ropes to the canvas was still in good condition. It was curious how the stitching of a sail or awning always rotted long before the cloth itself.

The poor old *Calypso* needed a new suit of sails, and the present ones should be struck below as spares. The trouble was that she was back at Chatham being paid off when the war started again after the Treaty of Amiens, and she had been hurriedly commissioned – which meant getting the yards across with new rigging, but the old sails were bent on again. The *Calypso* was merely one of many ships of war being commissioned in a rush, and Ramage had not been there to use cunning or influence to get new sails.

Nor was Captain Ramage himself much better off! One of his first calls in London would be on his tailor. Twenty guineas, probably more, for a full dress coat and epaulette (it was an economy being a post-captain with less than three years' seniority because he had to wear an epaulette on only one shoulder). Ten guineas for an undress coat. Five guineas for the gold-laced hat. Breeches, silk stockings, shirts, stocks, handkerchiefs…Silkin, his steward, had a long list which included table linen as well which needed replacing. Well, he did not complain about that: it was very irritating sitting down at a meal alone and restraining oneself, between courses, from poking the tines of a fork into a fraying patch. Silkin did his best to darn the patches, but new ones appeared every time the cloths were laundered.

He remembered Alexis' irritation, while they were having dinner on board the *Emerald*, when she noticed a tiny worn patch in the table cloth: she had frowned at the steward and glanced at it, and that was all. That was one of the advantages of being in a well-run merchant ship, which used fewer men for the same job than one of the King's ships, but the men probably worked harder because they were paid more and could be paid off at the end of a voyage if their work was unsatisfactory. They could also be picked up by a pressgang before the end of a voyage, too! Anyway, one frown from Alexis might be more effective than an outburst of anger from a post-captain!

He swung the telescope from *L'Espoir* to *La Robuste* and then to the *Jason*. All three ships were in good order, and for the moment none of the merchant ships showed any sign of dropping astern, although the sun had slipped well below the horizon. He had forgotten to look for the green flash. He had seen it hundreds of times in various latitudes, but it always amused him to watch for it, knowing that one blink at the crucial moment meant missing that bright green wink which lasted only a fraction of a second.

Young Kenton was standing over on the larboard side of the quarterdeck, having just taken over the deck from Martin. Ramage decided to go down to his cabin. Usually he did not like reading by candlelight in low latitudes because the flame made the cabin too hot, but they were now far enough north for it not to matter. More important, he had just found that the four volumes of letters edited by John Fenn and which he had bought three or four years ago and left in the bookcase, read more like novels than anything else.

Fenn (Sir John Fenn, he seemed to remember: was he not given a knighthood for his labours?) certainly gave the volumes a title which was accurate but hardly inspiring – *Original Letters written During the Reigns of Henry VI, Edward IV, Richard III and Henry VII, by Various Persons of Rank and Consequence, and by Members of the Paston Family.* To read the letters, as far as Ramage was concerned, was to be one of the Paston family of Norfolk at the time of the Wars of the Roses. Their neighbour was Sir John Fastolf, a soldier who fought at Agincourt (was that not in 1415?), and was changed by Shakespeare from a brave soldier in real life to the bawdy and drunken (but humorous) coward in some of his plays, the name changed slightly from Fastolf to Falstaff, a change too slight, Ramage thought, to avoid a Mr Shakespeare of today being called out by Sir John or one of his friends.

Still, Shakespeare's plays and the Paston family letters were (thanks to John Fenn) a joy to read. In fact he would be hard put to finish the final volume of the Paston letters before the Lizard hove in sight.

Gilbert looked puzzled as he tried to translate what was obviously a joke by Stafford. The trouble was that Gilbert's English had been learned in the eastern part of Kent, where country folk talked broadly and in a slow drawl, whereas the Cockney, Stafford, talked quickly, clipping words like a miserly tailor.

" 'Penten' – I do not understand it."

Stafford, sprawled along the form beside the table, the bread barge in front of him, was roaring with laughter, and Jackson tapped him on the arm. "That was all too quick for me, so how'd you reckon Gilbert is going to understand?"

"He asked me if I went to church or chapel," Stafford explained. "I said I didn't go to either (he meant a'fore I came to sea) but that some o' my friends said their prayers in St George's Fields."

"What's funny about that?" Jackson asked, and Rossi repeated the question, adding: "You can hurt yourself inside, laughing like that."

Stafford's features were now serious: he was faced with sheer ignorance, and he always delighted in instructing his shipmates. "I was making a little joke, see, about goin' to chapel. To the chapel in St George's Fields. There's only one chapel there – " he began laughing, " – and that's the one belonging to Magdalen Hospital, see?"

"No," Jackson said briskly. "This looks like one of your long jokes that has us all falling asleep."

"Yus, well, I'll shut up then and you can entertain the mess – song or story, eh Jacko?" Stafford asked sulkily.

"Oh come on," Rossi wheedled, now intrigued at the idea of a chapel in a place called St George's Fields. "Tell us about this saint. Why does he have his own chapel?"

"My oath," Stafford said despairingly, "I dunno, s'just a place darn the uvver end o' Blackfriars Road. Why's everybody suddenly interested in it?"

"Because of you," Gilbert said mildly. "You started to tell us a joke about it."

Stafford ran a hand through his hair and sat up straight, a look of desperation about him. "Chapel," he said slowly, as though feeling his way through a fog. "Church or chapel

Gilbert asked, and I said some of my friends went to chapel in St George's Fields…"

He rubbed his head, trying to restore the train of thought, but he had drunk his own rum issue and Gilbert had passed over his, and Jackson had paid him a tot for a favour done yesterday. Finally, he remembered. "Yus, well, I was really tellin' Gilbert that my friends were – well, young ladies who had to make their own living, if you get my meaning."

"Whores?" Gilbert asked.

"Well, yes, but that's a strong word."

"St George's Fields," Rossi said relentlessly. "*Accidenti, San Giorgio mi aiuta!*"

"Wotchew rattling on abart, then?" Stafford demanded suspiciously. "Speak English!"

"I was asking St George to help me," Rossi said, "but you need his help more. Now come on, start again. First, we have the chapel in St George's Fields."

"Well, the chapel belongs to Magdalen Hospital," Stafford said, as though that explained everything.

"And…" Jackson said encouragingly, "what sort of hospital is it? Like Greenwich Hospital, for seamen?"

"Nah, nah, nah!" Stafford exclaimed. "That's the whole joke – it's for 'The Reformation and Relief of Penitent Prostitutes'!"

"A sort of Stafford family home, like Mr Ramage has St Kew, eh?" Jackson asked drily.

"You don't believe me," Stafford complained, "but it's run by dukes and earls and rich merchants. Has a surgeon, several apotharies – "

"Apothecaries," Jackson corrected out of habit.

" – yes, s'what I said, and parsons. One's the chaplain and two more take it in turns to preach each evenin'. And the matron – she's a hard old biddy, I can tell you."

"How can you tell us?" Rossi inquired innocently. "Surely you've never been 'penitent'?"

Stafford realized he had talked too much, but as Jackson and Rossi (and Mr Ramage) knew that his job before the war, after an apprenticeship to a locksmith, was hard to describe, there was no need for secrets.

"One of my sisters," he said, offhandedly. "She got mixed up with that bad lot around Blackfriars and before we knew what had happened this pimp was threatening to cut her wiv a knife."

"Then what?" Jackson asked, realizing that there were still aspects of Stafford's past life he knew nothing about.

"Well, when Neilley (that's what we call her 'cos she don't like plain 'Nell') when Neilley got the word back to us, me and some mates went darn to Blackfriars and called on this pimp."

"And murdered him?" Rossi asked. Having spent a childhood in the Genoa slums, he was genuinely interested how the day-to-day problems of life in London were solved.

"Nah, that's 'gainst the law," Stafford said airily. "We just took Neilley and left 'im for dead."

"There is a difference?" Gilbert asked, who had been trying to translate for Louis, Auguste and Albert.

"Oh yus, indeed. Murder's a capital offence in England, you know that. Get topped if you're caught. You know," he explained, seeing the blank look on Gilbert's face, " 'topped' – hanged. So we just cut him up a bit, like he'd threatened to do Neilley, and if 'e died later 'cos he 'adn't the sense to stop bleedin', that's 'is affair."

"What about Neilley?" Jackson asked, puzzled by the connection with Magdalen Hospital and the dukes, earls and parsons who ran it.

"Oh, at first she took on a bit. She'd got a bit o' a taste for the life, if you get my meaning, but I persuaded her a stay at the Magdalen would put her right. Prayers and poultices, that's what she needed for a few weeks. She didn't agree, but she went all the same, and I used to go darn there a couple of times a week, just to make sure Neilley was paying attention to what all those dukes and earls and parsons and apotherums were telling 'er."

"Was she? Many peoples is talking," Rossi observed.

"She was listening an' prayin' an' taking her medicine," Stafford said. "The matron was watching her, special."

"What, you paid the matron for special attention?" Jackson asked doubtfully. It did not sound like Stafford who, he thought, had always taken what he wanted, providing the lock could be picked.

"Well, not exactly *paid* 'er," Stafford admitted, for the first time looking uneasy. "Just sort of 'inted to 'er that if Neilley wasn't right as rain by St Swithin's Day, an' penitent too, matron might find 'erself in need o' a lot of prayin' and medicalatin' too."

"Medicating," Jackson said. "You're a rough lot. What happened to Neilley? Was she the 'penten' you were telling us about?"

"Yus. Well, all that was going on abart the time the press took me up. My fault, 'cos I knew the word was out for a hot press, but one night I was drinking heavy down Fetter Lane an' reckoned I knew me way back 'ome without any of the gangers spottin' me, even though I couldn't see straight."

"And?"

"An' I was wrong. I sobered up in the 'old of a receiving ship anchored off the Tower with 'alf an 'undred other rascals that the pressgang had just rounded up, an' there we all were, screamin' at the top of our lungs that we'd fight the French wivart swords or pay."

Wide-eyed, Gilbert exclaimed: "You were all shouting that?"

"Well, not 'xactly shouting if you get my meaning, but we thought it. We was all recovering from too much drink, an' if anyone 'ad actually shouted, the noise would've done us an injury."

Jackson explained: "Staff sometimes exaggerates a little."

Gilbert nodded and turned to translate for the other Frenchmen, but if anything Stafford's story grew in the translation: like Stafford himself, Gilbert was not one to let facts spoil a good tale.

The Frenchmen listened wide-eyed, glancing at Stafford from time to time. Between them they had lived as fishermen or on the Count of Rennes' estate. Brest was small, built round its port, the river and the naval dockyard. A city like London, with its capacity for sin and which offered such scope for lively fellows like Stafford, was more than they could imagine.

Stafford, his ten minutes of glory at an end, leaned against the ship's side and went to sleep with the Atlantic swirling past his head, separated by only a few inches of oak.

"What a man," Louis commented in French, but Auguste winked. "What a woman, eh? Can you imagine life with the sister of a man like this?"

"I could, but I'm not going to: most of the time it would be like war! In England are all the women like that?"

"No, most certainly not," Gilbert said, shaking his head with the air of a connoisseur. "I met several I would like to have married."

Jackson said: "You are going about it backwards. I followed what you just said. Under English law if a foreigner marries an Englishwoman he can be pressed, because marrying makes him the same as an Englishman – leastways, as far as the pressgangs are concerned."

"You mean that foreigners are not pressganged?"

"Well, they are sometimes, but they can apply to their consul and be freed."

"So as Frenchmen...?"

Jackson frowned, suddenly realizing that of the seven men making up Mess Number Eight in His Majesty's frigate the *Calypso*, Stafford was the only Englishman.

"As Frenchmen, I suppose you rate as 'enemy' unless you're serving in one of the King's ships. Still, there's one thing about it, when we arrive in England you can marry an English-woman without fear of the press because you're already serving!"

"What about you? You're American, aren't you?"

"Yes, but our government gives us things called 'Protections'. These certify that we're American citizens, so we can't be pressed. But if we are, we apply to an American consul, and the Protection should get us freed."

"Why don't you have a Protection, then?" Gilbert asked.

"I've had one for years," Jackson said.

"Then why don't...?"

Jackson shrugged his shoulders. "I'm too old to change my habits and I like serving with Mr Ramage."

"But supposing you were transferred to another ship, what then?"

"We'll see. Mr Ramage and I have managed to keep together – and Rossi and Staff too – for several years now. And Mr Southwick."

"And Mr Orsini?" Gilbert asked.

"Yes, he's been with Mr Ramage for a couple of years or so."

"So when we get to England we can all stay together in the *Calypso*?"

Jackson shrugged again. "It'll depend how the *Jason* affair turns out. If this Captain Shirley has friends in high places, there's going to be trouble."

"But hasn't Mr Ramage friends in high places too?"

"Yes, but years ago his father – an admiral – was made the scapegoat for some government mistake, and people might attack our Mr Ramage to get at the father."

Gilbert sighed. "Politicians…they should all be made to go to that hospital Stafford was talking about."

"I've never heard of a penitent politician," Jackson said. "Anyway, I'll be damned glad when we get a sight of the Lizard and then anchor at Spithead, or Plymouth, or wherever we're sent, so we get the trial or inquiry over quick."

CHAPTER **THIRTEEN**

Ramage wiped the tip of the quill with the cloth, put the cork back in the inkwell, and started to read through his letter to Their Lordships. The report that would accompany it, seven pages in draft form, waited in the drawer. He had spent a couple of weeks on it: not two weeks of solid writing, but every day he had taken it out and read it through, at first changing whole paragraphs and then towards the end just substituting sentences or changing individual words.

The final draft, which his clerk would write out in a fair hand, did not bear much relationship to the first, in which he had let his anger with Shirley distort the narrative (surprisingly, Alexis had been the first to draw his attention to it), so that it read as though Ramage had expected trouble from the moment he sighted the *Jason*, whereas he had hauled his wind and gone up towards her expecting to find a friend and exchange news.

And that had been the problem in writing the report: to explain to Their Lordships the shock of the sudden attack and, much more difficult, to describe Shirley's behaviour without using phrases which, in condemning Shirley, would put Their Lordships immediately on the side of the senior captain.

Also (and perhaps more important) he had to bear in mind that the Board might be reading his report *after* receiving one from Shirley. Yorke and Aitken reckoned the advantage would rest with the man whose report was read first, but Ramage was not sure. Viewed from the Boardroom of the Admiralty it was a bizarre and utterly unimportant episode; to Their Lordships, discipline was probably the main question. For one British frigate to have fired on another could be an accident – that would be their first reaction. Then from both Shirley and himself they would read stories which (he assumed) flatly contradicted each other. Bowen had already reported, after his visit to the *Jason*, that Shirley regarded the *Calypso*'s captain as mad, and no one in the *Calypso* had any doubt about Shirley. But what about all those silent men in the *Jason*: officers and men who did and saw nothing…How would the Board regard them?

The whole story, whether from the point of view of the *Jason* or the *Calypso*, sounded mad: that was Alexis' view, and she had argued that Their Lordships would naturally tend to disbelieve the first report they read. So, she said, Ramage must make sure that Shirley's was the first to arrive. Then, with Their Lordships completely puzzled by Shirley's description, along would come Ramage's report which would supply the answer (without saying it in as many words) – that Shirley was mad.

Alexis' argument (with which Southwick agreed) was a good one until one started thinking about other letters that Shirley might be writing: what friends he had who, to be fair to them, might not have any idea of Shirley's lapses into madness.

Well, it would not be long now. With the Lizard in sight and the Liverpool, Dublin and Glasgow ships, eighteen of them, formed up as a small convoy and sent off yesterday for the St George's Channel with *L'Espoir*, and the ten Bristol ships separated this morning with *La Robuste*, the *Calypso* was left with forty-four ships, most of which were bound for London, Hull and Leith, after first anchoring in Plymouth to see if there were any last-minute orders from their owners. Often the shippers of a cargo originally consigned for, say, London had a better offer by the time the ship arrived in England, involving delivery to another port, and Plymouth was well placed if a ship then had to go to, say, Liverpool.

Ramage had quite expected the *Jason* to leave the convoy and go on ahead to Plymouth or Spithead, and she did so long before the Lizard was in sight. So far (with only a few score more miles to go) it had been a successful voyage for the convoy. Most of the slow ships had responded well to being hurried; only two gales had hit the convoy and although both had scattered the ships, in each case the convoy had reformed within a day. Then, in a final gesture, as the St George's Channel ships formed up into a small convoy to leave and the *Calypso* had sailed among them, helping *L'Espoir*, first one and then the remaining seventeen ships had fired an eleven-gun salute to the *Calypso* with their men lining the rails and cheering.

This gesture, combining their farewell with a genuine thank you, was not lost on the Bristol ships which this morning had also fired a salute as they were led off by *La Robuste*.

Now the *Calypso* frequently sighted other ships. One sloop coming down Channel had reported that a small convoy from the Cape of Good Hope and a larger one from the East Indies were already in the Channel bound for Spithead, and Ramage breathed a sigh of relief that the convoys had not met off the Lizard. There would have been collisions and confusion, Southwick commented, and Aitken added that a gale would probably have arrived as well to act as the spoon that stirred the brew.

They were now for all intents and purposes home: when the *Calypso* had been hove-to for a cast of the deep sea lead, they had found sixty-eight fathoms and a sandy bottom.

Nearly two months had passed from weighing anchor in Carlisle Bay, Barbados, to finding soundings near the Chops of the Channel. He had dined on board the *Emerald*, either alone or with various of his officers as fellow guests, nine times. Sidney Yorke and Alexis had been his guests on board the *Calypso* five times and on three other occasions the *Calypso*'s officers had (with his permission) invited them to dine in the gunroom and asked their captain to join them. He had dined on five other of the merchant ships and in each case returned the hospitality, though eating a heavy meal in the middle of the day with wine and having two or three hours' conversation with the master of the ship left him weary and bored, annoyed at wasting an afternoon that could have been spent with the Yorkes.

He put the draft of the letter in the drawer on top of the report. At the most, a day or night and they would be anchored in Plymouth. Then he would have to face what he had been driving from his mind for the past couple of months – where was Sarah? Thank goodness there had been plenty to keep him occupied. Commanding a convoy of more than seventy ships meant that all day and every day and often much of the night there was some problem or other with any one of half a dozen of the mules. Someone would furl sails without a signal and the ships astern in the column would be hard put not to collide; another would suddenly sail diagonally out of the convoy (done thrice by the same ship and each time it transpired the master, the man at the wheel and the lookout had drunk themselves into a stupor...). Then there was Shirley and the *Jason*. On the brighter side, the Yorkes had done so much to make the voyage pleasant. Sidney could be lively and charming but he could also be sober and wise. Alexis was much the same, a woman's instinct leading to conclusions men would never have found by logic.

Soon after dawn when the *Calypso* led the rest of the convoy into Plymouth Sound, one of the lookouts reported that the *Jason* was at anchor.

Once the merchant ships had anchored and the *Calypso* too had an anchor down, with the salute fired for the port admiral, the frigate's cutter was hoisted out. After rowing once round the ship to make sure the yards were square, Southwick went on shore to inquire what time would be most convenient for the port admiral to have the convoy commander call and make his report.

The old master, considerably agitated, returned to the *Calypso* with news and a large packet from the port admiral. The news was that the rear-admiral in Plymouth – the second-in-command, whose main function was to preside at court-martials – was Rear-Admiral Goddard, a man whose hatred of the Ramage family was long-standing.

The news of Goddard left Ramage strangely cold: for the moment he was more concerned with Sarah and getting the rest of the convoy round to London. He went down to his cabin. The packet obviously contained two or three letters, all inside a single sheet of thick paper folded and sealed with wax: the port admiral would not risk using a wafer, relying on gum. As he sat at his desk holding the packet, Ramage felt it was hardly necessary to break the seal and start reading: he could guess what they would say. This was the moment he stepped on the merry-go-round which was going to revolve for days, if not weeks.

He picked up the paper-knife, slid it under the seal, and opened the outer page which formed the envelope. He had been wrong in one respect: the first letter was a copy of one from the Admiralty to the port admiral, and after the usual opening, "By the Commissioners for executing the office of Lord High Admiral", it went on:

> Whereas Sir James Bustard, Vice Admiral of the white and commander-in-chief of His Majesty's ships and vessels at Plymouth, hath transmitted to us a letter of the third of September last, from Captain William Shirley, commander of His Majesty's ship *Jason*, requesting that you, commander of His Majesty's ship *Calypso*, might be tried by a court-martial for various matters falling under certain of the Articles of War, namely numbers XV, XVII, XIX, XX, XXII, and XXIII.
>
> And whereas we think fit the said Captain Shirley's request should be complied with: we send you herewith his above-mentioned letter, and do hereby require and direct you forthwith to assemble a court-martial for the trial of the said Captain Lord Ramage, for the offences with which he stands charged, and to try him for the same accordingly.
>
> Given under our hands the seventh day of September.

And there were the names of four members of the Board – only three were needed to sign such letters, so he should be flattered that a fourth should have been added. Was it significant that the First Lord, Earl St Vincent, was not among them? No, he was probably out of town that day, or there was a quorum of signatures without having to bother him. But Shirley had acted quickly to get his letter to London. How long did it take to get a letter to London by messenger? A week? Probably less.

He smoothed out the second letter and glanced at it: Admiral Bustard was merely telling him that he had received orders from the Admiralty concerning him (a copy was enclosed) and he had therefore given the requisite orders. He also enclosed a copy of Captain Shirley's letter, referred to by the Board. The deputy judge advocate appointed for the occasion, Admiral Bustard concluded, would be communicating with him.

The third letter had his father's crest on the seal and was brief: on the off-chance that Nicholas would call at Plymouth the Earl was writing to tell him about Sarah. Obviously his father knew that St Vincent had written to Barbados.

"We have no more news," the Earl wrote:

The *Murex* left the Fleet off Brest, and vanished. My own opinion is that she may have been dismasted or captured, and ended up in a French port to leeward, so Sarah will be a prisoner. Bonaparte regards civilians as combatants, so Sarah is probably a prisoner of war.

Your mother and I, and the Marquis, have done all we can to get news from France; St Vincent has been very understanding and pressure has been brought to bear on the French agent for the exchange of prisoners. I went to see him myself and am convinced he genuinely knows nothing.

Of Gianna – what a sad letter this is – we also have no news. Perhaps that is as well: we must prepare ourselves for the worst. We can be sure Bonaparte's men caught her, and he is a man without mercy.

The letter went on to give family news: Ramage's mother had spent most of the summer down at St Kew; the Marquis spent most of his time now in London, hoping for news of Sarah, and like the rest of the family eagerly awaiting Nicholas' return.

Ramage was just reading the final sentence when the Marine sentry outside the cabin door announced that the first lieutenant wished to see him, and Ramage called briefly: "Send him in."

Aitken, hat tucked under his arm, stood in front of Ramage's desk. "Another boat has come off from the shore and is heading for us, sir," he said, so lugubriously that quite unexpectedly it made Ramage feel cheerful.

"It'll be bringing a lieutenant – maybe even just a midshipman – with another letter for me, this time from the deputy judge advocate."

"The deputy judge advocate?" Aitken repeated, as though he might have misheard: in fact was sure he had.

"Yes – telling me the date of my trial, in which ship it will be held and asking for a list of my witnesses."

Aitken swallowed, and was obviously puzzled by Ramage's jocular manner. "So there's going to be a trial, sir?"

"My goodness yes! A mad captain and Rear-Admiral Goddard together in the same port are (for us) one of those unhappy coincidences, like a spark in a powder magazine. A bag of powder and a spark alone are each harmless, but put them together…"

"You don't seem very worried, sir," Aitken said, the relief showing on his face.

"I'm accused under – " he glanced at the Board's letter, " – under six of the Articles of War." He had read them out to his ship's company scores of times, as required by Admiralty Instructions, but he still had to recite them to himself by rote. "Only a few of them carry a mandatory death sentence."

Aitken said bitterly: "There's something wicked afoot when you're in more danger of death on board one of the King's ships than you ever were capturing the French frigates at Devil's Island, or rescuing those people from the renegades at Trinidade, or escaping the guillotine in France, or – "

"Aitken," Ramage said, dropping the usual "Mister" and indicating that the remark was man to man, not captain to first lieutenant, "we've set off on some adventures where our chances of survival were not very great. But I can't recall you ever standing there with a face as long as a yard of cold pump water saying: 'Sir, we're all *doomed!*' " He tried to give his voice the depth and emphasis of a Scottish cleric. "In fact, I always have the feeling that facing death cheers you up!"

"Ah, but there's a difference," Aitken said. "Then we went off knowing we all shared the risks. This time, you're on your own, sir. Every shot will be aimed at you alone."

There was a shout from on deck, and Aitken said: "If you'll excuse me sir, it sounds as though that boat has arrived."

The lieutenant on board had indeed brought another letter for Ramage and when Aitken brought it in Ramage told him to sit down for a few minutes.

Ramage then opened the letter – sealed this time by a wafer with the glue still wet – and nodded. "Yes, here's the deputy judge advocate. They aren't wasting much time!"

"But why is Captain Shirley charging you? You ought to be bringing *him* to trial!"

"He's senior, so he gets first whack!" Ramage grinned and then tapped the papers on his desk. "I haven't read his letter yet, but Their Lordships have sent me a copy of his complaint. I'll read it in a moment. Let's first see what the deputy judge advocate has to say."

The deputy judge advocate wrote in the stylized way laid down in the manuals:

The Lords Commissioners of the Admiralty having ordered Vice Admiral Sir James Bustard to assemble a court-martial to try Captain the Lord Ramage, and it being intended that I shall officiate as deputy judge advocate upon the occasion at the said court-martial, which is to be held on board the *Salvador del Mundo* at Plymouth on Monday next, at nine o'clock in the morning; I send you herewith a copy of the order for the trial on yourself [Ramage noted that the deputy judge advocate had forgotten to enclose it] and am to desire you will be pleased to transmit me a list of the officers and men belonging to the *Calypso* who are in this port, and of such persons, as you may think proper to call to give evidence in your favour, that they might be summoned to attend accordingly.

He passed the letter to Aitken. "You've probably never read one of those letters before. Consider it part of your education."

While the Scotsman read the letter, Ramage read Captain Shirley's asking for a court-martial. It was addressed to Sir James Bustard – did they know each other, or did Shirley know Sir James was the port admiral? Anyway, Sir James must have forwarded it to the Admiralty (by one of the special messengers who left for London every evening on horseback, passing on the way similar messengers who left the Admiralty every evening).

Shirley's letter was well written and set out his complaint clearly and Ramage admitted ruefully to himself that both Sir James and the Board, reading the letter, would have no hesitation in ordering a court-martial.

Shirley began by referring to his orders and giving the date he left Barbados. He referred to sighting the *Calypso* as she bore northwards for England, and then went on to relate how the *Calypso* had come alongside, using grapnels. Her men, led by an officer later identified as Captain Ramage, had then boarded the *Jason* and Captain Ramage had taken command...

Shirley explained that he had recognized the *Calypso* and seen that she was escorting a convoy, so he was completely unprepared for such an attack. Captain Ramage had then removed him from his command, giving no reason, put one of his lieutenants on board and ordered the lieutenant, by name Wagstaffe, to keep station astern of the convoy and to leeward of the *Calypso*. The *Jason* had been forced to comply with these orders until near the Lizard, when the *Jason's* commanding officer (Ramage allowed himself a wry smile at this description: Wagstaffe's version would, no doubt, be quite different) had managed to crowd on sail, ignoring Wagstaffe, and arrived in Plymouth safely. Shirley went on to say that Captain Ramage had given no explanation for his actions, although when he first boarded the *Jason* he was warned at once that his behaviour was in defiance of certain Articles of War, which were cited.

However, Captain Ramage had only laughed in reply and said he had a large convoy to defend and a long way to go with not enough frigates, so the *Jason* was needed to help. "I warned him that he would be called to account once the convoy arrived in Britain," Shirley wrote, "but he just laughed like a madman. His behaviour at all times while on board the *Jason*," Shirley added artfully, "was such as to raise very serious doubts about his sanity, and had the *Jason's* surgeon not, unfortunately died a week or so earlier, the surgeon would have been instructed to examine Captain Ramage to ascertain his fitness for command of the *Calypso* and advise me what steps were necessary to ensure that the King's Service should be properly carried out."

Ramage sighed because it was a clever letter. No wonder Sir James sent it straight on to the Admiralty, and no wonder Their Lordships promptly ordered a trial. Their Lordships must be shaking their heads and saying, yes, young Ramage has done splendid service in the past, but one of those wounds – perhaps that glancing musket ball that caught his head at Curacao (and where the hair growing round the scar was always a tiny white tuft) – had finally put him in a position where he was no longer responsible for his actions.

Well, the Board were not at fault: they did not know Shirley was mad. They might not know about the sycophantic Goddard, either. But he and the Yorkes were mistaken in thinking that the advantage would be with the writer of the second letter to reach the Admiralty: Their Lordships must have already ordered his trial before his letter had gone on shore.

"This deputy judge advocate hasn't wasted much time," Aitken commented.

"No, they give me enough time to read the Admiralty's letter and Shirley's complaint, and then the deputy judge advocate's letter arrives with the wafer still wet. Seems more like malice over at the port admiral's office rather than the efficiency of his staff."

"We can anticipate some more pettiness, I expect," Aitken commented. "I must make sure our boats' crews obey all the port regulations when they go on shore. Luckily Southwick brought back a copy of the Plymouth 'Port Orders', so we can carry out flag signals promptly. Thank goodness we are not having any work done in the Dockyards – the 'Daily Report' on progress has twenty-five headings and a 'Remarks' column, so a dockyard commissioner can always find fault somewhere and complain to the admiral."

"Yes, we're all going to have to tread carefully. I'm sorry I've made it difficult for everyone."

"Captain Shirley, not you, sir," Aitken corrected. "Now, sir, can I help you draw up that list of witnesses?"

Ramage thought for a few moments. "I'd prefer you to draw up a separate list, then we can compare them: that way, we're less likely to forget anyone. And listen, Aitken, think about this. They – Shirley and his cronies – seem to be in a hurry. There might be some reason, or it might just be the excitement of the chase. We can't slow up the proceedings (anyway I don't want to prolong all this nonsense), but let's see if we can't find some advantage in it, too."

Aitken nodded his head slowly. "Aye, I take your meaning, sir. They're up to windward of us, but we must try and make that to our advantage."

Ramage saw no reason why he had to be discreet in the present situation. "If you're unarmed and a man suddenly attacks you with a knife, I reckon you're justified in using unorthodox methods to defend yourself. 'Turning the other cheek' doesn't help!"

Aitken grinned for the first time that day. "Aye, I like that word 'unorthodox' – it has a pleasant unorthodox ring about it!"

After Aitken left the cabin, Ramage read through all the letters again. His defence. Well, all he had was the truth, though that might not count for much if Admiral Goddard was president of the court.

Time...yes, time was an enemy because he had no time to get his father and the Marquis to work at persuading Lord St Vincent to transfer the trial to, say, Portsmouth, with another president. But the more he thought about that – realizing it would take ten days or a fortnight to get a letter to London and the reply back to Plymouth – the more he understood how they were weighed down with Sarah's disappearance.

His father's letter made it clear that there was no news and how despondent they were. The Marquis must be distraught: he and Sarah were very close.

Now, burdened with worry over Sarah, it would crush them all to find Sarah's husband was in grave danger from the Articles of War. A week or more – the trial should be all over before news reached London. That decided him: no appeal to his father for help – the old man had suffered enough when that past government put him on trial – and no appeal to the Marquis. He would fight with the weapons he had. It did not do to think too much about the calibre of those!

Ramage and Sidney Yorke stood by the entryport as the chair with Alexis in it was hoisted up from the boat, swung inboard and gently lowered until it was just in front of Ramage. As Jackson and Stafford held it steady, Ramage stepped forward to flip back the wooden bar which held her secure, helped her step out on to the deck and, as Jackson swung the chair back out of the way, saluted her gravely. She curtseyed. "Good day, Captain, I trust my brother has already asked if our visit is discommoding you?"

"He has indeed."

"And what was your answer?"

Ramage was still standing close enough to her that by dropping his voice only she could hear his reply. "That your visit was very ill-timed because I was sitting in my cabin so miserable that I was thinking of doing away with myself!"

She laughed and said in a normal tone: "Oh good, as long as we have not interrupted anything of importance!"

With them seated in the cabin, Yorke said as soon as the sentry had shut the door: "We have been hearing a rumour."

"It is probably true. What does it say?"

"Leave the rumour for the moment. We have just heard officially that the convoy sails tomorrow with the London, Hull and Leith ships, and you are not named as the commander of the escort, nor is the *Calypso* mentioned."

When Ramage nodded, Yorke continued: "The rumour – which I don't mind telling you is upsetting all the masters considerably – is that you are being court-martialled at the instance of the captain of the *Jason*."

Ramage pointed at the papers on his desk. "That's not a rumour, I'm afraid. The Admiralty has ordered the trial and the date is already fixed – for the beginning of next week."

"But...but what about witnesses?" Alexis said angrily. "All the convoy will have sailed and the masters want to give evidence on your behalf!"

"That rumour-which-is-not-a-rumour is not the only one," Yorke said. "I hear that our old friend Goddard is the rear-admiral here. Does that mean...?"

As Ramage nodded, Alexis exclaimed: "Goddard? Who is this Goddard? Why do the pair of you have such long faces? Are you frightened of him?"

"Yes and no," Ramage said, and quietly explained to her how Goddard had entered his life, toadying to the old ministers and currying favour by attacking the Earl of Blazey's son.

"Sidney," Alexis said firmly. "We let the *Emerald* sail tomorrow with the convoy, and we move on shore to an inn. The King's Arms, I think; I refuse to stay at the Prince George – I dislike Foxhole Street and the place is always full of noisy shipmasters and foreigners."

Yorke agreed but warned that after so many weeks at sea, it would take a few days to find their land legs.

Alexis pointed at the papers on Ramage's desk. "Why are you so sure that this Goddard man will preside at the trial?"

"In Plymouth there is a port admiral," Ramage explained. "He is Vice-Admiral Sir James Bustard. I know nothing about him except he's getting on in years. He has a house – just near

Mount Wise and the Telegraph, and just across the Parade from Government House.

"Then there is a rear-admiral, who is the second-in-command. His main purpose in life is to preside at courts-martial. In a big port like Plymouth there are trials almost every day and they're held on board the *Salvador del Mundo*, an old prize which is well suited for the purpose."

"Trials almost every day?" Alexis exclaimed. "But what *for*?"

"Don't forget that a 74-gun ship (most of the ships you see here larger than frigates are seventy-fours) has at least seven hundred men on board, and the frigates about two hundred each. So take half a dozen seventy-fours and you have more than four thousand men. If only half a dozen of them desert, get drunk and start a brawl and hit an officer or mutter treasonable phrases in their cups – well, that makes half a dozen courts-martial a day!"

"Not to mention captains who misbehave out in the Atlantic and come in here to be punished," Alexis added mischievously.

"Indeed not," Ramage agreed gravely. "Poor Rear-Admiral Goddard must be a much overworked man."

"It's a pity you have to add to his burden."

Ramage laughed and said wryly: "I am sure he will think he's doing me a favour."

Sidney Yorke, who had remained unsmiling as Ramage and Alexis teased each other, asked quietly: "Am I being indiscreet in asking what you are charged with – and by whom?"

Ramage sorted out the papers on the desk and passed them to Yorke. "They're in order now. When you've read them all, you'll know as much about this as I do."

Alexis look questioningly and Ramage nodded. "Of course you can read them too."

"They'll make a change from the Paston letters which you lent me and which I've nearly finished. Not that I haven't found them fascinating, but I didn't know the Pastons and I do know you!"

She waited a few moments and then said quietly: "Why don't you come with us and stay at the inn? You have not slept on shore since – "

She just prevented herself putting a hand to her mouth, a gesture which in other women always irritated her, but there was no way she could recall the words. Ramage said easily: "Since Bonaparte's men chased us out of Jean-Jacques' château near Brest. No, but a captain may not sleep out of his ship without the port admiral's permission. That is just for a night. For longer, he needs permission from the Admiralty."

"And for the moment you do not want to ask favours of anyone."

Ramage nodded. "Anyway, I have plenty to do – lists of witnesses, draw up my defence, and so on."

"And rally your friends," Alexis added.

"A naval officer on trial for his life in these circumstances has no friends," Ramage said with unintended bitterness, and was startled to see Alexis' eyes beginning to glisten with tears.

"That is not true," she said quietly.

He said gently: "I spoke clumsily. Yes, I have friends. Very few, and of those the Yorkes are the most valued. I thought you meant that I should rally my friends in the Service, and I meant that I have none but in any case at a time like this, with a man like Goddard involved, anyone in the Service is well advised to keep away. In fact I'd tell him to!"

"But what about Aitken, and Southwick, and Bowen – ?"

"Oh dear," Ramage said. "I sound ungrateful but I'm simply tactless. I'm conceited enough to assume that all the Calypsos, like the Yorkes, are on my side. When I said I was on my own, I really meant *we* – the Yorkes and the Calypsos – can't look round for friends."

"But," Alexis said chidingly, "you forget the masters who were in the convoy, and surely the Count of Rennes and your father and father-in-law will help?"

"The Count saw nothing that you didn't, so there's no way he can help, and anyway he's probably on his way to London by coach. My father and the Marquis are stunned by Sarah's disappearance. I'm not going to add to their troubles."

Sidney said suddenly, an impatient note in his voice: "Think, girl! The Count is a friend of the Prince of Wales, and this wretched man Goddard is one of Prinny's favourites. Nicholas wouldn't dream of putting Jean-Jacques in such an awkward position."

"I would," Alexis said stoutly, "and Prinny too, if I thought the Prince of Wales' presence would make sure justice was done."

"You'll be sent to bed without any supper," Yorke said in a mock warning, and then turned to Ramage and said: "These Articles of War that Shirley's charging you under – what penalties do they entail?"

"Some leave it up to the court; guilty verdicts with others call for death, without any option."

There was the hissing of silk against silk and a gentle thump as Alexis fainted and slid out of the chair, and as he jumped up to go to her, Ramage noticed she had the most shapely legs.

"I should have left her on board," Yorke said, "but I'd have had to lock her in. She's taking all this business very seriously."

"So am I," Ramage said dryly. "Ah, she's coming round…"

"You're on board the *Calypso* and everything is all right," Yorke said hastily, and Ramage realized the hurried words were in case the dazed girl said something which might cause embarrassment. He asked her if she wanted a drink of water but she shook her head and Ramage was relieved. There was no need for a Marine sentry and his steward Silkin to know that Miss Yorke had fainted. That was the trouble with fainting – it could be caused by anything from a shock to pregnancy, from "vapours", intended to attract attention, to real illness.

Aitken and Southwick looked at Ramage, waiting for his answer, and the first lieutenant still held the list from which he had been reading.

"Wagstaffe – yes, I can't see how I can avoid calling him – he'll be called by the prosecution anyway. But I need only one of the *Calypso's* officers – he can give evidence about the challenge, lack of reply and being fired on."

"Yes, well, that's why I put my name at the top of the list," Aitken said. "But all the rest can and will substantiate that."

"Look," Ramage said firmly, "whoever gives evidence on my behalf will be a marked man in the Service from then on, so I want only one person."

Southwick sniffed: it was his "I don't care what you say, I'm going my way" sniff and Ramage tried to look at him sternly, but the old master simply grinned. "It'll be all or none, sir. No one is going to be left out. Or if you try to make do with just one of us, then that person'll be like the Jasons. Saw nothing, heard nothing."

"But there's no *need*," Ramage said. "Aitken, don't you see that giving evidence on my behalf will probably mean you'll never be made post?"

Aitken shrugged his shoulders. "Sir, thanks to you by way of prize money, I'd pass for a wealthy man in the Highlands. If what you say is true, I'll find myself a bonny bride and a middling sized estate, and if I never go to sea again I've tales enough to tell a dozen grandchildren – aye, and never the same tale twice!"

"That's how everyone feels, sir," Southwick said. "You've looked after them in the smoke of battle, and they're going to look after you – " he paused searching for the right phrase, failed to find it and ended lamely, " – well, at a time like now. They see you're in more danger from our own folk than the French, and that's enough for them."

"How do they know?"

"Too late to complain sir," Southwick chuckled, "but every man on board knows the six Articles of War that Captain Shirley is citing, and even now there's a copy of the *Articles of War* being passed hand to hand on the lowerdeck. The men were complaining that they only ever heard the Articles read out to them on the quarterdeck, and they wanted – those that can read – a chance to study 'em."

Ramage knew he was helpless to protect his officers from the price they would pay for their loyalty. Aitken, Wagstaffe, Kenton, Martin and Orsini: he had let them down. Southwick and Bowen were different – Bowen only continued serving in the Navy as a surgeon in order to stay with Southwick and Ramage himself: Southwick, like Aitken, had plenty in the Funds from prize money and had reached the age when retirement might seem welcome.

It had all started with a lookout sighting a sail on the horizon and he had decided to investigate it. If only he had ignored it – they had seen several others that day. At least he had not sent off *L'Espoir* or *La Robuste*: he shivered at the thought of the problems that would have arisen if the *Jason* had raked one of them.

Anyway, Aitken had the list of witnesses, and that was that! Then he remembered: "There are two more names to add to your list."

Aitken got up and sat at the desk, reached for a quill and taking the cap off the inkwell, said: "Yes, sir?"

"Mr Sidney Yorke, who will be staying at the King's Arms, in Britonside, and Miss Yorke, at the same address."

"Ah," said Southwick, "They're with us all right, then?"

"Yes. The *Emerald* sails for London with the convoy tomorrow, but they're staying for the trial. What evidence they can give, I don't know, but Miss Yorke should make an impression on the court!"

"She certainly makes an impression on me!" Southwick said. "And I'd sooner have her brother on our side than against us."

Ramage said: "I've been thinking about the masters of the merchant ships. I don't think we need any as witnesses. The captain of *L'Espoir* – he won't have seen what happened. The *Jason*'s first lieutenant, gunner and the cook's mate – "

"Cook's mate, sir?" Aitken could not believe his ears.

"Who better? Cook's mates are usually the most stupid men in any ship, and he has nothing to lose. More important, he probably has little understanding. But he will know if the ship fired a broadside or not."

"Shirley's fellows will get to him before the trial and tell him what to say," Southwick declared gruffly.

"Perhaps – in fact no doubt will. But if the man gets muddled enough in court, we might get some truth out of him."

"Truth isn't going to get a look in," Southwick said.

"No," Ramage agreed, "I doubt it. So we'll be as brief as we can. Few witnesses, few questions…The briefer the trial, the less time the other side have to gloat."

Aitken looked worried and he shook his head. "You don't seem to consider the question of being acquitted, sir."

"I've considered it," Ramage said, his voice neutral. "I'd like to be cleared, if only for my father's sake. But over there – " he gestured vaguely to the northwest, towards Cornwall, " – lies my home, with enough land to keep me occupied for the rest of my life. And over there – " he gestured seaward, " – is the answer to the question of whether I am a widower or a married man. Those are the two most important things in my life, and what lies in between – a trial on board the *Salvador del Mundo* next Monday – doesn't seem of so much consequence at the moment."

"Even tho' it could result in a sentence of death," Southwick said sharply.

"Right now I haven't a devil of a lot to live for," Ramage said bitterly. "My mother and father can't live forever, and I don't fancy wandering round St Kew Hall without Sarah for the rest of my life. It's a dam' big house and there are plenty of tenants on the land, and whoever runs it should have – well, some zest, and a wife, and that's what I lack now."

"Sir," said Southwick, "I'm going to presume on the length of my service with you and unless you order me not to, I'm going to speak my mind freely. I've talked it over with Mr Aitken, and to be honest, sir, you're worrying us, so what I have to say – if you'll allow me to say it – goes for both of us."

Ramage smiled and nodded. "I've never known you to ask permission before, but go on…"

"Well, sir, you've done more for King and country than most men, but apart from some of your despatches being published in the *London Gazette*, you've had no recognition and there are a lot of senior officers jealous of you. All that's normal. It took long enough for Their Lordships to give Lord Nelson his first real chance: those dam'd Antigua merchants nearly did for his career right at the start, when he went for 'em in the last war."

Ramage said impatiently: "I am not another Lord Nelson, Mr Southwick."

"No sir, but hear me out. There are some admirals who listen to what you say – Admiral Clinton off Brest let you go to Devil's Island on what must to him have seemed a flimsy story. Lord Spencer when he was First Lord gave you opportunities, and now Lord St Vincent has not signed that court-martial order from the Board, even though he is First Lord."

"He was attending a levee at letter-signing time," Ramage said. "Four other members of the Board had their pens ready – three is a quorum."

Southwick shook his head but said: "Have it your own way, sir. You can say you haven't had recognition for what you've done – "

"But I don't," Ramage interrupted. "I've had *Gazettes*, I'm on the Post List: I don't need anything else."

"Very well, sir, I'm wrong in that particular. But think of this: supposing you quit now, are found guilty but are not sentenced to death; dismissed from the Service, say. You go back and watch your tenants, course hares, milk the cows and make butter and cheese at St Kew, and smile at the young maids and kiss the hands of the wives of the local gentry – and then you find that Lady Sarah is alive and (because by then the war has ended) is about to be released and come home. Now you think what she'll find. A disgraced husband with no fight in him. The bottle, that'll be your mistress by then, sir, the bottle and not even bothering with a glass.

"Sorry, sir. Overstood the mark, I have, but I'm not sorry, but you haven't been yourself for many weeks, and we all know how you were waiting for news of Lady Sarah when you got to Plymouth, and instead you had this crash on your head. But right now those of us who've picked you up for dead several times in the past can't see any wound or blood, and we wonder why you've given up fighting. Don't seem like you, sir. Lady Sarah'd be ashamed."

Ramage flushed but said nothing. There was nothing to say except to agree with Southwick, because the old man knew he was right and did not need Ramage to tell him so; in fact would be heartily embarrassed if he did.

Both Southwick and Aitken picked up their hats. Aitken put the list of witnesses on the desk while Southwick led the way to the door, muttering that they would be back later.

As the door closed behind them and Ramage noticed for the first time the whine of a high wind in the masts and riggings – it sounded as though a squall was sweeping down on them, and he saw rain running down the glass of the skylights – he realized that apart from the reference to recognition, there was nothing that Southwick had said that he disagreed with or could deny. It was a shameful admission to have to make, and he was ashamed that Southwick and Aitken had been forced into such a position. Then, thinking of their embarrassment – trying to put some backbone into their captain – he remembered phrases spoken by the Yorkes which had not, at the time, made much sense. Yes, and glances between Sidney and Alexis which he had intercepted and assumed were something that happened between brother and sister (not having a sister he did not know) but which he now recognized were glances of despair or silent pleas for help or support for something one of them had said.

He felt hot and ashamed: hot from the embarrassment that four people, one of them Alexis, had inspected him and found him weak, and ashamed that he had in fact mentally given up without openly admitting it. Given up, he told himself bitterly, because of the threat of being beaten by a madman, or the fear that, with Sarah probably dead, he had no purpose left.

No, he protested to himself, that was not the whole problem. A major part of it was the Articles of War. Anything reduced to paragraphs invariably ended up as nonsense when applied to a living situation. Admirals and captains, since the Byng court-martial and execution, had to fight any odds in battle, however stupid it might be and however much wiser it would be to wait for reinforcements or even decline action, because of a phrase in Article XII, the phrase that did for poor old Admiral Byng – "*shall not do his utmost*". This could find a man guilty whether he was an admiral or a cook's mate. What was a man's "utmost" and who, not there at the time, could determine the circumstances?

It was curious how Southwick could read his mind. Ramage had sensed that the old man knew Ramage was not more frightened of the death sentence than he was of being killed in action against the French. Death was death, a big black curtain. But Southwick (and almost certainly Aitken too) knew that the man who accepted death in battle would be ashamed of dying at the hands of a firing squad carrying out the sentence of a court-martial – the fate of Admiral Byng, who had been outraged at the government's original intention, which was to hang him. All governments were capable of the vindictiveness that went with brutish stupidity (the treatment of Byng showed that).

CHAPTER **FOURTEEN**

The convoy sailed from the Sound next day and as Ramage and Southwick watched the ships weighing, shepherded by a frigate and two sloops, Southwick commented: "Admiral Goddard must be sure of himself…"

Ramage, thinking of the brief letter from the deputy judge advocate which was now locked in his drawer, nodded in agreement. "Still, they haven't realized yet who the Yorkes are. As a shipowner, Mr Yorke's word will carry some weight."

"Maybe, and maybe not," Southwick said. "But don't let's anticipate too much unhappiness. Have you heard from your father, sir?"

"Not yet: there hasn't been time. But I want him to stay out of sight. The Press will eventually make a great song and dance, although the *Morning Post* is likely to be on my side. It has never liked the Prince of Wales and perhaps it doesn't like Admiral Goddard either! Anyway, don't forget it takes about a week for news to reach London from here."

Southwick gave one of his famous sniffs, this time clearly indicating contempt, and after looking round to make sure no one else was within earshot, said respectfully but firmly: "Never lose sight of one thing, sir: it's what happens at the trial on board the *Salvador del Mundo* that matters.

"The Press can say what it likes, mobs can throw half-bricks through the windows of the Admiralty (and I reckon they will, once they hear about it: you're a hero to them) and Parliament can debate it all when it sits again – too late to do us any good: just our luck that this happens during the recess – but once the court gives its verdict, it's all over.

"Once that verdict is pronounced, then it becomes a matter of pride: the court will never admit it made a mistake, nor will the Admiralty, nor will the government. The law officers of the Crown can turn themselves into murderers – judicial o' course – without a moment's thought. Look at the Earl of Hardwicke in the Byng affair. He was Lord Chancellor and planned the murder."

"All three were newly created titles," Ramage said jokingly. "His Grace the Duke's title dates from Byng's trial, 1756, and the Hardwicke earldom came a couple of years earlier. I can't remember when Anson had his barony – probably owed it to his wife's father, after he sailed round the world."

"Well, my point is that once there's a verdict," Southwick said doggedly, "no one in authority is ever going to change his mind. Poor Admiral Byng was a good example. The court itself later said they never intended that he should be executed, but just the same he was led out and shot on the quarterdeck of the *Monarch*."

"I shall insist on the *Calypso*," Ramage said lightly, "even though you'll have to get the quarterdeck holystoned afterwards."

"Don't even joke about it, sir. Might I ask what that last letter was about?"

"Just a brief note from the deputy judge advocate telling me that several of the people I wanted to call as witnesses are no longer here and so won't be available for the trial."

Southwick's bushy eyebrows shot up in surprise. "Who are they?"

"A couple of the masters of merchant ships. They're not vital. The Yorkes have been notified – that other boat from the shore brought a note from them saying they'd each received a letter from the deputy judge advocate 'desiring' them to attend to give evidence. I listed them by their surname and initials, so the deputy judge advocate assumed they were both men."

"If he's like most deputy judge advocates I've ever seen," Southwick said sourly, "he could look at Miss Yorke and still not know the difference! But did the idea of giving evidence for you make her feel nervous, sir?"

Ramage shook his head, laughing at the memory. "On the contrary. From what she said and the look in her eye, I almost felt sorry for Admiral Goddard."

"They'll find a way, sir," Southwick said crossly. "They'll find a way to prevent the Yorkes giving evidence, you'll see. The admiral will remember Mr Yorke from that business in Port Royal."

"I know, but they want to help and I'm not going to disappoint them, so I put them on my list. They'll be able to see the trial, anyway."

"No they won't, sir," Southwick said. "They'll see the court assembling and the swearing in, but after that, as listed witnesses, they'll have to withdraw. You can't stay and listen to what's going on if you're going to give evidence later!"

Southwick pointed to another boat heading for the *Calypso* and about to be challenged by one of the Marine sentries. "Anyone would think we're the only ship in the Sound!"

Ramage looked at the boat through his telescope. "As far as Rear-Admiral Goddard is concerned, I expect we are! Another lieutenant – in his best uniform, too, complete with tarpaulin to keep off the spray. As the fishermen say: 'I think we have a live one here!' "

As the boat came alongside, Southwick growled that he would go down and meet it to keep Aitken company, commenting: "It's one of those lieutenants that never go to sea: they dance attendance on the port admiral's wife and her dog, and any daughters and nieces…"

The lieutenant was tall and willowy: he stood up in the boat swaying like a slender plant in a gentle breeze. He had that foppish air that Ramage knew always infuriated Southwick and aroused the contempt of Aitken.

Five minutes later, Aitken brought the lieutenant up to the quarterdeck, saluted Ramage and said, making no attempt to disguise his voice: "This individual claims to be Lieutenant Hill, or Hillock, and he says he has business with you, sir."

The lieutenant gave a languid salute and asked: "Captain Ramage?"

Aitken immediately said, his Scots accent very pronounced, always a sign that he was losing his temper: "You insert the word 'sir' between the name and the question mark."

The young man nodded graciously. "I do beg your pardon. You are Captain Ramage, sir?" When Ramage nodded, he held out the letter he had been carrying. "It is my duty to deliver this."

Ramage took it and thanked the man, who continued standing there. "You may go," Ramage said.

"Oh, I shall: but you come with me." The lieutenant was smirking and Aitken, without a moment's hesitation, walked to the quarterdeck rail, looked down at the Marine sentry and shouted: "Pass the word for Mr Rennick."

He continued waiting at the rail, obviously not intending to move until the Marine lieutenant arrived.

"I am Lieutenant Hill, sir," the lieutenant said nervously.

"Are you, by Jove," Ramage said. "Luck of the draw, I suppose."

"Er, who is your first lieutenant summoning, sir?"

Ramage thought, anyone else would have used the word "calling" but this fellow would also use "prior to" instead of "before" and "decimate" when he meant almost destroyed, quite unaware that it meant one in ten, from the Latin *decimus*, a tenth.

"He's calling for the Marine lieutenant. He may be going to arrest you for insolence, but I think he suspects you're an impostor."

"An impostor? Why, sir, I have just received my orders direct from Rear-Admiral Goddard and the deputy judge advocate. I, sir, am the provost marshal."

" 'Upon the occasion'," Ramage said.

"I beg your pardon, sir?" Hill said uncertainly.

"Someone has been rash enough to appoint you 'Provost Marshal *upon the occasion*'. I was just correcting your temporary title."

"Oh, yes indeed, and thank you, sir."

"Not at all," Ramage said politely, seeing out of the corner of his eye that Rennick and two Marines had arrived on the quarterdeck and Aitken was clearly bringing him up to date. Hill then noticed them and said even more nervously: "I do wish you would read the letter, sir: it explains everything."

"I know what it says," Ramage said. "My first lieutenant and I are trying to save you and your admiral some embarrassment."

"Me, sir? And Admiral Goddard?" Hill hitched the scabbard of his sword round and stood stiffly. "My orders are to take you into custody and deliver you to the court on the appropriate day at the appropriate time."

"Yes, indeed," Ramage said agreeably, "but if either you or any senior officer – " Ramage was careful not to identify Goddard, " – think that you will take me from my own ship, *which I still lawfully command*, and shut me up in a cell or cabin, then you had better bring a file of Marines. I shall present myself (in your company, of course) on board the *Salvador del Mundo* in good time for the trial on Monday. So unless you want to find yourself locked up on board this ship, guarded by Marines, under suspicion of being an impostor as neither my officers nor myself can credit that you *really* hold the King's commission, I suggest you leave the ship."

Hill took one more look at Ramage's deep-set eyes, which seemed to be boring into him, saw that Aitken, the Marine lieutenant and the two Marines were now marching towards him, gave a hasty salute and bolted for the quarterdeck ladder, having the presence of mind to grab his sword scabbard so that it should not trip him up.

As Aitken reached him, Ramage smiled. "Your bird has flown, but you timed it well. Mind you, we might have a file of Marines coming on board in an hour, but..."

"I have my doubts, sir: I think we've made the point!"

Promptly at seven o'clock on Monday morning Ramage followed Aitken, Wagstaffe, Bowen and Southwick down into the cutter. A cloudless sky and a light wind from the northeast left the Sound calm and the row to the great *Salvador del Mundo*, anchored half a mile away, would have been a pleasant outing, but for its purpose.

Jackson climbed from thwart to thwart, draping a piece of tarpaulin over the officers. The routine letter from Goddard to the officers who would form the court and those due to give evidence ended with the sentence, "and it is expected you will attend in your uniform frocks." This set stewards busy pressing their masters' frock coats and white breeches. Aitken, Wagstaffe and Southwick found their best stockings had been the dining-room for moths so they were now wearing spare pairs belonging to Ramage. All four men had their swords, but

Ramage alone had been careful to make sure that the two clips on the scabbard worked freely.

The boys who looked after the officers, and Ramage's steward Silkin, had been busy shining shoes and sword scabbards, and all of them had taken care in tying their stocks.

The result was interesting, Ramage thought, and as they sat in the sternsheets, being draped with Jackson's tarpaulins, Southwick looked (if one ignored the uniform) like a very prosperous farmer setting off on Lady Day to settle up some accounts; Aitken, from his serious expression and rather long face, could be a clever young surgeon not long ago qualified at Edinburgh. Wagstaffe looked just like a naval officer. Bowen, dressed in a pearl-grey coat with matching breeches, had the vaguely debauched air of a portly landowner come up to town either for a few days' gaming or to spend a night or two with his mistress.

Jackson looked at them all carefully as he placed the tarpaulins, watching for missing buttons, creased stocks, grease spots that might have been missed, and his memory went back several years, as though slipping back the pages of a book. He realized with a shock that all four men had aged: for years he had seen them every day and, he supposed, never really saw them, instead seeing only what he expected to see. But Mr Ramage was no longer the deceptive-looking young lieutenant: of course he was still taller than he looked, his shoulders were still wider than one expected. Those brown eyes were still deep-sunk under eyebrows that if anything were bushier. Hair still black and even with his hat on there was no sign of grey hair, except for that tiny circle of white that grew where the pistol ball caught him down in Curaçao. High cheekbones, slightly curved nose, face still tanned from the Tropics, a small web of wrinkles at the outer corners of the eyes caused by having them half closed against the bright sun.

Yes, he had matured rather than aged; now he looked what he was, the heir to one of the oldest earldoms in the kingdom, and one of the most famous frigate captains in the Navy. But all that was not helping him now. He was about to be court-martialled, Jackson knew without a moment's doubt, because the vendetta against his father, Admiral the Earl of Blazey, was still being waged by old men with long memories and younger men like Rear-Admiral Goddard who were trying to advance themselves by pandering to them. How long would all this go on? Jackson was far from sure. When the old Admiral retired, the vendetta had already passed on to people like Rear-Admiral Goddard, so the old grudge against the father was already born again and carried on as a vendetta against Mr Ramage, who had been a child when it all started.

Jackson pictured Rear-Admiral Goddard and for a moment felt sorry for him: the American knew instinctively that Goddard was one of the men who could only win by cheating. Jackson had long ago learned that certain men were so devious that it would never occur to them that it was possible (or indeed desirable) to be straightforward. They were the men who, asked the time of day, consulted their watches and gave a wrong answer in case the correct one gave the other person some advantage.

And Mr Aitken. Like whisky, he had matured and although he looked more dour each month, he had in fact long ago relaxed as he gained confidence. Mr Southwick – he had aged but only because his hair was whiter. But Mr Bowen had not changed much. Yes, he looked a lot better than the day he joined the *Triton* brig (that showed how long ago it was) a drunken sot who within weeks did not drink a drop, except water. What a time and a cure that had been! Dragons all over the deckhead, screams that made the men's blood run cold. But the cure, devised by Mr Ramage and Mr Southwick, had worked and to look at Mr Bowen now, no one could guess that drink had ever been a problem. And Jackson doubted if the Navy had a better or more popular surgeon.

Jackson scrambled back aft and took the tiller. At least the officers would now arrive on board the *Salvador del Mundo* with their uniforms unmarked by splashes of water thrown up when one of the men caught a crab. No matter what, someone always caught a crab…

Ramage looked across at the *Salvador del Mundo* as Jackson gave the orders to start the cutter spurting through the water. "Saviour of the World" – well, until she was captured by Sir John Jervis (as he then was: now an earl with his title taken from his victory) at the battle on Valentine's day off Cape St Vincent in 1797. Then she flew the flag of Spain, carried 112 guns, and was one of the largest ships in the world. Not as big as the *Commerce de Marseille*, of course, taken by Lord Hood at Toulon.

For a few moments Ramage recalled his own role in that St Valentine's day battle when he had lost the *Kathleen* cutter but had prevented the Spanish fleet escaping. Southwick, Jackson, Stafford, Rossi – they were all there and saw the great *Salvador* captured; they had all escaped death from drowning by a miracle as the little *Kathleen* had been rolled over. What were they thinking now?

Ramage's thoughts went on to the *Commerce*. It was ironic that the biggest ship in the Royal Navy should have been captured from the French and was now usually commanded by a lowly lieutenant because she was being used as a prison ship.

Ramage recalled that after being captured she was first taken to Portsmouth, where the dockyard authorities found that there was not a dock in Portsmouth big enough to take her, so she had to be sailed round to Plymouth. A pity such a great ship could not be sent to sea against her former owners: it was a sad thing that she would end her days in the Hamoaze, where she was now anchored and still home to French seamen, although as a prison.

Idle thoughts but they helped keep his mind occupied. His life seemed to be hedged round with signs saying *"Do Not"*. But his brain ignored the signs with the wilfulness of a confirmed trespasser – or poacher, rather. Do not think about Sarah. Yes, that was all very well, but what if he was thinking about her thinking about him? Was she alive to think about him? What had happened to the *Murex*? Why had no news come through from France? Normally the French agent for prisoners, stationed in London, received the names so that negotiations for exchanges could be started, but in the case of the *Murex* there had been nothing. Perhaps the system working before the Treaty of Amiens was taking some time to get going again…it was a possibility; no more than that.

Now the damned trial. To be fair (not that he wanted to be) this was not Goddard's fault or responsibility: sheer chance had placed him as the rear-admiral at Plymouth at the time Shirley had seen fit to go off his head and accuse the captain of the *Calypso*. Damn, damn, damn the man: Ramage felt murderous towards Shirley because of the effect the coming trial could have on the future of Aitken and the other lieutenants. The master was old enough to retire if the case went against him, and probably would, and Bowen could (and probably would) go back to private practice, but the rest of them, even if they did not give evidence, Martin, Kenton and young Orsini, would for ever be known as having been associated with the *"Calypso* Affair" (although perhaps it would become known as the *"Jason* Affair"). The Byng affair had affected (disastrously) the behaviour of senior officers in battle for fifty years, because of that "did keep back" phrase in the Articles of War. Would the Ramage verdict (as it was bound to become known) merely emphasize that unfit captains could not be replaced at sea except on cast-iron medical grounds? In fact none of them could even remember such a case: if only they could, they would have a precedent to cite at the coming trial.

They – which meant he, Aitken, Wagstaffe and Southwick – had spent almost a whole afternoon discussing the merits of hiring a counsel. It was allowed, but was it wise? The court would comprise no more than thirteen and no fewer than five of the senior officers available in the port, and they would be ordinary naval officers, captains and perhaps flag officers, with no legal training. How would they view an accused officer who was represented by a lawyer? Would they consider that the lawyer was an indication that he had something to hide? Would they be prejudiced against the lawyer who would (or should) know the law – and who might, in fact, trip them or the deputy judge advocate on points of the law?

Aitken, who had not yet been involved in a court-martial either as a witness or defendant (or, for that matter, prosecutor, even of a refractory seaman), had wanted him to get a lawyer, but Southwick had argued against, saying he was sure it would antagonize the court. Ramage had listened to all their arguments, added several of his own which had provoked more discussion, and then pointed out that even if they had decided to engage a counsel there was no time to find one in London and get him down here to Plymouth.

And already the cutter was going alongside the *San Joseph*, another of Lord St Vincent's prizes from the same battle as the *Salvador del Mundo*, to collect Lieutenant Hill, the "provost marshal upon the occasion". The day after the fellow had fled from the *Calypso* without his prisoner under arrest, a letter had arrived for Ramage from the commander-in-chief, written as though Hill had never been on board the *Calypso* and Aitken had never called for Rennick. It said that Lieutenant Hill of the *San Joseph* had been appointed provost marshal "upon the occasion" and would be responsible for taking Captain Ramage into custody and delivering him "in due time" for his trial, but in view of Captain Ramage's duties as the commanding officer of His Majesty's ship the *Calypso*, it had been thought fit that Captain Ramage should remain a prisoner at large on board the *Calypso* but should surrender himself to the provost marshal at least an hour before the time appointed for the trial.

Even as the cutter came alongside the *San Joseph*, Ramage could guess that petty minds were at work, and that none of them was going to miss an opportunity to try to humiliate Captain Ramage. The trouble with petty minds, Ramage had long ago decided, was that they contained only petty thoughts.

As the cutter came alongside and painter and sternfast were secured, a voice bellowed down from on deck: "Captain Ramage come on board."

Ramage leaned over and after a slight wink said to Southwick: "Just react to whatever I say; we'll have some sport with these fellows. Now," he said, raising his voice, "I've just remembered that I've left some documents on board the *Calypso* that I need for the trial."

Southwick slapped his knee. "Well, I'm blessed, sir: we'll have to go back and fetch them."

"We shall indeed, and we'll have to hurry or we'll be late."

By now Hill had appeared at an open gunport and he said, with as much sternness as he dare muster; "Captain Ramage – you're being hailed from on deck."

"Am I? Well, whatever they want, it must wait: I'm under an arrest and the provost marshal has to deliver me – " he stopped and dug into his pocket for his watch. He flipped open the front, then closed it down again and put it back in his pocket. " – to the court on board the *Salvador del Mundo* in half an hour. I've forgotten some papers so I have to return to the *Calypso*. Boarding the *San Joseph* will only waste time and I've no wish to get the provost marshal into trouble."

"But you can't go back to the *Calypso*," Hill yelped, "that – "

"Then you'll have to explain to the court why you prevented Captain Ramage making any interrogatories or presenting his defence, apart from explaining that you kept the court waiting because you insisted on Captain Ramage being taken on board the *San Joseph*."

"Ordering you on board is not my idea, sir," Hill protested. "I had – "

"Well, you'd better run along and explain your problems to whoever had the idea and owns the voice up there on the maindeck. I'd like to know the names and ranks, too, so that I can report them to the president of the court."

Hill vanished and, in what seemed only a few seconds, was scrambling down into the boat. "If you are ready, sir," he said nervously, "we can go back to the *Calypso*."

Ramage turned and nodded to Jackson. "Cast off and carry on."

Once the cutter was clear of the *San Joseph*, Jackson asked conversationally, "The *Salvador*, sir?"

Ramage nodded and ignored Lieutenant Hill's protest about going to the *Calypso*.

"Reminds you of old times, don't it, sir?" Jackson said. "The *Salvador del Mundo* over there, the *San Joseph* over here – " he pointed to the west. "Just needs the *San Nicolas* and *San Ysidro* and it'd be like the day we lost the *Kathleen*."

"Sir," Hill said, not realizing Ramage was unclipping his sword because his hands were hidden beneath the tarpaulin.

"Don't interrupt my thoughts," Ramage said severely. "What you don't know is precisely how the *Salvador del Mundo* and the *San Joseph* and the *San Ysidro* and *San Nicolas* were captured, but almost every other man in this boat can tell you exactly, because they were there."

"Indeed, sir," Hill said disdainfully, "how interesting."

"Yes, interesting because – " A sudden thought struck Ramage. "Tell me, lieutenant, have you ever had a shot fired at you by the enemy – cannon, musket or pistol?"

"Well, not exactly, sir."

"Have you ever been in action?"

"Well, no, sir."

"Then don't ever sneer at those that have," Ramage said sourly, realizing he was hardly being fair to the wretched lieutenant. "You can see the *Salvador* and *San Joseph*. The two ships not here are the *San Ysidro* and *San Nicolas*. They were leading the enemy fleet, and both ships were captured by Commodore (as he then was) Nelson."

"I know *that*, sir," Hill said petulantly.

"But do you know *how* the commodore caught up with the two Dons who were trying to escape?"

"Well, no sir, I don't know *all* the details of the battle."

"You ought to ask the seaman holding the tiller of this cutter."

"Sir, I can hardly – "

"Or any of the first six men at the oars."

"Oh, sir – "

"Or this gentleman sitting here," Ramage said relentlessly, indicating Southwick.

Southwick sniffed and said loudly: "You might even ask Mr Ramage, because if it hadn't been for him none of the ships would have been taken and Sir John Jervis would never have got his earldom!"

By now Hill's embarrassment and annoyance had gone: instead his curiosity was aroused. He was cautious enough to ask Southwick, rather than risk an encounter with Ramage. "Tell me, then, what happened?"

"Mr Ramage was a lieutenant then, with about as much seniority as you've got and from the looks of it a lot younger, and he commanded the *Kathleen* cutter, and to stop the four Dons escaping – "

"He ran his cutter across the bows of the leading one!" Hill interrupted. "I remember now! I'd forgotten the name of that lieutenant," he said apologetically to Ramage. "And I've just remembered a *Gazette* I read: in the West Indies you captured that frigate you command: I forget her French name but she was renamed *Calypso*."

Ramage pulled his sword and scabbard out from beneath the tarpaulin. "You'd better take this."

The significance of an officer about to be tried handing over his sword had never been cleared up. Something to do with surrendering a badge of office, perhaps. Anyway, the sword was put on the table during the trial, and if after the court considered its verdict the accused came back into the courtroom and found the point of the sword towards him, he knew he was guilty.

Ramage could see that Hill was a very puzzled young man. He was glancing covertly at Ramage, Southwick and Jackson and – probably much to his surprise – finding that none of them had tails like the pictures of Satan. Ramage realized that the wretched youngster was finding it impossible to reconcile what he had been hearing about Captain Ramage for the past few days with what he had just learned in the last few minutes.

"Sir," Hill whispered, "this Captain Shirley says you are mad. It's in the charge and he talks about it to anyone who will listen – "

"Mr Hill, you are the 'provost marshal upon the occasion' and I am under arrest in your custody," Ramage said in a low voice. "Any discussion of the case is most improper – you must realize that."

Hill nodded, although it was obvious that his thoughts were far away. "Is there any chance after the trial," he asked diffidently, "that you'll have a vacancy for a lieutenant in the *Calypso*, sir?"

Ramage smiled to make sure that Hill realized his proffered olive branch had been accepted. "Is there any chance after the trial that I'll still command the *Calypso*?"

Ramage was startled when Southwick and the other two began folding up their pieces of tarpaulin and glanced up to see that the great hull of the *Salvador del Mundo* was alongside them like a cliff face. Jackson was bringing the cutter alongside an elaborate entryport at which a sentry with a musket stood on guard. As two seamen hooked on with boathooks and held the boat alongside, Ramage climbed on board but before he had time to glance around him a voice in the gloom said sharply: "All boats must be secured at the boat boom." By the time the man had finished the sentence Ramage could just distinguish him: a lieutenant perfectly dressed and wearing a sword. At that moment Ramage felt a flush of temper surge through him, as though someone had opened a furnace door. Everyone, it seemed, was setting out to bait Captain Ramage, but since Captain Ramage had spent most of the last ten years serving at sea in the Mediterranean or West Indies, none of these Channel Fleet people could know him, so their malice was being led or inspired by someone else.

"Oh, I beg your pardon," Ramage said politely, turning round and ushering Hill back into the boat and following him. To Jackson, just waiting for the last of the officers to board the *Salvador del Mundo* before moving out to secure the cutter from the great boom which stuck out from the ship's side and from which boats were streamed, like horses tied to a rail outside an inn while their owners were inside having a pint of ale, Ramage said: "Carry on, Jackson, get a painter made up on the boom."

Jackson had served with Ramage too long to hesitate: seeing his captain coming back into the cutter was enough to warn him that something unusual was happening, and he snapped an order which had the seamen pushing off the cutter.

The gap between the cutter and the ship had grown to six feet when a lieutenant appeared at the entryport shouting: "Hey you! You have to come on board!"

"Ask him to whom he's shouting," Ramage said to Hill.

Hill, now a different man and realizing that even if he was under arrest, Ramage was still a post-captain – and a distinguished one – knew that lieutenants bellowing like that were asking for trouble.

But the lieutenant was a friend of Hill's, and Hill knew the reason for the behaviour, and thinking quickly he stood up and shouted back angrily: "Don't yell at me like that. There's a trial due to start in less than two hours' time. Do you expect us to swing under the boatboom like bumboatmen?"

The *Salvador*'s lieutenant stood, jaw dropped. "Come on, man!" Hill snapped. "You'll have a dozen captains alongside you within the hour – as long as you remember to hoist the court-martial flag."

"Very well then, bring your prisoner on board. But the cutter can return to its own ship."

"Most of the men on board, including those at the oars, are witnesses," Ramage murmured. "If this sort of thing goes on,

I shall have a long list of protests to make to the president of the court, with a copy sent to the commander-in-chief."

"And I wouldn't blame you, sir. Could you ask your coxswain to put us alongside again, sir? This fellow is a fool."

This time Hill was the first out of the boat, holding the scabbard of his own sword with his left hand, and with Ramage's sword tucked firmly under his left arm.

"The provost marshal upon the occasion and his prisoner, Captain Ramage," he said briskly. "Bring your men to attention!"

The Marine had already recognized Ramage and stamped to attention. The lieutenant was now examining a list with great concentration, but by now Hill had learned that Captain Ramage was usually several steps ahead of such games and beckoned Ramage to accompany him, making sure the witnesses followed.

"There's a cabin set aside for you, sir," Hill explained, "and another for the witnesses."

"I'd sooner walk round up on deck," Ramage said. "It's a glorious day and this ship interests me."

"Of course it does, sir!" Hill said. "This is the first...?"

"Yes," Ramage said and because Hill's question was unintentionally ambiguous left it at that.

When one saw the ship from a frigate, the name *Salvador del Mundo*, Saviour of the World, seemed – well, more than a little pretentious. But now, standing on the maindeck, one could see that the Spanish builders and the Spanish navy had built a ship of which they could be proud. She seemed more like a great cathedral of wood which should be standing four-square on the ground. Here in the Sound on a calm day it was hard to believe she could ever be fighting for her life in an Atlantic storm, barely able to carry a stitch of canvas and with great seas sweeping over the bow and thundering their way aft, and the planking working so that water spurted through the seams and dozens of seamen cranked the bilgepumps. Nor, standing here and knowing that the other ship must be just as impressive, did the name *Santisima Trinidada*, the Holy Trinity, seem so pretentious (or, to a Protestant ear, so blasphemous).

Curious how different countries have different styles in naming their ships. The British seemed to name ships almost at random; sometimes they used that of an old ship which had been scrapped, but if the ship was a prize they often kept the original foreign name, the rule apparently being only that seamen should be able to pronounce it.

Ramage could think of very few British ships in service which had been named by the Admiralty after a man or woman, apart from members of the Royal Family. Merchant ships and privateers were often named after their owners (or their wives). Certainly no names had any religious significance, except for prizes like the *Salvador del Mundo*. Who but the British, he thought, would have the 110-ton *Ville de Paris* as the flagship of the admiral commanding the Channel Squadron? She was not even a prize, but had been built recently in a British yard! At Chatham, in fact. Admittedly that *Ville de Paris*, which was almost as big as the *Salvador*, was named after a predecessor captured from the French, but Ramage could not imagine a French fleet sailing from Brest with the admiral's flag flying in a French-built ship called the *London*. Still, apart from a few big ships associated with places, the French seemed to have just as haphazard a way of naming ships as the British. The arrival of Bonaparte had made little difference, except that since the Revolution there was now a *Ça Ira*. The only danger of such a name was that the ship might sink in a storm, or be captured by the enemy...if the *Ça Ira* (a 112-gun ship, if he remembered rightly) was captured by the British, would Their Lordships keep the name? It would be a huge joke, although the King was said not to have a very strong sense of humour.

He suddenly realized that Hill had been deliberately walking towards the fo'c'sle, as though to lead him forward, and the familiar squawking of rope rendering through blocks, and then the flopping of cloth in the wind, made him glance up.

A hoist of three flags were now flying – the uppermost was a white flag with a blue diagonal cross on it – number two. The second, triangular and divided white and red, was the substitute, indicating that the upper flag was being repeated, so the signal so far was two two. The lower flag comprised three vertical stripes, blue, white, blue, and was number three. So the whole signal was number 223, and Ramage did not have to look it up in the signal book: *The flag officers, captains and commanders, and all other persons summoned to attend a court-martial, are to assemble on board the ship whose signal is shown after this has been answered.*

An italic note below the signal in the book said: *NB. The ship in which the court-martial is to be held, is immediately to hoist a union jack at the mizen peak.*

Ramage looked aft and saw the Union Flag being hoisted. Tiresome, he thought, that an official volume like the *Signal Book for the Ships of War* should make such an elementary mistake as calling the Union Flag a "jack" when it most certainly was *not* being used as a jack, which was a flag flown on a staff at the bow.

"The Union at the mizen peak" – seamen's jargon for a court-martial, and as well known as being "stabbed with a Bridport dagger", which was another way of saying being hanged, and a tribute to the fine hemp rope made at the town of Bridport.

"Sorry, sir," Hill said apologetically, "I was hoping you would not see or hear any of that."

Ramage grinned amiably. "I wouldn't have missed it for anything," he said. "Just think, a dozen post-captains are now blessing or cursing me because for today, and perhaps several more days, they're going to have to attend my trial, and either be kept away from very important work or escape something very boring. It's not every day that a very junior post-captain gets court-martialled, you know."

"I suppose not, sir," Hill said cautiously, uncertain whether Ramage was serious or not. This fellow, he decided, had the damnedest sense of humour and the most uncertain temper of anyone he had ever met. Captain Ramage could say something with an absolutely straight face and have a hundred men jumping to attention while another hundred, who knew him better, would be roaring with laughter. It was all very odd, though it kept you on your toes – in case you got your foot stamped on! He giggled at his own joke and Ramage glanced round.

"Sorry, sir," Hill said apologetically, "I was just thinking of something."

"You must have a thin time of it if you giggle every time you think," Ramage said with a straight face. "That's the first time I've heard you giggle."

At that moment Hill decided he would pull every string within his reach to serve in the *Calypso*. Providing, of course, there was an acquittal verdict…

CHAPTER FIFTEEN

Ramage recalled his allusion to a wooden cathedral when he followed Hill into the great cabin, which ran the width of the ship. It was more than fifty feet from one side to the other, and the whole after end – or so it seemed because the sun now shining through was dazzling – comprised sternlights: windows that if the ground glass was coloured and set in leaded shapes, would in size be more suitable for a cathedral.

He was walking on canvas painted in large black and white squares which covered the cabin sole like an enormous carpet (and reminded him of the mosaic floors in some Italian cathedrals). For a moment he felt he should be jinking from one square to another in a particular chess move – two ahead and one to the right or left, in the knight's move, or else he would startle everyone by walking diagonally, announcing he was a bishop. In fact, he told himself grimly, he was a pawn…

Apart from a Marine sentry at the door, a couple of seamen arranging chairs round a long table, and a couple more giving the top a final polish, with another man perfunctorily cleaning some panes of glass in the sternlights, occasionally using a little energy on a fly speck, the *Salvador*'s great cabin was as peaceful as the nave of St Paul's between services.

The long mahogany table, big enough to seat a couple of dozen for dinner, was set athwartships, so that those captains sitting along one side would have their backs to the sternlights and face into the darker cabin, while the other half would look at the sternlights.

The chair at one end of the table had arms, so that must be the head, while the chair at the other end was straight-backed and armless. There were more chairs down the sides, and in front of each place was a pad of paper, inkwell, quill and sandbox.

As Ramage faced the sternlights with the table in front of him, there were a couple of rows of chairs behind him in the darker part of the cabin with two rows of forms behind them.

Hill coughed to attract his attention. He pointed to two other chairs, placed at an angle to the table in a position so that anyone sitting at the head of the table (it would be the president of the court) had only to look half-left to see and talk. "We sit there, sir. You nearest to the president and me behind."

"So that you can spit me with your sword if I make a bolt for it."

Hill had learnt enough by now to answer gravely: "Exactly, sir. Pistols make such a noise."

At that moment the door was flung open and a fussy-looking little man wearing tiny spectacles and (almost startling, these days) a short wig bustled into the cabin, followed first by a thin and lugubrious seaman carrying an arm full of books, and by a boy laden with a large pewter inkwell, a bunch of quills, and some large pads of paper.

"Ah, Mr Hill and the prisoner, eh?"

"Don't introduce me," Ramage murmured, guessing the man, looking like a startled hedgehog, must be the deputy judge advocate. No one had yet decided where deputy judge advocates fitted into the naval hierarchy but in Ramage's experience so far they knew little of law and always wrote very slowly, making them little more than clerks.

The little man sat at the chair at the end of the table and looked up at the seaman, now standing beside him. "Ah yes, the Holy Evangelist – I want that right in front of me." He reached up and took it. "Now, the Crucifix, for those of the Catholic faith: that goes there. The books – in two piles here, with the titles facing me."

He dismissed the seaman and turned to the boy. "Now be careful of that ink. Place it there – " he pointed to a precise spot. "Now the quills – examine each one to make sure it is sharp. You have a pen-knife?"

When the boy looked sulky he was told sharply: "You forgot it last time!"

"Will this be a long trial?" the little lawyer suddenly asked Ramage.

Ramage glanced at the pile of books, the inkwell and the quills, and deliberately misunderstood the purpose of the question.

"Ah yes, you are paid by the day. Well, I'll spin it out as long as I can, and you can dawdle as you write down the evidence. And always read the minutes in a slow and deliberate voice. But come now, you must know all the tricks!"

The boy sniggered but hurried out when the red-faced lawyer pointed to the door.

"I asked you a perfectly civil question, Captain," the lawyer said crossly.

"And I gave you a perfectly civil answer," Ramage said.

At that moment three captains came into the cabin, nodded to the three men, and stood near the rows of chairs. Each man had a small roll of parchment in his hand, and as they continued their conversation several more captains came in and joined them.

Ramage said to Hill: "It's time we went outside and waited – the court convenes in five minutes."

Hill led the way out of the cabin and went on to a small cabin which was probably used originally by the Spanish admiral's secretary – it was still pleasantly painted in pale blue and white, with a built-in table at one end which served as a desk.

"Damn," Hill exclaimed unexpectedly, "I forgot to tell the Marine sentry where to find us."

Ramage had just looked at his watch and noted that the court should have assembled fifteen minutes earlier when the sentry knocked on the door. "The admiral is just coming on board, sir."

Hill looked at Ramage and said: "I suppose the provost marshal isn't allowed to say anything, but George Hill would like to wish you the best, sir. The more I think about this trial, the less I understand what it's all about."

Ramage smiled and nodded. "Thank you. And if you are puzzled now, remember to pinch yourself halfway through!"

Hill opened the door and led the way back to a point where he could just see the big door into the great cabin and the Marine sentry outside it. "We can see the admiral when he goes in, sir: there's no need for you to be waiting outside."

Waiting outside and a target for any unpleasantness Goddard wanted to hand out in passing: this young man Hill was thoughtful…and in addition to the extra four shillings a day he would receive for acting as provost marshal, he was learning a lot about both people and the Navy.

The sentry (Ramage realized that Hill must have given him instructions) waved to Hill, who asked Ramage to follow him. "They've just ordered the prisoner to be brought in, sir," the sentry said.

Hill looked round at Ramage and inspected him. "Excuse me, sir," he said and gave Ramage's stock a gentle tug. He removed a tiny piece of fluff from the shoulder and then, adjusting his own sword and making sure that Ramage's sword was tucked firmly under his left arm, murmured: "If you'll follow me, sir…"

The great cabin was full of men: six post-captains sat along one side of the table and six more the other, their backs to the sternlights. The fussy and bewigged deputy judge advocate sat at one end while Goddard sat at the other. Crouched, Ramage corrected himself: the fat, grey-faced man was hunched in the chair, holding the arms and looking like an aged toad preparing to leap. Except that now he was staring down at a pile of papers in front of him, deliberately ignoring Ramage's arrival. But all dozen members of the court were watching: the six facing the sternlights were twisted round on their chairs. Ramage did not recognize a single face. Every one of them wore epaulettes on both shoulders, indicating more than three years' seniority. Ramage realized that he was the only post-captain in the cabin wearing a single epaulette, on the right shoulder.

The rows of chairs and forms were filled with people – spectators and witnesses. He caught a glimpse of Yorke and wondered why he was sitting on a form, and he was just trying to think why Alexis was not with him when he saw her sitting on a chair in the front row, apparently on her own, the only woman in the cabin.

"The prisoner should be seated," the deputy judge advocate said pompously, pointing to a chair, but Hill ignored him. Walking up to Goddard and placing Ramage's sword on the table in front of him, he reported quietly: "The prisoner is delivered to the court, sir."

Goddard growled an acknowledgement and said brusquely to the deputy judge advocate: "Carry on, Mr Jenkins."

Ramage sat down and crossed his legs. Yes, there was Captain William Shirley, sitting in a chair close to Jenkins. He had been bent over earlier, adjusting his shoe, and Ramage had missed seeing him.

Jenkins' face was shiny and he looked harassed. Already he would have been busy, first checking the seniority of the captains by examining their commissions, and seating them so that the most senior were nearer to the president and the two men at Jenkins' own end were the most junior.

Now he searched through the papers in front of him, found a particular one and, tilting it slightly towards the sternlights, began by reading the letter from the Lords Commissioners of the Admiralty, a copy of which Ramage had already received, ordering the trial following the request by Captain Shirley.

Putting that page to one side, Jenkins searched for another, scattering the bunch of quills as he shuffled through several sheets. Finally he began reading, in an even more lugubrious voice, the commander-in-chief's warrant appointing him the deputy judge advocate for the trial of Captain the Lord Ramage. As he finished he stood looking round the court as though anticipating applause, and Goddard snapped: "Well, get on with it, man!"

Ramage, glancing at the row of spectators and witnesses, caught Alexis' eye and at the same time realized that all the officers in the cabin were glancing at her surreptitiously: she was dressed elegantly in a long dress of dark olive-green with a matching hat obviously inspired by the military shako. Her long-handled parasol was a lighter green – and it was looking at it that made Ramage realize that the hat was a slightly lighter colour too. And although he had not really noticed it on board the *Emerald* or the *Calypso*, but it made a contrast with the pinks and whites here, she was very suntanned: unfashionably so, he could hear the admirals' wives saying disapprovingly: that was why one carried a parasol. But these scrawny old harpies never went to sea, or if they did they never came up on deck. They had never learned that one could sit under an awning and never for a moment be in the sun, but after a few days would have a tan: the sun reflecting up unnoticed from the sea was almost as merciless as the direct rays.

Then Ramage realized why Alexis was sitting in the front row and on the larboard side while her brother sat on a form on the other side. Goddard had met Sidney years ago in Jamaica and might well remember him (probably would, since it was not a pleasant meeting for Goddard), but he had never before seen Alexis and could never guess they were brother and sister. Had Sidney thought up some trick? Ramage decided that was impossible: their evidence could be only about what they had seen. No, Sidney had probably decided there was no need for them to be associated on the off-chance that – well, Ramage could not think, but he found her nearness curiously comforting.

Now Jenkins was getting ready to administer the oath to each of the captains sitting at the table, and the president. He started with Goddard, who stood up, put his hand on the Bible held out by Jenkins, and read from a card which the deputy judge advocate held discreetly to one side: "I, Jebediah Goddard, do hereby swear that I will duly administer justice, according to the Articles and Orders established by an Act passed in the twenty-second year of the reign of His Majesty, King George III, for amending, explaining and reducing into one Act of Parliament, the laws relating to the Government of His Majesty's ships, vessels and forces by sea, without partiality, favour or affection; and if any case shall arise which is not particularly mentioned in the said Articles and orders, I will duly administer justice according to my conscience, the best of my understanding, and the custom of the Navy in like cases; and I do further swear that I will not upon any account, at any time whatsoever, disclose or discover the vote or opinion of any particular member of this court martial unless required by Act of Parliament, so help me God!"

Goddard had ended with his voice ringing through the cabin in what he assumed was an assured and righteous tone, and again Alexis caught Ramage's eye and by an almost imperceptible lifting of her eyebrows asked: "Do we have to listen to that another twelve times?"

An equally almost imperceptible nod of his head assured her and, as if that was the signal, Jenkins turned to the captain on Goddard's right, the most senior.

Holding out the Bible for him to rest his hand on, Jenkins showed the card and the captain, giving his name as John Swinford, repeated the oath. A stocky but lean-faced man, blue-eyed and speaking in a clear but not fussily precise voice, Swinford seemed shrewd – but he was at the right hand of a man who could do him harm by telling tales to the commander-in-chief although that was true for all the captains, Ramage reminded himself.

Jenkins was about to move round to take the next most senior captain, sitting on Goddard's left, when the rear-admiral said: "Carry on down that side of the table – I'm sure that God doesn't recognize the seniority in the Navy List."

Several of the captains gave appreciative smiles but Ramage sensed that had Goddard been a popular man there would have been outright laughs where now there were almost wary grins.

As Jenkins went on to the next captain, James Royce, Ramage sat back and watched Captain Shirley. The man was sitting perfectly still. On the deck under his chair he had several books, one of which Ramage recognized as being the master's log and another, from its shape and size, a captain's journal. He held a pile of several papers on his lap and two or three of them had seals.

What was curious, Ramage thought, was the fact that the man remained absolutely motionless: he did not move his head to follow Jenkins' progress round the table with the Bible, he did not glance at Goddard, and the cabin might well have been empty instead of crowded with witnesses and spectators. He never glanced at Alexis; he did not appear to see the knot of officers whom Ramage recognized as from the *Jason*. In fact Shirley did not seem to be in any way connected to the present proceedings. It was as though they were all in the front seats in church, but a man sat alone in a pew at the back, ignoring the preacher and never joining in the responses, and completely oblivious of the stirring notes of the organ.

Remote. That word alone described Shirley, and Ramage realized that when he had seen him on board the *Jason* the man was probably not ignoring what went on round him, he was just detached from it. Most men with papers in their lap shuffled through them at tedious times like these, when Jenkins or one of the captains droned on, going through their own part of the trial ritual. Any other man might look down at the pile of books to reassure himself that he had not forgotten one. But not Shirley. Remote, yes but, Ramage now realized, the remoteness of carved marble or – he could picture one without effort – a scavenging bird waiting on a tree stump.

Jenkins finally administered the oath to the last captain, sitting on Goddard's left, and this brought him into position for the last part of the trial ritual. Goddard stood up and said to the deputy judge advocate: "Give me the Holy Evangelist – now, with your hand on it, make your oath."

Jenkins took a deep breath and with a sanctimonious expression on his face intoned: "I, Hubert Jenkins, do swear that I will not, upon any account, at any time whatsoever, disclose or discover the vote or opinion of any particular member of this court-martial, unless thereunto required by Act of Parliament, so help me God."

Taking the Bible from Goddard, Jenkins strode back to his chair with all the self-importance of a bishop's wife. He shuffled through his papers again and, still standing, announced: "It is now my duty to read the letter of accusation against the prisoner."

He gave the paper a brisk shake, as though removing an unsightly crease. "The letter is addressed to the commander-in-chief at Plymouth and is dated on board His Majesty's frigate the *Jason* at sea. It begins: 'Sir, I beg leave to acquaint you that this day, Captain Nicholas Ramage, the commanding officer of His Majesty's ship *Calypso*, frigate, did board my ship with a party of his men and did remove me from command, putting in my place one of his own lieutenants, in breach of the spirit of the Articles of War. I request that you will be pleased to apply to the Right Honourable the Lords Commissioners of the Admiralty for a Court-martial to be held upon the said Captain Nicholas Ramage for the said offence, I am, etcetera and etcetera, William Shirley.' "

Jenkins then sat down with the smug look of a man who considered the important part of his task had been done. The captains had been assembled and ranged round the table in order of seniority; they had all taken the oath; and (unknown to Ramage) because this was now regarded as an important trial, Jenkins had taken affidavits from the witnesses who would be supporting the charges against Captain Ramage and, in accordance with the regulations, had given copies to the commander-in-chief and to Rear-Admiral Goddard as president of the court-martial, "but no other members of the court". The court-martial statutes, as Jenkins knew well enough, made no provisions for copies to be given to the accused. For the time being the affidavits, like grenades, waited in the pile of papers in front of him for the appropriate moment for them to be lobbed into the proceedings.

Goddard looked round the cabin and said abruptly: "All witnesses are to withdraw, except for the first witness in support of the charge."

The scraping of chairs and forms made Ramage realize that several of the men who had been sitting on the chairs and forms and who he had assumed were merely spectators were in fact Shirley's witnesses. He guessed there were two or three dozen, perhaps more. Ramage saw Southwick, Aitken, Bowen, Wagstaffe, the other junior officers and Jackson with three more seamen heading for the door, followed by Sidney Yorke. Ramage was suddenly conscious of a curious hush in the cabin and glanced round to see that Goddard and most of the captains at the table were watching Alexis. If she remained seated, she was simply a spectator, perhaps the wife or daughter of some important person that no one knew; if she left the cabin she must be a witness.

Although she knew none of this, Alexis unwittingly added to the tension. Anxious not to be associated with her brother and wanting to avoid getting caught up in the crowd of men at the door, she waited until the last moment, and then slowly stood up and walked out of the cabin, every man's eyes on her. She knew it and enjoyed it, but had only one of those men been watching, the man sitting in the chair with the provost marshal behind him and the only captain not wearing a sword, she would have walked with the same elegance.

As the Marine sentry now standing guard just inside the cabin shut the door and then stood to attention, Goddard looked across at Shirley (for the first time, Ramage realized) and asked: "Your first witness is ready?"

Shirley slowly stood up. "Yes, indeed, sir."

"Call him, then," Goddard said, already showing signs of impatience.

Shirley beckoned the lieutenant sitting at the end of the front row of chairs who walked across the cabin uncertainly, as though treading on ice. Shirley pointed to a spot a yard or so from Jenkins' chair, where the deputy judge advocate was already waiting with the Bible and a piece of card.

"Put your right hand on the Holy Evangelist and recite this oath." He held up the card and the lieutenant, every movement uncertain and his brow shiny with perspiration, read in a monotone and at great speed: "The evidence I shall give before this court respecting the charge against the prisoner shall be the truth, the whole truth and nothing but the truth, so help me God."

Jenkins sat down, dipped a quill in the inkwell, and glared up at the lieutenant. "Your name, rank and ship – and," he admonished before the man had time to say a word, "speak slowly: I have to write down everything you say. And that," he added, looking at Shirley and then Ramage, "goes for the interrogatories, too."

The lieutenant was silenced by Jenkins' manner, mistaking the deputy judge advocate's fussy briskness for hostility.

Jenkins turned to Shirley: "Sir, will you instruct this officer to tell us who he is?"

"Ridley, sir," the man said, "Jasper Ridley, first lieutenant of the *Jason* frigate."

Jenkins' pen squeaked as he wrote, repeating each word after the lieutenant. Finally he stopped and looked up at Goddard.

Ramage saw that Shirley was now holding a handful of slips of paper, the first of which he handed to Jenkins, who read it. Shirley, as prosecutor, had adopted a method which helped the deputy judge advocate and speeded up the proceedings. Jenkins had to record all the evidence – the questions asked and the answers given. If the prosecutor, for instance, had his questions written down on separate slips of paper, Jenkins had only to number each one, writing the number in the minutes and the answer given. Later, after the day's evidence when he was preparing the final copy of the minutes from his rough draft, he could write the questions out in full in place of the numbers.

As president, Goddard started the proceedings with what was the usual first question: "Tell the court all you know about the charge against the prisoner."

As the man stood, apparently struck dumb, Ramage remembered questioning him on board the *Jason*, where he and the rest of the ship's officers were being held prisoner by Shirley, a Marine guard at the door.

"Come on, come on!" Goddard exclaimed.

"I don't know where to begin, sir."

"Begin when the ship left Barbados."

"Very well, sir. We left Barbados bound, as I understood it from the captain, for Spithead. After two or three days we sighted a sail on our larboard bow. The lookouts reported that she had hauled her wind and was beating up towards us. I understand the captain gave the order to bear away and run down towards her. Soon after this, various other sail were sighted and it seemed the ship might be a frigate escorting a convoy to England. We knew one had sailed recently from Barbados."

"What happened then?" Goddard asked.

"I understand we hoisted the challenge and also our pendant numbers."

While Jenkins' pen scratched away, Ramage pencilled in some single-word queries on a pad he now had in his lap and, realizing that both Shirley and Goddard were watching him, made sure that he wrote a minute or two after Ridley had spoken the phrase he wanted to question him about later.

"Carry on, then," Goddard said.

"Well, the two ships approached but – well, I understand that because the *Calypso* had not answered the challenge and was French-built, Captain Shirley was about to give the order to beat to quarters when the *Calypso* suddenly wore round and came alongside us, throwing out boarding grapnels and securing herself alongside. Boarding parties came over and Captain Ramage took command of the ship."

"Did anyone on board the *Jason* try to repel the boarders or open fire?" Goddard asked.

"We had no reason to expect an attack, sir," Ridley said in a monotone. "We expected the usual visit from the captain of the *Calypso*, or his first lieutenant."

"So the officers and men of the *Jason* offered no resistance to the *Calypso*'s attack?"

Ramage thought for a moment whether to protest at the word "attack" but decided not to start an argument with Goddard over words which would probably end up simply antagonizing the other members of the court.

"No resistance at all, that I know of, sir."

"Where was Captain Ramage?"

"He was leading the first boarding party, I believe: then Captain Shirley spoke to him on the quarterdeck and they went down to the cabin."

"Where was the officer waiting that Captain Ramage put in command?"

Ramage stared at Goddard. The whole object of the trial was to decide whether or not Captain Ramage had superseded Shirley and put one of his own officers "in command": it was up to the court to decide whether or not he did after hearing the evidence for the prosecution and the defence. But here was Goddard, the president of the court (supposed not only to be neutral but the guardian of the court's neutrality), asking the whereabouts of the officer the prisoner "put in command".

Goddard glanced at him, obviously expecting an objection, but Ramage kept silent: he guessed Goddard was trying to provoke him, but he knew a full broadside was always more effective than the same number of guns fired singly.

"I don't know," Ridley said. "I wasn't on deck at the time."

Ramage made another note.

"You have some questions?" Goddard asked Shirley.

"I have, sir, and the deputy judge advocate already has the first, so if you will give permission…"

Goddard nodded and Jenkins read from the slip of paper. "When was the first time you knew that Captain Ramage had removed Captain Shirley from command of the ship?"

"He came down to my cabin with some of his officers and so informed me."

Shirley handed across another sheet of paper, and Jenkins read: "What reason did he give for such an action?"

"He claimed that the *Jason* had fired on his ship."

"Had she?" Goddard asked, obviously not wanting to lose the drama of the moment, which had provoked the captains round the table into sudden movement: some turned to look at Ramage, others were now watching Shirley.

"No, sir," Ridley said in a voice hardly above a whisper.

The captain on Goddard's right leaned over and whispered something. The admiral nodded and said: "Captain Swinford has a question to ask."

"What can possibly have led Captain Ramage to say such a thing to you?"

"I do not know, sir," Ridley said woodenly, and then looked back at Jenkins as he read from another of Shirley's slips of paper.

"Did the prisoner make any other allegations against Captain Shirley?"

"Yes, sir," Ridley took out a handkerchief and mopped his face, and Ramage noted he was the only man in the room who was perspiring at all. "Yes, sir: he asked me if I thought that Captain Shirley was mad."

"What was your answer?"

"Well, first I protested that it was a very improper question for someone of Captain Ramage's position to ask, and gave it as my opinion that Captain Shirley was not mad."

That answer clearly did not satisfy Goddard. "In your view, as a naval officer and first lieutenant of the *Jason* frigate, was there any circumstance which could lead Captain Ramage suddenly to ask you such an extraordinary question?"

Ridley shook his head. "No, none sir."

Ridley's whole attitude, Ramage felt, was that he wanted to run away: not because he was frightened of the court or overawed by being called as a witness. Rather – and that was it, he realized with a shock but was unable to think of the explanation – that Ridley was being blackmailed, and the questions Goddard was asking were coming close to the subject about which he was being blackmailed and about which he dare not talk.

Jenkins was holding another piece of paper and, when Goddard nodded, began reading: "Lieutenant Wagstaffe, the officer whom Captain Ramage left in command – " Jenkins paused for a moment, as if anticipating a protest from Ramage, who decided to continue his policy of making none at this stage, " – gave certain orders after Captain Ramage returned on board his own ship. What were they?"

"I understand they were to do with the *Jason*'s course and her future position in relation to the *Calypso*."

"Can't you be more specific?" grumbled Goddard.

"No, sir, I wasn't present at the conversations."

Jenkins received another slip of paper from Shirley. "What did the *Jason* do from then on until she arrived in the Channel?"

"She helped escort the West India convoy."

Obviously Goddard expected more. " 'Helped escort'? What did the ship *do*? Did Captain Ramage make signals, send messages over?"

"I understand the *Jason*'s orders – which meant, I suppose, the orders given to Lieutenant Wagstaffe – were to keep a cable to leeward of the *Calypso* and this was generally astern of the convoy."

"Captain Ramage did not send you off investigating strange sail, or anything like that?" Goddard inquired.

"Not to my knowledge, sir."

"He made no signals to the *Jason* and gave no orders?" Goddard asked incredulously.

"I believe that on several occasions we were sent to chase merchant ships back into position, although by and large they kept pretty much in position."

"Did this Lieutenant Wagstaffe have much to do with the running of the ship?" Goddard asked.

"To the best of my knowledge he took no part in the day-to-day running of the ship, sir: he was almost entirely concerned with keeping the ship in position."

Captain Swinford, after whispering to Goddard and apparently getting his approval, asked: "Did this lieutenant give any orders to Captain Shirley, or attempt to – er, usurp, Captain Shirley's position?"

Ramage leaned forward slightly. This could be one of the key questions in the trial, but Ridley still had that blackmailed look. Blackmailed? He could also be a timid husband nagged by an overbearing wife – or even a lieutenant, serving a port admiral, who was terrified of the admiral's wife. In fact, much of the time Ridley's face was a happy hunting ground for most of the timid expressions available to man.

"Not to my knowledge, sir. As far as I know," he said with a rush verging on garrulity, "he did not stand a watch, but he was on deck much of the time, and the only orders he gave were those that an officer of the deck would normally give to keep the ship in position."

Without asking Goddard's approval, Captain Swinford then asked: "During all this time, from the *Jason* meeting the *Calypso* until the convoy arrived in the Channel, was Captain Shirley prevented in any way from doing whatever he wanted?"

"I did not see any restraint being applied, sir," Ridley said cautiously. "He was on deck whenever he wanted to be."

The captain sitting next to Swinford – Ramage thought he had given his name as Royce – suddenly asked without reference to Admiral Goddard: "What in your opinion would have happened if Captain Shirley had ordered a couple of his officers to seize this Lieutenant Wagstaffe, and then sailed the ship away from the convoy?"

"There were never any – "

Ridley had no chance to finish his sentence because Goddard said harshly: "That question is disallowed. The opinion of a lieutenant upon what a senior post-captain might or might not have done in a hypothetical situation does not concern this court."

"But what the first lieutenant of a ship considers his captain might or might not have been able to do most certainly is, sir," Royce protested. "The witness has just said Captain Shirley was free to move about the ship."

"And I have just disallowed the question," Goddard said abruptly. "Next question, Mr Jenkins."

Jenkins had been writing quickly and took the opportunity of changing pens, carefully wiping the tip of the old quill with a cloth before putting it down so that ink should not stain the polished mahogany table. Trained by his wife, Ramage thought.

Jenkins licked the tip of the new quill so that the ink would flow freely, dipped into the inkwell and then looked inquiringly at Shirley, who shook his head. "I've no more questions to ask this witness."

"You may sit down over there," Jenkins said, "but listen carefully while I read back the questions and your answers: you will then be required to sign the minutes as a correct record."

As the deputy judge advocate read his minutes in a listless monotone, Ramage listened carefully and checked the evidence against the very brief notes he had made. There was no doubt that even when another man spoke his replies, Ridley sounded just like the man being blackmailed, but although Ramage could not escape the feeling he still could not account for it. Tone of voice, actual words, look on his face, stance…an impression which had been conceived in Ridley's cabin on board the *Jason* but was only just born? It was like trying to remember all the details of a dream: the complete story was ephemeral, but now and then brief episodes came to mind: not enough to give any cohesion; just enough to tantalize.

Ridley walked back to the table and Ramage realized that Jenkins had stopped reading and Ridley was now signing his name. He was just turning away again when Goddard snapped: "Stay there in case the prisoner has any questions."

Jenkins had made his first mistake in forgetting Ramage's right to question the witness.

Ramage stood up. "I have had no opportunity to write down my questions – "

"Very well, but speak slowly," Goddard said.

"Mr Ridley, in your evidence, the minutes of which you have just signed, you use the word 'I understood' very frequently. Is this just a habit of speech or were you not present at the events you describe?"

"What events have you in mind, sir?" Ridley asked carefully.

"When you refer to the *Calypso* coming alongside, for instance, you use the phrase 'I understand'. I would have thought that if the ship of which you are the first lieutenant (and thus the second-in-command) was being boarded by another frigate, however unexpectedly, then you would be on deck."

"I was not on deck at the time," Ridley said woodenly. As though, Ramage decided, he was repeating something by rote.

"Why were you not on deck?"

"I had other duties."

And, thought Ramage, there is no point in questioning you further about that. "Mr Ridley, you said early in your evidence that you understood the *Calypso* did not answer the challenge. Who told the seamen in the *Jason* what the challenge for the day was, and checked that they had bent the correct flags on to the halyards?"

"I assume the captain, because he had the copy of the private signals giving the challenge for the day."

"And Captain Shirley would have checked the flags?"

Before Ridley could reply, Goddard interrupted. "Mr Ramage, the question of the challenge for the day and who bent flags on to halyards has nothing to do with the charges you are facing, so please go on to your next questions or allow the witness to stand down."

Here we go, Ramage told himself. As far as Goddard is concerned, nothing helpful to the prisoner is going to be allowed. The question of the challenge has been disallowed – yet it is of vital importance leading directly to the next question. Very well...

"Mr Ridley, why was the *Jason* flying the wrong challenge for that day?"

"I did not see – "

"Mr Ramage, I have just disallowed any further questions about the challenge."

Ramage bowed ironically: Goddard's face was growing redder; his jowls beginning to quiver. Another half a dozen questions, Ramage estimated, and he would be unable to control his temper and then, with some luck, at least a few of the captains will have been insulted and start feeling sympathetic towards the prisoner...

"With respect, sir," Ramage said politely, "my next question is of considerable importance but the beginning must refer to the challenge."

"Ask it and I will decide whether or not to allow it."

Ramage looked squarely at Ridley, whose eyes dropped. "The question is: You say that the *Calypso* did not answer the challenge and she was recognized as French-built. Why did not the *Jason* beat to quarters on the approach of what might be a hostile ship?"

"Disallowed," Goddard said firmly. "Has nothing to do with the charges. Don't answer," he told Ridley.

Captain Swinford leaned over and whispered something to the rear-admiral, but Goddard shook his head vigorously.

Damnation, Ramage thought: as far as these dozen captains are concerned, there is the *Jason*, sailing along quite peacefully, and along comes the nasty *Calypso*. How does one explain to the court that in fact the innocent *Jason* was flying the wrong challenge, had all her guns loaded, and was steering down to attempt to ram and certainly rake one of the King's ships?

Very well, try surprise: even if Goddard rules the question out of order, a seed of doubt will be planted in the heads of the members of the court – damnation, it should be hammered home!

"Mr Ridley," Ramage said politely, "I want you just to cast your mind back: where were you when Captain Shirley ordered his men to fire a broadside into the *Calypso*?"

"Don't answer – question disallowed – has nothing to do with the charges!" Goddard shouted, his voice rising in a crescendo.

Ramage decided to fire another barrel before Goddard recovered. "Sir, since that broadside was the reason that – "

"Silence! Strike that from the record! No, I mean don't note that down, Jenkins. Now look, Ramage, any more questions like that and you will be in contempt of court."

"Very well, sir," Ramage said contritely, "I thought that as I stand charged with removing Captain Shirley from his command, that my reasons for doing so would be – "

"Ramage!" Goddard shouted. "You know what the charges are and unless you limit your questions to the circumstances of the charges you will be in contempt of court. Do you understand?"

"Yes, sir, I do *now*," Ramage said politely, and turned to Ridley.

"The lieutenant that I left on board, Mr Wagstaffe. Was he – in your opinion – a competent officer?"

"I understand so."

"Don't you know from your own observations?"

Ridley paused for a full minute, during which time Ramage reminded him he was on oath, and then said, reluctantly it seemed to Ramage: "Yes, I do; he was a competent officer."

"Did you see him giving any orders to Captain Shirley, or disobeying any orders that Captain Shirley gave him?"

Ramage glanced at Shirley. The man had moved; he had swung his head round to stare at Ridley. Was that anxiety, even fear, in his eyes: fear that Ridley might fall into the trap set by Ramage?

"I did not see him give any orders, but I was rarely on deck. I understand Captain Shirley gave him no orders."

Ramage saw from the expression on Shirley's face that the questions had been anticipated. Ridley's slow answers were due to the wretched man trying to remember what he had been told to say.

"I have no more questions to ask this witness, sir," Ramage said. Once Ridley again signed the minutes, Goddard waved him away and told Shirley to call his next witness.

CHAPTER SIXTEEN

The next witness was the *Jason*'s second lieutenant, and Shirley asked him the same questions that he had asked Ridley, and received the same replies. To Ramage it seemed that the lieutenant, an older man than Ridley, was merely repeating answers which he had learned; as though a tutor had carefully drilled a boy in anticipation of questioning by the father. And he too had the same manner as Ridley, as though he was being blackmailed. Because it *must* be blackmail and not bribery. These men were frightened: they did not have the confident look of men who had been bribed, either with promises of promotion or sums of money.

The next two witnesses were the *Jason*'s third and fourth lieutenants, and as Shirley started asking them the same questions again, Ramage saw Captain Swinford whisper another question to Goddard, who once again shook his head.

Captain Shirley's fifth witness was the one that Ramage was dreading, not because of any damage he might do to the defence but because Ramage did not want him involved.

"Call Lieutenant Wagstaffe," Shirley said, and for a moment his eyes flickered across the few feet to where Ramage was sitting. Was there a look of triumph in them? Or just the flat look of a madman playing some elaborate game of which only he knew the rules? Obviously Shirley would call Wagstaffe as a prosecution witness, and Ramage had made it very clear to Wagstaffe that he was to answer the questions completely and openly, whether or not he thought they might hurt Ramage's case. When Wagstaffe had protested, asking to be given some latitude, Ramage had told him: "We have nothing to hide. I put you on board the *Jason* because I thought Shirley was mad, and that's all there is to it."

But since Ramage had spoken to Wagstaffe, Rear-Admiral Goddard was so juggling the evidence by restricting the questions, that Ramage was now sure he was not going to be able to make a proper defence. Goddard (and perhaps the commander-in-chief and the Admiralty) must know that Shirley was mad, but apart from Goddard getting his own back on Ramage, neither the commander-in-chief nor the Admiralty would want it confirmed in open court (or even alleged in open court, let alone being confirmed by a verdict) that one of the Navy's captains was mad and had to be removed from his command not by some unknown commanding officer or flag officer of whom few had heard but by one of the country's most famous young frigate captains…

Wagstaffe took the oath and faced Goddard, assuming that the president of the court would ask the familiar question: "Tell us what you know…" but instead Jenkins started reading from one of Shirley's slips of paper.

"When did you board the *Jason*?"

"At eleven forty-three in the forenoon of July the twenty-first last," Wagstaffe said.

"What were the circumstances?"

"The *Jason* had nearly rammed – "

"Silence!" Goddard bellowed. "Confine yourself to the questions you are asked and to the substance of the charges against the prisoner."

"I am on oath, sir Wagstaffe waited until he was sure that Jenkins had written that down and then continued: "…and I shall not perjure myself, either by wrong statements or by omissions, sir."

"Nobody is suggesting you perjure yourself," Goddard said huffily, startled by Wagstaffe's statement and realizing the significance of his use of the word "omissions". "Just confine yourself to the questions and the charges," Goddard said,

Jenkins read: "Having boarded the *Jason* with Captain Ramage and various other people, what did you do?"

"I had a severe coughing fit," Wagstaffe said innocently, and before Goddard realized what was coming next added: "There was still a lot of smoke about from the broadside the *Jason* had just fired."

"Strike that from the record," Goddard shouted. "You have been warned once," he told Wagstaffe. "The next time you will be confined for contempt of court."

"Yes, sir," Wagstaffe said contritely, and added quietly: "May I be excused now, sir?"

Goddard, obviously wanting to make some amends for the shouting, had been looking amiably in Wagstaffe's direction, but now he looked first startled and then wary.

"The prosecutor – Captain Shirley – has more questions to ask you. And the defence, too," he added hurriedly. "Why are you asking to be excused?"

"Because, Sir, the court is trying to force me to commit perjury, and if I do that I shall myself be liable to be tried by court-martial."

Very neatly done, Ramage thought. Wagstaffe had not said a word earlier about how he would try to trap Goddard. Well, Ramage's only regret was that none of his other witnesses could see Goddard's face: the glowing red of a few minutes ago was replaced now with a whiteness verging on grey, and the flesh of his face, never taut at the best of times, now hung slack like a spaniel bitch's teats. He was having a whispered conversation with Swinford on his right, and then he turned to Captain Huggins on his left. Then he looked down the table at Jenkins.

"The witness is accusing the court of forcing him to commit perjury. What are the precedents for that, Mr Jenkins, eh? Let's have the precedents for *that*!"

Jenkins carefully wiped the tip of his pen and put it down on the table. Then he clasped his hands together, as though in prayer, and said carefully: "Sir, I have looked back over my minutes, and it seems that is not *quite* what the witness said."

"What the devil was he saying, then? I'm damned sure I heard him say the court was forcing him to commit perjury."

"His actual words – " Jenkins lifted the top sheet of his minutes and read down until he found the exact line, " – after asking to be excused, were (in answer to your question): 'Because, sir, the court is trying to force me to commit perjury if I – ' "

"There you are!" Goddard exclaimed triumphantly. "I was right. 'Force me to commit perjury.' "

Captain Swinford said mildly: "The phrase is that the court is *trying* to force him to commit perjury, sir."

"What the devil's the difference? Damned insolent young puppy! I'm – "

Jenkins interposed smoothly: "Sir, legally there – "

"Clear the court!" Goddard suddenly shouted. "Clear the court, I say!"

This brought Jenkins to his feet. "Sir, if you clear the court this lieutenant whose protest we are considering will have to leave the court, along with the prisoner and the prosecutor. If I may offer an opinion sir, I think it would be most unwise, most unwise." He shook his head as though more words could no longer help him.

Goddard sat silent for a full minute, staring at Wagstaffe with an expression about which Ramage was not sure if it revealed hatred or sheer disbelief.

"All right, the court will remain in session," he said finally. "The witness can be assured the court is not trying to force him to commit perjury. This court," he added, an unctuous note in his voice, "is concerned only with discovering the truth, without fear or favour."

Wagstaffe gave a slight bow and said politely: "Thank you, sir, I realize that. It was simply that when I described how the smoke of the *Jason*'s broadside made me cough, you – "

"Wagstaffe, you are under arrest! Jenkins, strike out his remarks! Send for the Marine officer!" Goddard started mopping his face with a large silk handkerchief, and Ramage remembered how, in the tropical heat of a trial in Jamaica, Goddard had a lieutenant sitting close and handing him fresh handkerchiefs from time to time.

Now Captain Shirley was standing up. He waited for Goddard to notice him and then said: "Sir, I still have several interrogatories to put to this witness."

Goddard's jaw dropped: he stared at Shirley with the same look of betrayal and disbelief that a man might look at a hitherto loving wife who mentioned casually at the breakfast table that she had been committing adultery with Dr John Moore, the Primate of All England, on Mondays, and Dr John Douglas, the Lord Bishop of Salisbury, on Thursdays, explaining that she could not resist prelates with the Christian name John, but the bishops of Hereford, Chichester and Oxford, although all named John, had so far rebuffed her advances.

"This officer is under arrest," he said flatly, "and as soon as a Marine officer has taken him away, the court will adjourn for today and convene again tomorrow at the usual time."

Ramage watched Shirley. The man's expression did not change as he lost what was probably his best witness. Instead he sat absolutely still as the Marine sentry passed the word for his officer, who took Wagstaffe away. He must be, Ramage reflected, one of the most contented prisoners ever to be taken into custody, judging from the expression on his face. Still, Goddard would not allow much of what he had said to appear in the minutes – which, Ramage suddenly realized, Wagstaffe had not signed, so they had no legal standing. As far as this court-martial (and thus the Admiralty) were concerned, Ramage guessed, Wagstaffe had never given evidence…And Goddard had known that.

CHAPTER SEVENTEEN

Next morning the court opened in the *Salvador del Mundo's* great cabin with the precision of a quadrille: the captains filed in, all wearing full uniform with white breeches and swords, and went straight to their seats, ready to sit in descending order of seniority; Jenkins made one neat pile of his reference books and another of the paper on which he would be writing the minutes. He examined the tips of his quills and made sure his pen-knife was close by in case any needed recutting, along with the small square of cloth he used to wipe the ink.

Goddard strode in last of all, trying to infuse dignity into his carriage, but the effect was marred by the protuberant belly (which no amount of cunning by his tailor could disguise) and by the heavy jowls which jerked up and down with each step with the springiness of geraniums displayed by an itinerant flower seller.

Goddard nodded an acknowledgement rather than a greeting to the court and sat down. The captains then scraped their chairs and sat down, and Goddard told Jenkins: "Have the prisoner brought in."

A call to the Marine sentry led to Lieutenant Hill marching in carrying Ramage's sword and followed by his prisoner. While Ramage sat down, Hill replaced the sword on the table and Ramage saw Captain Shirley walking in, holding books and papers but with the remoteness of a monk pacing the cloisters.

"Ah, Captain Shirley," Goddard said, in his first pleasant word or gesture of the day. "Are you ready to call your next witness?"

Shirley nodded and said to Jenkins: "Call Lieutenant Aitken."

Like Wagstaffe, Aitken was a witness for both the prosecution and the defence. He marched in briskly, took the oath, his Scots accent very pronounced.

Ramage saw Shirley pass several slips of paper to Jenkins, and noted that the usual procedure (not that there was any regulation about it) where the president of the court did most of the questioning was, as in the case of the other witnesses, being abandoned: Goddard was going to leave the questioning to Shirley.

At a nod from Goddard, Jenkins read out the first question.

"You are the first lieutenant of the *Calypso* and you were on July the twenty-first last?"

"I am, and I was," Aitken said, adding as though making it clear to a child, "on that specific date, too."

"When the *Calypso* boarded the *Jason* on that date, what was your role?"

Aitken gave a brief chuckle, as though both Jenkins and Shirley had, by asking the question, committed some solecism. "The *Calypso* did not board the *Jason* of course, but I ken what you mean. Aye, well, when Captain Ramage laid the *Calypso* alongside despite the risk of another broadside – "

"Stop!" Goddard shouted at Aitken and, waving to Jenkins, instructed him: "Strike it out."

He then swung round in his chair to face Aitken. "Listen, you were not in court yesterday but the second lieutenant of the *Calypso* is under an arrest for contempt of court from his refusal to answer the court questions properly. You will confine yourself to a direct answer to the question."

"Of course, sir," Aitken agreed and Ramage watched the polite smile on the Scotsman's face. "But sir," Aitken asked politely, "what part of my answer – or, rather, partial answer – did you find so provoking?"

With Aitken's accent the word "provoking" had a soothing quality, long drawn out, and Goddard's eyes rose to the deckhead as though seeking Divine help.

He was just going to answer when he saw the trap: if he said that he objected to the phrase "another broadside" he would – damnation, he thought: this young puppy Ramage must have spent hours with his officers guessing what Captain Shirley's questions would be and perfecting these double-edged answers. Goddard knew he had been very near the limit of his powers as court president yesterday, and he had arrested that other lieutenant for contempt of court because it seemed the only way of shutting him up. The charge would not hold, of course, and all that he intended was to keep the fellow locked up out of the way until after the verdict on Ramage was given. But two lieutenants cited for contempt in the same trial (in succession, too) would raise eyebrows at the Admiralty and draw attention to what he was trying to do.

All right, what *is* the answer to this impudent young puppy's apparently innocent question? Damnation, this cabin is so hot. Ah yes: this should hide the fact that he had not thought of an answer to the question.

"Lieutenant Aitken, let me remind you of this. The prisoner is accused of – "

Now this damned fool Swinford is whispering something. He had always considered Swinford as a reliable sort of man but, Goddard thought, he seemed to be adopting a very radical attitude in this trial.

Goddard nodded impatiently at Swinford and modified his second sentence. "Yes, as Captain Swinford points out, the prisoner is accused by Captain Shirley of removing him from his lawful command of the *Jason*, and he is charged under six of the Articles of War…numbers fifteen, seventeen, nineteen, twenty, twenty-two and twenty-three."

He gestured to Jenkins and told him to bring up a copy of the *Articles of War*.

He opened the black leatherbound volume with the bold gilt lettering on the front cover. "Let me just remind you. Number fifteen, the first in the charge, refers to 'Every person in or belonging to the Fleet' who shall desert (which does not apply here) or, and I emphasize that word, 'or run away with any of His Majesty's ships or vessels of war, in any ordnance, ammunition, stores or provision belonging thereto'…"

He tapped the small book. "I think you can see why the Board of Admiralty ordered that Captain Ramage should be tried under that Article. Let us consider the next one, seventeen. I will just quote the relevant parts, as it is long: 'The officers and seamen of all, ships, appointed for convoy and guard of merchant ships, or any other, shall diligently attend upon that charge…and whosoever shall be faulty therein… and submitting the ships in their convoy to peril and hazard…' and so on and so forth…"

"Increasing our escort by one more frigate can hardly be hazarding it, sir," Aitken said sourly but, Ramage guessed, by adopting a guileless manner, deliberately trying to provoke Goddard.

"Damnation, Aitken, don't you understand what a court-martial is all about?"

"I thought I did, sir," Aitken said, his accent becoming heavier, "I *thought* I did – until now."

He is trying to provoke me, Goddard told himself, and stabbed his finger down on the *Articles of War*.

"Listen carefully, now: the nineteenth Article…'If any person in or belonging to the Fleet shall make, or endeavour to make, any mutinous assembly…he shall suffer death…' and, in the same Article, '…shall utter any words of sedition or mutiny, he shall suffer death…'"

Now the pair of you, Goddard thought grimly, can have a taste of your own medicine. "Might I remind you, Mr Aitken, that plotting against a superior officer, removing him from his command, or even talking of doing so, is a breach of that Article, and no one is disputing that Captain Shirley was the superior of all the officers in the King's service in that convoy."

And that, you impudent Scot, Goddard thought, reminds you that you are as guilty as your blasted commanding officer: you helped him and if you were brought to trial and found guilty (as you surely would) the noose would go round your neck too.

"Aye, sir," Aitken said, "but there's a phrase in that Article you didn't read, though – about 'such superior officer being in the execution of his office'. Captain Shirley had no 'office' connected with the convoy."

"Don't be impudent," Goddard snapped. "He was the superior officer by virtue of his seniority in the Navy List, and that's all that matters." And before Aitken had time to argue that point Goddard said triumphantly: "Now we come to Article twenty – 'If any person in the Fleet shall conceal any traiterous or mutinous practice or design…he shall suffer death.' Later the same Article refers to concealing '*words*, traiterous or mutinous, spoken to the prejudice of His Majesty or tending to the hindrance of the service…'"

Goddard noted to himself that the whippersnapper had no answer to that and hurriedly went on to the next Article.

"Article twenty-two says that 'If any officer, mariner, soldier or other person in the Fleet, shall strike any of his superior officers, or draw, or offer to draw, or lift up any weapon against him...' then if found guilty that person shall be sentenced to death, and of course the same article deals with anyone disobeying lawful commands."

Goddard could not resist turning round and wagging an admonitory finger. "Mr Aitken, firing a gun comes in the same category as 'lift up any weapon', of course."

"Of course," agreed Aitken, "but in this case the *senior* officer fired a broadside at the *junior* one."

Goddard was quick to realize that, having no answer to the slip of his own tongue, it was best to ignore the remark and trust that Jenkins was not putting it in the minutes.

"Now, Mr Aitken, we come to the final Article to the charge, number twenty-three, which says that 'If any person in the Fleet shall quarrel or fight with any other person in the Fleet, or use reproachful or provoking speeches or gestures...' and so on."

"Thank you for reading them, sir. Of course I know them by heart but it must be very helpful to yourself as the president to be reminded of the precise wording."

Goddard, brought up in the old school where you were polite and considerate to your superiors, particularly if your promotion depended on them, shut the book with a snap and signalled to Jenkins to carry on with the questioning. In the meantime this wretched fellow Aitken's question about that phrase "another broadside" had been forgotten: he had guessed that nothing would smother it as successfully as reading from the *Articles of War*.

Then, to Goddard's horror, Jenkins, instead of going on to the next question, repeated the previous one about Aitken's role when the *Calypso* boarded the *Jason*, but the deputy judge advocate looked up in time to see Goddard's glare and tried to recover the situation, saying to Aitken: "You have already told the court how Captain Ramage had laid the *Calypso* alongside the *Jason*. Go on from that point."

"I led a particular boarding party and climbed over at about the mainchains."

"How were you armed?"

"Cutlass and pistol."

"And Captain Ramage?"

"If you mean 'how was he armed?', I think a cutlass and pistol – little enough when you think we'd just received a broadside."

Ramage almost laughed at the way that Aitken's quiet voice with its Highland lilt had lulled Goddard so that he could make what sounded as though it was going to be an innocent remark in fact be lethal. Lethal, Ramage amended, in a proper trial, but not in this travesty.

Goddard waved at Jenkins. He had learned enough now not to rely on using words with the witness. "Strike out all from 'little enough' – the witness has been warned to respond only to matter relevant to the charges."

Yet as Aitken gave a slight bow in acknowledgement, Goddard felt more than a little uncertainty. They were glib, these young scoundrels, and Jenkins did not seem to understand what was going on.

Jenkins picked up the next slip of paper. "Did you or your men shoot at or in any way attack any of the *Jason*'s ship's company?"

"It wasn't necessary – "

"Answer 'yes' or 'no'," Goddard snapped.

"No," Aitken said, and as Jenkins dipped his pen in the ink before writing down the single word, Aitken added: "The *Jason*'s men had left the 12-pounders and surrendered."

"Out! Out! Strike it out!" Goddard shouted. "Just 'No', that was his answer. Aitken, you've had your last warning."

Jenkins picked up the next slip of paper and, seeing Goddard nod, asked the question. "Did you see Captain Shirley at about this time? And if so, what was he doing?"

"I did, and he was standing abreast the mainmast," Aitken said.

Goddard nodded. The young puppy had at last learned the lesson, although God knows it had taken long enough.

Reading from the next slip, Jenkins asked: "Was Captain Shirley making any threatening gestures towards you or any of the *Calypso's* boarding party?"

"Oh no," Aitken said, as though shocked at the idea. "He was standing quite alone and watching us." He let Jenkins write down the answer and then added: "I also saw that none of his officers were making any threatening gestures." Goddard nodded – this was more like it: evidence was being given in a proper fashion now. Aitken continued: "In fact I was surprised – " he paused a few moments as Goddard continued nodding, " – because there was not an officer on deck: Captain Shirley was alone, apart from a few midshipmen."

Goddard's brow wrinkled and the six captains sitting with their backs to Aitken swung round and stared. Captain Swinford, without waiting for Goddard's permission, exclaimed: "What do you mean, there were no other officers on deck? You simply mean you did not see them."

"I did not see any, sir," Aitken agreed, and Swinford seemed contented with the reply until Aitken added quietly: "Within minutes I confirmed none was on deck because I found them all locked in the gunroom guarded by a Marine sentry."

"Indeed?" said Swinford, and looked at Goddard, whose face had gone white. The silence in the cabin was broken only by the slapping of wavelets under the *Salvador del Mundo's* stern, the distant mewing of seagulls, and the scraping of Jenkins' pen.

And that has nailed you, Admiral, Ramage thought. Now Goddard would have to ask questions concerning that evidence, and then there would be a chance of bringing out the details of Shirley's madness.

Goddard rapped the table with his signet ring and a startled Jenkins looked up.

"Read out the question again."

Jenkins again asked whether Shirley had made any threatening gestures.

"Ah yes," Goddard said calmly. "That was the question, and the witness replied that he had not, so the answer is: 'No'. Very well, carry on with Captain Shirley's next question. I have told the witness several times that he must answer the question. The court is not interested in his views on any subject not referred to in the question. We'll be hearing him preaching to us next – " he guffawed at the idea and added, without realizing that the captains were watching him silent and stony-eyed," – or even giving us his views on naval tactics!" Realizing his joke had fallen flat, he snapped: "Come on, Jenkins, we haven't all night. Next question. But perhaps, Captain Shirley, you have no more questions to ask this witness?"

The question was asked in a persuasive tone and accompanied by what Goddard no doubt regarded as his winning smile.

Shirley raised his head a fraction, as though resting from his survey of every thread in the canvas stretched over the deck. Before answering, he stood up and walked the three or four paces to Jenkins' place at the table, retrieved some slips of paper and returned to his seat. He reached under his chair for a leather pouch, opened it and put away the slips, taking out several more.

Only then did he look up at Goddard and say in a monotone: "I have no more questions to put to this witness."

Goddard sighed and then stared heavy-eyed at Ramage. "Do you have any questions? As he'll be called later as a defence witness, you must restrict your questions to the points raised by the prosecution."

"I have some questions, sir." He turned to Aitken. "The first question asked by the prosecution was to describe your role when the *Jason* was boarded. You omitted to describe my orders to you before the *Calypso* went alongside the *Jason*."

Ramage was conscious that Goddard's great bulk was tense; he could imagine the man's mind working quickly, trying to spot hidden meanings or traps.

"Your orders were brief, sir. I was to lead one of the boarding parties." He waited while Jenkins wrote the sentence and then looked at Ramage, as if waiting for the next question. Then he added: "And I was to help secure the captain."

Goddard neither shouted nor banged the table: he was learning quickly how to deal with questions and answers he did not want in the trial minutes. "Strike out the last part of that reply."

Ramage took a step forward. "May I ask why, sir?"

"Indeed you may; that is your privilege," Goddard said amiably. "The question is not allowed because it has nothing to do with the question asked by the prosecutor. I warned you about that a few moments ago, and your very first question ignored the warning."

"But sir, Captain Shirley asked about Lieutenant Aitken's role. Tell the deputy judge advocate to read out that part of the minutes. If Captain Shirley can ask Lieutenant Aitken about his role, surely I can – I am the one on trial!"

"Your question did not ask Lieutenant Aitken about his role," Goddard said, his voice oozing with reasonableness. "You asked him what orders you gave him."

"But *my* orders concerned *his* role!" Ramage protested. "He answered that he was to lead a boarding party – "

"Exactly," snapped Goddard. "That was the answer to the question. If the witness decides that is his answer to the prosecutor's question, that is the end of it. You can only question him on that."

Ramage knew that Goddard held too many aces. The president controlled what Jenkins wrote down in the minutes: he controlled the questions asked; he controlled the answers given because he could always order sentences struck out of the minutes on the grounds of them not being relevant. Who could argue – there was no record of – Ramage's question, the witness' reply or of Goddard's reason for striking anything out. In theory the safeguard for the accused (and the witnesses, for that matter) lay in the members of the court, the captains sitting round the table. But those captains, Ramage understood only too well, were serving officers with careers (and therefore promotion) to think about. The defect in the system was in making the president of the court the senior officer. In ports of the United Kingdom it was usually the second-in-command to the commander-in-chief; abroad a flag officer if available, otherwise the senior captain. It would be a bold and foolhardy captain who argued with a flag officer whose gossip, let alone a written report, would lose him his command and ensure that he would stay on half-pay for the rest of his life…on the beach drawing half-pay while the other captains round the table, who had kept their mouths shut, went on to find glory and prize money in battle.

Ramage bowed towards Goddard and said, speaking every word slowly and with deliberate clarity, and watching Jenkins to make sure he entered it all in the minutes: "In view of what you have just said, sir, there are no other questions I can ask this witness."

Goddard, seeing no ambiguity, said: "Very well, the witness may stand down."

Jenkins waved his pen at Aitken. "Wait, I must read the minutes back to you and then you must sign them."

As Jenkins read in a monotone, Aitken caught Ramage's eye and raised an eyebrow. Ramage gave an imperceptible nod. Aitken had a quick grasp in normal times: in these somewhat unusual circumstances he seemed to be even faster.

Jenkins finished reading and, looking across at Aitken, held up the quill. "Please sign here that the minutes are a true record of the evidence you have given."

"Ahhhh," Aitken shook his head, "now there we have a problem, mister. You know quite well the minutes are by no means a true record of the evidence I've been giving, so thanking you for your trouble, but I'll no be signing the noo."

Shirley continued looking down at the black and white squares painted on the deck canvas, but both Goddard and Jenkins looked at Aitken as though he was a barrel of powder which a fast-burning fuse had only a couple of inches to go.

Goddard smiled reassuringly but his thick lips betrayed his nervousness at this unexpected turn. "My dear Aitken, you must sign the minutes. The regulations, you know."

"That's not my understanding of them, if you'll forgive me, sir. I may be wrong," he added sorrowfully, and Ramage almost laughed aloud as he saw a flicker of hope cross Goddard's face. "Aye, I might be wrong, and for that matter so might you, sir. But of course that's why we have the deputy judge advocate, and why he's paid extra per diem while the court is sitting, to act as our legal adviser. Would you be good enough, sir, to have him consult the court-martial statutes?"

"Look here, Aitken, you'll save everyone a great deal of trouble if you just sign the minutes. It won't do your chances of promotion any good if you get a reputation for fussing about..."

Ramage was staggered at the barefaced threat and suddenly regretted having been responsible for getting Aitken in this, position, and yet curiously thankful that because of the prize money Aitken had earned under his command, he could resign his commission this moment and walk on shore wealthier, in all probability, than any of the twelve captains sitting round the table.

Captain Swinford said unexpectedly but firmly: "I think that the lieutenant has every right to hear what the court-martial statutes have to say on the matter. In all my years, I haven't come across the point before."

Captain Royce, sitting next to him, said: "Personally, I'm quite clear on the point. If the witness isn't satisfied with the minutes, he does not have to sign 'em."

Swinford said: "I must say, if a witness is expected to sign the minutes as 'a true record' of his evidence, then it seems only right that if they aren't 'a true record' he shouldn't sign 'em."

Goddard rapped the table. "Clear the court," he ordered.

"Sir," Jenkins said meekly, standing up, "the witness and the prisoner are involved in this argument, and if you clear the court, they will be removed from..."

"Oh very well," Goddard said petulantly, "why don't you cite some references?"

"I have several here, sir."

"Well, damnation, why didn't you mention it? What do they say?"

"They are clear on the point, sir," Jenkins said. "Quite clear."

"There you are," Goddard told Swinford and Royce. "Now I hope you will stop interfering. Sign and leave the court," he told Aitken.

"But sir," Jenkins wailed, "the statutes are clear upon the point that a witness should sign the minutes only if he is satisfied they correctly record his evidence."

Goddard sat with his eyes shut. Clearly, as far as Ramage was concerned, the rear-admiral was trying to recall the earlier part of Aitken's evidence because, of course, if Aitken refused to sign the minutes then none of his evidence would be admissible. Was there anything in that evidence that Shirley wanted? After a minute or two, Ramage decided that Goddard could not clearly remember. This was confirmed by Goddard's next words: "Very well, Lieutenant, if you do not sign the minutes you had better remember my words, and remember that the court can recall you as a witness any time it wishes."

Jenkins glanced down at his list and turned to the Marine sentry at the door. "Call Mr Southwick, master of the *Calypso.*"

Southwick was another of the men warned by both the defence and the prosecution that they would be required as witnesses, and he marched in to the great cabin looking unexpectedly smart, sword by his side, hat tucked under his left arm, freshly shaven, and only his hair the usual unruly white mop which had for many years defied brush and comb and responded only to a fresh wind.

Ramage suddenly realized that although he met Southwick many times a day (and had been doing so for several years) he rarely "saw" him in the sense of assessing his character from his appearance. In fact, watching him now as Jenkins administered the oath, Ramage felt he was looking at a stranger he had known well for years, admittedly a truly absurd contradiction. But Southwick obviously stood four-square, a bluff and kindly man, every inch of him a seaman;

a man who spoke his mind and whose honesty no other honest man could possibly doubt. That assessment, Ramage thought wryly, ruled out Goddard, who clearly measured every man by his own standards, thus ensuring he lived in a world apparently peopled only by scoundrels.

As soon as Jenkins was back in his chair, Shirley gave him several slips of paper. The man *glided*, Ramage realized. Again he had the picture of a sad-faced monk in long robes gliding gloomily along a cloister, head down, hands clasped behind his back – or even clutching a rosary to his breast. Quiet, remote from daily life, little understood by laymen who tried (and failed) to relate remoteness to holiness, and in turn understanding little of laymen.

Jenkins read the first question establishing that Southwick had been master of the *Calypso* on the relevant day and then, holding one of Shirley's slips of paper, asked: "What was your role in the encounter between the *Jason* and the *Calypso*?"

Ramage pictured Shirley sitting in the *Jason*'s great cabin, thinking hard and then scribbling away, thinking again and reaching for another slip of paper. He could not have thought of a more suitable question (from Southwick's point of view) to ask the master.

"Knotting and splicing rigging cut by the *Jason*'s broadside," he said matter-of-factly, in the same tone of voice that one prosperous farmer might use to discuss with another the improving price of wheat.

Goddard turned to look at Southwick. "I can't believe that you personally would be knotting and splicing rigging?"

"Masters of ships don't, sir," Southwick said politely. "You were expected to understand that I was supervising the work."

Ramage saw a cunning glint in Goddard's eyes: he had an ace concealed somewhere. "We can only take notice of what you say, not what you expect us to understand, so strike that answer out, Jenkins," he said. "I think in fact Captain Shirley wishes to withdraw that question."

Shirley nodded once without looking up, and Jenkins ostentatiously screwed up the piece of paper and put it to one side. He took up the next slip. Without reading it out he looked at Shirley and, when the captain did not glance up, walked over to him and whispered something. Ramage saw Shirley nod and Jenkins gave him the slip of paper and returned to his chair. That, Ramage guessed, was another question where Southwick's blunt answer could embarrass the prosecution. He watched as Jenkins picked up the next page.

"When you were on board the *Jason*, did Captain Shirley make any threatening gesture towards you, or employ any threatening words?"

"No, he seemed to be sleepwalking."

Goddard tapped the table with his signet ring. "The witness' answer to the question is 'No'."

Captain Swinford said quickly without reference to Goddard: "Mr Southwick, why do you use the word 'sleepwalking'?"

Southwick grinned. "You remember when I was serving with you in the *Canopus*, sir, back in – must be '92? We had that first lieutenant who from time to time would appear on the quarterdeck in his nightshirt, and a midshipman had to be told off to lead him back to his cabin without waking him? Well, he looked like that."

Goddard said sarcastically: "Reminiscing over old times is quite fascinating, but this is hardly the time for it. The reference to sleepwalking was struck from the minutes so your question, Captain Swinford, apart from not being asked through me as president of the court, is quite out of order."

"He was killed at Camperdown, sir," Southwick said, as though Goddard did not exist. "Had he lived, he'd have gone far."

"Quite," Swinford agreed, also ignoring Goddard. "That was why I'd picked him as my first lieutenant."

"Have you any more questions to ask this witness, Captain Shirley?" Goddard asked ominously.

Again Shirley did not look up. He shook his head almost imperceptibly, and after Ramage said he had no questions, Jenkins cautioned Southwick to listen while the minutes of his evidence were read aloud to him.

"Aye, that won't take long," commented Southwick. Then he walked down to the end of the table to where Jenkins sat, signed his name with a flourish and, giving Jenkins a broad smile as he thanked him for the trouble he had taken, put the quill back in the inkwell with just enough force to make sure the quill split slightly and ruined the point.

As Southwick walked out of the cabin – because he was to be called again, next time as a defence witness, he had to leave the court and join Aitken – Goddard said: "Your next witness, Captain Shirley."

Shirley stood up. "Mr Southwick was my last witness, sir. The prosecution's case is concluded."

"Very well. Mr Ramage, are you ready to present your defence?"

Yes, he was ready; but was there any point in making a defence? Goddard had blocked nearly all the answers referring to the *Jason* firing a broadside into the *Calypso*; he had blocked any hint that Captain Shirley might be mad. He had done all this very skilfully; anyone (particularly Their Lordships at the Admiralty) reading the minutes could not guess what had been struck out; indeed, might never suspect that even a comma was missing.

Yet upon those two facts, the *Jason*'s broadside and Shirley's madness, rested Ramage's entire defence: they were the two reasons why he took the step – which put his life in legal jeopardy – of removing a captain from his command.

How the devil then, could he defend himself against these charges, brought by Shirley himself, if the president of the court ruled out of order any reference to the broadside or madness? Oh yes, Ramage knew he could go to the commander-in-chief and complain, but the commander-in-chief (and the Admiralty too for that matter) would never accept his word against Rear-Admiral Goddard's, not because they particularly favoured Goddard but because the whole edifice on which the Navy was built depended on strict obedience to one's superior, whether an able seaman jumping when the bosun said jump or a lieutenant doing promptly what the captain said, or the captain carrying out his admiral's orders, or the admiral carrying out the Board of Admiralty's orders – and, finally, the Admiralty carrying out orders from its superior, which was the government of the day in the shape of His Majesty's Principal Secretary of State for the Foreign Department. Who, come to think of it, received his instructions from the Cabinet or the prime minister.

If any one of those men or bodies refused to obey, then the whole edifice would collapse or give a tiny shiver, depending on the level of the disobedience. The link between the Cabinet issuing orders to the Secretary of State and an ordinary seaman being harried by a surly bosun's mate might seem tenuous, but it was there and, Ramage had to agree, everyone from the prime minister to the bosun's mate was concerned with upholding authority.

The only problem arose when some unusual circumstance did not fit into the intricate structure of obedience which had been built up over the centuries. The structure had been modified by various Acts of Parliament from time to time; it was the best that men could contrive – up to now, anyway. As far as the Navy was concerned, it had one defect which either no one had noticed or (more likely) no one in authority would admit existed, yet that defect although small could eventually threaten the whole structure.

It was this defect, or flaw, which had trapped Ramage, and it was, quite simply, that there was no way that a captain of a ship of war could lawfully be removed from his command at sea by his officers if he went mad, lapsed into alcoholism, broke his back and could not leave his bunk or in some other way became unfit to command *unless* the surgeon was prepared to give his opinion in writing that the captain was unfit to command. Few surgeons would risk the consequences, and anyway the *Jason*'s surgeon was dead by the time his opinion was wanted. So the defect or flaw in the Admiralty's command structure became a gaping hole in the case of the *Jason* on that July day.

Still, there was only one question now remaining in Ramage's mind, and that was why none of the *Jason*'s officers or seamen would admit that she had fired a broadside at the *Calypso*. Goddard would block the question which, he recalled, led to another: why would none of the officers discuss the reason or even admit they were locked in the gunroom when the Calypsos boarded? Which brought a third question: why would none of the officers discuss the possibility of Shirley being mad with the very captain who was rescuing them from a madman?

So why the hell prolong the trial and give Goddard any more satisfaction? It was not Shirley's fault – he was mad and not responsible for his actions. The captains forming the court did not realize what they faced and could not be told enough

– except by the very evidence that Goddard had prevented being given.

Come to think of it, those captains (like Ramage himself) must wonder why the *Jason's* officers stayed stubbornly silent if they honestly thought Shirley was really mad. Yet that silence alone could be enough reason for them finding Captain Ramage guilty as charged…

How and why had he become involved in all this, he asked himself bitterly. Why had he removed Shirley from his command – because he would be back commanding the *Jason* as soon as the trial was over. Why had he freed the *Jason's* lieutenants – because now not one of them would speak a word even to help their rescuer.

Ramage looked at Goddard and the man's weak, sagging face made him angry. So did the thought of Shirley, and the *Jason's* lieutenants, who were behaving like sycophantic poltroons.

"Yes, sir, I am ready to present my case," he heard himself saying. "Could the first witness on my list be called?"

The first witness was Aitken, who strode into the cabin to be reminded by Jenkins that he was still on oath and therefore need not be sworn again.

The deputy judge advocate looked questioningly at Ramage, who shook his head. "I do not have my questions written out."

"In that case," Goddard said quickly, having seen that Ramage was not holding any sheets of paper, "you will write them out and ask them through me."

Oh no, Ramage decided: he had put up with enough in the trial so far and he was making a defence only because Goddard, Shirley and the wretched lieutenants had irritated him. "If you'll pardon me, sir, that is not required in the court-martial statutes; writing down questions has simply become a habit in some courts to save time."

"Nevertheless, you'll write down each question and pass it to me to ask."

Ramage took a deep breath and stared straight at Goddard. "In that case, sir, I have no defence to offer, and I insist that this dialogue be recorded in the minutes."

"You can't insist on anything," Goddard sneered. "You are the prisoner on trial for your life."

Swinford said unexpectedly: "Sir, as the senior of the captains forming this court – of which you are president – I must insist that Captain Ramage's request be granted. He has decided not to offer a defence because you insist on examining his interrogatories and asking them yourself. Your decision and his are both part of the trial and must be recorded. And if you'll forgive me, sir, Captain Ramage is correct about the court-martial statutes. This business of written interrogatories started to help deputy judge advocates write the minutes. In fact, it is bad because it gives a dishonest witness plenty of time to think of a way to prevaricate. We must remember the courts were set up to administer justice, not the comfort and convenience of deputy judge advocates."

Goddard was quick enough to know he was beaten on that point, and with a defensive half-smile at all the captains he said: "Of course, of course. I was simply trying to speed up the proceedings: we are now in our second day and only just beginning the defence." He turned to Ramage, his smile twisted and artificial, like the powder daubed on the face of a raddled old trull.

"Mr Aitken," Ramage said, "you have already deposed that during July last you were the last lieutenant of the *Calypso*, and now I want you to tell the court what you consider to be the beginning of the series of circumstances which has led to you appearing here as a witness in my trial."

Ramage looked round at Goddard. He had worked very carefully on that question because basically it asked an officer for his professional opinion on a relevant subject. Goddard could not object that the question had nothing to do with the charge or witness. But Ramage could see that as Jenkins wrote down the question, while he waited for the answer Goddard was trying to see what hidden significance might lie behind it.

Aitken saw Jenkins' pen stop moving and said: "Sighting a sail to windward which afterwards proved to be the *Jason*, sir."

"What in your view was the situation of the *Calypso*, with a strange sail sighted to windward?"

"Because the *Calypso* was escorting a large West Indian convoy, sir, she had to take immediate steps to be ready to defend the ships if necessary."

Goddard interrupted. "Pray tell me what has all this to do with the charges against you, Mr Ramage?"

"Only this, sir," Ramage said, not troubling to hide the sarcasm in his voice, "I am charged over matters concerning the *Jason* frigate and Captain Shirley. It seems relevant to my defence to introduce both of them."

Both Captain Swinford and, sitting opposite him, Captain Huggins, simultaneously coughed. Goddard glanced at each of them and then nodded to Ramage. "Carry on, then."

"Mr Aitken, what steps were taken that immediately concerned you, or which you initiated yourself?"

"Acting on your orders, I had the drummer beat to quarters. I then asked you for the day's challenge, and as soon as you gave it to me, I had the appropriate flags hoisted, along with our pendant numbers."

"You did not order any alteration of course or sail trimming?"

"No, sir. While I was attending to my duties, the master gave the orders which started us stretching up to windward."

So far, so good, Ramage thought. Goddard has at last woken up to the fact that some of the members of the court are concerned that the trial should be conducted according to the court-martial statutes. That did not mean they were on his side, but at least it hinted that they would listen to evidence fairly and give a verdict based on it. Yet, yet, yet…Would Goddard suddenly change his aim? No, there was no chance of that.

"What did you do after that?"

"I was concerned first with identifying the strange sail, and having done that, taking the appropriate steps to meet her."

"How did you identify her, and what steps did you take?"

Ramage saw that Goddard was looking worried. There was no way he could rule the questions out of order, in the light of Swinford's and Huggins' discreet coughs, providing Ramage was careful. But let Goddard object to one question and the flood would start…

"As we approached we (the officers and several seamen) recognized her as a British-built frigate, and her sails had an English cut. Then we saw she had a challenge hoisted, and read her pendant numbers."

Ramage waited until Jenkins indicated he had copied the answer down and then asked Aitken casually: "It was, of course, the correct challenge?"

"No, sir."

"What," demanded Goddard, "has this to do with the charges?"

"In my view, sir, it has a vital bearing on *all* the charges."

"In the court's view it has none. Strike it out, Mr Jenkins. Carry on, Mr Ramage."

"Having inspected the flags of the *Jason*'s challenge," Ramage asked, watching Goddard and ready with his protest should the admiral interrupt, "what did you then do?"

"I looked up her pendant numbers in the signal book and saw she was the *Jason*. As there was no need for the men to remain at quarters, I gave them the orders for them to secure the guns."

"What did you observe about the *Jason* at this time?"

"She was steering directly for us and I concluded she was going to pass within hail."

Ramage saw that Goddard was now tense, his eyes flickering from Ramage to Aitken and back. He knew that the time was fast approaching when Ramage would be asking about one of the critical parts of the case, the broadside, and knew he had to stifle the questions without being too obvious.

"Did she pass within hail?" Ramage asked again casually.

"No, sir, within gunshot, though."

"Wait," shouted Goddard. "Mr Jenkins, do not write that down. What has this to do with the charge?"

"I was just establishing a distance, sir. Pistol shot, musket shot, gunshot – these are all very well known distances and immediately recognized by seamen."

Goddard glanced at Captain Swinford before nodding: "Very well, carry on."

At once Ramage asked: "How do you know she was within gunshot of the *Calypso*?"

"She fired a raking broadside at us, sir."

"Stop! Silence, I say!" Goddard shouted. "Strike that out, both question and answer."

"Sir," Ramage said quietly, "if that question and that answer are struck out, clearly the court is being prevented from hearing this witness' evidence, and there is no point in me asking further questions. I request it be recorded in the minutes."

"If you choose to ask no more questions that is *your* affair," Goddard said bluntly. "As president of the court it is *my* affair that the proceedings be conducted as laid down in the court-martial statutes."

Ramage stared at him open-mouthed. The man's hypocrisy was unbelievable. "In view of that, I have no more questions to ask this witness," he said.

Aitken signed the minutes and Goddard said in a friendly voice: "You may stay in the court now you are not required again as a witness."

Aitken gave a deep bow. "You are too kind, sir," he said ironically, and walked over to the row of chairs.

"Call the next witness," Goddard said, as though to maintain some sort of initiative, and Jenkins called for Wagstaffe, who had been kept on board overnight in custody.

Ramage asked him preliminary questions establishing his role on board the *Calypso* up to the time she went alongside the *Jason*. Goddard did not object to any of the routine questions, then Ramage asked: "When you boarded the *Jason* with me, what opposition did you meet?"

"Wait!" snapped Goddard, but Ramage immediately interrupted.

"Sir, may I suggest you hear the witness' answer before objecting?"

Realizing that he was leaving himself open by not agreeing, Goddard nodded, but slewed his body round so that he could stare at Wagstaffe.

The young lieutenant said: "There was no opposition at all."

"Where were the officers?"

"I did not see – "

"Stop," Goddard said. "There is no opposition so any further question on that point is irrelevant."

"I want it noted in the minutes that I am not allowed to question this witness properly – sir."

Goddard shrugged. "If you can't frame your questions properly, that's your affair. It might have helped had you first written them down."

That none of the officers were on deck, that all the guns' crews were crouched beside their guns, that Shirley was standing there in a long black coat – Ramage knew there was no hope of getting any evidence about this past Goddard, yet that (and what he saw for the rest of the voyage to England) was what made Wagstaffe's evidence vital. Vital but impossible to have recorded in the minutes of the trial.

Ramage said no more, so that his last request still stood, although Goddard appeared to be ignoring it, impatiently gesturing to Wagstaffe to sign the minutes, having asked Shirley if he had any questions and receiving a dismissive reply.

Southwick was the next witness, but like Aitken he was prevented from giving any evidence about the broadside: Goddard was ready with several objections. Like Wagstaffe, the master was stopped from describing the absence of officers from the *Jason*'s deck. Finally Ramage said: "I have no more questions to ask this witness that would be permitted by the president of the court."

"My dear fellow," Goddard said blandly, "ask what questions you wish; just make sure that, as laid down in the court-martial statutes, they are relevant to the charges – after all, there are enough charges…"

There was no more point, Ramage decided as Southwick signed the minutes. All the evidence allowed would, like Goddard's manner whenever challenged, be bland. The other lieutenants, Paolo, Jackson, Stafford – whatever they said about the broadside would be disallowed so there was no point in calling them. In fact, that was the end of the defence. There remained only for him to make his defence statement.

Yet, he suddenly remembered, there was one witness who would be very offended if not called to give evidence.

Ramage said: "I wish to change my list of witnesses. May I be allowed to amend it?"

Goddard nodded and Ramage walked down to the end of the table. Jenkins gave him the list and handed him the pen. Ramage scored all through the names except one, added a few letters to it, and returned to his chair.

"Are you ready?" Goddard inquired, and when Ramage nodded he told Jenkins impatiently: "Call the next witness."

CHAPTER EIGHTEEN

Jenkins hesitated for several moments, reading his list a second time, and Goddard tapped the table impatiently with his signet ring. "Mr Jenkins, next witness!"

The deputy judge advocate turned towards the door, where the Marine sentry waited to repeat the name. "Call Miss Alexis Yorke," he said.

Goddard swung round to Ramage. "Who is this woman? What on earth has she got to do with this case?"

"She is a defence witness, sir," Ramage said, "and it would be quite improper for me to anticipate her evidence."

"Very well, have her sworn."

So, Ramage realized, Goddard did not remember the family name, and he was glad she and Sidney had sat apart. Nor did Goddard remember Sidney from Port Royal, Jamaica, and of course he had never seen or heard of Alexis before.

When Alexis walked into the great cabin, Ramage realized that most if not all of the court had previously only seen her at a distance across the cabin, sitting down in the rows of chairs for spectators, and then when she left the cabin. None of them – at least, not Goddard and presumably not the captains – had realized why Alexis was in the cabin. He guessed that they had assumed that she was the wife (a fiancée would need a chaperone) or mistress of someone interested in the trial. The thought of Alexis as a mistress was – he brushed the picture aside and watched her.

Goddard was impressed: he was already standing, a reassuring smile on his face. He gestured towards the chair which had been pushed to one side by the preceding witnesses. "If Miss Yorke will be seated there," he said. "We have one or two formalities to go through first."

Jenkins bustled round holding both the Bible and a Crucifix, and then had to scuttle back to collect the card on which the oath was written. Then obviously he decided to use one of the alternative forms, which did not require the witness to recite, and then remembered that he had not read all the details of the accused's list of witnesses. Finally he walked round to Alexis, who saw what he was carrying and stood up.

"Madam, do you subscribe to – "

"I belong to the Established Church," she said quietly, and took the proffered Bible in her right hand, holding it up.

Jenkins, more used to dealing with truculent, deliberately obstructive or stupid seamen, smiled encouragingly.

"Are you Miss Alexis Aureelia Yorke?"

"I am Alexis Aurelia Yorke," she said, quietly correcting the pronunciation of her second name.

"A spinster living at Bexley in Kent?"

"I am a spinster," Alexis agreed. Ramage could see she was puzzled over the address, since she and her brother owned homes in Barbados, Jamaica and London as well as Bexley.

"I have a home in Bexley," she said finally, "but I travel a good deal."

The point of the answer was lost on Jenkins, who took a deep breath and said: "Do you swear upon the Holy Evangelist that the evidence you shall give before the court, respecting the charge against the prisoner, shall be the truth, the whole truth and nothing but the truth, so help you God?"

"Oh indeed!" exclaimed a startled Alexis. "I mean, yes, it will."

Jenkins took back the Bible and returned to his seat while a smiling Goddard invited Alexis to be seated again.

Ramage was ready for Goddard's next move.

"Miss Yorke, as president of the court it is usual for me to ask questions of the witness, so my first question is if you know anything of the circumstances of the charges made against the prisoner?"

"The prisoner? No, I don't think I know anything about the prisoner."

Goddard gave Ramage a triumphant smirk. "Then, madam, would you mind telling the court why you are here?"

"Oh yes, that is quite simple. I am here to give evidence about Captain Lord Ramage – the gentleman sitting there."

Goddard swallowed hard, for a moment put about by the sudden use of Ramage's title, which would be normal enough in private life, but he failed to keep a sneer from his voice and a smile from his face: "But he *is* the prisoner."

"My goodness," Alexis said, "such a brave officer made a prisoner. Tell me, Admiral, have you ever read any of the *London Gazettes* when they print some of his despatches?"

Goddard's smile was trying to bolt, but he held on to it as best he could. "Madam," he said with icy politeness, "this is a court of law, and I have to ask *you* the questions."

"Oh, of course! Please do."

"I have to ask you what you know about the circumstances of the charges against the prisoner." Goddard now had the smirk fixed firmly in place: that question, he clearly thought, would dispose of this witness. It did not occur to him that he was dealing with an extremely intelligent young woman who was enjoying baiting him.

"Forgive me, Admiral, and it is probably against *all* your rules, but may I ask you a question?"

Goddard gave a slight bow; an inclination of head and shoulders which, accompanied by a smile, was intended to show this extremely elegant woman that admirals were indeed human and only too willing to attend to any feminine fads and quirks. "Of course, madam: feel free to ask."

"Well, you said – or, rather, I understood you to ask me – what did I know of the circumstances of the charges against the prisoner."

"Yes, that was the burden of my question."

"But how can I talk about 'the circumstances' when I don't know what 'the charges' are?"

Ramage kept a straight face. Goddard had walked straight into that trap, and Alexis had sprung it with perfect timing.

Red-faced and beginning to perspire freely, Goddard was obviously thinking of the tedium of reading aloud several Articles of War and, more to the point, could guess some of the questions Alexis would ask about them.

"We will put that question aside for a moment, madam," Goddard said, and went on with the question he thought should finish her business in short order.

"First would you tell the court all you know about the *Calypso*'s encounter with the *Jason*, and the voyage of the two ships back to Plymouth."

"That would take all night," Alexis said, "and anyway you can't really ask me any relevant questions about it because you weren't there. I am very anxious to help the court, but please, admiral – " she smiled sweetly, " – remember that I am but a woman."

Ramage knew that not a man in the court could forget that, and the six captains who usually sat facing the sternlights, their backs to the witness and the accused, were now twisted round in their chairs, watching Alexis.

"Why would it take all night to tell us?" Goddard asked patiently. "All the members of the court are experienced naval officers."

"Yes, I am sure they are," Alexis agreed, "but what Captain Shirley did is beyond the experiences of naval officers, or indeed any sane people."

Ramage had heard of the expression "a silence you could cut with a knife", but he had never experienced it before. Goddard was one of the last to pull himself together and, red-faced, mopping his brow with a handkerchief, he said: "Madam, you must not say things like that. The deputy judge advocate, as you can see, has to write down everything that is said. I regret that I must order him to delete that whole section."

"But why?" demanded Alexis. "Just look at him." By now she was standing and she gestured to where Shirley sat in his chair, still staring at the deck. "There you see a madman, a man who orders his own ship to fire a whole broadside at an unsuspecting *British* ship – no, don't you *dare* tell me to be silent," she told Goddard. "You weren't there and I was. I saw it all happen. That great puff of smoke was caused by all the *Jason's* guns firing into the *Calypso*, which was only sailing up to exchange greetings. *What* did you say?" she said quietly to Goddard. "You'll have me removed from the court?" She twirled her parasol. "Come, Admiral, this could be very amusing."

Captain Swinford leaned forward and, first glancing at Goddard to make it clear that he was going to speak to the witness no matter what the admiral might decide, said: "Madam, I am sure the president was speaking metaphorically: no violence will be offered you in this court. Would you please clear up one question which is puzzling myself and my fellow captains gathered round this table, which is how you were there?"

"Thank you for your reassurance, Captain," Alexis said softly, as though speaking only to Swinford and the captains, her face turned away from an officer who certainly was not a gentleman and who bullied women, "and I am only too pleased to explain.

"My brother owns a number of merchant ships – thirty-three, unless the French have captured another one recently. From time to time he decides to sail in one of the ships – usually to the West Indies. Occasionally I accompany him – I must admit," she said with a conspiratorial smile, "that I find London society rather boring: the attention of callow young men whether in uniform or not can become extremely tedious, although not as bad perhaps as the clumsy gallantries of politicians which, together with their uncommonly boring talk – always of politics – is rather like overhearing a den of thieves and murderers exchanging gossip about their latest crimes."

Ramage could see that Goddard could hardly restrain himself from interrupting but Swinford and the other captains were enchanted by this young woman who was giving them a fascinating glimpse of London society and saying with such insouciance what they wanted to hear about politicians.

"Please go on, madam," Swinford said. "You were telling us about your voyages."

"Ah yes, my brother Sidney – " she glanced at Goddard and saw that he had at last realized who she was, " – persuaded me to go on this last voyage to the West Indies because we wanted to make sure that our houses in Jamaica and Barbados were not being completely eaten by termites. They are a terrible nuisance, you know, and the houses are old, belonging to – oh, I forget how many 'greats' but to one of our ancestors. My rather strange second name – " she smiled at Jenkins, who bobbed his head, " – comes from the wife of that forebear – he was the leader of the Buccaneers, you know. He had a special rank but I can't remember…"

"That would be Edward Yorke, the Admiral of the Brethren of the Coast," Swinford said.

"That's him – how clever of you to know," she said delightedly. "He's always referred to as 'Grandpa Ned' in the family, although he's about fifth 'great', perhaps more. Anyway, Sidney persuaded me to go with him in the *Emerald* and that is how we came to be in the convoy."

"Could you describe where in the convoy the *Emerald* was sailing?" Swinford asked, expecting an answer full of feminine vagueness.

"Oh yes, we were leading the starboard column. You see, Captain Ramage – " she looked coolly at Goddard, " – perhaps I should say 'the prisoner' wanted a really reliable ship in that position, because the whole structure of the convoy depended on her, as you know. He knew my brother and he knew the master my brother employed. So we were leading the starboard column when the *Jason* approached on the starboard quarter to windward of all of us."

Swinford stood up and bowed. "Thank you, madam. Clearly you have a considerable knowledge of sea life!"

Alexis gave Swinford a warm smile before turning to Goddard as she remarked: "I have crossed the Atlantic half a dozen times, the first when I was about ten years old – which means all in wartime – but this is the first time I have seen a captain in the Royal Navy go mad."

Only Alexis could have lulled them (or Goddard, anyway) like that, with a stream of what seemed innocent chatter, amusing them and almost flirting with them, and intriguing them with the fact she knew about the sea and had made several Atlantic voyages. Then, having established herself as a knowledgeable and credible witness, she once again hammered home that vital point: Shirley was mad.

Goddard looked up warily, like a ferret emerging from a rabbit's burrow, and seemed to sniff the wind. The last time he had told Jenkins to strike out part of Miss Yorke's evidence he had unwittingly caught his head in the snare and nearly wrenched it off. Instead of saying anything he made a small scribbling gesture to Jenkins.

"To whom are you waving, Admiral?" Alexis inquired icily. "That seems to be more like an obscene gesture made by a street urchin…"

"No, no, I assure you, madam, it was quite routine."

"Then why is that clerk crossing out what I have just said?"

"Madam, I am sure – "

"Don't argue, Admiral, just go down and look at – what do you call them, the minutes – for yourself."

"Well, madam, I am afraid – "

"And well you might be," Alexis said scathingly. "You are censoring my evidence." She held up her hand as he went to speak. "Admiral, I know nothing of court procedure, and therefore nothing of court-martial procedure but I recognize censorship when I see it. That is the second time you have censored my evidence. No, be quiet, and listen. There are things going on in this trial which I do not understand and I do not like." She looked across at Swinford and Royce. "I do not think I am alone in my doubts. However, I do not depend upon your favour for promotion; if the Board of Admiralty is used only for ironing clothes or chopped up for kindling I do not care. But justice is a different matter. I am no Portia but don't forget Grandpa Ned, Admiral. He was establishing Jamaica when your forebears, judging from your behaviour here, were still poaching conies and making breeches out of moleskins. Please call a boat: I am leaving this ship."

Magnificent, Ramage murmured, and he heard Lieutenant Hill sitting behind him give a sigh of admiration. Both Swinford and Royce were standing and within a few moments the other ten captains were on their feet, a bewildered Goddard still sitting, his head cradled in his arms. Suddenly he was aware of the scraping of chairs and looked up to find everyone else in the great cabin on their feet, with even the Marine sentry at the door standing firmly to attention.

"Good day to you gentlemen," Alexis said to the court and swept out of the cabin, making an exit, Ramage was sure, which might have been equalled at St James's Palace but never surpassed.

The captains then sat down and Ramage realized that they were all looking at Swinford, who coughed to attract Goddard's attention.

"Sir," he said respectfully, "I have to request that you clear the court because there are certain points that some members would like to discuss."

"Ah yes, indeed, Captain Swinford. But it is late in the day and I have a statement which I have to make in open court, so I'll do that first. Tomorrow is the anniversary of the Coronation, and the day after both you Captain Swinford, and you Captain Royce, have to take your ships to the dockyard. On Friday, two other ships are to be drydocked. With two different captains absent on successive days, I propose adjourning the court until the usual time next Monday morning. Having made that announcement, I now formally adjourn the court, except that the court will continue in closed session.

"Provost Marshal," he said sourly and unnecessarily, "remove the prisoner. He can remain a prisoner at large on board his own ship."

CHAPTER **NINETEEN**

Ramage sat at his desk with Southwick as usual in the armchair beside it (in deference to his age, not his rank, since he was only a warrant officer among commission officers) and Aitken and Wagstaffe on the settee.

They had returned from the *Salvador del Mundo* an hour earlier, had a brief meal after removing their swords and changing into older uniforms, and then met in the cabin to talk about the trial.

Ramage found himself in the unexpected role of an apologist for Admiral Goddard, because constantly he had to remind himself that he was not still a lieutenant among lieutenants who were able to abuse admirals among themselves. As a post-captain he had to maintain a semblance of discipline and respect – ironical, when he thought of the officer concerned.

"What is the court considering, eh?" Southwick exclaimed. "Those captains will never stand up to the admiral, you can be sure of that."

"Captain Swinford – and Captain Royce, too – seem to me to have had enough of him," Ramage said mildly.

"Sir, do you think they're going to blast their futures on your behalf? It's a big jump from commanding a 74-gun ship to marching around on a three-decker, and when Their Lordships choose the names, anyone about whom there is the slightest gossip might as well resign his commission and buy a half-share in a privateer."

"Don't forget that when we first served under him, we knew him as Commodore Nelson and many senior officers disliked him. Now he's Vice-Admiral Lord Nelson..." Ramage said.

"Aye, and even more senior officers dislike him."

"Yes, but the Board of Admiralty were more persuaded by Cape St Vincent, the Nile and Copenhagen," Ramage said.

"If you'll excuse me, sir, fiddlesticks. He was pushed forward (quite rightly) by Lord St Vincent. Don't forget the row among the admirals, especially Admiral Mann, when as a very junior rear-admiral he was given the Mediterranean Fleet. No one else could win a victory like the Nile, but after that those who disliked him now hate him because they've a few quarts of jealousy to add to the brew."

Aitken said: "I think you're wrong Southwick. Obviously your general criticism is correct, but there are exceptions. Lord Nelson is one; Rear-Admiral Goddard might be another – "

"Not in the same breath!" exclaimed Southwick. "Please!"

Aitken grinned and explained: "I'm talking about the exceptions, who can be heroes or scoundrels. Seems to me that here we have one of each. Just as Lord St Vincent stuck by an unpopular commodore and put him in the way of promotion, someone has stuck close to Rear-Admiral Goddard, although I don't know who – "

"The Court," Ramage interposed quietly.

"So we have the King against us," Aitken mused.

"All this talk doesn't get the evidence down in the minutes," Wagstaffe pointed out.

"We were talking about what influence those twelve captains will have," Ramage reminded him.

"I'll put a little money on Captain Swinford," Southwick said. "He was a good man when he commanded the *Canopus* and he was standing up to the admiral at times."

"My oath!" exclaimed Aitken heatedly, "none of them were really standing up to him. We still have only one mention of the broadside in the minutes and not the slightest hint of Captain Shirley's madness despite Miss Yorke. *In the minutes*, remember that. Nor anything about the *Jason*'s officers being locked up in their cabins. In fact I don't know what the devil *was* left in the minutes."

"Don't worry about the minutes," Ramage said calmly, "minutes are for commanders-in-chief and the Admiralty to read after the trial – which means after the verdict. No matter what anyone might say and however much presidents might order stricken out, minutes are only useful as records, and for appeals. No matter what happens, I shan't appeal."

"So the only thing that matters is the verdict, 'Guilty' or 'Not Guilty'. And that verdict is going to be decided by those twelve captains."

At that moment Kenton arrived at the door to announce that Mr Yorke's boat was within hail, having approached in the lee of a 74-gun ship and out of sight, and he would be on board in a couple of minutes.

The moment Sidney Yorke walked into the cabin, preceded by the lugubrious Marine sentry's announcement, Ramage knew that something had happened: the man's face was drawn and the tropical tan now turned the skin an unhealthy yellow.

The young shipowner greeted the four men in the cabin and then nodded towards the coach. Ramage stood up and led Yorke into the smaller cabin, shutting the door behind them.

"It's Alexis," Yorke said, and for a moment Ramage was startled because he thought Yorke had already said that, and then realized he had imagined it.

"What happened?"

What *could* happen at an inn? Robbers, sudden illness, the building catching fire – perhaps their boat capsized: the boatmen plying for hire were –

"When I got back to the King's Arms expecting to find her there after giving her evidence, I was handed this note by the innkeeper."

He gave Ramage a single sheet of paper which had been folded and sealed with a wafer.

"My dear Brother," it said. "I should have talked about this with you but I was afraid you would try to dissuade me. If Nicholas is left at the mercy of that scoundrel Goddard, he will be found guilty, and I understand he would then have to be sentenced to death because the court has no alternative. I am therefore going to London because there lies authority. I shall be well along the road by the time you read this – your affectionate sister…"

"What 'authority' do you think she has in mind?" Ramage asked.

Yorke shrugged his shoulders. "She was very angry with Goddard – I gather he threatened to have her thrown out of the court. Most unwise of him to get athwart Alexis' hawse: even I don't!"

"Is it all right if the others know?" Ramage asked, gesturing towards the three men waiting the other side of the door.

"Of course! I just wanted to tell you first."

They went back into the cabin and before Ramage sat down he told the three officers: "Miss Yorke has gone to London on my behalf."

A startled Southwick said: "What is she going to do?"

"We're not at all sure, but from the way she dealt with Goddard today, I can imagine her coach and four turning into Downing Street!"

"Don't laugh," Sidney Yorke said. "She knows Henry Addington very well: in fact the last time she saw him was at Number Ten a few months after the signing of the Treaty of Amiens. She gave him quite a fright: she told him exactly what she thought about anyone who signed such a treaty with Bonaparte. He took it very well, I must say. Knowing what sycophants he usually has round him, that was probably the first time he'd heard the truth for a long time!"

"Could she really be going to see the prime minister?" an awed Wagstaffe asked.

Sidney Yorke pulled a face. "My sister knows an extraordinary number of people and she has a way of saying the most outrageous things without causing offence. In fact some people seem to like it."

"Should think so," Southwick muttered, "particularly if the way she settled the admiral's hash is anything to go by."

"I'm sorry I missed that," Yorke said, "but I had to wait in that damned cabin in case I was wanted as a witness."

"Well, she was magnificent," Ramage said. "One moment an empress and the next a tigress. Poor Goddard never knew whether he was going to be frozen by a regal stare or ripped by a hidden claw!"

"The courts sit again next Monday," Southwick said. "She'll have barely reached London by then. And then she has to see people."

"I inquired at the King's Arms," Yorke said. "Five days to London in a coach and four. Alexis hired her own coach – the postchaise costs tenpence a mile, with tips and turnpikes. She'd have saved money by buying her own coach!"

"There's the new telegraph from the Admiralty to Portsmouth," Aitken said. "They say they can get a message to the Admiralty and a reply in thirty minutes."

"Aye, a very brief message, providing there is no fog between the signal stations, all nine of them. Ten, counting the Admiralty itself," Southwick said.

"Is that true – half an hour?" Yorke asked.

Southwick nodded. "Yes, and the Admiralty is extending it along the coast to Plymouth. This telegraphic apparatus is a very simple thing to operate."

"And I'll bet that Southwick knows where every one of the stations to Portsmouth is built," Ramage said, "and plans to walk along the line of them from London, and then on to Plymouth and back, as soon as he's retired!"

Southwick looked puzzled. "How did you know that, sir? Not walk, though; I mean to do it on horseback."

"I guessed," Ramage said. "You once told me you had just copied out a list of where the stations were. Why would you want such a list, if not to follow the line of them?"

As Southwick nodded in agreement, Yorke said: "Where on earth are they?"

Like a child anxiously waiting to recite his poem at a party and once started unable to stop, Southwick said proudly: "From the Admiralty to Chelsea, Putney, Cabbage Hill, Netley Heath, Hascombe, Blackdown, Beacon Hill, Portsdown and then into Portsmouth.

"Then it is now being extended with stations at Chalton, Wickham, Town Hill, Foot Hill, Bramshaw, Pistle Down, Charlbury, Blandford, Belchalwell, Nettlecoombe, High Stoy, Toller Down, Lambert's Castle, Dalwood Common, St Cyres, Rockbere, Haldon, Knighton, Marley, Lee, Saltram, and then over to Plymouth Dock...how about that!"

Yorke had been listening carefully. "Yes, that would make one of the finest rides in England. There are other parts of the country where it'd be more beautiful for, say, twenty miles, but for a two-hundred-mile ride you couldn't beat that."

"When might we expect Miss Yorke back again?" Wagstaffe asked Yorke, "assuming she will need a couple of days in London?"

"Five days up and five back, plus two, which is twelve days," Yorke said. "Which means she can't get back until a week after the trial is over, even allowing that she'll drive the coachmen hard and may well sleep in the coach, stopping only for meals and change of horses."

Southwick nodded his head in agreement. "I can't see that young lady wasting time."

"No, she has hardly any luggage. Mine host at the King's Arms tells me that Alexis hired a coach and four and set off with one piece of luggage and a brace of pistols."

"A brace of pistols?" exclaimed Ramage. "A good idea for a young lady travelling alone, but where did she get them?"

"Oh, we always carry a brace each when we take a voyage," Yorke said. "Who knows, the commanding officer might go mad, apart from the risk of pirates, Frenchmen, privateersmen – "

" – and descendants of buccaneers," Ramage teased.

"It's because of our forebear that we are always well prepared," Yorke admitted with a grin. "Our forebear became rich because the Dons were never prepared. Anyway, you might well feel sympathy for the footpad or ravisher that stops Alexis' coach."

Ramage gave a shiver. "I'd rather not. I've never grown accustomed to being shot with a pistol, and by such a beautiful markswoman would be too painful. However, to get back to the point: what can we do now?"

"Have you anything else to present to the court in your defence?" Yorke asked. "Anything else for next Monday?"

"Nothing. Shirley will make his closing statement for the prosecution and then I make a statement outlining my defence, and the court is cleared while Goddard and his twelve captains consider the verdict. Then, when they've decided, I'm marched in again escorted by the provost marshal – who, incidentally, turns out to be a nice young fellow – and all the witnesses and spectators who are interested follow me in."

"And we all wait for the verdict to be announced," Yorke said.

Ramage laughed. "No. You've forgotten the trial you attended in Port Royal. I'll know the verdict the moment I walk through the door. I just look at my sword on the table: the hilt towards me means not guilty, the point, guilty. I then have a few anxious minutes waiting to see under which Articles of War I'm found guilty. You don't know them like the rest of us, but some carry a mandatory death sentence."

"So if the court…?"

"If the court finds me guilty on any one of those, it has no choice but to sentence me to death."

Yorke looked grim. "I wonder if Alexis is thinking only of that?"

Aitken said quietly: "She asked me for a copy of the *Articles of War*, and I gave her one, sir. I hope I did the right thing. And I marked the ones under which you're charged."

"You were quite right," Ramage said, and remembered Alexis' question in court about the charges, when Goddard had dropped the question rather than read through all the relevant Articles of War. So Alexis had known all the time: she had started provoking Goddard from the moment she began giving evidence.

He had to admit that seeing her sitting in the row of spectators' chairs, he regarded her as a very elegant ornament, much as one might be proud of a fine portrait in oils on one's dining-room walls. He had (he went hot at the thought) only called her as his last witness from fear that she would be offended if he left her out. Ye Gods: one day, when they were old and grey and reminiscing, he would tell her how close she came to never being a witness. But after being a lively witness she was now making a madcap dash to London in a coach and four with a brace of pistols close at hand. Gianna would have done that – and Gianna was at this moment probably dead, killed by one of Bonaparte's police agents. Sarah would have done it – but she had almost certainly died in the *Murex*. Would he always bring death to the women he loved?

The rest of the week passed slowly. The last days of autumn brought zephyrs which ruffled wavelets to make the sea look like hammered pewter. Each morning the *Calypso*'s cutter under Jackson's command went to fetch Sidney Yorke from the North Corner of the dockyard – the name given to the part close to the Gun Wharf and where North Corner Street met the jetty.

Yorke enjoyed leaving the King's Arms and walking the road from Plymouth itself, passing between the barracks and squares named after famous generals and skirting the Post Office as he strode down Cumberland Street to the noisy Market Place, where most things from cabbages to penny nails were being sold from the stalls.

Along Catherine Street and turning left a few yards into Fore Street brought him to the Dock Gates which seemed, improbably, to be guarded by the chapel just inside. A few more yards along Queen Street in the shadow of the dockyard walls brought him to the landward end of North Corner Street, with the jetty and the *Calypso*'s cutter at the bottom.

Walking along the streets, some cobbled, some surfaced with bricks, he passed men pushing laden carts and wheelbarrows, carrying baulks of timber, striding along with an adze over the shoulder or swinging a caulker's maul with, in the other hand, the wooden box of caulking cotton with its wide handle forming a seat.

A few sailors hurried along pulling a cart laden with coils of new rope intended for one of the ships anchored in the Hamoaze; a file of Marines marched to the sergeant's monotonous "leff...ri'...leff...ri' " – where were they going, he wondered?

He felt an air of unreality; everything seemed insubstantial, as though he was walking in a dream. The sun was still weak at this time of the morning but cast chill shadows across the narrower streets. The town of Plymouth Dock, he thought, comprised more angular buildings than any other place he knew, and every one of them caused a shadow.

Yet despite this strange remoteness affecting him, there was a sense of purpose about the dockyard area as a whole: workmen heading for the Dockyard gates, each man with his own tools and most of them with their midday meal wrapped in a bright bandanna; the seamen running with a cart, shouting and yelling, teasing each other and hurling well-meant abuse at men from other ships; the marching Marines, serious of face and giving the impression of a moving panel of white diagonal lines, a tribute to hours of pipeclaying. All had obvious links with the ships of war at anchor.

It all had a sense of purpose until he thought about the enormous *Salvador del Mundo* moored out there in the Hamoaze, and the *Calypso* riding at a single anchor. Could a man like Ramage, wounded several times, who had captured from the French the frigate he now commanded (apart from capturing the famous Diamond Rock, commanding the approach to Fort Royal the capital of Martinique), the hero of many attacks on the French in the Mediterranean, now be in desperate danger?

What was wrong with a system under which such a man could be tried for his life by his own people and, as far as Yorke could make out, be almost certain of being executed by them? Why was the Navy, no matter who represented it, about to do what Bonaparte most certainly would do, given the chance – kill Captain Ramage?

Ramage had written to his father, the Earl of Blazey, and told him not to attempt to interfere. Nicholas was obviously frightened that the old political vendetta which had made his father a scapegoat could somehow be renewed, so that the old man could be harmed. Could it? Yorke was far from sure. He only knew that any politician would always do unspeakable things to save his own political skin. Making a career out of murder, or prostitution, or burgling, or pimping, was against the law: society in its wisdom had decided that each was wrong. Politics came into the same category, but since politicians were also lawmakers, there was no law regulating politics; the only limit placed upon them was the natural contempt of honest men. Yorke for a moment felt sorry for a man who had taken up politics. Possibly in the early flush of youth the man had intended to do great things: then, probably quite slowly, he found that men outside politics whom he respected did not exactly shun him, but kept him at a distance, as though shamefully hidden beneath tailored breeches and silk coat he had the scabs of some vile disease.

Byng was fifty years ago. And today? Certainly members of the present government were intellectually barely equipped to run some of the stalls he was now passing in the Market Place. Addington, for instance, the prime minister, was a man so weak and vacillating that no one in his right mind would leave him in charge of a greengrocery stall.

Yorke recalled bitterly that Alexis might in fact be calling on the wretched man in three or four days, trying to persuade him to do something. Yorke was far from sure what Alexis had in mind, and he was beginning to realize that Nicholas and his officers were just being polite.

Yes, they were deeply touched that Alexis had impulsively hired a coach and four and was at this very moment hurrying to London; they were very grateful for her spirited appearance in court. They appreciated that Yorke was waiting to give what evidence he could to help.

Yorke now realized that the "but" was that nothing Alexis could do *would be in time*. She would hardly have arrived in London by the time the court sat again next Monday; by Monday evening, or Tuesday morning at the latest, the court would have returned its verdict and Nicholas would have been found guilty or not guilty. And that would be that.

Yorke had the feeling that they thought Ramage would be found guilty and sentenced to death, but that the Admiralty would order a reprieve. Poor Alexis. Yorke knew by now that his sister loved Ramage but, more important, had during the long voyage home from the West Indies, when she had seen a good deal of him as a guest on board the *Emerald* or when they were dining on board the *Calypso*, accepted that she had lost him before she found him, because he was married to another woman. Alexis had come to know that woman through the occasional remarks of Ramage and his officers, and as she had learned of the circumstances of the two of them meeting at some island off Brazil, and the honeymoon cut short by Bonaparte's police, she had come to admire her.

At the moment she was trying to save him because he was a friend of the Yorkes who needed help; but she was also trying to save him for Sarah, whom she had never met. Perhaps – who really ever knew all the details of a person's motives? – she had wild hopes that if anything had happened to Sarah (which seemed highly probable) she could take her place. Whatever Alexis was about now, though, she did not know (fortunately, he thought) that on board the *Calypso* brave men had in fact finally given up.

And there was the *Calypso*'s cutter, with Jackson standing at the top of the slippery steps ready to help him down. What did Jackson think? And Stafford and Rossi and all those other men who had fought beside Ramage and who never cared whether he was right or wrong, but only that he was their captain?

If their captain was in danger of his life in a French prison, they would be ready to follow Aitken and Southwick and the others in whatever desperate rescue attempt they decided to make. Now their captain was in deadly danger from his own people: from the very senior officers whom these seamen were supposed to respect.

As he said good morning to Jackson, and commented on the fine weather, the sun and the calm sea, he felt he wanted to do something violent: words had failed them all. He realized that he could watch Goddard fall into the sea and flounder around and drown, and his only emotions would be contempt and relief, in that order.

When Yorke arrived on board the *Calypso* and was met at the entryport by Ramage he was startled to find him grinning and obviously in high spirits, even though today was Sunday and tomorrow the trial was due to open again on board the *Salvador del Mundo*. There was one thing he had long ago learned about Nicholas, going back to those days when they were together on board the Post Office packet (which was when he first got to know and appreciate men like Southwick and Jackson). When a situation became what most men would regard as desperate, Ramage was likely to become ribald. Danger seemed to rouse him so that he brought zest to even the most routine activities. Loading a pistol, laying a sword blade on the wheel of a grindstone, all these became for Ramage not the prelude to some desperate adventure likely to put a term to his life but the bouquet which would bring a contented smile to a wine connoisseur. His modesty was not false: when he did something brave it genuinely embarrassed him to be congratulated because an action that seemed normal to him would be heroic for most other men.

"You have that contented look, mixed with excitement, of the cat that has stolen all the fish from the pantry and still has some left!" Yorke said.

"If she'll forgive the expression, our cat seems to have arrived!"

Yorke looked puzzled and Ramage led him below to the cabin, sat him down in the battered armchair, and gave him the letter which had been lying opened on the desk.

Yorke saw from the superscription that it was from the commander-in-chief, dated and timed earlier that morning, and telling Ramage:

I have received instructions from my Lords Commissioners of the Admiralty to postpone your trial for one week, and you are hereby informed that your trial will therefore be resumed seven days later at the same time in the morning...

"What do you think that means?"

Ramage shrugged his shoulders. "It could mean that Goddard has been taken ill with the colic, or the commander-in-chief wants to prepare the great cabin of the *Salvador del Mundo* so that his wife can give a vast first-of-the-season ball in my honour..."

"It could," Yorke agreed, "or perhaps the dockyard has run out of quills and ink so that Jenkins cannot delete evidence from his minutes, but I think there might be some other explanation. When did you get this?" he asked, waving the letter.

"The provost marshal brought it out an hour ago."

"Well, tell me; I'll never guess what it's all about."

"Alexis," Ramage said. "Obviously she's arrived in London."

"Alexis? What on earth has she got to do with this letter? She'll be in London in a day or so, yes, but this letter was written here in Plymouth."

"Ah, you're probably not the first brother who underestimated his sister. But let me tell you what I *know*, then we can speculate about the rest. The provost marshal (you met him, that young Lieutenant Hill) has been sitting behind me for the whole trial and he realized what Goddard is trying to do, so although officially he is my jailer, Hill is secretly on my side.

"Early this morning he was ordered by flag signal hoisted on Mount Wise to report to the commander-in-chief. He hurried on shore and was given this letter to deliver to me.

"Being an enterprising young fellow, he had a gossip with the commander-in-chief's secretary, who was somewhat ruffled and only too glad of a chance to describe how he had been called from his bed shortly after dawn – on a Sunday, too! – by a messenger who had ridden with an urgent signal from Portsmouth for the admiral.

"Apparently the Admiralty had sent a signal to Portsmouth by the telegraph – taking a matter of minutes – with orders that a messenger should immediately ride with it to Plymouth and deliver it to the commander-in-chief. The poor fellow has been riding for hours and has had a devil of a job getting fresh horses. Luckily there has been a moon, so that he could keep to the road at night.

"When the secretary – roused out when the messenger arrived – saw the instructions on the outside of the letter, signed and sealed by the port admiral at Portsmouth, he called his lord and master from his bed. The admiral read the signal, expressed his displeasure, and dictated that – " Ramage pointed at the letter, " – to the secretary, giving him precise instructions for getting it delivered to me. They're all the facts I know."

"So now we speculate, eh?" Yorke grinned cheerfully. "You start, because you know more about the bureaucracy than I."

"Well, why should the trial be postponed for another week? Goddard has already delayed things for a few days, because of the Coronation anniversary, and he wanted to square his own yards with the captains forming the court, and perhaps he also wanted to have a quiet chat with the commander-in-chief."

"Then, *why* the delay?" Yorke asked.

"I'm asking the question, not answering it! The question is whether or not the delay ordered by the Admiralty is the result of something done by Goddard or by..."

"Alexis?"

"Yes. I'm putting my money on Alexis and the Admiralty. I think she reached London earlier than we expected, and has been harrying authority on my behalf."

Yorke nodded his head slowly. "Yes...but why a *week's* delay? What happens at the end of that week?"

Ramage laughed. "One thing, for sure: Alexis will have arrived back here with her brace of pistols!"

"Yes," Yorke said seriously, "but surely the Admiralty wouldn't delay anything for even seven seconds because of

Alexis. I love my sister and have great faith in her abilities, but let's be realistic!"

"They may not be delaying anything *for* her but perhaps they're delaying the trial because of something she's done."

"Like seeing Lord St Vincent, or perhaps even Addington?"

"Or blowing up Parliament or attending a levee and complaining to the King."

Yorke gave a dry laugh. "You can joke about it, but I can see her doing one of those things. All of them, even."

"I wasn't really joking, either," Ramage said. "I can see her, prodding with her parasol. I seem to attract women who can flatten mountains by pointing at them."

"When you get women under your spell, they're inspired to do wild things."

"Oh, that's it, is it? Pity I can't do the same to admirals."

"Ask Alexis to point at Goddard: perhaps she can flatten him too."

"Why the delay, though?" Ramage mused. "A week. Seven days. What can happen a week from tomorrow that can't happen tomorrow?"

Yorke stood up and took the backgammon set from a cupboard. "Obviously the Board of Admiralty have something in mind, otherwise they wouldn't have ordered the delay."

"Don't make any mistake about the Board," Ramage said, helping Yorke set out the backgammon. "The Board of Admiralty and a backgammon board have much in common; both depend on the roll of a die. At least, sometimes I'm sure that's what Their Lordships use."

"Who exactly are 'the Board'?" Yorke asked.

"Well, originally there was the Lord High Admiral, but from Queen Anne's time the office has been administered by commissioners – the 'Board of Admiralty', also known as 'My

Lords Commissioners of the Admiralty', or 'Their Lordships'. I don't think there's a set number, but for the last few years anyway there have been the First Lord, who is usually a politician, and six other members, three of them naval officers and three politicians.

"It so happens that the present First Lord is an admiral of the white, Earl St Vincent, but he succeeded Earl Spencer, a politician. Lord St Vincent has no patience with politicians, so I imagine the prime minister gives him a free hand. Knowing the admiral, I can't imagine him deferring to Addington."

"Are the other naval members of the Board all admirals?"

"Usually, but not always. One of Lord St Vincent's present Board is Captain Markham, whose name must be seventy-five or so from the top of the Post List, while Lord Spencer's had two or three admirals."

"And the whole Board meet to make major decisions?"

Ramage shook his head. "No, a 'Board decision' needs only three members present. I think it is three but it may be four. Commissions, appointments, and orders, that sort of thing, usually have three signatures, sometimes four. I know that three or four Board members call in at the Admiralty in the late afternoon each day to sign documents and letters, but certainly with Lord Spencer – and I am dam' sure even more so under Lord St Vincent – the First Lord makes the major decisions and the Board members sign at the bottom of the relevant pages."

"No discussions, then?"

"Oh yes, the members usually meet daily in the Boardroom. Not all the members, necessarily, but usually the First Lord and two or three members and the Secretary to the Board, who is an important person with a good deal of influence. He gets paid a thousand pounds a year more than the First Lord! It's his job to keep the minutes of the Board meetings and see that decisions are turned into actions. Letters to the Board are addressed to him, and letters from the Board are usually written and signed by him in its name."

"What about the letter?" Yorke asked, nodding at the paper now on Ramage's desk. "Did he sign that?"

"No, because it's from the port admiral here," Ramage explained, "but I expect the original signal to Portsmouth was signed by him."

Ramage, who had finished setting out the counters, handed a leather dice cup to Yorke. "Shake," he said. "Unless you want to find a gipsy to tell our fortunes, let's concentrate on the roll of the dice."

The second week passed with numbing slowness. Yorke usually came over to the *Calypso* for dinner which was served about two o'clock, and Ramage tried to busy himself each morning with the paperwork necessary when the King's ships were at anchor in one of the King's ports.

Every port admiral had his own quirks as well as his own idea of what information he needed daily from the anchored ships. Most port admirals had their requirements printed in book form: a copy of the Plymouth Port Signals and General Orders was one of the first things Southwick obtained after the *Calypso* had anchored. Apart from the signals, which ranged from requiring a variety of people "to repair on board the Flag ship, or ship whose number is shown or pointed out by compass signal" to the last one, which was to "Return the Book of Port Signals and Orders to the Flag Ship", the orders were almost bewildering in their attention to detail. And Ramage guessed that in the present situation several people on board the flagship or in the Dockyard were keeping an eye on the *Calypso*, waiting for her captain to omit sending in even one of the daily returns listed in the book.

One of the earliest orders in the book, Ramage had noted, laid down that "Admirals, captains and commanders are to attend courts-martial in frock uniforms with white breeches, unless otherwise ordered."

The rest were mostly routine. "A return according to the prescribed form, is to be made daily to the Admiral, of all men impressed the preceding day: and it is to be observed that men are not to be impressed from outwardbound vessels..." In order to prevent any person being improperly taken out of His Majesty's ships, "no stranger shall be admitted on board till the real object for which he comes is made known" – a regulation to protect seamen from being seized for actual or alleged debt. Hard on creditors, perhaps; but a tradesman giving a sailor credit was an optimist.

Ramage, flicking through the pages of the orders, was always surprised by their scope. "Foreign seamen taken into the Service, if found to be married in England, the circumstance to be inserted in the ship's books." And, a page later: "All sick seamen, and Marines, are to be sent to the hospital in the forenoon...and are not to be victualled on board for the day they leave the ship" – whereas "Commission and warrant officers (except in the cases of accident or urgent necessity) will not be received at the hospital, unless their tickets are approved by the Commander-in-Chief."

Not all the instructions concerned a ship swinging at anchor and Ramage wondered if a port admiral had inserted one particular order as the result of his own experience or an Admiralty order: "It being a practice with the enemy, when they made a capture, to keep an Englishman in the Prize, to make answer when hailed by a British ship, particular caution is to be observed that no inconvenience occurs by this deception."

A ship's boats were not – except in urgent necessity – to be away at mealtimes: that avoided men missing their food. Working parties leaving the ship were "to have their breakfast before they are sent on duty". Well, he noticed, a captain or first lieutenant observing all the reports he had to make might reflect that those same irritating port orders also gave the men several safeguards.

On Sunday morning, knowing it was his only chance of finishing the remaining paperwork before the trial began again next day, Ramage reached across the desk for the pile of letters, completed forms, reports and surveys placed there the previous evening by his clerk, and started reading through them before adding his signature. He looked at the first one which, with luck, might be the dreariest of them all. "Account of Vouchers for Provisions" it was headed, but the page was divided to allow many more details. "When dated...When signed...Where signed...To Whom delivered" were the main questions, but eleven more columns needed precise details of weights and measures – "Bread, pounds...Rum, gallons... Wine, gallons... Beef, pieces...Pork, pieces...Pease, bushels... Oatmeal, bushels ...Butter, pounds...Barley, pounds... Molasses, pounds... Vinegar, gallons."

The figures meant nothing to Ramage, although once he signed the voucher he would be responsible for its truth. Well, the purser and the master, Southwick, would have cast them up. He signed at the foot of the page and reached for the next sheet of paper.

Signing papers was preferable, he supposed, to listening to Admiral Goddard. No, it was not! Crossing verbal swords with that wretched man certainly had won him no victories in the *Salvador del Mundo*'s great cabin, but Ramage was satisfied that he had put up a good fight. Unfortunately, every time that his sword pierced the wretched man and should metaphorically have drawn blood, Goddard refused to allow it to register. Stabbing Goddard was like fighting a duel with a straw-filled sack.

He signed his name and reached for the third. "Cooper's affidavit to Leakage of Beer" –120 gallons of small beer had leaked from two casks "as mentioned in the survey hereunto annexed". Ramage checked – yes, the second page was the survey to which the cooper was swearing the affidavit. Ramage signed and reached again.

"Vouchers for slops purchased" – the *Calypso's* purser had been restocking: now the frigate was in a cold climate the men would want to buy warmer clothes. For a year they had been wearing duck and many of them spent most of the day without shirts. Ramage read through the list. "Jackets, one hundred, at 10s – £50; waistcoats, one hundred at 4s 3d – £21 5s 0d; shirts, one hundred, at 5s 3d..." He noted that trousers were 3s 2d a pair now, shoes 5s 10d and stockings 3s...He signed and wished he did not feel so drowsy. The unaccustomed lack of movement of the ship and the noises of a big anchorage, with guard boats rowing round all night, prevented him from sleeping properly. The noise and, he had to admit, worry about the trial...

Yorke should be along very soon. Ramage had conducted Divine Service an hour earlier and although in port he usually tried to brighten up the morning with a short sermon, today he had fallen back on the Articles of War. By regulation they had to be read aloud to the ship's company once a month, and most captains used them instead of a sermon, or homily. Ramage had been startled by the fervour of the men in singing the hymns. The way the men sang hymns was always regarded as a good yardstick for measuring how contented they were, but Ramage had never had to wonder whether or not he had a contented ship's company. Anyway, today the men bellowed the hymns, and it was clear they were hurling defiance at the port admiral, Rear-Admiral Goddard and anyone else connected with the trial. There was nothing Ramage could do to make them sing in a more restrained fashion and, damnation take it, he did not want to. But this display of loyalty left him worrying about Sarah: feeling empty when he puzzled about her fate, yet thankful she was not sharing the doubts and fears of the trial. He knew he had better not trust either his own voice or choice of words in a brief sermon, and he had ploughed through the Articles of War in a completely neutral voice. Even then he had been startled by the men's low murmuring, little more than the noise the wind made in the rigging, or the faint sawing of a yard when the ship rolled at anchor, as he read the Articles under which he was charged.

One more page, one more signature. He scribbled a signature and reached for the piece of cloth to wipe the pen. Suddenly, without any call by the Marine sentry, the flimsy door of the cabin was flung open.

CHAPTER **TWENTY**

She came into the cabin shyly and closed the door behind her. "Nicholas," she said, "forgive me: I waved to the sentry at the gangway and to Mr Kenton not to announce my arrival, and Mr Kenton came down and told your sentry to stay silent. Was I *very* naughty?"

By now he had recovered enough to stand up and move towards her and before either of them knew quite what was happening, Ramage found himself patting her head (she was smaller than he realized: the top of her head was below the top of his shoulder) and she was crying as he murmured: "No, no, of course not; everything will turn out all right; you mustn't upset yourself..."

Then she stood back, trying to laugh away her tears while tidying her windswept hair. She smiled uncertainly but the effect was spoiled by her sobs.

"Alexis..." Ramage began tentatively, "you shouldn't have gone off to London like that...you upset and tire yourself..."

She was pale and the golden tan of the Tropics was now yellowish, because of the obvious weariness, and there were dark smudges under her eyes.

"We did the journey in well under five days," she said, her voice now becoming excited. "We changed horses many more times than the coachmen said was necessary, but we kept them galloping...Through the nights as well, and how lucky we were that there was a full moon…oh, but we were so tired."

"We" – she kept referring to "we". Not "we" meaning her and the coachmen because she had mentioned them separately.

"Who are 'we'?"

"Oh dear, I'm so tired that I'm muddled – "

Ramage suddenly realized that they were both standing in the middle of the cabin. "Sit down – you know that old armchair. Sidney should be coming on board in half an hour or so for dinner. Do you want to stay and see him here, or shall I send you to the King's Arms in the cutter with Jackson? Is – er, well, I can't come with you because I'm under arrest and have to stay on board – "

"Oh Nicholas, that's what I'm trying to tell you. It's going to be all right. I have the witness that you want, and a member of the Board is here in Plymouth and will attend the trial tomorrow – but you're not to say anything until the trial begins. I'll explain how…oh Nicholas, I want to laugh and cry and giggle and faint and explain all at once…"

"So the best thing we can do is to sit here and wait for Sidney to arrive," Ramage said. "That way you won't have to tell the story twice, and you'll be more composed. Brothers like to see their sisters composed," he said, making a weak attempt at a joke.

She was obviously almost stunned with weariness, but she tried to smooth the creases in her skirt. "I feel so grubby," she said. "I must look a scarecrow – I haven't changed my clothes for two days, and the only wash I've had since breakfast time yesterday, is rubbing my face with a damp cloth."

"Alexis," he asked gently, "what made you bolt for London like that without telling us?"

"You thought you were beaten," she said simply, and her directness hit him like a blow. "I thought there was a chance, although I knew if I listened to you and Sidney, I'd be persuaded there was not. So I arranged for the coach, wrote a note to Sidney, and left before the mail coach. I knew Sidney would be late back to the inn and would go straight to his room."

He watched her as she sat in the low armchair, apparently concentrating on her creased clothes, and he felt ashamed: yes, he *had* felt defeated, and so had Sidney, and Southwick, Aitken and Wagstaffe, too, for that matter. Anyone thinking about it logically would know he was beaten, but this tiny girl did not bother with logic; she knew instinctively what was wrong and how to put it right. The famous Captain Ramage, he jeered at himself, could slash with a cutlass, or fire a pistol or bring his ship alongside the enemy and board in a cloud of smoke and survive it all, and be called a hero by people who did not know about these things, but he had surrendered at a time when this girl had only just begun to fight.

"I hadn't realized how far it was to London," she said. "Usually when Sidney and I visit the West Country, we come round in one of our ships. But oh dear, how dusty are those roads. The thudding of hooves and the rumbling of the wheels, too: it gives me such a headache, and it is hard to talk..."

Talk? With whom? Was she not travelling alone? Well, apparently not, but, he told himself sternly, it was none of his business.

He heard Kenton shouting down through the skylight: "Boat bringing Mr Yorke will be alongside in three minutes, Sir!"

Her face was tearstained. "Go through to the bed place," he said, gesturing to the cabin in which he slept. "There's a basin and a jug of fresh water. I'll find you a fresh towel."

A couple of minutes later, the Marine sentry called: "Mr Yorke, sir!" and a moment after Ramage replied, Yorke came through the door and stopped suddenly as he saw Alexis. "How the devil did – "

Alexis looked at Ramage. "You see how he greets his loving sister – the next thing is he'll be grumbling about how much money I've spent. Then I remind him it is my own money and – "

" – he says you waste it. Right," Yorke said, "that takes care of the greetings. What happened?"

"I had an appointment with my dressmaker," she said coolly. "And my shoemaker. And one or two other people."

Yorke looked across at Ramage. "She seems to be in one of her skittish moods. Has she told you anything?"

"No, we were waiting for you, so that she didn't have to tell the story twice."

"There are really three stories," she began, "but I'll start at the King's Arms."

Yorke groaned. "Surely we don't have to hear all about your journey to London, at tenpence a mile including turnpike charges and tips."

"No, but you have to hear about the beginning because that's where I met the young man who escorted me all the way to London – to Palace Street, in fact, to Nicholas' home."

She looked at the two men with what seemed to Ramage to be an impish grin, as though she was enjoying teasing them. "Yes, I had just arranged with the innkeeper for the hire of the coach, and paid half the fare in advance, when this young man burst in, very agitated because all the seats were taken in the London mail coach."

"So you offered him a seat," Yorke said crossly. "A complete stranger! He could have been a footpad's accomplice!"

"He could have been, but I only offered him a seat after I'd discovered he was someone we were looking for."

"Who? An honest politician?" Yorke asked sarcastically.

"No, a witness for Nicholas."

"We don't lack for witnesses," Yorke said bitterly. "We just lack witnesses who know what happened on board the *Jason*."

Alexis nodded contentedly and smoothed her skirt. "This one does."

"And we need to be able to get his evidence into the minutes of the court's proceedings."

"Yes," she said demurely, "that's arranged, too."

"Look here, Alexis," Yorke exclaimed angrily, "this isn't a joking matter."

"I'm not joking," Alexis said, "just listen, without interrupting. It's not often I get a chance to talk for a whole minute so – "

Ramage coughed and Alexis glanced round, smiling.

Then she told how the young man – in fact, only a youth of seventeen – proved to be a midshipman who was leaving his ship and the Navy. He had seemed overwrought, and did not have enough money to get to London: he wanted the innkeeper to accept a ten-day bill of exchange drawn on his father, who was a Member of Parliament. She had felt sorry for the youth, who was clearly well educated, and then discovered he was leaving the *Jason* for a reason which seemed to hang over him like a shadow.

"So I offered him a seat, and I told him his father could pay for his place when we reached London. I warned him that we would be driving day and night, and that he would have to eat and sleep in the coach, and he agreed: he could not get away from Plymouth quickly enough."

So each of them had climbed up into the coach, the postboys had slammed the doors and swung up the steps with the usual crash, the coachmen had whipped up the horses and they had thundered through the night, both Alexis and the midshipman trying to sleep. When they stopped next morning to change horses they had a hurried breakfast and the midshipman had commented on Alexis' tan, and she had taken a chance and mentioned very casually that she had just arrived in England from the West Indies. As she had intended, this had led to the midshipman exclaiming that his ship had been part of the escort for that convoy.

Alexis explained how she had sensed that the youth – his name was Edward Blaxton, son of one of the Members of Parliament for Maidstone – wanted to tell someone about some awful experience he had undergone, but she had decided she would hear the story more fully if she let him tell it bit by bit, as the days went by during the journey to London. And that was what happened. He would mention one episode when they stopped briefly for dinner, she would hear of a later one when the coach stopped to change horses and there was a quarter of an hour's quiet. An earlier episode might be related while they had a hurried supper as the horses were changed and the coach axles greased.

The journey itself, Alexis admitted, became a nightmare: soon she could remember no other life than being confined inside a coach and breathing the smell of mildew and old leather. Occasionally she and Edward would try to clean it up, because eating a snack amid all the jolting meant that crumbs and pieces of cheese and cold meat would slip down under the leather seats.

Gradually the coach made its way towards London: eventually Exeter, Honiton, Axminster, Bridport, Dorchester, Blandford, Salisbury, Andover and Basingstoke became memories, places where horses had been changed, surly or bowing and scraping innkeepers served or refused meals, where a horse went lame or an axle ran hot. Then the place names became more associated with London than the West Country – she particularly remembered a good dinner at Bagshot, where they also changed horses, with a good road on to Sunningdale. Then Staines and another change of horses, and on to Heston and another change at Brentford. By then, as they approached Westminster, she knew everything that had happened on board the *Jason* and she had made a dangerous decision: she had told Midshipman Blaxton the reason why she was hurrying to London, and he had immediately volunteered his father's help. His father, it seemed, also knew Addington well and had a London house. She had left Blaxton at his home in Berkeley Square, with him promising to bring his father to Palace Street as soon as possible.

"I had to risk upsetting your father," she told Ramage, "but I needed somewhere as a headquarters. I could have used our own house, but that seemed to be wasting time: I needed to talk with your father and at the same time have somewhere to meet young Blaxton's father. And of course, Palace Street is so close to the Admiralty and Parliament."

She gave a nervous laugh. "To be honest, by now I was frightened to death at what I'd done. I wasn't at all worried until we reached Hyde Park Corner, but when Edward left the coach in Berkeley Square, I suddenly felt very lonely, and I knew that if I opened up our own house I'd just sit in my bedroom and weep. So although I didn't know your parents, I decided that if I was going to weep I'd sooner do it in their company."

"Were they very frightening?" Ramage was curious about the impression they made on a stranger.

"Frightening? My goodness, if I'd been their daughter they couldn't have made me more welcome, even though I must have looked like a street woman who hadn't changed her clothes for days. I hadn't since leaving Plymouth, of course, and I was probably wild-eyed. I was certainly incoherent when your butler – a delightful old man whose spectacles kept sliding down his nose – opened the door. I could only ask for 'the Admiral', but your mother heard me, and all I could say to her was 'Nicholas', but that was enough."

Alexis described how the Earl had taken her into his study and she had poured out an almost incoherent description of Rear-Admiral Goddard's behaviour at the trial. At this point the Earl had become angry, she said, because he had just received a letter from Nicholas telling him to refrain from interfering. "That letter hurt him: I think you must have written tactlessly."

She then told Ramage's parents how she had decided to come to London to get help. The Earl had asked very bluntly, she said, whether or not Nicholas thought he had a chance of being acquitted, and she told him that it was Nicholas' acceptance of defeat which had started her off on the road to London.

" 'Defeat' is pitching it a bit strong," Sidney protested but Ramage shook his head.

"I don't know about you," he admitted, "but I was feeling defeated. I couldn't – still can't, for that matter – see a way of getting round Goddard, and only two or three of the captains seemed prepared to argue over all that deleted evidence. Three votes out of twelve means an almost unanimous verdict of guilty, particularly since the junior captains vote first."

"The junior vote first?" Alexis was puzzled.

"When all the evidence has been heard and the prosecution and defence have stated their cases," Ramage explained, "the president of the court (after it has been cleared of everyone except the members) asks each member whether or not he considers the accused is guilty or not. He asks the most junior captain first, and then the next most junior, and so on. The theory is that the juniors give their opinions without being influenced by the seniors, but he'd be a mutton-headed officer who reached the end of a trial without seeing or guessing his seniors' views."

"Well," Alexis continued, "your father thought you seemed to feel defeated, and so did I and," she added with a grim laugh, "the opinions of the two of us carried a lot of weight in Palace Street.

"Then the fireworks started. Your father had been fairly calm until then: your mother could control him, in other words. But when I told him young Blaxton's story he swore and swore. I must say that as soon as your mother reproved him – she was concerned for my young ears – he changed to Italian, which I don't speak, but even then his meanings were quite clear since I read Latin."

She described how by then the room was beginning to spin because she was so tired, and the Countess had insisted that she had some sleep. In fact she slept for nine hours and when she woke and washed she rushed downstairs in a panic – to find that the Earl, Sarah's father the Marquis of Rockley, and Sir James Blaxton, with the young midshipman, had already been along to the Admiralty and waited on Earl St Vincent.

"Your father says the First Lord is dour, the sort of man who is miserly with words. Lord St Vincent made it quite clear he could not interfere with the court-martial, apart from delaying it for a week, to give us time to discuss it, but what he could do was make sure that all the legitimate evidence – your father says he laid great stress on that phrase 'legitimate evidence' – should be heard and recorded in the minutes."

Yorke said bitterly: "How can that be done with Goddard sitting there?"

"Wait a moment, Sidney," she said. "It seems that the First Lord is a worldly man and he acted as though there was no point in sending orders to the port admiral here in Plymouth. The inference was (although Lord St Vincent did not put it into words, of course) that Goddard probably influenced him. All that was needed, the First Lord said, was someone in authority making sure that the trial was conducted properly, and that is why he delayed it a week."

Yorke groaned. "You don't mean to say that after all your efforts, you left it like that and came back here?"

She nodded and Ramage guessed that Sidney Yorke had underestimated his sister. Perhaps brothers always did because the important impressions were made during childhood. But Sidney was not only underestimating his sister, he was underestimating the Earl of Blazey, the Marquis and Sir James Blaxton. And come to that, the Countess of Blazey as well.

"Sidney, there are times when I could shake you." The exasperation showed in Alexis' voice. "It seems to me that this man Goddard has bewitched you. Well, he hasn't bewitched me; he's just made me very angry. And he's had the same effect on Nicholas' parents, the Marquis and Sir James Blaxton – and perhaps Earl St Vincent, but I wasn't present."

She rearranged her hair, a womanly gesture that Ramage found quite beguiling.

"So this is what has been arranged. By chance one of the Lords Commissioners of the Admiralty (Nicholas' father says he's one of the officers most highly regarded by Earl St Vincent) was at Portsmouth. He is Captain John Markham, son of the Archbishop of York. Do you know him, Nicholas?"

Ramage shook his head. "Only by sight and reputation: he's a well respected officer. It's not often captains are made sea lords, and Earl St Vincent neither suffers fools gladly nor plays favourites. He must have advanced Markham because he is competent."

"Good. Well, Captain Markham was in Portsmouth on some Admiralty business, and the First Lord immediately wrote to him and sent the letter to Portsmouth in the night bag – apparently the messenger leaves in the evening and gets to Portsmouth early next day. Captain Markham was told to get to Plymouth by any means he chose, but he had to be on board the *Salvador del Mundo* by half past eight next Monday – that's tomorrow morning – and sit as the First Lord's observer at your trial."

Ramage nodded, scarcely able to believe his ears. "That's all we need," he muttered. "Just a fair hearing." He rubbed the scars on his brow. "Just a fair hearing," he repeated. "No more, and no less."

"You're going to get that," Alexis said. "And I've brought Midshipman Blaxton back with me: he's staying at the King's Arms. I've told him to be waiting at the North Corner in the Dockyard at four o'clock, when you'll send a boat for him. You can talk to him and he'll be ready to give evidence tomorrow. Oh yes, Lord St Vincent has told Captain Markham not to wear uniform. I gather that Rear-Admiral Goddard does not know him by sight, so he's unlikely to recognize him sitting among the spectators in court, and that's so much the better, as far as Lord St Vincent is concerned."

"Dinner," Sidney Yorke said. "Nicholas, you are the host and my sister looks exhausted."

"I am too sleepy to eat," Alexis said. "Can I sleep here for an hour or two while you dine, then I can go back with Sidney? I'd like to be here to introduce young Blaxton."

Ramage went to the door and told the Marine sentry to pass the word for the captain's steward, and then he went through to the bed place. The cabin in which he slept was tiny and his bed was the usual cot, a long, open-top box fitted into what was in effect a large hammock which was suspended from the deck beams. The box was fitted with a mattress, and he checked that the sheets were clean.

"Two blankets – will they be enough?"

"Plenty – I'm too sleepy to feel the cold. Wake me when my Mr Blaxton arrives."

CHAPTER TWENTY-ONE

Rear-Admiral Goddard looked at each of the captains seated round the table and noted that there were many more spectators sitting in the chairs and forms at the back of the cabin – among them that wretched young woman who had made such a scene the day he adjourned the court. Jenkins was sitting behind his pile of reference books and papers. He saw that Captain Shirley was sitting in the prosecutor's chair and, as usual, staring fixedly at the deck – like, he thought unexpectedly, a man who had dropped a golden guinea and just seen it roll down a crack between two planks. A seam, he corrected himself.

This should be the last day of the trial: Shirley had to make the closing statement for the prosecution; then Ramage had to make his for the defence. Clear the court and let these twelve dunderheads talk about it all, and then, with their verdict returned, twist the sword round so that it pointed to the door, and have Ramage brought back in...

At last he felt cheerful. Swinford, Royce and Huggins had made a lot of trouble at that last session, after the court had been cleared. Fussing about what should be recorded in the minutes and what should not: they were like a trio of virgins pleading for their honour. But they had eventually submitted. A hint that there were many more captains on the Post List than ships for them to command had been enough: they seemed suddenly to be able to understand the position of unemployed virgins…

Goddard waved cheerfully to Jenkins. "Have the prisoner brought in."

Lieutenant Hill led Ramage to his chair, and when Ramage, after bowing politely to the court, took his seat, Hill sat down behind him.

Goddard spoke the preliminary words declaring the court in session and was just about to call on Captain Shirley to begin his statement when he heard a chair scrape and turned to see Ramage on his feet.

"Well?" Goddard asked coldly. "What now?"

"I have two more witnesses to call before closing my defence, sir," Ramage said politely.

Goddard raised his eyebrows in feigned surprise. "I thought you'd already called your last witness, that young lady. You made a rather melodramatic gesture of crossing out all the other names on your list. Since *you* crossed out the names, the court is satisfied that it has heard all the witnesses you requested. Jenkins, my understanding of it is correct, is it not? You have no outstanding witnesses waiting to give evidence for Captain Ramage?"

"Indeed not, sir," Jenkins said unctuously.

Ramage walked the length of the table and put a sheet of paper on the table in front of Jenkins. "Two fresh witnesses," he said.

Without looking down, Jenkins waited for Goddard who said, before Ramage returned to his seat: "Too late, far too late. A trial would drag on for a month if the court allowed the defence to keep on producing witnesses. Captain Ramage should know," he added in a patronizing voice, "that that is the reason why the deputy judge advocate writes to the accused before the trial to ask for a complete list of defence witnesses."

Without sitting down, Ramage said: "With respect, sir, there is nothing in the court-martial statutes that forbids the calling of extra witnesses should further evidence – or witnesses, for that matter – become available."

"I am the president of the court," Goddard said heavily, "and the court rules that you have had your chance to call the witnesses you requested."

"But I am requesting two more, so – with respect – that ruling is hardly fair."

"I've already explained to you," Goddard said angrily. "If you forget to put witnesses on your list, it's no good you coming along a fortnight later and making additions. You are overruled, and that's that."

Goddard was surprised that Ramage did not sit down. Instead he turned to the spectators, and Goddard saw a man nod to him, whereupon Ramage turned back to face the court.

"Sir," Ramage said politely, "I must with great respect ask you to reconsider your ruling on my request for two more witnesses."

"You're wasting the court's time," Goddard snapped. "Sit down: we now have to hear the prosecution."

Ramage remained standing, his eyes fixed on Goddard. "With your permission, sir, I would like you to hear the opinion of the gentleman sitting in the second row of spectators, the third chair from the far end."

"Ramage, you strain the court's patience. We were very considerate when that young lady gave evidence; it is sheer impertinence for you to ask the court to listen to some stranger's opinion on a point of law. I presume that's what you intended."

"I suggest you let the gentleman speak for himself," Ramage said.

"I'll do no such thing!" Goddard shouted.

"I'll introduce him then," said Ramage. "The gentleman is one of my Lords Commissioners of the Admiralty, Captain Markham."

Goddard sat wide-eyed for a full minute, clearly not fully able to comprehend what Ramage had said. Captain Swinford leaned over and whispered to him, pointing at Captain Markham, who was now standing.

Suddenly Goddard pulled himself together. "Captain Markham!" he exclaimed. "All these years in the King's service and I have never had the pleasure of meeting you! Please come over here!"

Goddard's fawning manner had no effect on Markham, who walked up to within a couple of yards of the table – far enough away, Ramage noticed, that Goddard could not attempt to shake his hand.

"Markham," he introduced himself brusquely. "I'm here by virtue of orders from Lord St Vincent. Apparently the prisoner wants my opinion on the validity of his request for extra witnesses because new evidence has become available since he submitted his first list." He spoke slowly, glancing at Jenkins, who hurriedly began writing down the words. "It is not a point on which I need give an opinion. I suggest, Admiral Goddard, that you consult the deputy judge advocate – he is there to advise you on points of law and regulations."

With that Markham turned and went back to his seat, leaving Goddard like a small boy who had just had his hand slapped in front of visitors.

"Ah, Mr Jenkins, of course it was remiss of me not to ask you," Goddard said. "Are you familiar with this point?"

"Sir, it has arisen before and the ruling is that whether the request is from the defence or from the prosecution, it should be granted – providing the witnesses are available."

"You heard that, Ramage? *Are* these witnesses available?"

"Yes, sir," Ramage said. "Mr Jenkins has the list: could the first one be called?"

"Of course, of course!" Goddard said, his voice now friendly and hinting that Ramage had offended him by doubting his intentions.

Ramage looked towards the deputy judge advocate, who was now staring at Ramage's list like a rabbit paralysed by a stoat's stare. Finally he stood up with a muttered: "I think you should see this, sir," and walked to the head of the table, putting the list in front of Goddard.

The rear-admiral read the two names and glanced sideways to where Markham was sitting. Then, with a show of impatience he returned the list to Jenkins and said loudly: "The defence is entitled to witnesses. Call the first one!"

Jenkins scurried back to his chair, put the list down as though it had suddenly become red-hot and in little more than a whisper said: "Call Captain William Shirley..."

There was a gasp in the court as though half the people present had suddenly been jabbed in the ribs by an elbow. Shirley suddenly sat upright and then, as he saw Jenkins coming towards him with the Bible, stood up.

"There's no need to admininster the oath," Goddard snapped. "After all, he is the prosecutor."

Ramage stood up and clasped his hands behind his back. "In this case I must insist upon it, sir. It's customary for all witnesses to give evidence on oath."

With a nervous glance towards Captain Markham, Goddard motioned Jenkins to carry on. Shirley held up the Bible and read the oath.

Ramage remained standing and waited for Jenkins to return to his seat. The great cabin was silent except for the distant slop of the waves butting the *Salvador del Mundo*'s hull, and he asked Captain Shirley the first question.

"Did you on a certain day in June last murder Henry Barker, the surgeon on board His Majesty's ship the *Jason* frigate, which you commanded?"

"Yes," Shirley said in a conversational voice. "He was irritating me. You see, he continually claimed I was mad; indeed, he wanted to confine me and put the first lieutenant in command of the ship. I couldn't allow that, of course, so I ran him through with m' sword."

Ramage nodded, as though expecting the answer which had brought a gasp from almost everyone else in the cabin. "Did Barker attack you? Did you act in self-defence?"

"Oh no, I was the captain, you see. But he had been nagging me for weeks."

"Always claiming that you were mad?"

"Mmm, yes," Shirley said. "Always the same thing, like a litany. Pity about Barker, he was a good surgeon. But just imagine it, the first lieutenant in command!"

Shirley began to laugh; a laugh which went on and rose in pitch until it was a maniacal scream and the man's face, mouth open and teeth bared, seemed to be a skull over which parchment had been stretched.

Ramage stood still, startled by the man's reaction, and Markham was the first to recover. "You! Provost Marshal!" he shouted at Hill. "Take Captain Shirley into your custody. Guard him carefully: make sure he doesn't harm himself."

As soon as Captain Shirley was led away, with Goddard still mopping his brow and the twelve captains recovering enough to whisper to each other, Ramage said quietly: "Can my next witness be called?"

Goddard stared at him as though he had burst into song. "But my dear fellow, obviously the case is closed! There is no need for more witnesses!"

Ramage shook his head stubbornly. Goddard was either numbed by what had just happened, or a cunning scoundrel whose brain was working very fast, trying to calculate whether or not Shirley's madness (with his confession made in open court and, thanks to Ramage's insistence, on oath) could affect him.

"With respect, sir, the case against me is most certainly not closed. I am still charged with breaches of various Articles of War, several carrying a mandatory death sentence, and I insist on the opportunity of clearing myself."

"Quite unnecessary," Goddard said. "As soon as I clear the court, we shall consider our verdict. In fifteen minutes you will leave the ship a free man without – well, without a stain on your character. As of course," he added smoothly, "we all knew you would."

At that moment, Ramage was sure that Goddard was being cunning; that he had not been numbed: he had already calculated that any further evidence given for Ramage would reinforce a case against Shirley, who obviously now faced a charge of murder (and possibly more), and it was in Goddard's interest to stop the proceedings at once.

Ramage finally turned to the spectators. "Captain Markham, I must appeal to you again."

"No need, no need!" Goddard exclaimed. "No, you are quite right. The court will hear your next witness."

"Call Midshipman Blaxton," Jenkins said.

As the young midshipman came into the cabin, Ramage took several sheets of paper from the flat canvas pouch beneath his chair and walked over to Jenkins, who looked up nervously.

"A copy of the questions I shall be asking," Ramage said.

"Oh – thank you, sir: I am much obliged."

Blaxton, who was not in uniform, was nervous yet self-possessed. He held up the Bible, read out the oath from the card, and identified himself.

Goddard coughed and said: "The court will question you."

At once Ramage said: "This is a defence witness and I have prepared questions." He allowed impatience to creep into his voice as he added: "I am aware of all the circumstances and the court is not, and I know you wish that the witness' knowledge be fully investigated."

"Oh, very well," Goddard said sulkily, seeing the trap in front of him, "but of course the court reserves the right to take over the questioning."

Ramage ignored the remark and asked Blaxton: "Please tell the court of the events concerning the handling of the *Jason* frigate, in which you were serving, in June last."

"Come now!" Goddard exclaimed. "Are we to hear of every time she tacked or wore for two months?"

"Not *every* time," Ramage said carefully, and told Blaxton: "Confine yourself to the main events."

"On the first day of June as soon as it was daylight and the lookouts had been sent aloft, Captain Shirley gave the order to back the topsails, and for one hour we made a stern board. Then he let the topsails draw for an hour, and then ordered them backed again, so that we did another stern board – "

Ramage interrupted him. "For how long did this manoeuvre continue, going ahead for an hour and astern for an hour?"

"Until dusk, sir."

"And the *Jason* was on passage from where to where?"

"From Port Royal, Jamaica, to Carlisle Bay, Barbados, sir."

"So that occurred on the first day of June. Very well, what happened on the six successive days, between dawn and dusk?"

"The same, sir."

"What happened during the second week of the passage?"

"Captain Shirley had the ship beating to windward for an hour, and then running off for an hour, with stunsails set."

"This happened every day during that second week?"

"Yes, sir," Blaxton said, obviously as puzzled now as he was then.

"Was the *Jason* closing with Barbados?"

"No, sir. What with the westgoing current and running off and the wind dropping at night, the first lieutenant calculated that on average we were losing three or four miles easting an hour."

"What happened during the third week of the passage?"

"We had a very bad outbreak of yellow fever, sir, and we became very short of water."

"Why were you short of water? After all, you were only two weeks out of Port Royal."

"Captain Shirley refused to water the ship there, sir."

"Do you know – of your own knowledge, not from what anyone else may have told you – why this was?"

"Yes, sir. I was with the first lieutenant in Port Royal when he asked permission to send off the boats with the casks, and Captain Shirley refused."

"Did you hear him give a reason?"

"Yes, sir; he said he was not going to have the ship laden down with a lot of extra weight."

"How many cases of yellow fever did you have?"

"It started with three men, sir. There were nine the second day and twenty-eight the third – "

"How many men had died before the ship reached Barbados?"

"Twenty-three, sir."

"Did the surgeon, to your certain knowledge, make any representation to Captain Shirley?"

"Yes, sir, several times each day, and always after we had funeral services, which were held daily."

"Did you hear Captain Shirley's replies?"

"Most of them, sir. He said that the deaths were 'condign punishment' for the men's wickedness in plotting against him."

"To your knowledge, were the men plotting against him?"

"No, sir."

"After the ship reached Barbados, was water embarked?"

"Yes sir, but Captain Shirley allowed only twenty tons."

"Did the officers comment?"

"Two lieutenants went with the first lieutenant to see the captain, to protest we needed fifty tons for the passage to England."

"Do you know what happened then?"

"Yes, sir, because I was present: the captain assembled all the officers and the midshipmen and said he was charging us with mutinous assembly."

"Did he in fact charge you all?"

"Not exactly charge, sir..." Blaxton was at a loss for words.

"What then?"

"Well, sir, he made us all sign a document he drew up. We also had to witness each other's signatures, so we signed twice."

"What did the document say?"

Blaxton's brow wrinkled with the effort of remembering. "I can't recall precisely, but across the top it said something to the effect that all the undersigned admitted making a mutinous assembly, and then there were two columns. Each officer signed in the first column, and the witness to the signature signed in the second."

"Why," asked Ramage, "can't you remember more exactly what statement you and the lieutenants were signing? It is a serious admission for you all to make."

"Oh, but that one was only one of several," Blaxton explained.

"How many more were signed and what did they say?"

"I signed seven more, and so did each of the commission and warrant officers. Seven in addition to the first one. The rest of the ship's company signed two."

"Do you mean to say the commission and warrant officers all signed eight documents at the same time, and all the ship's company were mustered to sign two?"

"Oh no, sir!" Blaxton exclaimed. "They were signed at various times on the passage between Barbados and meeting the *Calypso*."

"What did the various documents say? Begin with the ones signed by the commission and warrant officers."

"The first was making a mutinous assembly; the second was the same plus concealing a 'traiterous or mutinous practice or design', falling under Article twenty. The next four were mutinous assembly again, Article nineteen. The next two followed the sighting of the *Calypso*, Article twelve, 'every person in the fleet, who through cowardice, negligence or disaffection, shall in time of action withdraw or keep back, or not come to the fight...'"

"Wait," Ramage said. "What was the occasion of Captain Shirley making you all sign an admission at that particular moment?"

"We had just sighted the *Calypso* and the convoy, and identified her from her shape and pendant numbers, when

363

Captain Shirley announced she was an enemy ship and he intended to attack her. The officers protested and pointed out the convoy, which had to be British. Captain Shirley accused them under the twelfth Article and made them sign."

"You say 'made them sign', but how could he force them?"

"He already had admissions (confessions, I suppose they were) of breaches of other Articles of War, sir, and he threatened to ask the *Calypso* for assistance in confining us all."

"But he had just identified the *Calypso* as an enemy and planned to attack her!" Ramage protested.

"Yes, sir," Blaxton said soberly. "That was the trouble: he was completely mad."

Ramage waited for Goddard to order that remark to be deleted from the minutes, but the Rear-Admiral was slumped in his chair, apparently dazed.

"So by the time the *Calypso* arrived, the commission and warrant officers had signed eight of these 'admissions', or confessions. What about the two signed by the rest of the ship's company?"

"They were admissions of 'mutinous assembly' on various occasions, and Captain Shirley told the men that under Article nineteen death was the only punishment."

"So everybody signed? What about the men who could not write?"

"They put down a thumbprint and an 'X', and this was witnessed by shipmates who *could* write. Captain Shirley had the clerk copy the names out of the Muster Book: it was no more difficult than a weekly muster."

"So in all how many 'admissions' did Captain Shirley have?"

"I don't know offhand, sir. We mustered more than two hundred, so there must have been more than five hundred signatures."

"But why," Ramage insisted, "did you all sign so freely when you thought Captain Shirley was mad?"

"The officers signed that first admission because they were frightened that they had in fact taken part in a 'mutinous assembly' and they thought Captain Shirley would bring them to trial. Later, when they became absolutely certain that he was mad, they knew that with the surgeon dead they could never prove it, and Captain Shirley used that first admission to force them – to blackmail them, I now realize – to sign the later ones."

And that just about covers Captain Shirley's madness as far as I am concerned, Ramage thought: from now on the Board of Admiralty has to decide what to do with him. There was just one last episode to clear up.

"When the *Calypso* was first sighted from the *Jason*," Ramage said, "you gave evidence that she was immediately identified."

"Yes, sir: she has a distinctive shape since she's French-built, and we all knew of her because she's your command, sir. And she was flying the correct challenge, and we could see her pendant numbers."

"But Captain Shirley did not agree with the identification by his officers?"

"No, sir. He didn't doubt she was the *Calypso*; he just insisted she was an enemy ship."

"Even though he was told I commanded her?"

"He never doubted that, sir," Blaxton said, looking embarrassed. "He just said that everyone knew you were a traitor."

"Describe what happened in the *Jason* after the *Calypso* was within five hundred yards."

"Well, sir, Captain Shirley sent the men to quarters and the guns were loaded with roundshot. He had told the gun captains to aim for the hull. In fact," Blaxton explained, "the men agreed among themselves to aim high, even though Captain Shirley had just threatened them with the admissions. Well, we approached larboard bow to larboard bow, as though both ships intended to pass within hail. All the officers had been sent down to the gunroom under Marine guard, and Captain Shirley had the deck to himself. At the – "

"Wait," Goddard snapped. "How do you know this? You were under guard in the gunroom."

"No sir: if you recall," Blaxton said politely, "the midshipmen's berth in a frigate is separate, forward of the gunroom. Anyway, we four midshipmen remained on deck."

"Please continue," Ramage said.

"At the last moment, Captain Shirley turned the *Jason* to larboard and bore across the *Calypso*'s bow, as though he intended to ram, and as we passed he gave the order to fire."

"You heard him and the actual raking?" Ramage asked.

"Yes, sir: everyone in the *Jason* heard."

Ramage turned to Goddard and said quietly: "I have no further questions to put to this witness."

Goddard nodded. "Let him listen to the minutes being read back, and then he can sign them."

When Blaxton had done this, Ramage said to Goddard: "Does the court wish me to make a statement in my defence?"

Goddard shook his head wearily. "That will not be necessary." He looked down the table at Jenkins. "Clear the court," he said. "We will now consider our verdict."

Lieutenant Hill had not returned from taking away Shirley, and Ramage walked to the door of the great cabin, meeting Alexis on the way.

"It worked," she murmured, and as they paused, waiting for the crowd of spectators to leave the cabin, she added: "It worked just the way I dreamed it would when I slept in your bed at Palace Street."

"You have slept in two of my beds now," he said, and then had to turn politely as Captain Markham walked up, smiling and with his hand outstretched.

"What he did on board the *Jason* takes more courage than attacking a ship of the line," Markham commented to Alexis, taking her arm and leading her out of the cabin.

"Yes, I know," she said, "but what happens now?"

"Captain Shirley will be examined by doctors: I'm sure he's not fit to stand trial. The *Jason*'s officers and men – nothing will be held against them."

"And that poor surgeon?"

"Murdered by a madman: it doesn't help him much, but that surgeon probably saved the *Jason*," Markham said soberly.

"And – and what about Nicholas? About Captain Ramage, I mean?"

"He'll go back in there in a few minutes and find his sword hilt towards him, showing he is acquitted."

"And then?"

"Well," said Markham, smiling at Alexis, "for the moment he seems to be in good hands; but very soon he will have to take the *Calypso* to sea again."

Dudley Pope

Governor Ramage RN

Lieutenant Lord Ramage, expert seafarer and adventurer, undertakes to escort a convoy across the Caribbean. This seemingly routine task leads him into a series of dramatic and terrifying encounters. Lord Ramage is quick to learn that the enemy attacks from all angles and he must keep his wits about him in order to survive. Fast and thrilling, this is another highly-charged adventure from the masterly Dudley Pope.

'All the verve and expertise of Forester'
– *Observer*

Ramage's Challenge

The Napoleonic Wars are raging and a group of eminent British citizens have been taken captive in the Mediterranean by French troops. The Admiralty traces their location and sends the valiant Lord Ramage to effect their release. As Ramage and his crew negotiate the hazardous waters off the Tuscan coast, they soon begin to doubt the accuracy of their instructions. Ramage comes to realize that in order for his mission to succeed he must embark upon a fearful and highly dangerous escapade where the stakes have never been higher.

Ramage's Challenge is another action-packed naval adventure from the masterful Dudley Pope.

DUDLEY POPE

RAMAGE AND THE GUILLOTINE

As France recovers from her bloody Revolution, Napoleon is amassing his armies for the Great Invasion. News in England is sketchy and the Navy must prepare to defend the land from foreign attack.

Lieutenant Ramage is chosen to travel to France and embark upon the perilous quest of spying on the great Napoleon. His mission is to determine the strength of the French troops – but his discovery will mean the guillotine!

'The first and still favourite rival to Hornblower'
– *Daily Mirror*

RAMAGE'S PRIZE

Lord Ramage returns for another highly-charged and thrilling adventure at sea. Instructed with the task of discovering why His Majesty's dispatches keep unaccountably disappearing, Ramage finds himself involved in a situation far beyond his expectations. Based on true events, *Ramage's Prize* is another gripping story from Dudley Pope.

'An author who really knows Nelson's Navy'
– *Observer*

Dudley Pope

The Ramage Touch

The Ramage Touch finds the ever-popular Lord Ramage in the Mediterranean with another daring mission to undertake. He soon makes a shocking discovery which dramatically transforms the nature of the task at hand. With the nearest English vessel a thousand miles away, Ramage must embark upon a truly perilous and life-threatening course of action. With everything stacked against him, he has only one chance to succeed...

Ramage at Trafalgar

Lord Ramage returns to fight in the most famous of Britain's sea battles. Summoned by Admiral Nelson himself, Ramage is sent to join the British fleet off Cadiz where the largest battle in naval history is about to take place. Finding himself in the front line of battle, Lord Ramage must fight to save his own life as well as for his country. The result is a thrilling, hair-raising adventure from one of our best-loved naval writers.

'Expert knowledge of naval history'
– *Guardian*

OTHER TITLES BY DUDLEY POPE AVAILABLE DIRECT
FROM HOUSE OF STRATUS

Quantity		£	$(US)	$(CAN)	€
	FICTION				
	ADMIRAL	6.99	14.50	21.00	12.00
	BUCCANEER	6.99	14.50	21.00	12.00
	CONVOY	6.99	14.50	21.00	12.00
	CORSAIR	6.99	14.50	21.00	12.00
	DECOY	6.99	14.50	21.00	12.00
	GALLEON	6.99	14.50	21.00	12.00
	RAMAGE	6.99	14.50	21.00	12.00
	RAMAGE AND THE DRUMBEAT	6.99	14.50	21.00	12.00
	RAMAGE AND THE FREEBOOTERS	6.99	14.50	21.00	12.00
	GOVERNOR RAMAGE RN	6.99	14.50	21.00	12.00
	RAMAGE'S PRIZE	6.99	14.50	21.00	12.00
	RAMAGE AND THE GUILLOTINE	6.99	14.50	21.00	12.00
	RAMAGE'S DIAMOND	6.99	14.50	21.00	12.00
	RAMAGE'S MUTINY	6.99	14.50	21.00	12.00
	RAMAGE AND THE REBELS	6.99	14.50	21.00	12.00
	THE RAMAGE TOUCH	6.99	14.50	21.00	12.00
	RAMAGE'S SIGNAL	6.99	14.50	21.00	12.00
	RAMAGE'S DEVIL	6.99	14.50	21.00	12.00
	RAMAGE'S CHALLENGE	6.99	14.50	21.00	12.00
	RAMAGE AT TRAFALGAR	6.99	14.50	21.00	12.00
	RAMAGE AND THE DIDO	6.99	14.50	21.00	12.00
	NON-FICTION				
	THE BIOGRAPHY OF SIR HENRY MORGAN 1635–1688	10.99	18.00	25.00	17.00

ALL HOUSE OF STRATUS BOOKS ARE AVAILABLE FROM GOOD BOOKSHOPS
OR DIRECT FROM THE PUBLISHER:

Internet:	www.houseofstratus.com including synopses and features.
Email:	sales@houseofstratus.com info@houseofstratus.com (please quote author, title and credit card details.)
Tel:	Order Line 0800 169 1780 (UK) International +44 (0) 1845 527700 (UK)
Fax:	+44 (0) 1845 527711 (UK) (please quote author, title and credit card details.)
Send to:	House of Stratus Sales Department Thirsk Industrial Park York Road, Thirsk North Yorkshire, YO7 3BX UK

PAYMENT

Please tick currency you wish to use:

☐ £ (Sterling)   ☐ $ (US)   ☐ $ (CAN)   ☐ € (Euros)

Allow for shipping costs charged per order plus an amount per book as set out in the tables below:

CURRENCY/DESTINATION

	£(Sterling)	$(US)	$(CAN)	€ (Euros)
Cost per order				
UK	1.50	2.25	3.50	2.50
Europe	3.00	4.50	6.75	5.00
North America	3.00	3.50	5.25	5.00
Rest of World	3.00	4.50	6.75	5.00
Additional cost per book				
UK	0.50	0.75	1.15	0.85
Europe	1.00	1.50	2.25	1.70
North America	1.00	1.00	1.50	1.70
Rest of World	1.50	2.25	3.50	3.00

PLEASE SEND CHEQUE OR INTERNATIONAL MONEY ORDER
payable to: HOUSE OF STRATUS LTD or card payment as indicated

STERLING EXAMPLE

Cost of book(s):...................... Example: 3 x books at £6.99 each: £20.97

Cost of order:....................... Example: £1.50 (Delivery to UK address)

Additional cost per book:............... Example: 3 x £0.50: £1.50

Order total including shipping:........... Example: £23.97

VISA, MASTERCARD, SWITCH, AMEX:

☐ ☐ ☐ ☐ ☐ ☐ ☐ ☐ ☐ ☐ ☐ ☐ ☐ ☐ ☐ ☐ ☐ ☐ ☐ ☐

Issue number (Switch only):

☐ ☐ ☐

Start Date: **Expiry Date:**

☐☐/☐☐   ☐☐/☐☐

Signature: _____

NAME: _____

ADDRESS: _____

COUNTRY: _____

ZIP/POSTCODE: _____

Please allow 28 days for delivery. Despatch normally within 48 hours.

Prices subject to change without notice.
Please tick box if you do not wish to receive any additional information. ☐

House of Stratus publishes many other titles in this genre; please check our website (**www.houseofstratus.com**) for more details.